Hope you enjoy Lee and Emmaleigh's story!
Happy Reading!
Love
Emma
Ling
xx

Copyright © 2022 by Emma Luna

All rights reserved. No part of this publication may be reproduced, stored or transmitted in any form or by any means, electronic, mechanical, photocopying, recording, scanning, or otherwise without written permission from the publisher. It is illegal to copy this book, post it to a website, or distribute it by any other means without permission.

This novel is entirely a work of fiction. The names, characters and incidents portrayed in it are the work of the author's imagination. Any resemblance to actual persons, living or dead, events or localities is entirely coincidental.

Emma Luna asserts the moral right to be identified as the author of this work.

Emma Luna has no responsibility for the persistence or accuracy of URLs for external or third-party Internet Websites referred to in this publication and does not guarantee that any content on such Websites is, or will remain, accurate or appropriate.

Designations used by companies to distinguish their products are often claimed as trademarks. All brand names and product names used in this book and on its cover are trade names, service marks, trademarks and registered trademarks of their respective owners. The publishers and the book are not associated with any product or vendor mentioned in this book. None of the companies referenced within the book have endorsed the book.

First edition

Ebook ISBN number: B0B6DYL727

Paperback ISBN number: 9798373113069

Editing: Amber Nicole

Proofreading: Abrianna Denae

Cover Design: The Book Cover Boutique

Graphics For Paperback Formatting: Lou J Stock

Formatting: Emma Luna at Moonlight Author Services

CONTENTS

Blurb	vi
Author Note	viii
Trigger Warning	x
Prologue	1
1. Emmaleigh	3
2. Lee	13
3. Emmaleigh	23
4. Lee	33
5. Emmaleigh	45
6. Lee	57
7. Emmaleigh	64
8. Lee	78
9. Emmaleigh	89
10. Lee	96
11. Emmaleigh	105
12. Lee	123
13. Emmaleigh	136
14. Emmaleigh	142
15. Emmaleigh	165
16. Lee	174
17. Emmaleigh	180
18. Emmaleigh	195
19. Emmaleigh	206
20. Lee	215
21. Emmaleigh	229
22. Emmaleigh	236
23. Lee	244
24. Lee	250
25. Emmaleigh	262
26. Emmaleigh	271
27. Lee	278

Acknowledgments	292
About Emma Luna	295
Follow Emma Luna	297
Also by Emma Luna	299

Blurb

I was always yours, but are you mine?

I've been on every bad date you can think of, and I'm still traumatised by some of them. I know I'm a curvy girl, but I still deserve a nice guy.

I decide to give Internet dating one last go, and that's when I meet Lee. He's the perfect guy—smart, funny, and incredibly sexy. He brings out a praise kink I didn't even know I had, and I just want to be his good girl.

Sadly, Lee doesn't want a relationship, and instead proposes we be friends-with-benefits.

The more time we spend together, and the more benefits we enjoy, the more my heart is put on the line. So why can't I walk away?

Then when life throws me a deadly curveball, and I lose all hope, I push everyone away. But as Lee fights to be a part of my life, we both have to reevaluate what we're really looking for.

Is there any chance we were both meant for each other?

I Was Always Yours is a heartbreaking, friends-with-benefits, contemporary romance featuring a curvy girl looking for love and the guy who shows her what life and love is really about. This book is intended for mature readers and there are plenty of spicy scenes featuring praise kink.

Author Note

Although this book is not as dark as I normally write—by a long way—it does still come with a trigger warning. Please read it carefully, and if you have any further questions, please don't hesitate to reach out.

Please note - this book is set in England, UK. Because of its setting, and the fact I'm also from the UK, this book will feature English (UK) spellings and phrases, so please keep that in mind when reading. If you think you have found any errors, which no doubt will happen because me and my team are human, please don't hesitate to contact me. If you reach out to me directly, it's the quickest way for me to get the issue rectified.

Please **do not** report spelling or grammar inconsistencies via the Amazon reporting system. Often they don't pass these issues along to authors to be fixed, and when they do, it's usually with a warning that

AUTHOR NOTE

they could pull the book from sale. This is obviously bad for readers too, as you won't be able to read, or finish reading, the book.

Finally, I just want to say a massive thank you for picking up **I Was Always Yours** and giving this story a chance. I hope you love Emmaleigh and Lee as much as I do. If you enjoy the book, I would be very grateful if you could leave a review anywhere you're able to. Reviews help me grow as an author, but they also help other readers decide if this is a book they should read. So, if you enjoyed it, please recommend it as much as you can.

Your help, support, and love is very much appreciated, and I can't thank you all enough for giving my book baby a chance.

Happy reading, and stay safe!

Em xx

Trigger Warning

Please note - this trigger list may not be exhaustive. I acknowledge that people have things that are triggers for them, but they aren't for others. So, while this lists the main triggers featured in the book, if you have something that triggers you, and it's not listed, please don't hesitate to reach out via social media or email, letting me know what your trigger is. I will respond swiftly, and in the strictest of confidence, letting you know if your trigger features in the book or not.

Please do not feel like you can't contact me. Your mental health is very important to me, and I would never want anyone to be triggered by something they read in this book.

So please, read this list carefully, contact me if needed, and stay safe. But, if you don't have any triggers listed... enjoy!

TRIGGER WARNING

Lack of body confidence
Mental Health issues
Suicidal thoughts and ideation
Suicidal attempt
Self harm
Physical ill health issues
Discussions around long-term health and disability
Breath play
Dom/Praise kink

Dedication

To Mel

My dear friend who sadly lost her battle with cancer at just forty-five years old.

*Every day, you faced the world with a smile and a positive attitude.
No matter how bad things got, you kept going.
You never asked for too much, just a little more time.
A little longer with the people you love.*

*You left behind the love of your life, and three beautiful children.
I know the pain I feel at your loss, and so I can't imagine how they feel.*

*One thing you always taught me is that no matter how bad life gets,
no matter how much it rains,
you can always put your Wellies on and dance in the rain.*

You taught me that no matter the diagnosis, it doesn't change who you are.

You had cancer, but it never had you!
Even on my darkest days, I will remember your strength,
I will remember how you remained positive,
even when everything seemed bleak.

I'm going to enjoy my life, and live it to the fullest
Because more than anything,
you taught me that tomorrow is never guaranteed.
Do what scares you.
Kiss your loved ones.
Make up with those you've fallen out with.
Life is too short.
Just live it, surrounded by the people you love, with a smile on your face.

Thanks for being in my life, Mel,
And for making it a brighter place.
You will be missed!

I WAS ALWAYS *Yours*

USA TODAY BESTSELLING AUTHOR
EMMA LUNA

Emmaleigh

PROLOGUE

Hope is a word I stopped believing in a long time ago. It's one of those words that people throw about so casually. Hope you are well. Hope you have a great day. Hope you feel better soon.

But what does it really mean? For someone like me, hope is a pipe dream. Something I gave up on when I grew up, a bit like Father Christmas. As my dad used to say—once I finally stopped believing—"There's only one fat man who brings presents to this house... me."

I know I probably sound depressed, and you would be right. I believe my doctor's files say something along the lines of moderate depression, generalised anxiety disorder, and suicidal ideation. Basically, I feel exactly the same as most people do at some point during their lives. But that's the thing, this isn't just a passing phase, this is my permanent existence now.

I once had it all. High-flying career as a nurse, an amazing guy I saw great potential with, friends I enjoyed spending time with, a loving family who all live nearby, financially self-sufficient. I even had my own fucking car. On paper, my life was perfect, until it wasn't. Until the day hope became nothing except a wish.

I fought so hard to get everything in life, but the idea of having to fight each day for something so far from my original vision was just too hard. The world never tells you that you can't have it all. My parents, just like every other child's parents, used to tell me that I can do anything I set my mind to, but they were wrong. There are some things you just can't do.

Sometimes in life, through no fault of your own, you have to take a path you never saw coming. You have to leave the path covered in hearts, rainbows, and sunshine, to walk down the dark, dreary lane, hoping the whole time that it will get better. After all, nobody can see what the road looks like ahead. But, for me, I knew the life I'd envisaged for myself was gone. I just didn't know how I should feel about this new life, and the new options that were in front of me.

Last week my life changed forever. I stopped being the Emmaleigh Wayward I had always known, and I had to figure out what this new me looked like. Sadly, as each day passed, I stopped searching for that better version of me, for that better life. I pushed away everyone that ever cared about me, and the only hope I dared to have is that it would all be over soon.

I like to remember the days from before, when I didn't know what life would bring, and I just thought my body was failing me. I remember laughing to myself, joking about why it was always me that seemed to have no luck. I never saw this new life coming, but now I can't stop wondering if my life will ever be the same again.

They say everyone has one good story in them, and this is mine. This is the story of how my life turned dark, and how I became encapsulated by the darkness, in a position I never thought I would be in. Until a bright bolt of electricity zapped me back to life, and helped me to see that small bit of light in the darkness. Hope.

Emmaleigh

> **EMMALEIGH**
> I know this probably seems like a stupid message, but I just wanted to clear something up. I really did want to meet you and go on a date. When I said I couldn't go because I broke my foot, that wasn't an elaborate cop-out. A way to get out of meeting you. It's the truth. I have loved talking to you, and think we could get on just as well in person. But I know you are dating someone else now, so I wish you all the best. Was nice talking to you, Carlos.

Fuck. Could I sound any lamer?

Without thinking too much about it, I press send. I don't normally send such desperate, pathetic sounding messages. But at the present moment, my life literally can't get any shittier.

It's three in the morning. I'm sitting in a bathroom that screams 'owned by a guy' while his cum dribbles down my legs.

I wish I had some incredible sex story to share, that I could tell you all about how he had magic fingers that he knew how to use, but it was nothing compared to his dick. That I saw stars and couldn't catch my breath as I came so many bloody times.

Ha. I fucking wish. Let me tell you what really happened. I was stupid, and I made the mistake I kept telling myself I needed to stop making.

Drew, the guy who I can hear snoring from two rooms away while I cower in his bathroom, is one of those people that looks fucking gorgeous. He exudes bad boy, with tattoos on top of his lean muscles and a perfectly sculpted face to match. His short, spiky black hair, that admittedly featured far too much gel, and the cocky smirk, round off that bad boy vibe. They were the idealistic things I focused on when I stupidly hoped—there's that word again!—that I could change him. So I ignored the fact he wore tracksuit bottoms everywhere, smoked roll-ups, which I fucking hated, and he didn't want any kind of sexual activity to take place while he was watching reality TV. They are just the everyday issues. The other ones were even worse. Still, I ignored all this, and the shit times I'd had before with him, hoping that this time would be different. That maybe, just once, I will be the one to cure the bad boy.

Newsflash... I'm not that girl. Then Drew took his dickish behaviour even further and I think back to the beginning of the evening, wondering how the hell I got myself in this position.

"*Emmaleigh, I need to ask you something, and I expect you to be honest. Are you dating anyone else?*" *asks Drew, and instantly my mind travels to the texts I had been sending Carlos, whose real name is Lee... It's a long story! We had been texting a lot, but we never met. We had been talking about it, until I went and broke my stupid fucking foot with my clumsy, off-the-chart bad balance. I think he thought I was blowing him off, as so many people who meet on dating apps do, but that wasn't the case here, and it hurt that he didn't see that. He went on a date with someone else, and he likes her, which is why he messaged me this morning to let me know we couldn't talk anymore. I haven't been able to reply yet.*

How do you tell the guy you had started to fall for over a damn dating app, it's okay if he moves on? It's not okay. Out of all the guys I've talked to on this shitty app, he was the only one I could ever hold a conversation with, who asked me about my day, and who didn't send me a dick pic—winner in my book.

Instead, I found myself back here, sitting on Drew's shitty old couch, wondering how much further I can stoop.

We had been seeing each other off and on for the last few months. Nothing serious, just the odd hang out and hook up. Other than the first time we met, we've never even been on a real date, and to be honest, that's okay. We have zero in common, and I don't think I could stand a date with him.

I can already hear the judgement. If this guy's such an ass, why are you still meeting him? Worse than that, why are you still fucking him?

And the honest answer is so fucking depressing to admit. I'm using him to make up for my shitty, low self-esteem. He's hot, and I'm in a place right now where I hate everything about me. I can't even tell you how often I feel like my body fails me. I'm exhausted all the time. Sometimes, for no reason, I can't feel my leg, or my vision will go blurry. Doctors say I'm just stressed, but I can't help worrying it's something more.

The more my body fails me for no reason at all, the more depressed I get. So, when this hot guy started showing an interest in me, I jumped on it. I ignored the fact we have nothing in common. He's dull as dish-water, and he wouldn't know a clitoris if it whacked him around the head. Still, I keep showing up at his apartment late at night so that nobody can see me making another big mistake.

Tonight I'm probably the lowest I've been in a while. I know you shouldn't get your hopes up with guys you meet on a dating website, but I honestly thought Lee was different. I thought we had great potential. And even now, as I'm sitting on another guy's sofa, all I can think about is him. But when Drew asks me if I'm seeing anyone else, I can answer honestly. If I'd arranged to meet Lee, I would have told Drew right away. I don't believe in leading two guys on, or dating two people at once—even though I'm definitely not dating Drew. I still only sleep with one person at a time.

Trying to put all thoughts of Lee's message out of the way, I answer

Drew honestly. *"No, I'm not seeing anyone else. I thought we talked about that the other week and agreed that if we ever wanted to go on a date or fuck someone else, we would tell each other. We aren't exclusive or dating, but it just feels polite to tell each other when it gets to that stage. I would have done that anyway, but it was you that suggested it."*

Drew shifts his gaze to the floor, and thankfully for him, his reality show starts up again after the commercial break, and he clarified that we don't talk while his show is on. I should have run the minute he enforced this rule on date number one. I'm such a twit for still being here.

I zone out for the next half an hour, playing with my phone, rereading Lee's message and trying to think of an appropriate reply. I'm pulled back to the room when the show's theme tune blasts out of the television speakers, and Drew talks again. *"So, are you looking for us to be exclusive?"* he asks, as he turns the volume down—not off, just down!

"I don't think I said that specifically. What I said is that I won't sleep with someone who is fucking other people. We don't have to be boyfriend and girlfriend, and do all the soppy shit. I just want to know that the person I'm with isn't with someone else, too." I don't think that's an unreasonable request, and when Drew ducks his eyes, looking down at the cigarette he's rolling up, I should have been suspicious, but I'm not. Or maybe I am and I'm just choosing to ignore the obvious?

"You know I don't do girlfriends. I don't like to be tied down. But I'm happy to just see one person," he states as he takes a drag from his cigarette, lounging back on the opposite sofa.

"Okay," I add, not really understanding why he's bringing up something we hashed out weeks ago when we first started sleeping together.

"Good. Now, why don't you come over here and give me a blow job?" Fuck, is that romantic?!

I know I should read between the lines, questioning him on why he would bring up something like that when we sorted it out a while ago. But, I guess the saying ignorance is bliss really is true.

"I thought this time you were going to go down on me, show me the magic fingers you tempted me with when we first started talking," I ask, remembering all the messages we sent over the dating app. He was hot, sexy, and kept telling me exactly what I wanted to hear. All about his magic fingers that could find my G-spot without even trying, and about

how much he loved to lick pussy. Not to mention his giant cock and the fact he liked to get rough and dirty when he fucked.

That was exactly what I was looking for. A guy to throw me around, spank my ass, and call me his slut. So, when we first had sex, to say it was a letdown was an understatement. I gave him the best blow job of his life and got him nice and ready, but then a few pumps in doggy and it was over. I barely had time to think about getting wet, and my G-spot was nowhere to be seen, let alone an orgasm. I didn't even give a shit that he lied, and his penis was just average sized. I've been with men who are average, and if they know how to fucking use it, that's all that mattered. Yet, Drew neither had the size he boasted about, he lacked the skill too.

I can hear the screams again. Get out of there. Why are you back for another round? What can I say, I'm an idiot.

"I will, but it has to be the right time. I have to be in the mood. So, why don't you help me get in the mood with that fucking amazing mouth of yours?" he asked, his voice taking on that low husky tone he gets when he's horny.

I drop to my knees, feeling the last drop of self-esteem fall to the floor with me, and I crawl towards him as best I can without knocking my broken foot. By the time I'm sitting in front of him, on my knees, he has his sweatpants and boxers off, and his cock is standing to attention, pre-cum dripping from the tip.

Pushing all thoughts of my dignity to one side, I lower my mouth around his cock and am rewarded with a loud groan as he thrusts his hips upwards until his dick hits the back of my throat. I suck hard, bobbing up and down the shaft, twirling my tongue around the head and along the vein on the underside—that really drives him wild. He threads his fingers through my hair, but doesn't take control, so I continue sucking the way I know he likes.

It's not long before his hips thrust frantically, his breathing becomes more erratic, and his cock pulses in that telltale way. I know he's close, and so much to his disappointment, I pull away from his cock. "Nooo. Em, what the fuck?" he groans, as he slams his hand down on the sofa next to him.

I look up at him, hoping he can see the annoyance clear on my face. "Because, Drew, if you come in my mouth now, you won't be able to fuck *me. You will fall straight to sleep, and I will have hobbled all the way over here with a broken foot just to blow you."*

He looks at me with a face that says, 'and what's wrong with that?'. I shake my head and stand up, making my disapproval clear thanks to my glare. I'm sure he rolls his fucking eyes at me, but thankfully he stands and pulls his T-shirt off so he's fully naked. Without saying a word, he walks towards his bedroom, just expecting me to follow—which I do—stupid me!

Upon entering his bedroom, I try not to look at all the mess surrounding the room. I'm sure underneath all the laundry there's a carpet to be seen. There's just crap everywhere, over every surface, but thankfully his bed looks clean with new sheets. As soon as he turns his bedroom light on, and the fucking hideous red bulb coats the room in a crimson glow—reminding me of the red-light district in Amsterdam—I remember why I usually tell him to keep the light off. I already feel slutty, without a fucking red light adding to it.

He doesn't make any move to undress me, just sits in the middle of his bed, stroking his cock in one hand while pointing for me to join him with his free hand. I slowly remove my clothes, although why I'm dragging this out is beyond me.

"Come on, baby. Get on your hands and knees," he purrs and I feel disgust ripple through my body. Shocker, of course, he wants to go for doggy-style again. I should have known.

Crawling onto the bed, naked, I get onto my hands and knees the same as always. I feel the bed dip as he shifts into position behind me.

He lightly strokes his finger through my slit, and for just a second I get my hopes up that this might be the start of some foreplay. Instead, he simply uses his fingers to part my lips so he can aim the tip of his cock. Unfortunately, he doesn't aim it too well and the first couple of attempts bounce off my perineum.

"Open up for me, baby." Argh, it's not a matter of me opening up. It has a lot more to do with you hitting the right fucking target.

Realising he needs a bit of guiding, I reach around and take hold of the tip, guiding it to the right area. I expect him to ease into it, to get me ready first, but he doesn't. He plunges his cock straight into my dry pussy, and I yelp from the burning sting of skin against skin.

As soon as his cock bottoms out, he doesn't wait for me to get a little more ready. He just continues thrusting in and out at a ridiculous speed. I *realise then that he doesn't have a care in the world about if I'm enjoying it or not. I'm literally just a hole for him to use to get himself off, and the more that realisation sinks in, the shittier I feel.*

It's over all too quickly—although at that point, I didn't exactly want to prolong it. I don't think I even have a chance to consider getting wet, let alone for it to actually happen. I feel him pull out, and as I feel his cum trickle from my pussy, I spin around so fast, my eyebrows pulled together as I look at him with venom in my eyes.

"Why the fuck didn't you use a condom?" I snap. I didn't check with him before we got started because I didn't think I needed to. We'd had this conversation weeks ago when we first slept together. He knew what I expected, and he'd never done it without one before. How the hell did I not feel it when I touched his cock to guide him in? I guess I was so keen to get it over with, it didn't even occur to me.

Shrugging his shoulders, he leans back against the headboard and lights up a roll up that sends a billow of smoke up into the room, and the smell causes my nose to wrinkle. "I ran out of those latex free condoms you bought, and when I went to buy more, they were so fucking expensive, so I just bought normal ones. I figured we could just not use any, since I know you aren't fucking someone else, and you're on the pill."

There's so much wrong with that fucking sentence. I don't know where to start. I feel like I should start by punching him between the eyes for deciding by himself about something that concerned us both. I don't give a shit that I'm on the pill. I never wanted to have sex without a condom until I was in a long-term, committed relationship.

"I'm so fucking pissed at you right now," I fume, as I try to roll off the bed. At first I try to do my best to not drip cum everywhere, but then I think, fuck it. It's his cum, he will have to deal with it. I pick up his T-shirt and pull it over my head, trying desperately to ignore the nausea-inducing cigarette smell that clings to it. "How dare you make a decision like that, and not at least discuss it with me?"

He shrugs his shoulders, that blank expression remains on his face as he snuggles further into the bed, pulling the duvet cover up, like I'm not even there. "Chill out, babe. We can talk about this later. I'm tired now. Come on, just go to sleep."

I get ready to argue, but there's no point. He isn't even listening to me, and within minutes, he rolls over and begins to snore. I'm just about to head out to the bathroom when a buzzing rings from on the bedside table where Drew carefully placed our phones before we had sex. There's definitely no all-consuming passion where we can't hold it in any longer and we rip off each other's clothing, letting them fall where they may. Even the act of getting naked is boring and dull.

I go to pick up my phone, until I realise the vibration wasn't in fact from my phone, it came from his. I would never normally read another person's phone without their permission, but it's just sitting there, the message preview staring at me, tempting me to look. All I can see is that it's a message from someone called Tiff, and she enjoyed...

Well, that's more than enough of a reason for me to open the phone and read the rest. The idiot doesn't even have a passcode on the phone. That's how cocky—or stupid—he is.

> **TIFF**
>
> I enjoyed hanging out with you last night. That thing you did with your tongue was amazing. I know you said you are seeing another girl and can't get serious, and that's okay with me. I don't mind being the other woman. But, when you say she gives the best blow jobs, I'm determined to prove I'm better. Then maybe one day you can get rid of her for good. But for now, this is fine. What do you say, can I be your dirty little secret on the side?

Fuck! My mind whirls as I try to take in all the fucked up things with that message. Looks like the reason he wanted to clarify that we were still only fucking each other was because he was secretly fucking someone else. And, by the sounds of it, he actually showed her a good time. If I felt like shit before, it's nothing like how I feel now.

I know that if I look further into his phone I will find more. I don't know how I know that, I just do. I guess maybe it's something I knew all along, I just wanted to ignore. The bad guy never changes, and the short, curvy girl never gets the guy.

Picking up my phone, I head to the bathroom, and that's when the message I've been trying to send all day finally comes to me.

. . .

I message Lee, using our joke name of Carlos, and I bare my soul. I tell him I thought we had a connection, and that I really wasn't trying to blow him off, that my broken foot is real. I wish him all the happiness in the world with this new girl, and as I press send, I know in the pit of my soul that I don't mean a single word. I can't explain it, there's a pain there that hurts more than all Drew's deception.

The idea that this is the last time I will ever speak to Lee physically hurts me. There's a part of me, I think it may be my heart, telling me that Lee is important and that I shouldn't let him go. But therein lies the problem. I haven't let him go. He left me. He decided to date someone else, just like they all do in the end. After all, who wants to date a short, curvy, sarcastic girl with an incredible ability to fall over a leaf and break her foot? There's nothing about me that screams date me, love me. I'm one hundred percent forgettable, replaceable.

I clean myself up, and as quietly as I can, move around the flat, picking up my clothes so I can get dressed and leave this fucking shit hole, never to return. Once I'm fully clothed, I debate waking Drew up, but there's no point. We don't need to have a conversation, it won't go anywhere. I just need to forget all about this little mistake and accept I'm going to grow old with hundreds of cats—or maybe dogs, since cats scare the shit out of me. There's no denying that one day a cat is going to rise and take over the world. Just look at them. They have that evil dictator look about them, all of them.

It's three in the morning, but I order a taxi on my phone. Opening the front door, I'm shocked to see the person in the flat opposite is also coming out of their door too. I hadn't expected to see anyone. My hair is all messy, my make-up smudged, and my dress is all wrinkled from when I threw it on the floor. It's obvious I'm making the walk of shame, and to be honest, that wouldn't be a problem at all, if it wasn't for the fact I recognise the person coming towards me.

"Emmaleigh, what are you doing here?" asks Neelam—my boss!

"Erm... I-I was just... visiting a friend. Now I'm heading home." Yeah, that doesn't sound suspicious at all. I watch as her gaze travels over the slutty dress I'm wearing, and the big boot I have on to support my broken foot.

I suppose now would be a good time to mention that I work in the hospital as a nurse, and of course, given the broken foot, I'm currently on sick leave. "This is an odd time to be leaving, Em. Should you be on your foot at all? I don't want you injuring it further," Neelam states, and I can hear the tone of disapproval in her voice.

I mumble my response, trying not to act like a child being chastised by a parent. "I'm just heading to the taxi. I have my crutches at home. That's part of the reason I'm going home. My foot hurts. What are you doing here?" I turn the tables on her, although she doesn't look like she's making the walk of shame. She's in her jeans and T-shirt, and honestly she looks as perfectly put together as she always does at work.

"This is where I live. I'm on call, and they are short staffed on the ward, so I'm just going in to help." I can't help but wince, thinking I could be responsible for their staff shortage. I try to visualise my off-duty in my head, and I let out an audible sigh when I remember I definitely shouldn't have been working tonight. So, technically, it isn't my fault, but I still don't enjoy hearing that my colleagues—my friends—are struggling. We work as a team on our ward and I hate that my body means I am letting them down.

"Oh well, hopefully things will get better." What else am I supposed to say? I can't exactly help at all.

Neelam gives me a small smile. "Make sure you rest, please. Then when you get back to work, you can tell me all the gossip about why you are sneaking out of a boy's apartment at three in the morning."

She gives me a small wink as she walks past me towards the door that acts as an entry for the whole block of flats. I follow behind her, hobbling at a slower pace, trying not to wince. Fuck, I'm really regretting not bringing my crutches right about now.

She jumps in her car and my taxi appears. I wave her off as my body begins to sag. It's typical she spots me at the worst moments of my life. I can't really get much lower. A girl so desperate to be loved that she will settle for someone as fucking disgusting as Drew. I think now is the time when I really need to concentrate more on loving myself than on finding a man. Which is a fucking good idea since I'm out of options. My mind wanders to Lee, and I can't help but think about what we could have been if we had just had our chance.

Lee

"Ugh, I had the worst date ever last night," I groan as I flop down onto my best friend, Craig's, rumpled double bed. It's well after two in the afternoon, yet it still looks like he's just rolled out of it because he knew I was on my way over.

"Who was it this time?" he asks, as he munches on a chocolate bar he had on his computer desk. I can see he has a few, but he doesn't bother to offer me one. Typical. I almost roll my eyes at him.

Our friendship has never really been any different. Don't get me wrong, he's still the closest thing I have to a best friend, but that doesn't make him very good at it. We've been friends since we first met in school, around the age of five, and we have been close ever since. But the thing about Craig is that he's flaky as fuck. It's almost like if he sees something new and shiny, he will ditch me for a bit while he goes to play with that. I've come to learn that the newness always wears off, and eventually he always comes back. What I've never quite understood is why, each and every time, I let him.

"Is this the one with the massive tits?" he adds, as if that helps to clarify the situation.

Shaking my head. "No, that was the singer I met the week before last. This was the babysitter."

Craig has this lightbulb moment when he suddenly remembers who I'm talking about, and as he gets a mischievous glint in his eye, I remember why. "Oh fuck, yeah. Please tell me you fucked her and spanked her ass for being a bad babysitter," Craig jokes as he stands up, puts one foot onto the edge of the bed, and begins thrusting his pelvis while spanking his own ass.

Rolling my eyes, I push at his chest, not wanting his gyrating hips anywhere near me, thank you very much. "You watch too much porn, man," I chastise, before explaining that if I'm not her boss, I can't treat her like a bad babysitter.

He ignores me, like he never heard a word I said. "Okay, so you didn't have sex, is what I'm hearing?"

I can't help releasing a groan as I pull my fingers through my short jet black hair. This is what every failed date boils down to with him, and honestly, we are twenty-three years old, so I don't fucking blame him. But still.

"Look, I'm not like you. I have to get to know them slightly before I fuck them. And every date I've been on lately has been so monumentally fucking bad that I just can't get past their shit to even kiss them, let alone go for more," I explain, trying to hold in the groan as I think back to all the horrendous dates I've had over the last few months since I joined that fucking awful dating website.

They say that it's the men on there that are sex mad, and we're all sending dick pics within the first few minutes, talking dirty instead of asking how they are. But, in my albeit very limited experience, the women on there are just as horny. I've had pics of nipples, cleavage, and pussies sent my way all before I'd even asked how they are. So, as much as men get a bad rep on those sites—and it's probably well deserved— there are a few women that are just as bad.

I can feel my balls shrinking the more I talk about wanting to get to know a woman, and if I'm being honest, I'm not looking for a long-term relationship. I just don't want to fuck around with someone who is fucking around with ten other people. I guess you could say I have standards. Or, as Craig would say, I have blue balls thanks to my standards.

"Okay, so what was wrong with the babysitter?" Craig asks, and I feel a shiver of disgust ripple down my thoughts as I tell him all about my evening.

"So, you know how she invited me over to her house last night?" I ask, and he nods, but says nothing, so I continue. "Well... it turns out it wasn't actually her house. She was babysitting this young kid."

"Ohhh my naughty nanny porn is coming to life before my very eyes," Craig jokes, and I can't help but laugh at his crazy antics.

"Nah, it was nothing like that. I was so self-conscious. I mean, she's supposed to be watching the little kid, who thankfully was asleep the whole time, and yet she was more concerned with the joint she had with her."

"Wait! So, not only did you have a bad babysitter situation going on, she also provided you with weed. I'm failing to see what was wrong with this girl. Did she have a third boob, because at this point, I might be on board with that?"

I flopped back so that I was lying on the bed as a loud groan escaped my lips, frustration over my best friend more than clear. "She didn't have a third boob. It just felt weird. We were in a stranger's house, and she was getting high while we were responsible for a little kid. Whenever things started getting interesting and we started making out on the couch, the baby monitor would go off, interrupting us. But that wasn't even the worst part."

"So far I'm failing to hear a worst part, but please continue."

"She went to settle the kid down, and as she came back, she had some cash in her hand. I wondered what she had got it out for, and where from—since her jeans were so tightly plastered against her body, I would have noticed if she had a purse in her pockets. And I knew her bag was on the floor in front of me. That's when she told me she found it in the parents' bedroom, and sometimes she helps herself to stuff they won't miss. Then, as she put the money in her bag, she also put what looked to be an ornamental dog in there, too. She informed me she had done some research, and it was worth a couple of hundred pounds. I said surely it wasn't a good idea to steal from her employers, and she just said they're so rich they probably won't even know, and that they should have been paying her more. I hightailed it out of there and never looked back."

Silence fills the room, which is very unlike Craig, so I sit up to look and see what he's thinking. He's stuffing his face with another chocolate bar, and replies with his mouth full, which makes my stomach roll as nausea takes hold. "Okay, so you probably did the right thing there. Who are we dating next? What happened to the naughty nurse?"

My mind flicks back to Emmaleigh—or Gertrude, as I jokingly call her. She's the only person on the whole fucking app that knows how to hold a conversation. We had been talking every day for almost six weeks, until a couple of weeks ago. We had finally got to the point where we felt comfortable meeting, and if I'm being honest, I was actually very fucking excited about meeting her.

I dread the other dates now, wondering what fresh hell I will have to encounter, but there was just something different about her. I had a good feeling, but all that was long forgotten when she blew me off. It was the shittiest excuse, too. Something about breaking her foot by falling over a leaf. Yes, you heard that right—a leaf from a tree. I mean, she could have come up with something better. I was just sick of waiting. I didn't want a relationship where we just text every day. I wanted to meet her, but obviously she didn't want the same thing. So, I told her I was moving on, that I was seeing someone else. But it was her message a day later that broke me.

She told me she really had broken her foot, and that it was never an excuse. Apparently, she really wanted to date me and she was gutted that we couldn't meet. She wished me happiness with the girl I was dating, but I could tell she didn't fully mean it. It's like one of those things you say just because it's the right thing. You say one thing, but inside, everything is screaming the opposite. Don't date someone else. Don't be happy with someone else. What happened to giving us a chance? And you know what, I've been asking myself the same thing every day.

It's only been around a week since I got that message from her and I already miss her. Not having her there at the end of the day to message, talk about our day together, and generally someone to have a laugh with. It's actually been unbelievably lonely, which I know sounds absurd. How can you miss someone who has never really been part of your life? Particularly since I've never even laid eyes on her, but it's true

—I miss her. But, just like every other fucking thing in my life, I messed things up with her, too.

Craig clears his throat, dragging my attention back to him, and I see he's still staring, waiting for me to answer him. Taking a deep breath, I try to push Emmaleigh from my mind, and tell him to do the same. "I already told you, I've moved on from her. She was making excuses not to meet, and so I started seeing the babysitter."

"Ha, look how well that turned out. What do you mean by excuses?" I can practically feel him rolling his eyes at me, like it's more about my excuses than hers.

"We had planned to meet, but then she said she broke her foot. I don't know. I just got the feeling she was blowing me off so—"

Before I get the chance to finish my sentence, Craig interrupts me. "You would be fucking lucky if a girl blew you off. For fucks sake, Lee. You have got to stop making excuses. And more than that, decide what it is you really want. You say you want nothing serious, that you just want to fuck around, yet you are vetting these girls like you are looking for a wife. If you really just wanted a no strings fling, all you need to know about them is if they are hot, into you, and looking for sex. You keep going on dates, and then ditching these women because they aren't right. You are giving me fucking whiplash, so I can only imagine what the girls are thinking."

Shit, he's right. I don't know what the fuck is wrong with me. Maybe I just don't have it in me to sleep around. But I sure as hell know I'm not looking for a girlfriend. I can barely deal with looking after myself without having the needs of someone else to think about. Besides, even at twenty-three, I already know that I never want to get married or have children. So, what's the point in looking for a woman to settle down with when I can't—or won't—give them what they are looking for?

"Look," Craig says, as he flops down onto the bed beside me, grabbing my attention from the darkness that was engulfing me. "Just give the girl a chance. I know you've already blown her off, but it's fixable. Give her a week or two, tell her she's been on your mind, but that you were waiting for her foot to heal. Then ask her out. If you don't, you are always going to keep wondering. In the meantime, what about the swimmer you were talking to?"

He's got a point, I don't think I will be able to just forget about Emmaleigh as easily as I have the other girls. It's only been a few days, and I can't get her off my mind. Craig's right—fuck, I hate saying that—I should give her foot some time to heal, then go for it.

It's been a long couple of weeks, and I'm wondering why the hell I'm bothering going on dates. They are just one failure after the next. I really tried not to think about Emmaleigh. I tried telling myself that I broke things off with her and that I need to learn to live with that, but I just couldn't. With each new person I spoke to on the dating app, I compared them to her. They didn't ask me how my day had been like she always did. They didn't get my humour the way she did. They didn't make me laugh the way she did. So, in the end, I bit the bullet.

CARLOS AKA LEE

> Hey, Gertrude. I hope you are well and your foot's healed. I know you probably never thought you would hear from me again—maybe you never wanted to, in which case you can delete this message. But, I really hope you don't. You see, I thought I could easily move on and forget about you, since you blew me off—or so I thought. But the truth is, I haven't forgotten about you. I keep thinking about you, wondering what you are up to, and if you are thinking of me. If you've already moved on, then I completely understand that, but if you haven't, I would love another chance. What do you say, will you go on our long-overdue date with me?

I sent that text two days ago now, and I've been glued to my phone ever since. The one thing I fucking hate—and kinda love—about WhatsApp is their delivery system. You can see when someone has got your message, which is a relief, but then you wait for them to read it. Even worse than that is when they read it, but they don't reply. That's essentially what happened to me.

Emmaleigh read the message almost as soon as I sent it, but she hasn't replied. I've been checking every hour, hoping that she hasn't been back online, as that would mean she isn't ignoring me. She's just busy. But each time I check and see the time she last logged in has changed, that's when I realised she probably will not reply. It doesn't change the fact I have been glued to my phone. Every slight notification, every message ping, I'm there in a flash to check if it's her. Then I have to ignore the ache in the pit of my stomach when it's not her name.

I've started talking to another girl, Frankie, and honestly, she seems nice. We have a lot in common, and I probably should just ask her out on a date, but there's something holding me back. I never date or talk to two girls at the same time, it just doesn't feel right, and so accepting a date with Frankie would be like admitting that I've blown it with Emmaleigh. Something I'm just not quite ready to face yet.

I'm laying on my bed, just staring up at the ceiling when there's a knock on my bedroom door. Did I forget to mention that I still live at home with my parents? I know some people would frown upon this, and that they are in a mad rush to get away from their parents, but that couldn't be further from the truth for me. I love mine, and I have such an amazing relationship with my mum—she's like my best friend. So they give me freedom to come and go as I please, and they treat me like an adult, not a kid anymore, which was important to me.

But the biggest factor was that I only have to pay like a hundred pounds a week, which means the rest of my wages belong to me. Not a bad price considering I get all my food cooked, washing and ironing done, and all my bills are included, too. Why anyone would want to move out and give up all those benefits is beyond me. But, my number one rule when I decided to stay at home is that my room is my safe space. Nobody comes in without my permission, and especially not if I'm not here. Mum agreed to this as long as I agreed to keep it tidy.

Looking over, I see the sliding lock isn't on, and so I call out for whoever is on the other side to come in. Mum pushes the door open and comes to sit on the edge of the bed.

My mum's only a small lady, probably around five feet tall, and she looks good for her age. All the Zumba classes she goes to means she has the body of a thirty-year-old, despite being in her sixties. Her shoulder-length brunette hair is always perfectly styled, and her face is always made up to fit the occasion. Even around the house, she's rarely without makeup. Her flowery, baggy linen trousers, and her white flowy blouse make her look smart, even though I know she isn't going out today.

Mum smiles at me with one that matches my own, and I sit up to hear what she has to say. "So, I want to talk to you about something important, if that's okay?" she asks, her voice sombre, and that's when I see the sadness on her face and that her smile doesn't quite reach her eyes.

"Are you okay, Mum?" I ask, fear gripping me as I wait and wonder what she's going to say.

"I was talking to your sister earlier. Unfortunately, she's had a bit of a falling out with Cain. You remember how she found out he was sleeping with one of her friends that she worked with? Well, Lena put her name down to get an apartment near here. She's worried Cain won't be with her for the long-haul so she wants to be close to us, to give her the support she needs with Hayden. They're still working out all the move details, but Lena feels like Cain is dragging his heels. Personally, I think he's depressed, but Lena's obviously worried he's cheating again. So, she's asking if she can come and stay with us until she finds an apartment nearby. I think she's hoping some time away from them will make Cain realise what he's missing. Hayden's only a couple of months old, so he really shouldn't miss too much of these early years. I know having your sister move back home, along with baby Hayden, will be a big upheaval, so I wanted to get your opinion." Mum picks at her hands as she talks, and the minute she finishes talking, she bites at her cheek. She's worried I'm going to say no.

Initially, my instinct is to say that I don't want to live with Lena, or have a baby in the house. But, the more I mull it over in my head, the more I realise that's a massive douche move. My sister wouldn't want to move home unless it was the absolute last resort. She loves having her freedom, and when we were growing up, the more she rebelled, the more she argued with our dad. She couldn't wait to move out, so I'm guessing moving back, particularly when she had her whole future planned out with Cain, is not what she wants.

"Shit, I can't imagine how Lena feels right now. Am I thrilled to have her home, or to be living with a baby? No, of course I'm not. But she's family, and she needs our support, so I can get on board. Besides, it will give me a chance to spend a little more time with Hayden," Before I've even finished speaking, Mum throws her arms around me and pulls me in for the biggest hug. For a little woman, she sure gives big, squeezing hugs, and I love them.

Breathing a sigh of relief, I realise Mum was worried I might kick off. "I was worried you would say no."

Shaking my head. "I know I can be an asshole, but Lena needs somewhere, and I know you would never want to turn her down." Mum chuckles and then playfully whacks me across my arm the way she does every time I swear in front of her.

"Language, Lee. So, you got another date tonight? When am I ever going to meet one of these girls?" she asks with a pout and I can't help but roll my eyes.

"Oh, I don't know. Maybe the twenty-fourth of never!" I joke and again she playfully whacks my arm as she laughs. I grab hold of my bicep where she just hit me, and as dramatically as I can, I groan and fall backwards so I'm now laying on the bed. I make it sound like she's injured me and she just laughs. We both know I'm distracting her from answering the date question. The truth is, I don't know if she will ever meet one of the girls. At this stage, it will be a fucking miracle if I actually go on a date with someone I like. And even if I do, I don't ever want a long-term relationship.

My mind drifts back to Emmaleigh, and I can't help but think how much I've royally fucked that up before we even had a chance. Thankfully, Mum is here to distract me. She drags me downstairs for some dinner, which isn't really a hardship. I don't know anyone who would complain about having good, home-cooked food given to them every night without even having to ask for it.

After spending an hour or so just hanging out with Mum, I head back upstairs, realising I'd left my phone on my bed when I came downstairs. I actually had a moment when I thought how refreshing it was to not be staring at the damn thing every minute of every day. But when I pick it up and see the new notification that I missed, I can't help but curse out loud.

Motherfucker. I leave my phone for an hour, and she finally messages me. I take some deep breaths and try to calm myself while I ignore the butterflies in my stomach and the jitter in my hands. Fuck,

I'm not a teenage girl. Why am I getting so anxious and excited over a fucking text? What if she tells me to leave her alone? I know she would have probably just ghosted me for that, but you never know.

With shaky fingers, I take a deep breath, and press on the button to read the text from Emmaleigh.

> **GERTRUDE AKA EM**
>
> Hey, Carlos. Sorry for the late reply. I've been on nights and my body clock is all over the place. Thank you for your message, I've got to say I was a little surprised to hear from you again. My foot is almost healed. I still have a bit of physio to do, but it's getting there. If you still want to go on a date, I would love to.

Holy shit! After all the crap that's gone on between us, I never thought she would ever want to hear from me again. But she does, and she wants to meet me! Looks like I'm going on a date.

Emmaleigh

Standing in front of the mirror, I take in my outfit and my mind runs rampant. My dark ripped skinny jeans cling to my curves in all the right places, and they hold in my flabby bits just right. The off the shoulder black top is casual enough for a pub date, but the little display of skin and my bra strap makes it a little sexy. I've worn my best push-up bra too, since let's be honest, guys love boobs.

My long, dark purple hair is curled and clipped up so that it hangs perfectly around my shoulders, with a few stray tendrils hanging to frame my face. I'm wearing a bit of makeup, including my dark eyeliner and mascara, to make my blue eyes pop even more. The bright red lipstick compliments my black attire and makes my plump lips look inviting. I know in my head I look good, but I can't stop the anxiety from getting the better of me.

What if you aren't dressed up enough?
What if he's looking for someone a bit more girly?
Maybe you should wear a skirt?

Do those jeans make you look too fat?

All those thoughts are swimming around my mind, and I can't quieten them. A loud ringing pulls me out of my head, and I turn the alarm on my phone off. I set it so I would know exactly when I needed to leave. I have a tendency to turn up to things a bit late, but with him, I can't wait.

Pulling on my Converse, I look over at my heels but think better of it. Not only is my balance more horrendous lately, but my foot hasn't properly healed yet, and I don't want to do anything to hinder its recovery. I pull on my favourite leather jacket, grab my bag, and head out the door.

I arrive at the pub, Floods, just in the knick of time. We agreed to meet outside the door, and when I see nobody standing there, my stomach flips and the nerves begin. I'm glad I ate nothing before I left, as it would definitely make the nausea that's just settling in worse.

Looking down at my phone, there's no message from him. Do I wait here or go and look inside? There's no fucking point me looking inside. I don't really know what he looks like, other than the few pictures I've seen on his profile, and honestly, you never know how accurate they are.

What if he's stood you up?

Fuck off, brain.

I lean against the side of the pub, trying not to think about that possibility. He said he would be here, and so he will. I try my best not to look at my watch, but I can feel the minutes ticking by. Then, suddenly, I hear loud footsteps approaching rapidly, like someone is running. I look up to see Lee running towards me. He looks just like the pictures on his Internet dating profile, which is a novelty. I've met guys and the pictures they used were from five years previous, and they couldn't look more different. So, to see Lee looking exactly how I expect is great.

He stops right in front of me, taking a few deep breaths so he can slow his breathing down after his run, and it gives me the perfect opportunity to check him out.

The first thing I notice about Lee is his smile. It's warm, inviting, and it lights up his whole face, including the little dimples he gets in his cheeks that are very cute. His bright blue eyes shine beneath his dark-rimmed glasses—that really do suit and compliment his face. He's obviously chosen a pair that is made for him. His short, dark hair is so black it almost has shades of blue and purple when the light hits it.

My gaze rakes over his body and I take in one thing Lee told me he was most self-conscious about. He's only around five foot six, which, compared to the average male height of five foot eight, isn't all that much shorter, but to him it is. He thinks there are a lot of girls out there who would judge him based on that, but honestly, compared to my five foot two frame, he is tall. That's all that matters to me. Honestly, if he'd not told me about it, I probably wouldn't have even thought much of it.

The rest of his body is something to behold. Dark jeans wrap tightly around his muscular thighs, and I feel sure that when he turns around, the view of his ass will be incredible. His tight black T-shirt clings to his muscular chest. I can tell that he's a runner because his frame is more lean than bulky muscles. His body is toned and hard, and I know that the view underneath will be quite something.

Focus, Emmaleigh. This is only the first date. Show some restraint!

Lee catches me checking him out, and one side of his smile lifts into a cocky grin and fuck, does he look hotter. We both have that awkward moment where we wonder how we should greet each other. While this is the first time we are meeting in person, we feel like we know each other. We've been texting nearly every day for months now—minus the couple of weeks when we ended things—so just saying hello doesn't quite feel right. I'm close to doing something socially awkward, like hold my hand out for a handshake when thankfully Lee takes the lead and holds his arms open. He doesn't move in straight away, it's like he's letting me know what his intentions are so that I can pull away if I'm not comfortable. With a nod of my head telling him to continue, Lee wraps his arms around my shoulders and pulls me in for a hug.

The minute he pulls me against him, and I'm enveloped by his scent, I feel myself sag. It's such a weird feeling to explain, but it's almost like I found where I'm supposed to be. Like having his arms around me is all I need to feel safe and happy. I know that sounds totally bloody bonkers, given I've only just met him, but I can't change how I feel.

Eventually, he pulls away, and I try to hold back a groan. With a smile on his face, he finally introduces himself. "Hey, I'm Lee. It's so lovely to finally meet you. You look amazing, by the way. Can I buy you a drink?" It all comes out in a bit of a rush, like he's nervous and the words are coming out quicker than he can organise his thoughts. I know that feeling well.

"Thank you! I'm Emmaleigh. You look great too. Yeah, shall we go in and get a seat?" I ask, raising my arm to point at the entrance.

With a smile, Lee holds out his arm, too. "Ladies first."

We walk into the bar and get settled in the back room, next to the big pool table. I look over the list of drinks that's written on the wall, but I don't know why I bother. I always have the same. "Can I get a cider please?" I ask, pointing at my favourite brand. Lee lets out a little chuckle, and I wonder what's funny about my choice?

"That's exactly what I was going to order. I love the apple and raspberry flavour," he explains. "Great minds think alike." He winks at me and fuck, I think I actually swooned like a teenage girl watching a boy band live. I don't know what it is about this guy, but I can already tell I really like him.

"What do you say to a friendly game of pool?" I ask, tilting my head towards the empty table beside us. His brows furrow, but his cheeky grin remains.

"Oh, I will play pool, but there will be nothing friendly about it. I know I probably shouldn't let you see this side of me on a first date, but I'm ruthless. I will not let you win. I will take you down," he jokes and I can't help the girly giggle that bursts free from my lips.

"Wow, competitive much," I tease as he stands and heads to the bar, telling me to save the pool table so that nobody else can grab it before us.

He returns with our drinks, and the balls and cues we need to play with. He takes a sip from his glass before shrugging off his jacket, showing off his muscular biceps. As he leans over to set up the balls on the table, I take the opportunity to check out his ass, and fuck, it looks just as good as I thought it would.

Though, as Lee turns around and hands me my cue, it's clear by the cocky grin on his face that he knew I'd been checking him out again. I take a gulp of my drink, hoping the movement will hide the blush spreading across my cheeks.

"Shall we make this interesting?" I ask, biting my lip as I try really hard not to come across as too eager. I can see I've piqued his interest, appealing to his competitive side.

"I'm listening."

"How about, each time I pot a ball, I get to ask you a question that you have to answer?"

That cocky grin of his makes my stomach flip. "I like the sound of that. What about if I pot a ball? Will you answer any of my questions?"

Shrugging my leather jacket off and placing it on my chair, I shrug. "Of course."

"Then let's play. Who is going to break?" Lee asks.

I take a coin out of my purse and tell him we should flip for it. I call heads just as it lands heads facing upwards and with as sexy a shimmy as I'm capable of; I go to stand at the head of the table. As I lean over to line up the white ball, I'm suddenly very glad I wore my good bra—and given the direction of Lee's gaze right now, I think he feels the same.

I smack the cue ball with as much power as I can, absolutely no skill involved, just brute strength and sheer dumb luck. Thankfully, two balls with stripes on them go straight into the pockets and I hold two fingers up at Lee, making sure they are the right way around, so he doesn't think I'm swearing at him. "That's two questions you owe me."

He leans against his cue with one hand, while he takes a sip from his cider in the other. "Okay, first question."

I make a big deal, pretending like I'm thinking hard about what to ask him. Actually, I'm not pretending all that much. Obviously, it's the first question, so I can't go in with anything too personal, and I can't turn it sexual—yet.

"Okay, so let's make it an easy one. Tell me a secret that nobody else knows about you."

He ponders that for a moment, and we look at each other in companionable silence while I wonder if he's going to answer or not. "I don't want to be an adult." Well, that's not quite what I was expecting him to say.

"What do you mean? And no, that isn't the second question," I clarify, before he cheats me out of my second question on a technicality. He chuckles like that's exactly what he had been thinking.

"I don't like the responsibility that comes with being an adult. Everyone agrees, but nobody says it out loud. I can barely take care of myself. I don't want the added responsibility of having to look after or care about someone else. That's why I never want to get married or have kids," he says firmly, but I can tell he's a little wary about bringing up such a heavy subject on our first date. I might not know how I feel about his answer, given that I very much do want to get married and have kids, but I appreciate his honesty. I like that I know I'm getting the truth whenever I talk to him.

"Does that mean you aren't looking for a relationship?" I ask. I don't mean to, it just kinda slipped out, and I can't take it back. Fuck, I'm going to look like a stage four clinger asking about relationships when we aren't even an hour into our first date.

Lee just laughs. "If I answer, I'm counting this as your second question," he explains, and so I nod my head in confirmation, my heart racing as I wait to hear his reply.

I don't know what it is about him. I mean, I only met him less than an hour ago, and already I've got butterflies in my stomach, and my heart is racing while I wait to find out if he's looking for a relationship. Is that what I want? Do I want to date Lee? What if he doesn't want a relationship? Would I be happy with a friends-with-benefits type situation? Fuck, all these things are going through my head, and I try to quieten them down so I can actually hear his reply.

"Honestly, I don't know. For the right girl, I think I would, but it would take a fair bit to get me there. I would want to just be friends first and see how that goes," Lee explains, and I see his cheeks flush slightly as he answers. I mean, it's not a bad answer. I guess there's always hope for us!

I take my next shots and pot nothing, but when Lee steps up, he nets a spot on his first try, doing a very cute little happy dance to celebrate. "Okay, now I need to come up with a good first question that doesn't make me sound too pervy," he muses aloud, and I can't help but laugh.

"Oh, we can go straight for the sexy questions if you want." I wink before giving him a cheeky grin. Where the fuck did that come from? I absolutely don't need to be telling him about the shittiest sexy times that have come before him.

"We will get there, there's plenty of balls after all." We both laugh at his double entendre before taking drinks from our glass. "Right, I've got a good one. If your mum could change anything about you, what would it be?"

"What kind of a question is that?" I ask, confused by why I need to tell him about my mum's thought process.

"Well, we all have stuff that we hate about ourselves. So, if I ask what you would change, that would be easy. But mum's love everything about their kids, even sometimes blindly. So, I want to know what your mum would change."

I laugh because he's right. I have a list as long as my arm that I would change, but Mum loves all of it. Except for maybe one or two things. "I guess it would probably be one of two. She would either say my mouth because I can be incredibly bossy and I talk a lot. Or she would say my clumsiness. My body has this incredible ability to fail me at the worst possible times, leading to me injuring myself more times than I can count. The broken foot was just one in a long line of issues. In fact, Mum used to be scared every time she took me to the hospital that social services would ask questions. In today's world, they definitely would have."

He laughs, and the rest of the date flows easily from there. We spend the next couple of hours just playing pool, asking each other funny or personal questions, having a laugh, and just generally getting to know each other.

As the pool games progressed, we got more touchy feely. I would try to distract him by running my foot up his leg, or leaning over the opposite side of the table so all he could see was my cleavage. He would retaliate by blowing in my ear, or covering my back with his front, pressing himself against me to put me off. It worked.

By the time the date was coming to a close, I knew I liked him. My face ached from the amount of smiling. My heart was racing just being near him, and I didn't want the date to end. I knew I wanted to see him again, but that brought up the awkward question of how he felt about me.

"Would you like me to walk you back to your car?" he asks, after I explain it's a few streets away because there was no parking nearby. I only had the first cider, swapping over to Coke after that first drink, so I knew I was fine to drive. It turns out Lee only lives around the corner from where I parked, so I take him up on his offer to walk me to my car. I'm actually glad about it, as I don't want the night to end yet.

As we leave the pub, Lee takes hold of my hand in his and it's like bolts of electricity are shooting through my arm. My whole body feels like it's on fire, all because I'm near him. I let Lee lead the way, this is his town and he knows it much better than me. I only live about thirty minutes away, and since my best friend lives in this town, I know where I'm going, yet he still seems to show me new routes.

We stop in front of a thin alley that barely looks wide enough to fit us both in side by side. It's completely dark, the moonlight that had been aiding the street lamps on our journey so far is no longer visible. There are no street lamps lighting the way, and the darkness is so pitch black, we can't even see the other end of the alley.

Lee goes to move towards the alley, but I hesitate. He looks between the alley and me, and eventually I see the moment the realisation hits. He can see I'm apprehensive about going down a dark alley, with a complete stranger, who I may or may not be very fucking into. "Okay, so this is the ultimate test. I like to call it the dark alley test. Do you trust me enough to let me lead you down a dark alley, all alone at night? I promise you it will come out right beside the street where you parked your car, but you have to trust my word. Do you trust I'm not lying to you and do you trust me?"

His bright blue eyes fix on mine, and I take a moment to appreciate how gorgeous the colour blue is. It's like looking into a stunning clear sea. I don't know how I know, and I certainly can't explain it, but I do trust him. I'm the girl who never trusts, who never takes a chance on anyone but herself. Yet, right now, I want to go with him.

"Do you often lead young girls down dark alleys at night?" I joke, and Lee laughs.

"None as beautiful as you," he winks, before moving towards the alley, keeping hold of my hand. Though he never pulls me, he just keeps hold to guide me.

I follow behind him, trying to ignore the way my heart races when he says I'm beautiful. The deeper we get into the tunnel, the darker it gets. I trust Lee, but that doesn't mean there are no other murderers and rapists lying in wait in the damn alley. Just as I'm thinking that, street light shines on Lee's face, and as we come out of the other end of the alley, he throws a bright smile my way.

"You really weren't scared at all in there, were you?"

I can't help but chuckle. "No, I would have taken out anyone who attacked us. I'm feisty like that," I say before pointing at the Ford behind him. "That's my car, by the way. Thank you for walking me here."

We both stand in front of my Ford Fiesta, just looking at each other, waiting for someone to say something, anything. I want to ask him if he wants to go on another date, but his silence has me worried. Maybe he's not that into me. Maybe we have crossed wires. Fuck, I really need to quieten my head sometimes.

Before I have a chance to say anything, Lee takes a step towards me and I'm caught off balance, causing me to stumble backwards. Luckily, I land with my back against my car, and Lee closes the distance easily. He leans forward, his hands on the car roof either side of my head, caging me in, and he's so close I can feel the heat from his body. His breath fans across my face, causing my breath to hitch. I bite my bottom lip nervously, but Lee moves one of his hands and gently tugs my lip free. He then leans over and whispers in my ear as a shiver ripples down my spine. "Don't do that. Only I'm allowed to bite your lip."

Fuck! If that's not the hottest thing a guy has ever said to me, I don't know what is.

While I'm busy considering that, he leans forward and presses his lips against mine. It's soft and gentle at first, but the moment our lips really connect, passion sparks through us. My hands fly to the back of his head, my fingers threading through his hair as I frantically try to pull him closer. I can feel his body, his hardness, pressed against my front, and I can't hold back the moan of pleasure that comes out.

As soon as he hears my desperate sounds, he pulls his head back, but doesn't leave my space. He keeps his body against mine, and I can feel my core throbbing with need. I don't even care that this is a first date, or that we are in the middle of a very public road. Thankfully, Lee is thinking with his head and not his dick.

"Wow. You do not know how difficult it was to pull away from that. But this is a first date, and you deserve better. How do you feel about a second date?" I can't believe after the way I just lost control kissing him, he still looks unsure of what my answer might be.

"I would love to go on another date with you."

He gives me a little smile before he steps back out of my personal space, and I can almost feel my body throbbing from his absence. A strange, almost sad expression crosses his face for just a moment before his face becomes a blank mask again.

"Em, I have to remind you about what I said in the pub. I'm not looking for a relationship right now. If it turns into one, then so be it, but until then, I only want friends," he explains, his voice a little sheepish, like he's worried I won't accept his terms.

I nod my head in confirmation. "I remember you saying that. Now it's my turn to clarify something. When you say you want to be friends, do you mean just friends or friends-with-benefits?" I feel my cheeks flushing, and I want to look away, but I can't. I don't know if I can be just friends with Lee and not want to kiss him again after that.

"Well, I'm still a guy, and you are a beautiful woman. So, of course, if you wanted to add the benefits part, then I would be very on board with that. But I would also be happy with just friends too. I've enjoyed chatting with you every day, even before we met."

I give him a big smile before I lean in and capture his lips for a moment. It's nowhere near as deep and sexy as before, and it's over in a flash, but it was full of passion and spoke a thousand words. Though I made sure he knew exactly how I felt. "So, why don't you come over to mine next time? We can do takeaway and a movie?"

"It's a deal. Bring on date number two," he says, as he captures my lips again for another short but intense kiss.

He helps me into the car, and I can honestly say I don't remember a single thing about driving home. All I could think of was his laugh, his smile, the way his eyes light up. Not to mention how hot his peachy ass looked in those jeans. My heart races and my body tingles from where he was touching me. I can still smell him on me, and I feel like I'm in heaven.

I don't know what the hell I'm thinking, but the one thing I know. Lee has got beneath my skin. He's burrowing his way under, and I do not know what to think or feel. I want him—badly. I guess we'll just have to see how date number two goes. I'm still struggling to believe a guy like him could truly like a clumsy, accident prone, bossy, sarcastic girl like me. A girl can only hope.

Lee

"So, how did it go?" Craig asks the next day as he sprawls out on my bed like it's his own. Before I even get a chance to answer, he reaches over and turns on the Playstation. Good to know he really does give a shit about what I have to say.

"Surprisingly, it went okay," I reply, as I think back over the date I had with Emmaleigh last night. I've had a very long run of bad dates recently, and so I didn't really have any expectations for this one.

Okay, so that's a complete lie. I wanted to like Emmaleigh. I wanted her to be different from all the other miserable, failed dates I've had to endure over the last few months. I tried not to get my hopes up, particularly after all the hassle we faced actually trying to schedule the damn date, but I think deep down, I wanted the date to be good.

Whenever we text each other, it would always be the way you expect a conversation to go. She answers my question and then asks one of her own. It's like conversational tennis, where we each make an effort to keep the conversation started. I know this sounds like a standard thing, something everyone should know how to do, yet they don't. So many times I've sent a message to a woman and got a one word reply. You wouldn't believe the amount of times I've asked a girl how her day's been, listened intently to the answer, only for her to reply with a monosyllabic, one word answer. Never once thinking of asking me about my day.

With Emmaleigh, it's always been easy, but still I didn't hold out too much hope for the date. I've come to realise who people are on the internet, or even when you speak to them through text, it isn't always who they really are.

Craig groans, pulling me back from my memories of the night before, which is good because the more I think about the feel of her lips against mine, the more uncontrollable my dick becomes. "Just okay? What does that even mean?"

He sounds so frustrated as he runs his hand through his short brown hair. I can't help but chuckle at his exacerbated expression. "It means that we had a good time. She seems nice, and it was fun."

"Why does it sound like there should be a but at the end of that sentence?"

With a groan I flop down onto the bed beside Craig, who has just started another game of FIFA on my Playstation. Even though he's responding to my questions, and he's clearly interested in what I'm saying, his gaze never once leaves the screen. "I don't know. I guess I'm just worried we want different things. I did make it clear I'm not looking for a girlfriend."

"So, what's the problem?" he asks, his eyes flitting over to me for a second before going back to the screen.

"Honestly, I get the impression she wants more. I told her I don't want a relationship, and I just want to be friends. That's when she asked if that means friends-with-benefits, so—"

Craig drops the controller after pausing his game, and he holds out his hand to interrupt me. "Wait, so she's the one who suggested that you be friends-with-benefits?" he asks and as soon as I nod in confirmation he starts to laugh. "Fuck, Lee. You have just got everything you have been looking for, and you're moping around here like your dog died. What the hell is the matter with you?"

"What do you mean?" I ask incredulously.

"You met a girl that you like. She's hot—if I'm remembering the right photo you showed me. She is easy to talk to and you get on well. Then on top of all that she's happy with a friends-with-benefits set up. This girl sounds perfect. So why don't you seem pleased?" His voice gets more and more high pitched as he talks, as he gets more irked at me. I can see his point. If I listed all the things I was looking for in a girl, she would be very close to getting full marks. So why am I so hesitant?

"I have no idea why," I grumble, only for Craig to laugh.

"Maybe you wanted her to want more." He chuckles as he picks up the controller again and starts playing.

My brow furrows as I try to take in what he said. "What do you mean?"

"Well, you've always been sure that you don't want a relationship, and so every woman who does want one, that's a great reason for you to push them away. But, when this girl comes along, a girl you actually like, and she doesn't give you a reason to push her away because she wants the same things you do. So now you have to find some other reason why she isn't right. You have pushed so many girls away that I don't think you know how to actually date someone." His words are innocent. Hell, he doesn't even take his eyes off the television when he says them, but it's like they stab me deep. They cut through the armour I didn't realise I had in place.

"I didn't realise I pushed people away. I... it's just none of them were right," I mumble, and this time Craig does pause the game to look over and fix his gaze with mine.

"Even if none of them were right, this girl is perfect. You like her, and by the sounds of it, she likes you. She's agreed you can just be friends-with-benefits and see what happens, which is exactly what you said you wanted. So, why does that scare you so much? Are you worried that you might actually fall for her?" he asks, his gaze feels like it's examining my every move and I feel almost naked and exposed. This is so out of character for Craig. Yes, we've been best friends for as long as I can remember, but we don't do this touchy-feely bullshit.

"Since when do you ask me about my feelings?" I snap, hating how exposed I feel.

Craig holds his hands up like he's surrendering, his eyes wide and full of confusion. He doesn't see me snap or get angry often, since I prefer to hide my emotions away from other people. I feel like I play a role in front of others, to be the person they want me to be, or who I think I should be. That means holding back the real me, even from my friend.

"Sorry, man. Chill out, I was only asking. Just go on your date with her and see how things go. You never know, things might just have a way of working out in the end," he says, as he turns back to the game.

Maybe he's right, and I just need to go on another date and see what happens. We've texted each other since the first date, and it's still easy to communicate with her. I didn't know if it would be weird after our kiss, but we haven't talked about it, which is fine with me. Though that doesn't stop me from dreaming about it. About the taste of her on my tongue. The heat spreading across my skin wherever she touched me. The way my heart raced as the kiss became more passionate. Not to mention that my cock was hard as a rock until I got home to take care of it. Or the amount of times I've wanked thinking about her since then. There's something different about this girl and that scares me. I need to keep her at arm's length before she's able to burrow underneath the carefully erected barriers I have protecting my heart. She has the potential to smash my heart to pieces, and I can't let that happen.

"Breathe in, two, three, four, and breathe out, two, three, four," the soft, melodic voice echoes through my car as I try to practise the mindfulness technique people rave about.

I'm sitting in my car, around the corner from Emmaleigh's apartment, and I'm freaking the fuck out. The whole thirty minute drive over here, all I could focus on was the pounding of my heart, the ringing in my ears, and the sweat on my palms that's making the steering wheel clammy.

I don't know why I'm freaking out so badly. We had a great first date, and this is going to be so much more relaxed. After Emmaleigh hinted about this being a friends-with-benefits type situation, then inviting me over to her flat, it doesn't take a genius to work out where this might go. So, why am I so nervous?

Let me be very clear about something... I've had sex before. Granted, for a twenty-three year old to say I've only been with three girls, that's probably not anything to brag about. Even worse is that each experience was a little worse than the last. Not through anything I did wrong, I might add. The first girl, we were sixteen at a party and she cried afterwards. Said she regretted it as she always planned to wait until she was married, since her dad was a preacher. I got out of that one rapidly.

The next one was fine, but there was just no connection between us. I think maybe because we both knew that, we just didn't really make that much effort. She didn't tell me what she liked, and that made things very difficult. I guess you could say I learnt a lot about reading women from her.

The final girl was arguably the worst. I just couldn't get her to come, no matter how hard I tried—literally. I tried it hard, I tried it slow. I used all the techniques I learnt from porn and the internet. But nothing. I even tried asking her what she likes, and did exactly what she told me, but still no fireworks. Naturally, we broke up, and three days later she met the love of her life and announced she's a lesbian. So it wasn't necessarily that I was trying too hard, it was just that I had a cock. You should have heard Craig's jokes about my cock having the ability to make girls into lesbians. I still haven't lived it down.

So, no, my sexual history isn't exactly anything to sing home about. Maybe that's why my stomach is doing flips. Because my body definitely wants to take things further with Em. Hell, that's all I've been thinking and dreaming about since our last date. My cock has been hard as granite for the last week, uncomfortably so. So why does it feel weird to think this is just a meet up for sex?

Fuck, I thought it was supposed to be women who over-analyse everything and question every little thought, fear, or feelings. I honestly feel like a teenage girl reading into every word or gesture. I told Emmaleigh that there could be nothing between us. That I only wanted a friends-with-benefits situation, and she agreed. So that should be the end of it... right? Then, why am I thinking about waking up beside her in the morning?

Focus, Lee, I mentally chastise myself. I can't sit out here for the rest of the fucking evening. I'm already five minutes late. I need to pull up my grown-up pants, get out of the car, and just walk over to her apartment. One step at a time—literally. I don't need to analyse how the date could progress, but I do need to actually turn up for it before she thinks I've stood her up.

Taking some big deep breaths, I follow my own advice and get out of the damn car. With every step I take closer to the apartment building, my heart starts to race. At first I think it's nerves, but there's also a level of excitement there too. I enjoyed hanging out with Emmaleigh last time. In fact, it's the most I've laughed in a very long time. She's fun and easy to be around, which is probably why I'm looking forward to seeing her.

Once I reach the door for the apartment block, I pull out my phone to double check what number she lives at. Once I've confirmed I have the right place, I take a big deep breath and press the buzzer. The loud, shrill buzzing rings out loudly, and it's not long before a tinny version of Emmaleigh's voice echoes around me.

"Come in, I'm on the first floor, on the right," she shouts, as another lower pitched buzzing sound indicates she's opened the door for me.

I push the main door open, and am greeted by a set of stairs. There's a corridor to the right of them that no doubt leads to the ground floor flats. It looks like the stairs are in the middle of the building and there's one flat to the right of the stairs and one to the left. Looking up, I can see there are only two flights of stairs, and Emmaleigh's flat is in the middle.

Once I reach the top of the first set of stairs, there's a window looking out over the shared car park at the back of the building. To my left there's a wooden door that's identical to the one on the right—except for the metal number plate in the centre of the door. Turning to the right, I'm just about to knock on the door I believe to be Emmaleigh's when it swings open.

Emmaleigh is standing there, a bright smile on her beautiful face. She's wearing her dark rimmed glasses, but her bright bluey-grey eyes still sparkle from beneath them, accentuated further by the light strip of dark eyeliner that she's wearing. It doesn't look like she's wearing much makeup. I get the impression, same as I did on our first date, that she's not a big makeup kinda girl. And to be honest, she doesn't need it. She looks stunning without anything on. Though, that sexy shade of red lipstick does a great job of making her full red lips look plump and inviting.

The skinny jeans she's wearing cling to her curvy hips, making her look even more shapely and sexy. The rips along the thighs and knees give me a glimpse of the milky skin that lies underneath, and once again my dick is hard as nails. What the fuck is wrong with me? I'm not a pre-pubescent teenager who has never seen a naked woman before, yet I'm getting turned on by a bit of exposed skin on her thigh. As my gaze travels to her top half, I'm surprised I don't blow my load in my boxers.

Emmaleigh is wearing an off the shoulder white top that hangs down to her jeans on one side and stops just above her belly button on the other. The lacey white strap of her bra is showing, and I can't keep my eyes from the exposed skin around her navel. A twinkling of light catches my eye, and as she moves and the top rides up a little more, I catch sight of a silver belly button bar. I have to bite my lip to hold back the groan.

Fuck, this girl looks perfect. Don't even get me started on the way her top falls off one shoulder exposing very generous cleavage. If my cock gets any harder, it will pop the zipper on my jeans and free himself.

"Hey," Emmaleigh mutters, a shy smile spreading across her lips causing a little dimple to appear on her right cheek as she pulls her T-shirt down, trying to cover up the exposed skin. Fuck, that's so adorable. Did I notice that last time? "Do you want to come in?"

I realise I'm just standing there in the doorway to her flat, staring at her while she looks around nervously waiting for me to end the awkward silence. "Oh… yeah. Erm, sorry. I-I would love to," I mutter, sounding like a complete nervous wreck. So much for all the relaxing breathing bollocks. I did all their breathing exercises and I sure as shit don't feel any calmer.

Opening the door wider, she leads me into her apartment. There's a corridor that leads from the main front door, round a small bend to the right and then straight down into a large open plan kitchen and living area. As I'm walking through the short corridor, I take in the bright white walls that are lined with family photos, and the entire wall of bookshelves that are full of a wide array of books. There's a door to the left that Em tells me is the bathroom, and the first door on the right is the master bedroom and en-suite, and the second is the spare bedroom.

As she leads me through her flat, I'm pleasantly surprised by how big the place is. From the outside it doesn't look anywhere near this size, but it's quite spacious, and the clean magnolia walls make the rooms look larger. The living room has a dining table in one corner, with some flowers sitting in the middle, and there's a three-seater black leather sofa taking up one wall and a smaller two-seater against the opposite wall. It's actually an exquisite home, and I'm impressed Emmaleigh has been able to do all this on her own at such a young age.

"Welcome to my humble abode," Em jokes as she spreads her arm out and spins around dramatically, as if she's unveiling the place for the first time.

I drop my bag onto the floor beside her dining table before shooting her a smile. "It's lovely. You have a really great place here."

I watch as a blush spreads over her cheeks, and I can tell this girl isn't used to compliments. Which is actually unbelievably sad. What is so wrong with the male population? A girl this beautiful should be used to receiving compliments. I bet if I were to ask her she's received more dick pics than she has flattering remarks.

"Thanks. I like it. Please, make yourself comfortable and I will get you a drink. Do you want a cider or just a soft drink?" she asks as she heads towards the connected kitchen on the left.

I freeze, my mind going over all the different scenarios, trying to think of what the correct answer to this question should be. I know it sounds like an easy question, but it's not. If I have cider, that's me admitting that I plan on spending the night here. I live just over thirty minutes drive from here, and I never drive after I've had even the slightest bit of alcohol. The roads are windy and dark, and I'm not risking it. So, if I take the cider, I can't drive, and I would have to stay here.

Who would have thought a question as simple as what do I want to drink could turn into a complex mathematical equation. I need to stop overthinking this. We've already agreed to friends-with-benefits, and let's be honest, if it's shit, I can walk away. And even if it's mind-blowingly amazing, then we can just keep on doing it with no ties.

"I will take a cider, please. How have you been?" I ask, finally finding my voice as I move towards the sofa. I try my best to analyse whether or not she has a preferred side, as I know most people do, and there's nothing worse than someone coming and plopping themselves down and ruining the careful balance your ass has created.

As Emmaleigh gets a cider out of the fridge, I can see her watching me out of the corner of her eye, the slightest hint of a smile on her face as she sees my inner turmoil. She waits a good few, painful seconds before indicating that I can sit on the left hand side, as she usually takes the right.

Once we're both settled on opposite ends of the sofa, and I've taken a much needed swig of cider in the hope the alcohol will help to calm down my nervous brain, she breaks the awkward silence. "Welcome to Casa De Em. And, I should probably make it very clear that I speak no other language than English, and even that's a struggle. So, I hope whatever I just said didn't offend an entire nation."

I can't help but chuckle at the cute way she babbles when she's nervous. She told me on the last date that awkward silences make her nervous, and she tends to try to fill them. However, as she's already super anxious, she may have a tendency to make the situation worse. Actually, I find it rather endearing, and as a blush spreads across her cheeks, I can't help but shuffle a little closer.

"I don't think that was a bad attempt. So, how has your week been? Have you been down any more dark alleys with complete strangers?" It's supposed to be an innocent enough question, but I can hear a tone in my voice that I'm not used to hearing. It takes me a while to decipher what exactly I'm getting at, but I think Em gets there a lot quicker than I do.

"Are you asking me if I've been on any other dates this week?" she asks suspiciously, her gaze narrowing as they meet mine.

Am I asking her that? Is that what that feeling is—jealousy? Oh shit, I definitely do not like that.

"Well, I wasn't meaning it like that. Maybe I'm just wondering if other guys can come up with as cool a date idea as mine. I know it's tough to beat, but they can but try," I joke. Her eyes flicker in a way that calls bullshit, but she sidesteps my obvious blunder.

"Well..." she starts, a shy smile spreading across her face. "I haven't been on any dates this week, and I definitely haven't ever been on one with a potential serial killer who does freaky dark alley tests." Her tinkling laughter rings out at the end, and just like it did at the pub last week, it sends tingles throughout my body and is like music to my ears. I wouldn't class myself as a funny guy, but I love to see the way this girl lights up every time she laughs.

Feigning offence, I hold out the hand that isn't holding the cider can, in a stop sign. "Whoa, serial killer is a little harsh."

"I said potential serial killer," she replies, before taking a sip of her can and shuffling into a more comfortable position on the sofa, with her leg underneath her ass. I don't miss the way her new position puts her closer to me, and she's now leaning in my direction. It wouldn't be hard for me to pull the exact same move until we're both sitting right beside each other, almost touching.

"Why would you go down a dark alley with someone you thought could be a serial killer?"

With a big smile on her face, she pulls herself up so that she's sitting up taller and looks a lot more confident than she did just a second ago. "Well, it probably had something to do with the fact I knew I could take you."

If I'd had a mouthful of cider at the time, it wouldn't have been the perfect moment for a spit take. A short, sharp 'ha' escapes my lips and her brow furrows as she stares at me intently. I raise my eyebrows questioningly, and I can tell that only pisses her off further.

"I may be short and a girl, but that doesn't mean I don't know how to throw a punch or throw down. I used to be a bit of a fighter when I was younger," she explains, looking incredibly proud of herself, and I can tell she's serious.

"What do you mean?" I'm sure the confusion is evident on my face, but I clarify it aloud just in case.

A blush spreads across her creamy alabaster skin, and there's a definite twinkle to her eye that I've not seen before. "When I was a teenager, I just used to be really angry. I guess you could say I had a lot going on in my head and I really didn't know how to deal, and it caused me to lash out. I may have been a relatively small girl, but I had no issues throwing down with the tallest guy in the school if I had to. I guess you could say I got a bit of a reputation as being a brawler. It's not something I'm super proud of, but I know how to take care of myself. Which is why your dark alley test didn't scare me."

"Because you knew you could kick the shit out of me if I tried anything." I say the thing we both knew was left unsaid from the end of her explanation.

Fuck, I'm not sure how I feel knowing this beautiful girl in front of me likes to get in fights. I've been speaking to her, minus the time we took a short break, for a little over a month, and I had no idea. She's never brought it up before. Does it bother me?

Emmaleigh begins shuffling in her seat, looking a little uncomfortable as her gaze rakes over me. "Just for the record, that's not who I am anymore. I haven't thrown a punch since I turned eighteen. So that's well over five years ago," she mumbles, averting her gaze to look down at her hand that's picking at a piece of fabric on her jeans.

"I'm not bothered by it, Em. It's actually kinda hot to know you can take care of yourself. Did you actually win the fights against guys?" I didn't know I really meant the words until I said them, but it's true. I've never been a fighter. Hell, if a guy threw a punch my way, the only chance I stand is if I run. I'm a fast runner, but my face would break faster than if I dropped an old lady's china tea service on the floor. So the fact this girl can hold her own is more than a little hot.

"Yeah, I beat them all. But to be fair, after I slapped one around the face with a ruler in the middle of class, most just kept out of my way after that," she says with a smile, and I can't help but laugh. "What? He deserved it. He was picking on my best friend for being ginger, and so I made sure he knew that wouldn't be tolerated."

"You were a badass," I state, as I shuffle to close the gap between us on the sofa before reaching over to take her hand in mine.

The cool of my skin against her warm flesh causes tingles to ripple against my palm, shocking me completely. I've never felt anything like that before, and it startles me so much, I almost pull my hand back. But Em laces her fingers with mine, tightening her hold, and she looks up at me through hooded eyes, her baby blues glisten as she smiles at me. Our gazes lock together and for a moment we're frozen, neither of us moving. I'm not sure if I should close the last small gap between us and capture her lips with mine, or if I should pull back and carry on the conversation. I don't want her to think we're rushing.

My heart's racing so fast I can hear it whooshing in my ears, and as Em pulls her lower lip between her teeth, I can't help but smile. This gorgeous girl has no idea how stunning she really is.

I know I said nothing can come of this, and that all I'm interested in is a friends-with-benefits type of situation, and I really meant it, but I'm worried Emmaleigh isn't the type of girl who doesn't want anything meaningful. She strikes me as a hearts and flowers type of person, and if that's the case, this will never work. I know what I'm capable of, and I need my alone time. I wasn't made to be in a relationship, and I'm hoping I've made that clear to Em.

Emmaleigh

After a bit of a slow, almost nervous start, my second date with Lee definitely improved. At the end of the first date, we both made it clear what our intentions are, and that neither of us is looking for anything serious. Honestly, I'm not totally sure I was being honest with Lee when I agreed to us being just friends. I spent a lot of time mulling it over after the date, and I think I just said what he needed to hear so that I could see him again.

I've never met anyone like Lee, and I very quickly became addicted to how he made me feel. Not only could he make me laugh—which is super important to me—he also made me feel sexy, which isn't something I'm used to.

Don't get me wrong, I'm not hideous to look at, but I have my hang-ups just like every other girl. I see the way my hips puff over the belt of my jeans, causing a little muffin top, and the fact there's definitely no gap between my thighs. My ass is full, and even with a good pair of jeans, it's impossible not to notice the extra padding I have there.

Weirdly, my waist is smaller than my hips, and that's what gives me my curvy hour-glass figure. My boobs are a decent size, whilst not being too big, and I appreciate that. A handful of booty I can handle, but extra cleavage is harder to work with.

Despite being what society would call a plus size girl, Lee never made me feel this way. He looked at me with a big smile on his face, those sexy as hell dimples appearing as his sparkling blue eyes checked me out. I always feel a bit self-conscious when it's obvious guys are checking you out, as you never know how they're going to respond. But Lee licked his lips before biting down on his lower one, and it was obvious he found something about me attractive, which was a good thing, because I was more than just attracted to him. I liked him, and that led me to do something stupid.

Before going on the date, I told myself this would be the one. I was done sleeping around, dating jerks who never really cared about me. This was me taking a step in the right direction, getting onto the dating ladder. That meant, no matter how much I might like this guy, no sex on the first date. If I want him to be serious about me—which at the time I very much did—then I need to make sure he has a reason to keep coming back. I had it all planned out before the date, and then he dropped the bombshell—he doesn't want a relationship.

When he first told me, I didn't really know what to say. I just remember feeling a bit deflated, though I tried my best to hide it. I wanted more, of course I did. I've kissed more than my fair share of frogs, and I was done with it, but that could only happen if I started dating someone. I thought Lee was that someone.

When Lee asked if I would be interested in a friends-with-benefits type of situation, I don't know what the hell I was thinking. I mean, that couldn't be further from what I was actually looking for with a guy. I should have told him no, and ended the night there and then. We weren't on the same page, and by the sounds of it, we wouldn't ever be, so I should have run. No matter how depressing dating is, it's still the only way forward to find someone who wants the same thing I do. So why the hell did I say yes to his proposal? Why did I agree to be his friend-with-benefits?

That answer is more simple than it should be... because I like him. When he looks at me, I get the gooey butterfly feeling in the pit of my stomach. When I think about him, or get a notification to say he's messaged me, my heart races in anticipation. When he flashes that sexy dimpled smile my way, my cheeks flush and my core heats.

I like this guy, and that means I'm not ready to let him go just yet. The only problem with that is that we both have different expectations for this relationship, which means there can be no good outcome for us. I'm not sure if he just wants sex, or if it's more the friendship he's after and the sex is a bonus. While I've agreed to be friends-with-benefits, I'm secretly hoping the more time we spend together, the more I can convince him to enter into a real relationship.

I know my emotions are on the line here. There's a very good chance I could get my heart broken, and that this will end badly, but I have to try. What if this guy is the one, he just needs a little help to see that. I can't walk away from him. I just need to guide him in the right direction.

Throughout our second date, I constantly tried to remain casual, to not let him see what I was really thinking or feeling. Every time he looked nervous or unsure, I took hold of his hand and just gave him a chance to relax. I know I'm probably playing with fire, and that the only person who will get burned in the end is me, but that doesn't change how I feel. Some part of the universe, maybe fate, is calling to me, telling me that Lee is someone I shouldn't let go of. I can't let him slip through my fingers because I just know he's supposed to be someone important in my life. I'm not entirely sure how, but I know he is.

"This food is delicious," Lee groans, pulling me out of my musings as he shovels more of the Mexican food I made into his mouth.

I'm not the world's best cook, but I can make fajitas, tacos, and nachos—albeit a very dull version, since neither of us is a fan of much spice. I'm sure if an actual Mexican person were to try my awful attempt at Mexican food, they'd be offended. But for people who don't like a lot of spice, and prefer the flavour over having a chilli that blows your head off, this is the perfect compromise.

Normally, the first time a guy comes over to my house, I would order in... usually a pizza. But, with Lee, I wanted to make a bit more of an effort. I know deep down I'm doing it because I want him to realise we have the potential for more than just fuck buddies, but I'm pretending they aren't my motives. I just want to cook for him... end of discussion.

"I'm so pleased you like it. I know you said you don't like spicy food, so I tried to dull it down a bit," I reply, giving him a smile before scooping some sour cream onto my nacho as I shovel it into my mouth. The flavour bursts across my tongue, heat and cool all at the same time, and I try my best to hold back the groan threatening to escape my lips.

As we eat, things between us become more relaxed, like the first date. I think maybe Lee was nervous about being in my flat, and the expectations that come along with that. I know that probably sounds stupid, since sex is an obvious part of being friends-with-benefits, but I'm just going by what I see. Besides, we don't have to have sex straight away. We can get to know each other a bit better first, if that's what he wants.

After eating, we put a movie on and settle down on the sofa together. As I pull a blanket over us, he shuffles a little closer so that he can share it with me. He's so close, the heat from his body is warming my side, causing my nerve endings to prickle with anticipation.

A few minutes after the movie starts, Lee reaches over and takes my hand in his, clasping our fingers together so they're interlocked. His hands are so warm compared to mine that are naturally cold, and the heat spreads up my arm, warming me to my core. As Lee begins to swipe his thumb across the back of my hand, I'm frozen, all my attention is on the sensations he's producing with such a simple gesture.

I cast a glance over at him, and he looks to be enthralled with the movie, not even really noticing the effects he's having on my body. I try my best not to shuffle, to eradicate the feelings deep in my core. I'm not even sure squeezing my thighs together would be much help right now.

Without warning, Lee shuffles again, only this time he's getting more comfortable by laying on the sofa, with his head resting on my boob. As his head moves across my nipple, I try to ignore the tingling sensation. He's not doing anything even remotely sexual, but my body doesn't know that. When he pulls my arms around him, so we're cuddled up together, our fingers still interlocked, a strange sense of calm passes over me. It's like this is how we're always supposed to be.

I try to push those strange thoughts from my mind. Yes, I do believe in soulmates, but I also think it takes significantly longer to work out who your soulmate is. You can't tell just based on how relaxed you feel curled up with him on a sofa. But I can't deny the fact this feels right, like it's how we're supposed to end every night for the rest of our lives.

Fuck! I can't think like this. This isn't a relationship, and it has an expiration date before it's even begun. No matter how much I like him, we want different things. He doesn't want a relationship, and I do. I can be his friends-with-benefits hook up, but at some point, he's going to want to see other people, fuck other girls. He may even decide he wants to date someone else. Maybe he just said he doesn't want a relationship, because he knows he doesn't want one with me. When the right girl comes along, he will walk away, and I'm starting to realise the mess he will leave behind him. My shattered heart will be left in pieces… I just hope I can put it all back together again once it's done with.

The movie is drawing to a close, and it's obvious we're both exhausted. We've been taking it in turns to yawn for the last half an hour. He releases my hand to stretch a little, and I try not to look at the way his hard muscles stretch tight beneath his T-shirt. It takes every piece of willpower I have not to look at the patch of skin that emerges between the bottom of the shirt, and the top of his jeans. Fuck it, I look, and I'm not ashamed of looking. He's got one of those deeply defined V's that most men crave, and women go crazy over. He also has that little happy trail that makes women lose their minds, and I have to admit, I can feel myself drooling ever so slightly.

As Lee casts his crystal blue eyes over to meet mine, I'm suddenly not feeling all that tired. The way his gaze rakes over my body, I suddenly feel very exposed. His lip creeps up at one side as his eyes darken with lust, clearly happy with what he sees. A blush creeps across my cheeks, and I know he caught me checking him out, and so he was only too happy to return the favour.

I don't know how he's capable of making me feel so incredibly sexy with just one glance. Yet, that's exactly what he does. My core heats and my skin begins to tingle all over, anticipation building as I wonder where this will go. It may have started as an innocent glance, but it doesn't feel so innocent any more.

Lee shuffles slightly until we're facing each other, our knees touching. He reaches out with his hand to swipe a stray lock of purple hair away from my eyes, tucking it behind my ear. As he does this, his fingertips lightly sweep across my skin, and it feels like he leaves a trail of fire behind his touch. Instead of dropping his hand, he gently cups my cheek, rubbing the pad of his thumb over my sensitive skin.

I bite my lip to hold back the moan that's trying to escape, but that doesn't stop me from leaning into his touch. It's such a chaste move, but I feel it deep within my core, and I feel myself leaning in without even thinking about it.

Lee must have done the same because before we know it, our mouths are so close I can feel the warmth of his breath fanning across my face. Using the thumb that was sweeping across my cheek, he reaches up to my lip and gently pulls my lower lip free from where I was biting it before running the pad along my lip. A shudder runs through me as my heart starts to race.

As soon as he drops his hand, I lean forward and press my lips against him. Soft, warm, and incredibly inviting, from the first moment our lips touch, I can't hold back. I try to take things slowly, but it's like my body is already becoming addicted to his taste, and I can't get enough.

Thankfully, Lee has no problems deepening the kiss, and our lips crash together harder and more frantic than before. As soon as he requests access to my mouth with his tongue, I don't even think about hesitating, I open for him.

As his tongue explores my mouth, and I savour every bit of his taste, the need to have him closer consumes me. My fingers rake through his hair, gripping tightly enough to cause him to hiss into my mouth. But it doesn't seem to bother him. If anything, it spurs him on as his hands that were resting gently on my hips begin to move.

Lee's hands explore my body, sweeping underneath the hem of my T-shirt to make contact with my skin. Everywhere he touches feels electric, and my skin prickles from his touch. He starts off just exploring my lower back, before moving higher and grazing the underside of my boob, along the bottom of my bra.

My nipples harden with anticipation, hoping he's going to explore underneath my bra, but he doesn't. Instead, his hand trickles across my stomach, causing shivers of pleasure to ripple across my abdomen, and I can't hold back the moan that spills into his mouth.

Each touch has me more excited, and our mouths continue to crash against each other until we have to pull away, desperately gasping for breath. I drop my hands from his hair so he can move back slightly, his chest heaving as he tries to pull in the oxygen he needs. I'm panting just as heavily, but he doesn't move his hands from my body, and they feel hot against my back.

A mischievous smile spreads across his lips, as his stunning, crystal blue eyes sparkle at me. "I know we said this would be a friends-with-benefits type situation, but that doesn't mean we have to go all the way tonight. We can take things slow, if you like?"

I give him a small smile, grateful for his words. I'm not sure if he's saying it because he wants us to go slow, or because he thinks that's what I want. Is it what I want?

Fuck, I have no idea what I want. If this thing between us had the potential to be a relationship, then I probably would want to take things slow. I've had too many bad fucking experiences where I've slept with people too early on, and it's never gone anywhere. My mum always used to say if you give them freebie snacks the moment they arrive, they are going to fill up on those, and they'll never order from the menu. I hate the analogy, but she's probably right. Fuck, I hate saying that, but it's true. My mum is right a lot more times than I would like to admit.

But with this situation, it's different. Lee has made it clear, no matter how much I may want it, this will never be a long-term thing. He doesn't do relationships, and even if he suddenly decides he does want one, it won't be with me. I don't really know how the fuck I should take that. Most people would tell me to walk away, and in fact, that's exactly what my friends have told me to do. But I can't. There's something drawing me to Lee, something telling me that even when he's trying to push me away, I need to hold on.

I guess that's what makes this decision so hard. If all we're ever going to be is friends-with-benefits, then we might as well get to the benefits part sooner rather than later. Hell, it may be that we don't connect in the bedroom. It wouldn't be the first time I've had high hopes for a guy, only to be let down drastically when the clothes come off.

Fuck it. I'm gonna have my cake and eat it too, since the cake supply could stop at any moment. I just need to check if Lee's on the same page or not. "Is that what you want? To take things slow?"

My breath hitches as I wait for him to respond, while I try to ignore the way his fingers are drawing circles against the skin on my lower back. I want to reach out to touch him the way he is me, but my hands are frozen on my lap. Just waiting for his response.

"I don't know," he replies, barely above a whisper, and a short sharp laugh escapes my lips.

"Well, that doesn't help me much," I mumble, trying to hide how disappointed I am. It's fucking typical. I decide to throw my carefully crafted rulebook out the window, breaking all the rules, so I can fuck him on the second date, only for him not to feel the same. I mean, he's already gutted me by saying we can never be anything more, the least he could do is act like he wants to fuck me.

Is it too much to ask to find a guy who is so fucking attracted to me he can't contain himself, he's desperate to rip my clothes off and throw me onto the bed? Who the fuck am I kidding, things like that don't happen to girls like me. I'm far too curvy for anyone to be throwing around. I don't even want to see myself naked, so why should a guy as hot as Lee.

I can feel my body physically deflating with each negative thought that floods into my head. I thought I'd been able to chase them away, to push them down for the night so I could enjoy my time with Lee. I should have known my demons weren't too far away. They never fucking are!

Lee must notice the way my face falls, my eyes dropping to look at the way my fingers are picking at the skin around my fingernails, my whole body deflating. He removes one of his hands from my back, and brings it around so that his thumb and finger are holding my chin. He tilts my head up until my gaze is locked with his blue eyes. I'm taken aback at first as the normally glistening blue is darker, his eyes hooded with what looks to be lust.

"Hey... don't look away from me. I'm saying that I don't know if we should take things slow because I want to do this right with you. I know we're not gonna have a relationship, but I'd still like for us to be friends. To me, that's the most important thing. I don't connect with people very often, but with you, talking is easy. We have a laugh together and you just get me. I don't want to mess the start of a good friendship up by rushing into something. But that doesn't mean I don't want to have sex with you right now. You really do have no idea how beautiful you are, do you?"

His words shoot straight to my heart. When he asks if I know how beautiful I am, I can't help but look away. He's right, I don't think I'm pretty. But the way he says it, with such conviction, I can feel my resolve wavering. My heart races as I think about how sure he sounds. He really does want to fuck me, he's just unsure about messing up the start of our friendship. It almost sounds unbelievable, but I can hear it in his voice. I may not have known this guy for long, but I'm certain he's telling the truth.

Shaking my head, I confess something I've never admitted aloud before. "You're right. I don't think I'm beautiful. I think that's the reason I'm not in a real relationship. Guys are happy to be my friend, or have the odd fuck, but it never leads to more. In fact, most of the guys I fucked in the past, they either preferred I just blow them, or they wanted doggy, most likely because they didn't have to see my naked body. So, I get it, Lee. You don't have to try being nice to me."

Well, fuck, that really brought down the tone of the room. Not only have I depressed us both with talk of my flabby body, I've also mentioned other guys I've fucked. Great conversation for a second date.

Shit, maybe my mouth is the reason I'm not in a relationship. I really need to start thinking before I speak. Guys don't want to hear about how much I hate how I look.

The silence between us is deafening, and I can't wait any longer to find out what he's thinking. I look up at him through hooded eyes, and I'm shocked to see he looks almost angry.

Once he's sure he has my full attention, and that my eyes aren't wavering from his, he replies. "There is so much wrong with that statement, so I'm gonna break it down. Firstly, the guys you've dated or fucked in the past are clearly twatwaffles. I mean, I'm not defending them when I say this because it's clear they could have treated you better, but I can also see why they would want you on your knees. I mean, you have the sexiest plump lips that would look amazing swallowing a cock. And all guys love doggy because we can take control and get deeper. I can't speak to the other guys, but for me personally, I do it because it feels good, not so I don't have to look at the girl I'm fucking. They should never have made you feel like that. And for the record, I think they're fucking crazy because you are beautiful, and I can't wait to get you naked. But, if we could stop talking about the other guys you've fucked because I can feel myself getting angrier," he snaps, and my brow arches as I look on at him in confusion.

"Why are you angry?"

Shaking his head, he takes my cheeks in both hands to make sure I don't look away from him, and the intensity of his fiery gaze is making me want to shrink away but I can't. "I'm angry because the dipshits who came before me have clearly left you with no self confidence and that should never happen. Although I'm glad none of them worked out so we could be here doing this, I would never want you to have such bad experiences that it ruins your self esteem. That shit reflects badly on my whole gender. But the main reason I'm so angry is thinking about the guys you fucked in the past. I know we all have a past, but I hate the idea that they got to be with you, while I may have fucked things up so early on, all because I was attempting to be fucking chivalrous."

As soon as the words leave his mouth, I can't help the rushing exhale of air as I sigh loudly, so fucking relieved to hear him say that. My cheeks flush a pinky colour as I realise Lee is having a case of the green-eyed monster. I don't know how he does it, but even at a time where I can feel my insecurities overwhelming me, he manages to make me feel special. I've never met a guy who can do that.

"I don't think you've ruined anything," I mutter, barely above a whisper, but as his eyes widen, it's clear he heard me.

He looks like he's trying to find the words to articulate how he's feeling, and I know that sensation, so I try to make things easier on him. Without hesitating I close the small gap between us and press my lips against his.

The instant our lips touch, our frantic nature returns and we begin clawing at each other, our tongues consuming one another like we just can't get enough. I act on instinct alone, no longer afraid of what I should be doing with my hands, or thinking about if we're going too fast. I want Lee, and we could wait, but what would be the point? I may as well enjoy what we have now while we have it, since tomorrow is never certain.

This time as Lee's hands go to the bare flesh on my lower back, I shiver with pleasure, before reaching out to the hem on his T-shirt. I don't try to put my hands underneath and instead, I pull frantically to remove it. I don't get far before Lee lets go of me, and takes over helping me to remove his shirt. As he does, he shuffles backwards until his back is against the sofa, and once he's thrown the shirt on the floor, I find myself frozen, staring at his body.

In my opinion, he's got the perfect version of a male body. His biceps aren't bigger than my thigh, but he's still very clearly ripped. Lee is a runner, and that's obvious just by looking at him. He's lean, with muscles in all the right places. His chest and pecs feature a few dark hairs, but nowhere near levels to be classed as furry. His abs are ripped, with closer to an eight pack than a six, and without even really thinking about what I'm doing, I reach over and start tracing the ripples lightly with my fingertips. I love the way he shivers beneath my touch.

I'm so distracted staring at his abs and the little happy trail sitting in the middle of the perfectly defined V that scoops around his hips—something I'm not at all ashamed to admit—that I miss his quick movements. He reaches over, grabs my hips like I weigh nothing and pulls me until I'm straddling him, my legs on either side of his thighs.

I shuffle into position, hating the idea that I might be crushing him, but Lee doesn't seem to care. In fact, he places both hands on my ass cheeks and pulls me closer to him, closing the gap between us. My sensitive nipples rub against my bra as my boobs are pushed against his hard chest. Then, with a slight tilt of his pelvis, I feel his hard length pressing against my covered pussy. Even though we're both wearing clothing still, I can feel how big he is, and the delicious way he rubs against my sensitive clit is driving me insane.

Lee doesn't give me any chance to think about all the overwhelming sensations. Instead, he grabs hold of the bottom of my T-shirt and he begins pulling it over my head. As soon as he's removed it, he takes a moment to rake his gaze over my body.

My instinct is to cover up, but before I even begin moving my arms, the look in Lee's eyes stops me in my step. His bright blue eyes are darkened with lust, and he's looking at me like a starving man seeing a cheeseburger for the first time. His hooded eyes rake over my bra covered breasts, and over my stomach, paying close attention to the belly button bar in my navel.

The more his eyes rake over me, I realise he's not seeing what I see.

He's not paying any attention to the purple stretch marks I have on my hips, or the cellulite patches that are on my lower abdomen. He's looking at me, all of me, and if the desire blazing in his eyes is anything to go on, he clearly likes what he sees. He makes me feel so incredibly sexy. He's not just staring at my tits like most guys do—though his eyes do flare as he takes in my generous cleavage. He's looking at me in such a way that I really do believe he thinks I'm beautiful.

Lee looks at my body for so long, I start to feel almost awkward, and I can't wait for him to move. Though, when he does finally lean forward and capture my lips, it's in a short bruising kiss, one that's over far too fucking soon.

As he pulls away, he keeps his forehead resting on mine, and a genuine bright smile crosses his face. He reaches up to tuck a stray strand of hair away from my eye, behind my ear, and he cups my cheek with his palm. "You really are beautiful, Em. Are we doing this? Because if so, I plan on righting all the wrongs the fuckups before me caused. I want to fuck you so well you will feel me next week. I want to make your legs tremble and your pussy gush. But, more than that, I'm going to worship your body and show you just how fucking sexy you really are."

He pauses, looking at me with such intensity it causes my heart to race and my palms to become sweaty. Fuck me is he saying all the right things. Even if I hand over the keys to my body, and he really does show me what it's like to be worshipped, I need to keep the key to my heart firmly locked away. I have an awful feeling that if Lee keeps saying things like that, and making me feel the way he has so far, my poor little heart could get smashed into a million pieces.

Is it worth the risk? Hell yes.

"What do you say, Beautiful? Are we doing this?" he asks, his voice sounding hopeful, and I can't help but smile.

"Fuck, yes. Of course we're doing this. Friends-with-benefits, here we come," I joke, and as Lee's laughter rings out around me, I can't help but smile.

I'm not sure if I've just made the best or worst decision of my life. I guess we will have to see. But for now, I'm going to enjoy every pleasure he gives me, and we can worry about the rest later.

Lee

From the minute Emmaleigh lets go of everything in her mind, it's like she's a completely different person. Hearing her talk about the guys from her past literally caused my blood to boil. I'm not a jealous person, and never have been, but I have to admit that hearing her talk about being with other men caused the green-eyed monster to raise his ugly head.

But, if I thought how they treated her made me angry, that was nothing compared to the way I felt when she was talking about herself, and how she hates her body. At first I thought maybe she was joking, until I saw the darkness descend over her eyes. Her face became a blank mask, her gaze the only giveaway of the real pain she was feeling.

I honestly don't know why she feels the way she does, because to me, she's fucking gorgeous. I mean, I know she's not your typical supermodel size, but to me, that's a good thing. She's got curves in all the right places, making her look like a real woman. She's got an hourglass figure that I know a lot of girls would crave. Where she sees imperfections, I see beauty. So what if she's got a little bit more curves to her hips than other girls. To me, that just gives me something to grab hold of. I meant every word when I told her she was beautiful, and it pisses me off that she doesn't already know that.

Men have seriously let her down in the past, and I have to admit, that did add to my hesitance when it comes to rushing into having sex with her. If you asked my dick alone, he would say 'yes please' in an instant. He's been painfully hard, straining to break free from my jeans since we got here. So of course I want to have sex with her, I'm just worried. Even though she said she's okay with the whole friends-with-benefits situation, I can't help but think she doesn't really mean that.

When we were talking online before meeting, she always talked about wanting to find a long-term guy, after all her failed dating attempts that have come before. So I know she's looking for something serious. Yet, as soon as I told her I didn't want anything serious, she was still on board. I expected her to walk away after the first date, but she didn't. So, here we are, and now I'm faced with the possibility that I will be just another asshole who hurts her.

I know my situation is slightly different, since I've been honest with her from the start about what I'm looking for. But it doesn't change the fact all she's known in the past is twats, and I'm adding to that. I should let her walk away. Tell her to go and find her dream guy who can give her everything she's looking for. But I can't. I don't even know how to explain it, but there's a pull to this girl that I can't avoid.

Call me selfish, but I want her. I want to fuck her, to own her body. I meant it when I said she was beautiful, and that I could understand why other guys liked seeing her on her knees. Since she mentioned it my heads been full of visions of her on her knees, swallowing my cock.

So, for once, I'm letting my selfishness run free. I want Emmaleigh, and so I'm going to have her. All thoughts about her deserving better are pushed from my mind, and I focus completely on the fucking gorgeous girl that's currently straddling my thighs. There's no way in hell I can push her away while her sweet little pussy is grinding on my fabric covered cock.

Our mouths are battling for dominance, and whenever she runs her tongue along the inside of my lower lip, I'm assaulted by her taste and it makes me desperate for more.

My hands rake up the smooth skin on her back, loving the way she trembles beneath my light touch. Once I reach her bra, I gently swipe my fingers around the edges, softly scraping along the underside of her boob. As soon as I reach her nipple, the hardened bud is pressed firmly against the cup holding it in place, and I want to see it without the bra.

But first, I lightly swipe the pad of my thumb across her right nipple, and the moan that escapes into my mouth sounds so fucking hot. I repeat the motion on the left nipple, and Em arches her back, exposing her chest to me further. Clearly her nipples are sensitive, and she wants to feel more, which is something I'm only too happy to help her with.

As I bring my fingers to the back of her bra, I unclasp it with one hand—which took far more practice than I would like to admit—and with my other I help to pull it away from her body. As I do that, Em breaks our kiss, leaving us both panting and trying desperately to catch our breath.

When I throw her bra onto the floor she chuckles a little, and my brows shoot up in question of what's so funny. "You are really good at that."

I can't help but smile at how fucking adorable she looks when she's gazing at me with such a beautiful smile, a sligh flush spreading across her cheeks. "It took me more practice than I'd like to admit."

She groans loudly, dipping her head as she starts to laugh. I ask her what's so funny. "Well, firstly, I don't like the idea of you taking any other woman's bra off, so there will be no more talk of that," she grumbles, her face crumbling into a mixture of displeasure and jealousy. I try to hide the smile that is creeping in. I guess I like seeing her a little jealous. Em then lifts her head and continues, only this time her lip is raised in disgust. "I said the same thing to my last proper boyfriend, telling him I was impressed he could take my bra off one handed, and I'm still traumatised by his response."

A smile creeps on my lips. "Now this I have to hear."

"He told me that he practised a lot, and was determined to get good at it. I thought, nothing wrong with that, other than a little jealousy over hearing he'd been with other girls. But then he ruined it all by saying he practised on his grandma, who was the person raising him. After that, every time he removed my bra, all I could see in my head were flashing images of my boyfriend removing his grandma's bra. To say it was a mood killer is an understatement."

I can't stop laughing, the more she talks. I bite my lip to try and hold back the full belly laughs I'm struggling to contain. "Fuck, you weren't kidding when you said you had a bad romantic past, were you?"

She starts to giggle, shaking her head. "That's a fucking understatement. But I have a feeling you might be the one to break my weirdo streak."

My lip curls up into a cocky smirk, as her words go straight to my inflated ego. "Oh I'm definitely a weirdo. But that doesn't mean I don't know how to show you a fucking good time."

Before she has a chance to respond, I lower my head and capture one of her nipples in my mouth, sucking on the hard bud. As I flick my tongue over the nub, I take the other nipple in my hand, tweaking it with my thumb and forefinger, before tugging on it gently. As I do that, Em's moans echoes around the room, and I can feel her shudder beneath my touch. The more I suck and tug on her nipple, the more she arches her back, giving me even more access. Her fingers are gripping onto my hair, tugging to the point I feel that delicious sting. Don't even get me started on the way she's grinding her sweet little pussy against my denim-covered cock. I can feel myself getting impossibly harder, my engorged head feeling sore and full. I need to get my clothes off, and soon.

As I continue swapping my mouth from one nipple to the other, Em's moans become more frantic and wanton. She nibbles along my ear before sucking on the spot just below that causes my lower abdomen to tighten, and a groan to rip from my lips. I've always known that was a sensitive spot for me, but I've never had someone suck on it in such a way that I feel it in my balls.

Em gently presses my shoulders back, making it clear she wants me to stop the attention I'm giving her nipples. As she leans back, I can't help but ogle at how fucking sexy they look; swollen, glistening with my spit, standing on a peak that looks almost painful.

I'm pulled away from admiring my handy work when Em shuffles off my cock—much to my disgust—with a mischievous glint in her eye. Before I know it, she slides off my lap, down onto her knees in front of me, in between my legs. She's looking up at me through hooded eyes as she sucks her lower lip into her mouth. Fuck, I didn't know this girl could get any sexier, and then she reaches for the button on my jeans, and I'm a goner.

She unfastens the button and begins to pull the zipper down. I place my hand over hers to stop her, but not for the reasons she thinks. I know for a fact, the moment her lips touch my cock, I'm going to want to feel her pussy swallowing my hard length, so we may as well be prepared.

Taking my hands underneath her shoulders, I gently pull her until she's standing, as I do too. With one hand cupping her cheeks, I reach down and place my hand over her denim-covered pussy. She moans against my cheek and I can't help the shit-eating grin that spreads across my face. I press down, harder than I normally would, so she can feel the pressure against her clit. It has the desired effect when she cries out in pleasure.

Placing my lips beside her ear, I whisper all the filthy words I'm thinking aloud. "I want to feel your lips around my cock more than anything, but I already know where that will lead. I will want to fuck you. If you are okay with that, then I think we can make things easier on ourselves and get the awkward discussion out of the way now."

She turns her head slightly, her dark, lust-filled eyes stare at me, but her brow furrows. "What awkward conversation?" she mutters.

"Contraception. I tested negative recently, and I'm happy to use condoms, if you'd like. Honestly, I've never had sex without one before," I admit.

"Does that mean you want to have sex without one with me?" she asks, voicing the question I've been asking myself for the last few minutes.

Since she fell to her knees between my legs, all I've been able to think about is sinking my hard length into her bare, naked pussy. The desire to feel all of her, her heat and how tight she grips my cock is overwhelming me. Obviously, the sensible side of me says I should use a condom all the time. It's not just about the whole baby issue—which I would absolutely fucking hate—but it's also a safety thing. A girl can say all her test results have come back negative, but that's just her word. So, why am I considering going against everything I believe for this girl? Why is her pussy calling to me in a way no other does?

"I went to the clinic just a couple of weeks ago, when I found out the last guy I was sleeping with was also sleeping with the girl at the fish counter at my local supermarket," she explains with a grimace. "My results were all negative, and I haven't been with anyone since. I also have the implant, so there's absolutely no chance of me getting pregnant."

"My negative result was from a few weeks ago too, and I haven't been with anyone since," I confess, before gently rubbing my fingers against her pussy. Her pelvis tilts and she presses herself harder against my hand, groaning loudly as she does.

"So you want to do it bare?" she whispers, turning her face away, as though she's too embarrassed to make eye contact with me after saying that.

"I can't explain why, but I do. I'm happy to wear a condom though, if you want to. It's all your choice. I also need to know that you will tell me if I'm doing anything you don't enjoy. I want to make this as good for you as I can. You can show me what you like, and I will learn what makes your body sing. We can cover fantasies and other things later, but do you prefer it a little rough, or gentler?"

A blush spreads across her cheeks as she turns her head back to meet my eye contact. There's a fire burning in her eyes that is so fucking sexy, but I can tell she's a little shy talking about this sort of stuff. I don't usually discuss this sort of thing with a woman before we have sex, I usually just go with the flow. But Em's had so many bad experiences, I don't want this to be another story to add to her list. I want to know what she likes and what makes her body sing. I want to bring her pleasure and show up all the guys that came before me. I think maybe that's why I want to do it bare, because nobody ever has. I get to be her first, and that idea makes my heart race a little faster.

"I can tell you what I like, as long as you do the same. I've never had a guy completely dominate and tell me what to do, throwing me around and being rough, but I've always liked that idea. I want to try it rough and see if I like it," she admits, looking up at me through hooded eyes, which roll in her head when I flick my finger over her clit.

"I can show you rough. Just say mercy if you want me to slow down, and halt if you want me to stop. Do you understand? Repeat the words," I instruct firmly.

She straightens, pulling her lip out from between her teeth as she tries to ignore the slow, lazy circles I'm drawing on her pussy so that she can respond. "Mercy to slow things down, and halt to stop it," she repeats proudly. I lean down and press my lips against hers, a hard and fast kiss in praise for her doing as she was told.

"Good. So, condom or no condom? You decide," I mutter, as I press harder against her clit, causing her to cry out loudly, and her legs begin to shake. She's getting closer to the edge, but I'm not ready to see her fall apart just yet, so I pull my hand away, much to her annoyance. A loud groan fills the room, as she looks at me with wide pleading eyes. I hold my ground, waiting for her to answer. I meant what I said, this is all on her. If she chooses a condom, I will respect her wishes. But that doesn't mean I'm not standing here, silently praying to whatever deity is listening, that she chooses the no condom option. Thoughts of sinking into her warm, wet cunt are overwhelming me.

"No condom," she says, as she begins to slowly shimmy her jeans down her legs, removing them completely so that she's just standing in a little pair of black lace boy shorts.

I can tell by the way she lowers her gaze, and her hands swing around like she's not quite sure what to do with them, that she's nervous being this naked in front of me. I need to get the sexy, confident Emmaleigh back. The one who was sliding off my lap, a mischievous glint in her eye as she prepared to swallow my cock. I need that Em back.

Reaching out, I place my hand on her hips, gripping them harder than she expects, causing her to raise her head until she meets my gaze. "I mean it when I say, you are without a doubt, one of the sexiest girls I've ever seen. Your curves are incredible. So, I need you to see what I see. I need you to get back that confidence you had a moment ago. I want you to remove my trousers, drop to your knees, and show me what a sexy fucking vixen you can be."

Emmaleigh

I'm standing there, almost completely naked with just my little lace shorts in place, and of course, I can't help that little bit of self doubt that creeps in. I mean, I'm more than aware of all the little flaws he must be able to see at that moment, but he doesn't care about them. He still calls me beautiful, and strangely, the more he calls me that, the more I believe him.

He tells me that I need to find the confidence I had a moment ago, and that I need to drop to my knees, and I can feel my legs trembling with the desperate need. Talking to Lee about the type of sex I like was a bit embarrassing, because the truth is, I've only ever had vanilla—and that's been various shades of shit. So, I guess, I've never really given myself the opportunity to think about what I like. What gets me wet between my legs. But now, I have a feeling, Lee is going to be very interested in pushing my boundaries, seeing what I like and what I don't. And I'm very, very here for that.

In a normal situation, I don't think I'd appreciate a guy telling me what to do. But the minute we're naked, and he's looking at me with lust-filled eyes, I wanna submit to him. I want to do as he tells me, to hear his praise. So, when he tells me to drop to my knees, I waste no time doing as I'm told.

Knees on the floor, leaning back against my heels, I pull my arms behind my back, arching it and causing my tits to push forward. I look up at Lee through hooded eyes as he removes his jeans, and I'm mesmerised by the bulge in his black boxers. Don't get me wrong, the rest of him is really something to look at too. He's not the tallest guy, but you know what, his muscles make it barely noticeable. He's ripped like a Greek God, and that is more than enough to look at. Then he goes and pitches a very large tent in his boxers, and I can feel myself salivating as my pussy pulses with need. I was already moments away from an orgasm when he was rubbing my pussy through my jeans, so now it's throbbing with a deep need to be touched in some way. I can feel myself getting wetter just at the thought of what Lee could do to me.

I stay there silently, on my knees, waiting for my next instruction—like the good girl I am—and I love the way Lee smiles at me, praising me for not getting ahead of myself. I was tempted to just reach up and get started, but it's like this primal part of me knew that would be the wrong thing to do. I'm supposed to do as I'm told, and wait for instructions. So as much as my hands are twitching with a need to reach up and touch him, I fight against that instinct.

Lee reaches down and cups my cheek, and I lean into the warmth of his palm, loving the way he strokes me gently. He's also using his hand to direct my gaze, making sure I'm looking at him the whole time. He then crouches down and captures my lips with his. It's a short and bruising kiss that's over before it's even begun, but it was so full of passion that when we pull apart, I'm panting, desperate to pull in the oxygen I just lost when I was consumed by him.

"Good girl. I know you said you've never done this before, so that would mean you're a natural. Do you want to see my cock?" His praise makes my heart race, and I feel like a child getting told "well done" for the first time. I feel on top of the world, and I realise, it's important for me to have his approval. I want him to be proud of me and to call me his good girl.

I mean, don't get me wrong, at some point I would like to be a bad girl, just to see what he does, but mostly, I just want him to know I'm doing whatever I can to make him happy. I know it sounds crazy, and I feel a little insane, as I've never had any feelings like this before. Then again, I've never been in this situation with a guy before.

I did date one guy who said he wanted to try kinky stuff, but he was a massive fucking let down. The kinkiest he got was pushing me against a wall so he could kiss me against it. No sexy foreplay, or anything like this. In fact, he's still one of my worst memories to date, and one of the guys who managed to chip away at another piece of my self esteem. We were actually half way through fucking—doggy-style, of course—and he stopped. He actually just stopped in the middle, without coming, and said that he wasn't into it. That he wanted to be kinkier, but that I didn't take the lead when I should have.

I had never felt shittier, and I couldn't have got him out of my flat any quicker. I obsessed for weeks over it, thinking it was all my fault. That I couldn't turn him on properly. But, I now know that it wasn't me doing it wrong, it was him. If he wanted to have kinky sex, where things get a little rough and he dominates me, then it was on him to make that move. I think maybe he liked the idea of him being an alpha male who takes charge in the bedroom, but that's not who he was. Some guys have it, others wish they have it. He was the latter, whereas Lee is the former. He just exudes dominance, which is ironic because in a non-sexual situation, he doesn't come across as an alpha male. He's a shy, tech geek, but when the curtains get drawn, a new Lee emerges, and I'm so fucking here for that.

Lee raises to a standing position again, and this time when I look up at him through hooded eyes, my lower lip between my teeth as the anticipation starts to feel overwhelming, the corner of his lip tips up into a cocky smirk. He knows the effect he's having on my body, just by standing there while I'm on my knees, panting and waiting desperately for his touch.

"You can begin now." His voice is deep and gravelly, so different from what I'm used to, but it's clear he is just as affected by this as I am.

Without hesitation, I kneel up higher so my face is eye level with his bulging crotch, and I reach up to grip the elastic waistband of his black boxers. I allow my fingertips to trail gently over his abs as I do, loving the way his body shivers beneath my touch. He feels so warm, and I can feel my heart starting to race as I slowly lower the boxers down.

I pull them just a short way, and that's all it takes for his cock to break free. For a moment, I just kneel there frozen, taking in his hard length. I've never really thought of a penis as beautiful before, but Lee's is kind of perfect. It's big without being massive—just big enough, I think. The silky skin stretched along the shaft looks so smooth and soft that I can't wait to touch it, and the bulging vein running along the underside is just begging to be licked. The swollen head is red and angry looking, with beads of pre-cum pooling on the tip that I'm desperate to taste.

Reaching out with my hand, I grasp the base, trying to wrap my fingers around the shaft as best I can, struggling to get my fingers to touch. It's girthier than I expected, but that's not a bad thing. The skin feels just as soft as it looks, but the length is continuing to grow the harder he becomes. I feel like he has a bit more growing to do, so I squeeze the base, probably a little harder than intended. The deep, guttural moan that escapes from his lips is like music to my ears.

Thrusting his hips forward, he tries to get me to move the hand that's currently circling the base of his shaft, but with a mischievous smile on my face, I look up at Lee to let him know that it's my turn to be in charge, just a little. I want to watch him fall apart the way he did earlier with me. The moment he realises what I'm doing, he rolls his eyes at me before giving me a pointed stare that tells me I should start moving my hand unless I want to be punished. I mull that idea over for a few seconds, and I have to admit, the idea of being punished does sound a little appealing, but I think for now, I just want to feel whatever pleasure he can give me. We can experiment later.

That thought spurs me on, and I stick my tongue out to lick the tip. The beads of pre-cum that are collecting on the top are scooped up into my mouth, and the bursts of salty flavour that explode across my taste buds have me salivating. I want more.

After circling my tongue around the head a few times, I know I want more. So, whilst my hand stays tightly gripping the base, I lick along the shaft like it's my favourite lollipop. I can feel the vein pulsating beneath my tongue, and the silky smooth skin means I can glide over his hard length with ease.

Once I've got the shaft completely covered with my saliva, I slowly start to move my hand up and down the shaft, licking the tip in between strokes. I watch on in amazement as his length grows impossibly harder, more pre-cum pooling on the tip just waiting for me to devour it.

Lee's groans spur me on and as he becomes more vocal, I slowly start to take his cock into my mouth. I remove my hand from the base and swallow as much as I can into my throat.

He's fucking massive, so it's not easy, but I'm thrilled when I'm able to get at least three quarters into my mouth.

I continue bobbing up and down, running my tongue along the shaft as I do, I relish in the way Lee's losing control under my touch. His hands that were initially just by his side are now threaded through my hair, fisted tightly to the point I can feel the sting of it on my scalp every time he tugs harder. I find that I actually don't mind, and I quite like the pain.

Swallowing his cock all the way down my throat again, I'm impressed to see I only have one or two inches left to take. I let his cock sit in my throat, Lee's hands on the back of my head acting as a guide. It feels like he's holding me in place, but I know if I backed away, he would allow me to move. I swallow, loving the way his cock feels deep in my throat, and each time my throat muscles tighten around his cock, Lee growls with desire.

The longer my throat is filled with Lee's cock, and I'm without oxygen, I can feel my lungs start to burn. My eyes start to water and my pulse races. But I'm determined to take all of him. With another swallow, as I gently push forward the last of his long length slides into my throat, my nose touching the small patch of pubic hair just above his dick.

I hold it there for a few seconds before I have to pull back. I'm panting and gasping for breath, my lungs burning as I desperately take in the oxygen I've been missing.

"Holy fuck, Em. That was incredible," Lee exclaims, his voice deep and breathy too. He sounds almost as out of breath as I do, and I can see beads of sweat forming on his brow as the hard muscles on his chest rise and fall rapidly.

I look up at him from my position on my knees, I can't help but feel proud at the way he's looking at me. Reverence— that's the only way to describe the way he's gazing at me right now. Nobody has ever looked at me like this, and I can feel my confidence growing so much, as I feel so unbelievably confident and sexy.

As I try to catch my breath, I stroke my hand up and down his shaft, loving the feel of him beneath my touch. I lick around the tip again, and along the shaft, coating his cock in my spit as I prepare to take him in my mouth again.

Once he's coated, I open my mouth, preparing to take him again, but Lee shakes his head. "No. Fuck, no. As much as I want to feel your mouth on me more, I can't. I don't want this to be over yet, and I will blow my load if you put my cock back in your mouth."

I sit frozen, quite proud of myself for being able to bring this gorgeous guy to his knees.

With a mischievous grin on his face, he leans in and captures my mouth with his, before reaching down to clasp our fingers together and pulling me up until I'm standing in front of him in just my boy shorts. I try not to look at him in all his glory, but I can't help it, he's fucking gorgeous, and I try not to think about what the hell he's doing with me. Instead I focus on the here and now.

"Remind me where you said the bedroom is again," Lee instructs as he begins walking me out of the open plan living room.

"Second door on the left," I mumble, letting him pull me along behind him. Even though I know I prepared for this, I can't help but mentally run through my checklist that lets me know I'm ready to have sex.

Clean underwear. Check.

Shaved legs. Check.

Clean bed sheets. Check.

Tidy bedroom. Check—I mean, it's tidy to my standards. It'll never be tidy by Mum's standards, but I don't think Lee is going to be paying too much attention to the crap I have in my room. The sex is going really badly if that's the case.

Waxed vagina. Check, and no matter how many times I have it done, it really fucking doesn't get any easier. I've been going to the same beautician now for almost five years, and I still thank the lord that I don't bump into her in or around town. She's seen more of me than anyone else, and she still manages to do it with a smile on her face. Every time she asks me to roll over onto my side and hold my ass cheeks open so she can get to the little hairs around my entrance and ass, my cheeks flush red with embarrassment. It also fucking stings, and nobody can argue with that.

I'm more than prepared, and I have a very good feeling this could be the best sex I've ever had.

With those high hopes, I allow Lee to lead me into my bedroom. I'm barely sitting on the bed when Lee pushes me until I'm laying back, my legs hanging off the end, as he climbs over my body. He's careful not to put any of his weight on me, propping himself up with one arm beside my head. His lips meet mine in a bruising yet all too fucking short kiss. Then, with that mischievous smirk on his face he begins kissing his way down my body.

As his mouth begins to devour my left nipple, my back arches and a sound I've never heard before rips from my lips—I'm almost purring. But the way he sucks on my nipple before grazing over it with his tongue, while his fingers tug and rub my other nipple, it's like sensory overload, but in a good way. My skin feels almost electric, like all the little nerve endings are standing on end and prickling away under the surface, and each time he touches me, my body lights up. The feeling pooling in my lower abdomen causes me to clench my thighs together to try and alleviate the delicious ache that's forming.

Lee notices me squirming, but instead of taking his mouth from my nipple—thank God—he lowers his free hand down to the front of my panties. As he reaches the waist band, it feels almost like he has a moment where he's trying to decide if he should remove the panties or not. I want to reach down to help him, or at the very least, lift my ass up to help him get them off, but I'm not exaggerating when I say I'm so hypnotised by the sensations he's causing across my body, I can't move. Well... I mean, technically I could move, but I don't want to. I want to stay caged under his body, being assaulted by his touch for as long as possible.

Thankfully, Lee doesn't want to stop either. Instead of going under my waistband like I expected, his hand slowly lowers down to my pussy, the fabric keeping him from touching my hot skin. He gently swipes a finger through my slit, pressing the fabric into my soaking wet pussy, and as soon as he touches my clit, my groans of pleasure fill the room.

It's like the little nub was pulsing, just waiting for him to touch me, and the anticipation built it up so much that when I did feel him, it was overwhelming. My back arched, pressing my nipples even further into his mouth, my body pressing against his hard muscles.

My fingers grip tightly into his back, and I'd be very surprised if he doesn't have crescent shape indents where my nails were. The more he sucks on my nipples, alternating between them while his fingers show attention to the other, and his remaining hand continues to swipe up and down my slit, circling my clit and rubbing over my entrance, the louder I moan. I can feel the pleasure building as my heart starts to race. My whole body is starting to coil, and I'm becoming more frantic, trying to grasp hold of him whilst I mumble incoherently, begging for more.

Pulling his mouth away from my nipple, I hiss as the cold air hits my wet, hard nub. At first I think he's going to kiss me, but instead he moves his mouth across to my ear. He begins nibbling and sucking on the sensitive spot under my ear, and to say that feels amazing is a fucking understatement. My last real boyfriend I dated for close to a year, never realised this is one of my most sensitive spots—other than the obvious ones—yet, Lee's been here for a couple of hours maximum and he has worked it out. I don't know what it is about Lee, but it's like he has a direct line to my pleasure sensors. He knows how to make me moan and groan like a porn star, and I love it.

Whilst I'm distracted by the sensations on my neck, he moves his hand underneath my panties, and I don't realise what he's doing until I feel his warm fingers sliding through my slit. Twirling his finger around my entrance, he then continues to swipe through my lips and up to my clit. He circles around my clit, driving me even more crazy, before he finally rubs his fingers over the swollen, sensitive nub.

My cries of pleasure echo loudly around the bedroom, and if I wasn't in a blissed out state of lust, I would be a little self-conscious over how loud I'm being. I don't particularly want my neighbours to hear me having the best sex of my life, but since I clearly can't keep quiet, I may as well put on a show and let them know exactly how much fun I'm having.

His breath hits my ear, and a shiver ripples down my spine as he whispers, "You are so wet. Is it all for me?"

I nod my head, unable to find the right words as he continues to flick his finger lightly over my clit. Just enough to drive me insane, but not enough to get me to that peak I'm desperately trying to reach. But, when he realises I'm not going to answer him, he stops touching me and I let out a loud, frustrated groan.

"Use your words, Beautiful," he mutters into my ear, before gently nibbling on the lobe.

I cough to clear my throat, my mouth suddenly very dry as I try to form words, ignoring the throbbing in my pussy that is begging for him to put his fingers back where they were. "Yes, I'm wet, and it's all for you. I don't think I've ever been so turned on," I add with a laugh, and the smile it brings to Lee's gorgeous face makes my heart flutter.

No! Stop! No feelings. This is just sex, nothing more, and I need to keep reminding my stupid heart of that.

Thankfully, Lee's sexy, dirty mouth distracts me again. He's staring at me, his sparkling blue eyes locking with mine as he purposefully brings his fingers up so they are resting between us. His first two fingers are glistening from the juices that are coating them—my juices. A small part of me wants to shrink away, embarrassed that I'm so wet, but then I remember that Lee doesn't want me to hide from my sexuality. He wants the confident, sexy version of me.

"You are so wet, and I can't wait to see what you taste like," he states before bringing his fingers to his lips, and whilst maintaining eye contact, he swipes his tongue across his digits, devouring my taste.

Fuck. That's quite honestly one of the hottest things I've ever seen. There's that small part in the back of my mind telling me that should embarrass me, not turn me on, but the fire in Lee's eyes is impossible to ignore.

Once he's licked every last bit of skin on his fingers, he leans forward to whisper in my ear again, and this time I bite my tongue to try and stop the shiver I know he saw last time. But the minute his warm breath hits me, I can't control my body's involuntary reaction. As my body quivers, he chuckles lightly against my ear. "You taste delicious, and now I've had a sample, I'm ready for the full meal."

My eyes widen at his words, and before I have time to process what he's doing, he pulls my soaked panties off and throws them onto the floor in the corner of the bedroom while he sinks to his knees beside the bed. He throws my legs over his shoulders, opening them up wide, my core spread open just inches from his face.

I don't know why I do it, but I can't help dropping my hands so they are covering my exposed core. I guess I can tell myself to be sexy, but sometimes instinct just takes over and the self-conscious version of me wins out, even when I don't want it to.

Lee reaches up and takes hold of my hands, each one surrounded by his large, calloused fingers as he moves them to my side, pressing them there, making it very clear I shouldn't move them. I risk opening my eyes and look down to see his fierce, piercing blue gaze. The intensity in his stare makes me want to look away, but I don't—or I can't. I'm transfixed, looking at Lee who is staring at me like I'm one of the wonders of the world, and I don't even know it.

"You are so fucking gorgeous, I can't wait to taste you," he growls, leaning forward as he lets go of my hands, so he can use his to spread apart my thighs. I've never been so exposed, and I guess, vulnerable. But the way he's looking at me, it makes me feel almost safe.

"You don't have to do that, honestly. I know not all guys like to do it, and I understand…" Great, now I'm babbling and I can't stop talking. I don't know why I'm trying to talk him out of it. I've been wanting to know what this really feels like for a long fucking time.

You see, the guys I've fucked in the past have either been too caught up in seeking their own pleasure to send any my way, or they have just never wanted to do it. One guy said the idea repulsed him, but of course he wanted me to swallow his cum. I did have one guy 'give it a try'. He did one of the most pathetic licks through my slit before saying he didn't like it, his face scrunched up in a look of revulsion. I've never felt so disgusting in all my life, and after that I never really encourage guys to try it anymore. It was just another thing I thought was wrong with me and my body.

But, if the way Lee is looking at me right now—like he wants to devour me whole—is anything to go by, I don't think the problem all this time has been me. More likely the guys I've been picking. Although, I think deep down, I kinda already knew that.

"I will say this again… the other guys you've been with are tools. I am going to taste you, and have a pretty good feeling once I do, I'm only going to want more," Lee growls, his voice a mixture of anger—no doubt at the other guys—and something that sounds a little like amazement. Like he can't quite get over how much he wants to taste me.

He doesn't even wait for me to respond. Instead, he uses his fingers to part my pussy lips, and as the cold tips of his fingers connect with my heat, a delicious shiver races up my spine, and I have to bite my lip to stop myself from moaning. He leans forward, pulling my legs farther over his shoulders, forcing my legs to open wider, and as soon as I feel his warm breath against me, I'm a goner.

The warmth of his breath is nothing compared to the feeling of his wet, hot tongue sweeping through my folds. All my nerve endings down there feel like they are on fire, and it's a sensation I've never felt before. This time I can't hold back my moan of pleasure, and I'm surprised to hear Lee groaning too.

Once he knows we're both enjoying it, that seems to be all he needs to hear as his movements become frantic. His tongue sweeps through my slit, his tip circling around my clit before flicking over it, driving me fucking crazy. But, if I thought that felt amazing, it was nothing compared to when he pressed his tongue into my entrance, making sure to swirl all around, tasting all of me and getting me impossibly wetter.

My moans become more feverant and every time Lee moans, I feel it vibrate around my clit, which is a totally new sensation, and one I happen to very much fucking love. Once I get over that initial embarrassment, and just live in the moment, I open my eyes and look down at Lee. He's looking up at me through hooded eyes, a devilish glint in his gaze as he rakes his tongue through my pussy lips, and that's when I notice movement out of the corner of my eye. I look down to see him fisting his cock, stroking it up and down slowly. His head looks even more purple and swollen, beads of pre-cum pooling on the tip, making me want to taste him again even more.

Lee continues devouring my pussy, licking and sucking until he's driving me mad. The muscles in my lower abdomen start to tighten, and the nerve endings across my body feel as though they're about to explode. Beads of sweat are pooling on my forehead, and my heart is racing as I chase the orgasm I know isn't far away. No guy has ever given me one before, and so I'm surprised Lee was even able to get this far. But he doesn't just get me close, he goes all the way.

My orgasm crashes into me, completely unexpected, and it's like fireworks are exploding around my body. My eyes clamp shut, and I try to open them, as I want to see what he thinks of me falling apart, but I'm too lost in the moment. My legs shake and my body goes rigid for a moment, but Lee doesn't relent. He keeps casually flicking his tongue over my sensitive area as my moans of pleasure fill the bedroom. My fingers are clamped in his hair, and it's not until I start to come down from my orgasm that I realise I was pulling his hair pretty fucking tight. His skull must be stinging badly right about now. He doesn't seem to mind, and I'm not exactly functioning enough to apologise.

Once my body starts returning to normal, the feel of his tongue against my sore clit is too much, and I use my hold in his hair to pull him away from my sensitive area. I hear his breathing get louder, intermingled with grunts and moans, and that has me opening my eyes straight away. I see Lee fisting his cock harder and faster now, his movements becoming more frantic, and it's clear he's close to the edge. I want to see him fall apart and so I find my sexy, confident voice.

"Come for me, Lee. I want you to come on me, now," I instruct, grabbing his attention with my breathy yet firm voice.

Lee stands up, towering over me as I continue to lie on the bed. He stands between my legs, his cock just above my exposed pussy. Lee increases his movement, making sure to rake his thumb over his engorged head, spreading the pre-cum beads with each swipe. His moans become more desperate, and I can feel my core clenching as I watch this gorgeous man fall apart before my very eyes.

It's not long before he finds his release, coming with a loud roar as spurts of cum shoot from his tip, coating my lower stomach. He continues to pump slowly, pulling rope after rope of cum out and spreading it across my skin. I look down to see the creamy white patches of cum splattered across my lower stomach and pubic area, and I can't help myself. I lower my finger and scoop up a bit of his cum. I feel his eyes on me as he watches what I'm about to do next.

I don't hesitate to bring my fingers up to my lips, sucking his cum into my mouth. The salty liquid explodes across my tongue, and it's even more of an intense flavour than the pre-cum, but there's something oddly good about it. I think it's because I know it's Lee's, and I would devour as much of him as I possibly could.

I'm so lost in the moment, that it takes me a few moments to even realise what it means that he's finished now. I mean, I know I encouraged him to come, and fuck do I absolutely not regret that, but at the same time, I'm not ready for the evening to be over. I wanted so much more. I can't keep the disappointed look from my face, and I know the moment Lee sees it, because his brow furrows like he's confused, and I don't blame him. How do I explain that I'm sad this night is over? I know we can do more next time, but I'm still so fucking turned on, and all that talk of fucking without a condom has me so wet and desperate.

"What's the matter?" Lee asks, and I try to avert my gaze, but he reaches out to take hold of my chin, raising it until I have no choice but to meet his gaze.

My voice comes out barely above a whisper. "I'm just not ready for this to be over. I kinda wanted more... I mean, it's okay. I understand, it's just..."

Fuck, Em. Can you please stop babbling? I lecture myself, reminding my messed up brain that sometimes saying the first thing that comes into my head isn't always the best thing to do. I mean, what we have done has been fun, and it was so fucking hot I can hardly blame him for blowing his load. But of all the ways, and particularly after all that sex with no condom talk, I had such high hopes for more. I don't want to basically accuse him of premature ejaculation, which I think I may have just done, but dammit he asked!

His chuckle shocks me and it pulls my eyes to meet his instantly. That sexy, mischievous look is plastered across his face, and I can't help but draw my brow together as I wonder why he's laughing. Nothing I just said is funny. Quite the opposite, in fact.

"Em, just because I've just come doesn't mean the night is over. I mean, I will probably need a minute or two to get going again, but looking at you and that sexy, wet cunt of yours, it won't be too long," he replies, and I can't help but cast my gaze lower, trying to see if he's telling the truth. I know I shouldn't doubt him, but I've never been with a guy who was able to go again after coming. I thought it was just something women wrote about in romance novels, or put in TV shows to make men seem amazing, but real life men are never able to live up to that standard. Hell, I thought it was a myth.

I'm also pretty sure that women—well, me—can't have multiple orgasms. For me personally, even by myself using my favourite toy, it's hard to reach one orgasm, but there's no way on this earth would I ever be able to achieve two. I was impressed Lee was able to get one out of me, but I would have loved to feel him inside of me while I came around his cock.

Oh well, I suspect there will be plenty more times for me to find my orgasms with Lee. Since he's done it once, I have high hopes that he'll be able to do it again.

His dirty, delicious words make me shiver and clench my thighs, as I allow my vision to wander over his body some more. I try not to focus on his fucking hot abs, or that sexy V that drives all women crazy. And sure enough, as soon as my gaze lands on his cock, I see it start to twitch, beginning to harden again. I can't keep the smile off my face. It looks like I really am in for a good night.

Be still my beating heart, this is just sex. I can't keep Lee, no matter how much I might want to.

Lee

Emmaleigh is laying on the bed, her legs spread wide as her wet little cunt glistens just for me, and I can feel my dick springing back to life. I should be offended that Em thought I was only capable of one lot of cum. But then I remember all the tools that came before me, and if they weren't capable of showing her any pleasure, they probably couldn't get it up multiple times. I knew the moment I looked at Emmaleigh's beautiful, silky smooth naked body that I wouldn't have a problem.

It makes me so mad that Emmaleigh can't see how gorgeous she really is. Curves and all. It just makes her look more like a real woman. If I take a girl out on a date, I want to know she's going to order a massive burger and fries, and attempt to demolish the lot—then I get my money's worth. I don't want a girl who orders a salad and a glass of water, and who looks at my chips longingly the whole time. I absolutely hate sharing food, so she can stare as long as he likes, she ain't getting any chips. If she wanted them, she should have ordered them. I would have paid. Hell, I would have enjoyed finishing off the extra chips. It's a bloody good job I run every day, otherwise I would be a lot bigger than I am.

Emmaleigh lets out a soft little moan as she bites her lip, her gaze fixed on my growing erection, and it's more than enough to pull me out of my own head. There's just something about this girl. She makes me want it all, and she makes me want to give her the world. She fucking deserves it.

I waste no time crawling up her body, her legs widening to accommodate my hips. Kissing my way up, I show a little attention to her already stiff, pebbled nipples. They are super sensitive after her orgasm, and as soon as I take one in my mouth, her back arches and she moans loudly. I continue that a few times, alternating from one nipple to the other. My hardening cock is nestled between her pussy lips, and I can feel her juices spreading across my shaft each time she tilts her pelvis. If this feels fucking amazing, I can't even begin to wonder how incredible she will feel when her tight walls are surrounding my hard length.

Her legs wrap around my ass, her ankles locking together as she holds me in place, her nails gripping tightly into my shoulders, and I wouldn't be surprised to see more half moon shaped bruises in the morning. But I would never complain. I love that she feels comfortable enough with me to take the pleasure she desperately craves.

I place my lips against hers, and as soon as we taste each other, our kiss deepens, becoming more frantic and passionate. Our bodies are pressed together as I use my forearm to prop me up a little, making sure I'm not squashing her. I can feel her wetness coating my cock, and it's not long before he's fully erect and ready for more.

Reaching down between our bodies with my spare hand, I fist my cock before sliding the tip through her wet slit, the head pressing against her clit causes her to groan loudly as she tilts her pelvis again, desperately seeking more contact.

I pull my lips away from hers and gently kiss my way to her ear. Once my breath hits her ear, I feel her shiver beneath me. "I want to fuck you now. Is that what you want?" Even though in a way I'm doing this to establish consent, I already know she wants this, I'm just using this as a way to talk dirty to her. I don't miss the way her thighs clench and she bites her lip whenever I say dirty things to her. She may not know it, but she's definitely into it.

"Yes," she mutters, barely above a whisper, but that's not good enough for me.

"Tell me exactly what you want." The tone I use leaves no room for discussion, and I love watching the blush spread across her cheeks as she fights against her own embarrassment. I have no doubt the sexy side of her will come out very soon.

"Erm... I want you to fuck me." Not a bad start, if you ignore the shakiness in her voice, but I know she can do better. I pull away from her, so my dick is no longer touching her pussy, and I'm hovering over her, meeting her gaze. As she groans in frustration I try my best not to chuckle. I also have to give my hard shaft a little squeeze, to help curb the excitement.

"I'm going to need more than that, Beautiful. Tell me *exactly* what you want." My emphasis on the word exactly makes it very clear what I'm looking for. I can see it in the fire in her eyes, she wants to be my good girl.

"I-I want your cock... in my pussy. I-I want... to feel you deep. I... I want to please you, and be your... erm... good girl," Emmaleigh mumbles, and it's clear the more she forces her voice to be heard, the more she stutters and stumbles over the words. But, she tells me everything I want to hear, so who am I to deny her.

"You are my good girl. But, next time, I don't want to hear any hesitation. You know what you want, what your body craves, so don't ever be afraid to ask for it again," I state firmly, as I run the fingers of my free hand through her silky, purple hair. I didn't even realise I was doing it until I finished talking, but fuck does it feel nice. Maybe a little too intimate though. We both know what this is, and I have no intention of crossing any lines here.

"So you will fuck me now?" she asks, her eyes wide as she sounds hopeful.

I don't bother giving her an answer, instead I place my hands on either side of her hips and shuffle her so that she's in the middle of the bed. She clearly didn't expect me to manhandle her, if the loud squeak that escapes is anything to go by. Once she's in position in the middle of the bed, I spread her legs wide and kneel between them. With my fist wrapped around the shaft again, I give myself a couple of slow strokes, loving the feel of her wetness combined with my pre-cum as I spread it over my cock. Once I'm rock hard, I line myself up, but instead of plunging in, I gently rub my head up and down her slit. Her moans get louder as I slap the head of my cock over her clit, and I can tell my movements are driving her crazy.

"Lee, stop teasing me. Just fuck me!" Her voice is firm and authoritative, making it very clear exactly what she wants. Usually I don't respond to instructions, much preferring to hear my girls beg for it. But with Em it's different. For this first time, it's much more important that I show her how to be confident, how to listen to her voice and know exactly what she wants. She needs to not be afraid of taking whatever pleasure she wants. A beautiful woman like her needs to have the confidence to tell her sexual partner exactly what she likes. Em doesn't have that right now, so it's not surprising she's only ever had shit experiences.

Obviously, I can't speak for any of the guys who fucked her, but as a gender we are pretty lazy. If it's getting us off and the woman is making the right kind of noises, then of course we will keep doing that. Nobody knows your body the way you do, so we need women to show us exactly what they like, and then we know we're getting it right. But, if the girl is like Em and doesn't have the confidence to tell us what she likes, then of course we're going to keep getting it wrong.

"In future, I won't take instructions. If you want something, you better learn to beg for it. But just this once, because it's fucking hot seeing you take what you want, I'm going to do it for you. Just remember, good girls beg for cock."

Without hesitation, or waiting for Em to reply, I start pushing the large, angry looking head of my cock inside her waiting hole. Her face tells me she feels that delicious sting, that mixture of pleasure and pain as I stretch her out. Pushing in almost painfully slowly, I take my time so she can adjust to my larger than average size. Of course there's a part of me that just wants to get on with it, to plunge all the way in as quickly as I can, until I'm enveloped by her heat before I finally fuck her.

But that's not a good idea, so I keep my movements slow. I can see in her eyes that it's driving her crazy, and so I'm not surprised when she tries tilting her hips to pull me further into her. My cock slips in a little deeper, but I hold back my movements, more now out of punishment. No matter if she can handle me, or if she thinks she's ready for more. I call the shots, I'm in charge, and she knows that.

Holding her down harder with my hands circling her hips, in a way that will no doubt leave a bruise, I make it very clear what's expected of her. I see the internal battle going on behind her eyes. She's torn because there's a part of her that's desperate and just wants me to fuck her, and she will do what ever she can to get all of my cock. Whereas the other version wants to be my good girl, and to do that she will have to listen to every word I say.

The idea of me dominating her outside of the bedroom seems abhorrent to her, since she's most likely worked hard to prove she's a strong independent woman. And honestly, I have no intention of taking that away from her. The way *I* play is in the bedroom only, and I think she's slowly starting to realise that. Still, that doesn't stop the internal debate over if she should follow my instructions. I knew something like this would happen with her being new to this kink, but I can see that she likes the idea of experimenting with me, and she wants me to show her exactly what it is that her body craves.

I've already given her one pass for getting impatient and demanding I fuck her, and so she's on thin ice if she disobeys me again. I can see that she wants my cock, the way her eyes look down at where our bodies are connected, hunger evident in her gaze. That's the moment she decides to do as she's told and just embrace the sensations. Something I'm only too happy to help with. The look of pure bliss on her face as I stretch her walls is almost enough to make me come. She's so fucking tight around my cock. It's like I'm sliding into a glove that's a couple of sizes too small, but as soon as I start stretching her, she molds to me perfectly, that delicious squeeze going straight to my balls.

Leaning down so that my body is practically on top of hers, it does fucking amazing things at this angle as my cock seems to slide in that little bit deeper. I lean down and press my mouth against her soft, full lips, and what starts off as a short kiss soon deepens into something full of heat, as we both pull away, panting as we desperately try to gasp for air. I don't know what it is about this girl, but she takes my breath away, in more ways than just the kiss. And if I'm being perfectly honest, that scares the shit out of me.

I continue my slow, torturous movements as I move my cock deeper into her tight, wet pussy. The urge to just slam into her is overwhelming, but I know she's not ready for that. Besides, even though this slow pace is killing me, I love seeing the frustration on her face as she wars with herself over whether to tell me what she wants or be the good girl she's supposed to be. And honestly, I'm not sure which I want either.

"Please, please. I-I would love it if you would fuck my tight little cunt as hard and as deep as you can. I can take it all, I promise. If it hurts, or I need you to stop, you have my word that I will tell you. But I can't take much more of this, you're driving me fucking insane," she states firmly.

I can hear the tremble in her voice when she starts talking, embarrassment sneaking in for just a few seconds, but she pushes that aside quickly. I watch as she becomes that confident version of herself that I love. She knows what she wants, and she's making sure to tell me exactly what that is.

A mischievous chuckle slips from my lips, causing my body to shudder against hers, and I'm sure she feels it. I lean over until my mouth is close to her ear, my warm breath hitting her sensitive skin as I whisper to her. "So impatient, Beautiful. Trust me, you will thank me for going slow. I'm almost all the way in, and when I bottom out, I will freeze for a few seconds, as your pussy needs to become familiar with my cock, and adjust to his size. That way, you won't get sore, and I won't have to worry about hurting you if I decide I want to fuck you again in a couple of hours."

My voice is low and deep, sounding slightly breathy, and I hope she can't see just how painful it is for me to say that. I mean, it's hot as hell, but I don't want to hurt her. She tilts her face so that her breath is now fanning across my face and I try as hard as I can not to groan—fuck, that feels amazing.

I had no idea having a girl breathe just below my ear would get me so fucking turned on, but it has. She distracts me from the sensation by whispering in my ear. "You feel so fucking amazing inside me, but I don't want to go slow any more. I want to feel you—all of you. Even if it leaves me feeling sore, at least it will be a fucking good memory. Surely your cock is in pain going this slow?" she asks, hopeful that I will be honest and tell her how I'm really feeling.

Apparently I've done a piss poor job of hiding how infuriatingly painful it is going at this pace. I'm supposed to be doing it for a reason, but all those thoughts fly out of my mind upon hearing her dirty words.

While she's waiting for me to reply, I pull my body away from her until I'm kneeling in between her legs again, pushing them open even further, as wide as they will go. Without saying a word, I fix my intense gaze on hers as I slowly pull my cock out completely. A groan of disappointment rips from the beautiful girl below me, and I can't help but smile as I think about how much I'm able to affect her.

Taking the base of my shaft into my hand, I fist it a couple of times to spread her glistening juices across the smooth skin, placing the tip at her entrance. Using my hand that's tightly wrapped around the lower part of the shaft, I swirl just the head around her aching hole, doing my best to stretch her a little more with each circle. Her back arches involuntarily as a loud, sexy as hell moan rips through her.

I can feel her pussy getting wetter, soaking the head of my cock even more, which is exactly what I was hoping for. As I look down at the beauty spread out beneath me, I notice her eyes are clamped shut as the sensations overtake her. I don't want her eyes closed, I want to watch her fall apart.

"Open your eyes, Beautiful. I want your eyes on me at all times," I instruct, watching as she has to force her eyes open to meet my gaze. Her dazzling bluey-grey eyes darken as she sees the lust reflecting in mine.

As she keeps her gaze locked with mine, that overwhelming urge to do as she's told ruling her head, I can't help but wonder how the hell I got this lucky. I mean, this is only the second time I've met this girl, and even though I had a good idea this is how tonight would go, I had no idea it would be this fucking amazing.

Normally, it takes a couple of times and a lot of discussion to reach this level of comfort with a girl. Learning what each other likes, and what they want to experiment with, that takes time. Trust isn't something that comes easy. So, usually the first couple of times together can be trial and error, but with Em, it's been nothing like that. With the exception of her lack of body confidence, which is something I think will need a lot of work on, it's all fallen pretty naturally. I mean, I'm sitting here, completely naked with the head of my cock nestled between her hot, wet pussy lips, and it feels fucking intense.

The more I look over her delicate, naked body that's writhing around beneath me, the more I can't understand her lack of confidence. She really is fucking gorgeous, with curves in all the right places giving her the perfect hour-glass figure. I just wish she could see what I see. Yet, the more I think about how gorgeous and perfect Em is, the more it freaks me out. I try to convince myself it's just the sex talking, and that I feel this way every time my dick gets wet, but we all know that's bullshit. I feel some weird kind of connection with Emmaleigh, and I don't even want to think about it. I don't do relationships, and I won't be starting now. No matter how much I like her.

Thinking thoughts like that is dangerous, and I need to quickly get out of my own head. I'm surprised my brain's even capable of thinking about other things given the way her tight pussy keeps squeezing my dick. I know Em is doing it deliberately to drive me crazy, and since the sensation is enough to pull me out of my dangerous thought process, I don't punish her. Instead, I give her exactly what she wants.

"This is your reward for being a good girl."

As soon as the words leave my lips, her face lights up, blush spreading across her cheeks. She loves when I call her my good girl, and I love the way her pussy clenches around the tip of my dick as she basks in the compliment. I didn't even want to think about how she didn't know she was into praise kink before now. Her cunt gets even wetter each time I praise her, and I love seeing the smile it brings to her face. She has more than earned her reward.

Without giving her time to process what I'm about to do, I quickly push my hard length all the way into her waiting pussy. I don't go slow this time, and I don't give her any more time to adjust. If she says she can cope, I will believe her. So, as I bite my lip to try and avoid the sensation in my dick becoming too much, I push until I'm all the way in, bottoming out as my cock sits deep inside her.

Emmaleigh's hips tilt as her back arches, and that only makes my dick slip in deeper, causing matching groans to escape from us both. My eyes remain fixed on hers, and I can see the way her face is scrunched up in a mix of pain and ecstasy, but her eyes remain open and on me as they blaze with passion.

Leaning over her, with my cock sitting deep in Em's pussy, I press my lips against hers. It's short and sweet, but somehow it feels kind of perfect for this moment. As I pull away from her, I feel like I need to say something. Tell her how amazing or how beautiful she is, but I don't want to give off the wrong impression or mislead her—friends-with-benefits is all we can be. So, I keep quiet, and instead I start to move.

Pulling my cock out slowly, I make sure she can feel every inch of me, until the tip is sitting just inside her entrance. I don't pull out completely, but it's just enough for her to feel empty. Though that only lasts for a second as I quickly plunge back in until my balls hit her ass and my cock is as deep as it will go.

I continue this motion, pulling almost all the way out before slamming back in, each time hitting that sweet spot deep inside her pussy that has her back arching and moans of pleasure echoing around the room. Her cries become more wanton, and I can feel her chasing that peak. Her fingers that just moments ago were holding onto my back are now raking down it, digging in deep. The delicious sting mixed with the tightness of her wet cunt have me groaning loudly.

Each time I thrust in and out, getting a little faster with each stroke, she grips me like a vice and it feels fucking incredible. The more I embrace the feeling the more frantic and uncoordinated my thrusts become. I continue hitting that sweet spot deep inside and it drives Em crazy, her moans becoming louder.

I can feel that she's starting to build to an orgasm, her pussy walls quivering around me. Her body begins to tremble beneath me and the more I focus on the feeling of her bare cunt against the silky smooth skin of my hard length, the quicker I can feel my release building. My stomach clenches as my balls begin to tighten, and I have to bite my lip to hold off as long as I can. It doesn't help that she fits around me like a glove that was made just for me, and my pleasure.

It doesn't take long before Em starts to fall apart beneath my touch. Her walls clamp down on my cock, gripping me in place as she spasms around me. Her body quivers slightly as loud moans of pleasure sound out around me.

"Oh my God. Lee. Fuck, Lee. I'm coming. You're making me come. Fuck," she yells, her voice deep and breathy as she pants and calls out my name like I'm a God.

The combination of her screaming my name, and her pussy clamping down on my cock, means it doesn't take long for me to reach my peak. My movements still and with a loud roar I shoot my load deep inside her. My body shakes as squirt after squirt of hot cum fills her up, and my grip on her hips becomes bruising. I reach down and smash my lips against hers, swallowing her screams that are all for me.

When we both come down from our orgasms, I roll off to the side to avoid crushing her, and we both just lay there panting. As soon as my cock pulls free, it feels wrong. Like it's not where I should be, and that's a scary thought. I've always known women hold a lot of power in their pussies, but I've never known one to hold that kind of power over me. So much so that I actually feel incomplete without it.

Needing to distract myself from those thoughts, I quickly stand up and walk to the en-suite. I grab the flannel and wet it with warm water. As I walk back in the room, Em's looking at me with furrowed brows, like she's not sure what I'm doing. She's closed her legs, so I waste no time wordlessly nudging them open. Like the good girl she is, she does as she's told.

As I move the flannel towards her, it dawns on Em exactly what I'm doing and she reaches down with her hand to stop me. I look up and her face is flushed even redder. "You don't have to do that," she mutters, her eyes dropping from my gaze as embarrassment takes over.

"Of course I do. It's my cum, the least I can do is clean you up. Besides, I want to look after you." Her eyes widen at that last part and I curse myself internally. Why the hell did I say that? I hadn't meant to, it had just slipped out!

She eventually moves her hand away and as the warm washcloth connects with her sensitive pussy, she whimpers softly. I move as gently as I can, and once I'm finished, I quickly run it back to the en-suite before returning to her side. I reach down and press a quick kiss to her lips, and like every other time, a quick one is never enough. As soon as I taste her, I always want more. But, now is not the time. It's late and I can see the tiredness in her eyes.

She shuffles herself over to the right side of the bed, pulling the duvet covers over her naked body, and a moment of sadness overcomes me that I can't see it any longer. There's this awkward moment between us as we both remain frozen. She's sitting up on the right side of the bed, and I'm standing beside her. Is this the time where I get dressed and go? I've had a couple of ciders, so driving's probably not a good idea, but I could go into her spare room. Is that what I want? In the past, I've always left, but for some reason it doesn't feel right this time.

I tell myself it's because I want another round with her overnight, but I'm not sure if I'm bullshitting my brain.

With a cute, shy smile on her face she pulls the duvet back revealing the empty left side of the bed. "Wanna get in?" she asks nervously. Fuck, she looks so cute when she gets all nervous and embarrassed like this. The blush spreads fast across her cheeks and neck.

I don't even hesitate. I move to the open side of the bed and climb in. At first I worry it's going to be awkward, since we still don't really know each other, but I have nothing to worry about. As soon as I'm lying down, Em rolls over and tucks herself into my side. She throws her leg over my thigh, and I can't help but think how well we fit together, and how natural it feels. There's no awkwardness at all.

We don't say anything more. Em lays with her head on my chest as her hand traces circles across my abs. I try to ignore my dick attempting to spring back to life, and instead focus on stroking my fingers through her silky purple hair. It's like we are both at peace, comfortable in each other's company, and it's not long before we both drift off to sleep.

Emmaleigh

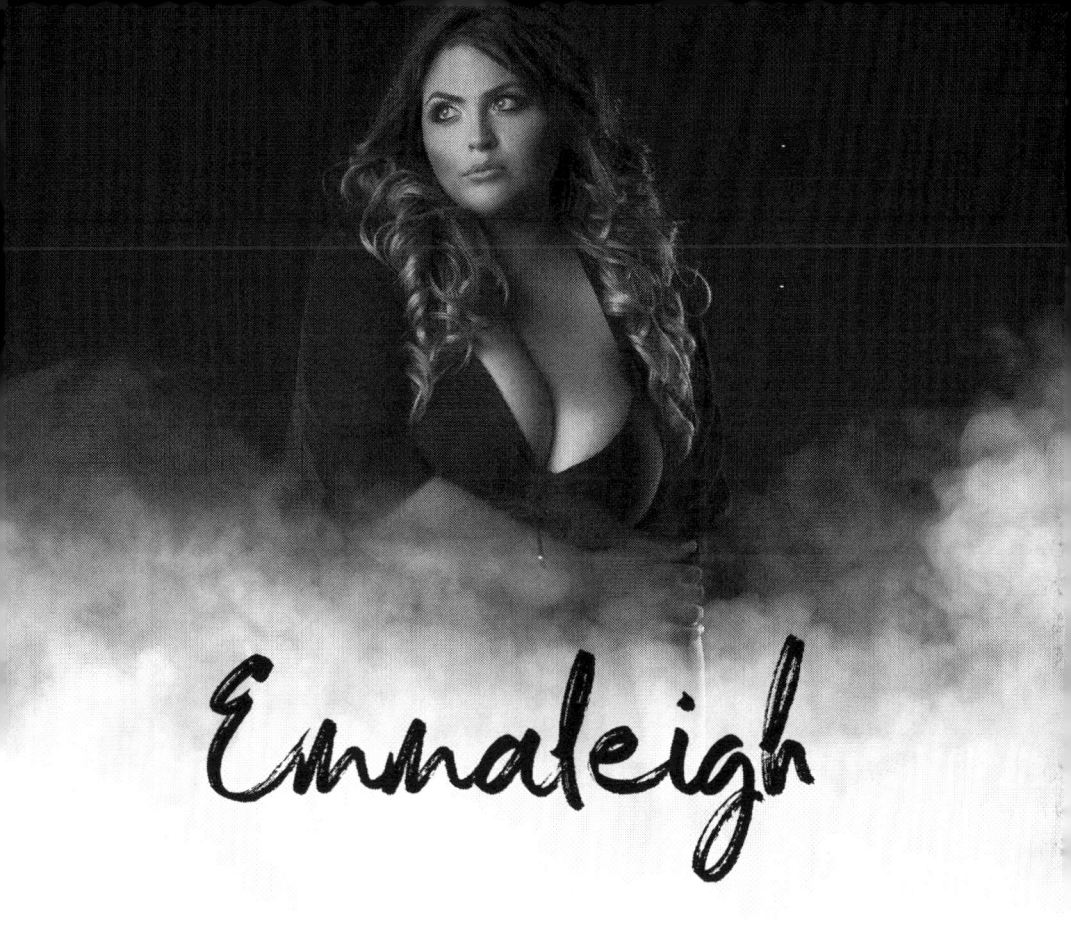

My eyes flutter open, and the minute I wake up, I just know something feels different. That's when I feel the hot, hard body beneath me, and the night comes flooding back to me in exciting waves. Lee and I had amazing, rock my world type sex, and as soon as it was over, I expected him to flee. There's no point staying around and doing all the stuff afterwards. I may have never had a friends-with-benefits relationship before, but I don't see cuddling and falling asleep curled up in his arms being on the list of things to expect. If anything, fleeing is the only thing that makes sense.

Whenever I've had a one night stand before, I'm usually so fucking humiliated, let down, or just deflated once the sex is over, that I almost push them out the door. None of them have ever stayed over, and I've never wanted them to.

Yet, as soon as the sex was over with Lee, I never got any of those feelings. I was sleepy, but the biggest feeling I had was that I didn't want him to leave. So, I invited him to stay. But even then, I didn't expect him to actually do it. After the night we had, I'm kinda glad he did stay though.

Falling asleep in his arms with my head on his chest scared the crap out of me because I enjoyed it so much. I've never felt so warm, secure, and... I'm going to use the words cared for here, because anything else would be far too dangerous to think about.

But if I thought falling asleep with him was amazing, it had nothing on waking up. You see, Lee woke me up twice overnight, and both times resulted in more mind blowing sex. The first time he woke me up with his tongue between my legs, and holy shit, that's the way all women should wake up from now on. To say at the beginning of the evening, I'd barely been able to have an orgasm, and if I did it was always by myself with the help of BOB—my Battery Operated Boyfriend. But Lee didn't need any toys or any help. The more we fooled around, the more he learnt my body, and by the end of the night, he knew every sensitive spot on my body, and he knew how to make me cry out, begging his name.

What surprised me more is how much confidence I gained the more we had sex. The more I did as I was told and he called me his good girl, the more I felt good about myself. He makes me feel so comfortable and beautiful. So when he suggested trying new positions, of course I said yes. He remembered what I'd told him about doggy style affecting my confidence, and when he asked if we could try, I was hesitant, but I wanted to please him.

The whole time he kissed and caressed my back, played with my nipples, or pulled my hair so my back was arched. He started off soft and gentle, so I got used to it, but then he fucked me with a wild abandon that I've come to love. The way his cock hits that spot deep inside has my eyes rolling into the back of my head as I scream his name. He managed to quickly change my opinion of that position, and the way he manages to get so deep means I will be more than willing to try that again.

The position I struggled with the most was when he asked me to get on top. Alarm bells started screaming in my head, and all thoughts of being a good girl and wanting to please him flew out of the window. I couldn't think clearly. I'd never done the position before for a reason. I was convinced I would crush him. Or, once I was on top, I wouldn't know what to do or how to move. I can dance a little, but I wouldn't class myself as being a very sensual person. And that's exactly how I've always seen that position.

I've seen porn. I've seen the way those beautiful women roll their hips, or bounce up and down on his cock. I want to be able to do all that, to give that to Lee after the amazing orgasms he's given me, but for some reason, I can't get the fear out of my head. I know I'm being irrational, but that doesn't make it disappear.

Eventually, Lee talked me into it, after a lot of telling me that I can do it, and that I'm really not as big as I think I am. I want to believe him, to think he's right, but it's hard. Years of conditioning can't be changed in a matter of minutes. But, even with the fear, I can still be brave and give things a try, and I'm glad I did.

What resulted was the most mind blowing sex of my life. The deepness of the position was overwhelming, but it was the fact I was in control that I loved. It turns out, rolling my hips, or bouncing up and down on his cock, was not as hard as I imagined, and I definitely didn't crush him. Quite the opposite in fact. I loved watching him fall apart beneath me.

The way his face scrunches up and his little button nose twitches when he's trying not to come. The feel of his hard pecs beneath my palms as I press down on his chest to help stabilise myself. We both finished at the same time, and it was honestly one of the best orgasms I've ever had.

So, after the most amazing night, I wake up more than a little anxious about how this is going to go. With friends-with-benefits, there really are no rules. It might be weeks before he calls me for the next booty call, or it could be tomorrow. Hell, I may never see him again—though the thought of that causes an ache in my chest.

All these thoughts are running through my mind as I roll over to climb out of bed. My mouth is really dry, and I need to grab a glass of water from the kitchen. Before I have the chance to stand, I feel a warm hand caress my back.

"You wouldn't be trying to do a runner, would you?" Lee jokes, his voice thick and heavy with the lack of sleep we had last night.

I know I should feel self-conscious as I sit here, the duvet falling around my body to reveal my breasts as I turn to face him, but honestly it's a little late for that. He's seen so much more of me, and I'm not embarrassed around him like that any more.

Giving him a small smile, I try to keep my voice friendly, hiding as much of the trepidation as I can. "Well... since this is my house, I don't think I can do a runner. I was just going to get a drink," I explain. "Why? Do you want me to leave?" I don't think I do a very good job of keeping the uncertainty from my voice as I ask the final question.

That bright, mischievous smile that he always seems to wear lights up his face, one side of his lip tilted up in the sexiest way. "You're right, it is your house. Maybe you want me to leave?" He keeps his voice light and playful, but there's definitely a hint of something that I can hear. Is he anxious and feeling awkward about this too?

"Well... it would be rude to kick you out without at least offering you some breakfast," I joke, as I lean down to grab the first item of clothing I can find. It's the T-shirt he took off last night, and I don't hesitate to pull it over my head. It's a little snug around my hips and boobs, but it hangs low around my thighs—the joys of being short. I try not to focus on all the ways it feels too tight, and instead try to exude the confidence he's helped me find.

Standing up, I walk towards the bedroom door, but I look back over my shoulder before I leave, waiting for his reply. He can see the back of my bare thighs, and the T-shirt doesn't leave much to the imagination. The fire and hunger in his gaze is enough for me to bite my lip and clench my thighs together.

"I can definitely think of something I want to eat right now."

Fuck! That has to be one of the hottest things I've heard, and the deep gravelly tone to his voice has me growing wetter at just the mere thought of his tongue between my legs. I got a taste for it last night and I definitely won't say no to him.

I open my mouth to respond, but then he starts climbing out of my bed, the duvet falling around him to reveal his lean, hard muscles. My eyes rake over every patch of his delicious skin, travelling down his body until I latch onto his hardening cock. He's not completely erect yet, but he's starting to get there, and as he grows bigger, I stare in awe that I was able to fit that monster inside me.

Reaching down, he pulls on his boxers before walking over to me. I blink a few times, still frozen at the door. As he gets closer that's when I finally snap out of my moment, and I see the knowing grin on his face. I was more than caught checking him out. I was frozen just ogling his body, and so of course he noticed, particularly when I was staring at his dick.

He reaches my side and my cheeks flush red with embarrassment at getting caught—though I wasn't exactly being discreet. He stops in front of me, his mouth so close I can feel his warm breath against my lips. He waits for a second, and I hold my breath, waiting for his next move. I could close the distance, but this feels like it has to be his choice.

Leaning forward, he captures my lips with his in a sweet, short, but bruising kiss. If I wasn't already holding my breath, he would have without a shadow of a doubt taken my breath away. My stomach is flipping like a teenager with her first crush. As he pulls back, I try to get control of my emotions. Kisses like that really don't help me to see this as just friends.

"I would love some breakfast, if you have something?" Lee asks, pulling my head out of the dangerous place it was just travelling to.

Nodding without saying a word, not able to trust my voice to come out normally, I simply lead the way back into the open plan kitchen-living room. I motion for Lee to take a seat on the sofa, and after finding out what he likes, I set about making some food. I don't have a great deal in the house, I'm in between shifts, which means I will be going shopping later today. Thankfully, I have enough to make him some beans on toast, which he seems happy with.

Over the next hour, we sit at the table together just talking about random things. It's like we are back on our first date all over again, and the conversation just flows naturally. He tells me about his job working in IT, fixing people's computer and technology issues. He asks me about my job, and I tell him about the ward I work on, and how hard the work actually is. People read about nurses in the media, and they think they know us. Yes, occasionally we go on strike over pay, but it has to get really fucking bad for us to reach that state.

"Is it a hard decision for you to go on strike?" Lee asks, leaning forward with his elbows on the table, looking like he genuinely cares about my answer.

It occurs to me, he's the only person that's ever asked me that question. I mean, my family knows that we were balloted and as a whole we decided to strike, but they never asked me how I voted or why. It's nice that he's interested, and that's why I decide to tell him the truth.

"Honestly, it was the easiest decision I ever made. I've worked so many shifts on my own, running a ward with over twenty sick people in it all by myself. Some days I might have the help of a health care assistant, but I'm the one in charge. I have nobody to relieve me. Nobody to take over if I want a wee, or if I want to have something to eat. If something goes wrong, and I have to call for help, they aren't on the ward with me—meaning I have to keep the patient alive until help arrives from wherever the specialist team is in the hospital. We have so much responsibility, we work overtime with no pay, and we miss out on spending time with our family to take care of someone else's.

"The least we deserve is to be paid fairly for it. The cost of living is rising, yet our wages aren't. We are working harder for less money, and only when it gets dangerous do we ask for help. I know the media is never happy with us striking, but we only do it when there's no other choice."

I know I sound like I've just stepped off my soap box, but this really is something I feel passionate about. I love my job, but I want to be able to do it safely. It's not necessarily about the money, it's about the government taking notice of how hard the people in the NHS work, and it's about us being appreciated.

I look over at Lee, expecting him to look a little bored after my rant, but he's got the biggest smile on his face, and it lights up the room. He waits for me to stop talking fully before he replies. "Honestly, I think everyone who works for the NHS deserves better pay. I don't blame you for striking. We've only been chatting for a couple of months, but even in that small space of time, I've seen how hard you work. The nights you've come home after working thirteen hour shifts without a break, and you've been knackered. The times you've barely been able to text me because you've had such a hard day. Or when you work night shifts and for like four days you don't speak to anyone other than those you see at the hospital, since you're like passing ships in the night with your family. I know you love your job, and honestly, I think you are amazing for loving it so much because you sure as fuck don't have it easy. When the day comes for you to strike, I'm sure you'll have a lot more support than you realise."

He reaches over and places his hand on top of mine, and I hate the way it tingles from his touch. My stomach flips as I try not to think about how much my body is drawn to him. I need to keep my emotions in check, and ignore the damn fluttering in my chest.

His smile is wide, and it causes his beautiful blue eyes to light up. With his free hand, he rakes his fingers through his dark hair, causing it to spike up all over the place, giving him the perfect bed hair—that I'm only a little jealous of. Despite running my hands through my long, purple hair, it's still sticking up at all angles. I'm lucky it's perfectly straight and doesn't curl, otherwise I'd look like a frizz ball right about now.

"So, now we've eaten, are you kicking me out, or shall we go out and have a bit of fun?" Lee asks, the cheeky glint in his eyes lets me know he's got an idea in mind for what he wants to do.

Do friends-with-benefits go out on dates? Is it a date, or just two friends spending the day together? Fuck if I know. All I know is that I have a long list of things I need to get done today before I start back at work tomorrow on day shifts. But that list goes out of the window completely as now all I can think about is spending the day with Lee.

"What do you have in mind?"

Lee

I don't really know what the hell came over me when I asked Em to spend the day with me. I mean, I don't exactly know what the rules are with regards to a friends-with-benefits situation, but surely this could fall under the friend part. Two people hanging out and having a laugh together—the very definition of friends.

So why, as I sit on the seaside wall, eating chips with one hand and Em's hand clasped with my other hand, does this feel a little more like something other than friends?

As soon as I mentioned spending the day together, I knew exactly what I wanted to do. We drove to the nearest beach just under an hour away from us. The whole way there, we just talked, and the conversation flowed easily. It's like we've known each other for a very long time, instead of just a few short months—and even that contained a break where we didn't speak. Still, things with Em are easy, and I actually like being in her company. It is a weird concept, given I prefer my own company to anyone else's.

As soon as we got to the small seaside town, and we parked up, I took hold of Em's hand and started dragging her toward the pier. I choose not to think about why I clasp our fingers together, or how tingly my hand feels connected to hers. I could say I'm holding her hand to make sure I don't lose her in the crowd, but we all know I'd just be bullshitting my brain. I feel a level of protectiveness over her.

Last night was without a shadow of a doubt the best sex I've ever had. I have messed about with other girls, and have done a little bit of Dom stuff with them, but I've never had a connection with any of them that has meant I can fully let go. In order to take control fully, I have to have trust with the girl. I have to know she will tell me before she reaches her limit, not after I've gone too far. Initially, with Emmaleigh having so little self confidence, I was worried she wouldn't be able to tell me how she felt or what she liked. I thought she'd just do whatever I wanted to please me.

There obviously was an element of that, and she got off massively on the praise kink—as did I—but she also learnt to tell me what she wants. I loved watching her become more confident as the night went on, and towards the end I even felt like she was embracing her beauty.

I enjoyed the sex so much more when I didn't have to worry about whether the girl was into it or not. Em let me know what she enjoyed, and made it very clear she liked things a little rough, a little less vanilla. And that made her so much hotter to me.

Once we reached the pier, we gazed at each other before looking around at all the fairground rides. Em told me pretty early on when we started talking that she used to live in a little seaside town, but she moved to the city to get a better job, as the prospects weren't great in her town. Even though she's never looked back after the move, she told me there are elements she misses. She told me she took the beach, and the rides there for granted. Because they were always there, and were seen as more for tourists, she never really got the chance to experience them.

So, I decided the nearest seaside town would be the perfect place to give her a taste of her old town. I grew up here, and have never lived anywhere else, so I've been coming to this little seaside resort my whole life. It actually feels kinda nice to share this with Em, to give her a little bit of insight into what my early life was like.

I've always glossed over talking about my family and my childhood.

Not necessarily because I had a bad one—I didn't. I have lots of good memories, but I also have some that I'm not proud of and don't want to share. So, it's often easier to give minimal information and try to change the subject as quickly as possible. Though I have noticed Em is able to get little bits of information out of me, things I wouldn't normally share. I don't think she even notices she's doing it, and I don't realise I've opened up until afterwards.

"So, which ride should we start with?" she asks, her eyes wide as she looks at the lights flashing brightly around the pier.

"You choose," I tell her, not bothered with what she picks. I know, chances are, I'm not going to like any of the rides. I only go on them to make myself look more masculine. I mean, don't get me wrong, once I'm on the rides, I enjoy them, but the actual build up and getting on them, I'm not a fan of. At first I thought it was because I don't like heights, but the more I thought about it, the more I realised it's because I have a very healthy fear of falling.

Em's eyes light up as she scans across the fairground rides, and given the laser focus in her gaze, she knows exactly what type of ride she's hoping for. Let's hope she starts with something nice and small to ease me in. Before I even have a chance to suggest that, she starts jogging towards the opposite end of the pier, a big smile on her face as she pulls me along behind her.

"Do you like the waltzers?" she asks with a giggle, and I can't help but groan. They are most definitely not what I would count as starting out small. They may not do anything overtly dangerous, like loops or plummeting from a great height, but it's the way they spin. It does fucking awful things to my head and stomach. And even though today is very much not a fucking date, I really don't feel that we're at the stage where I can vomit in front of her just yet.

Once we're in front of the large ride, I stand there just staring as the individual waltzer cars travel around the track. If it were just that movement the ride would be quite pleasant, albeit a little boring. But then, on top of travelling around the track, the damn waltzer cars spin around, and by the looks on things, they move so quickly people are pinned to the back of their chairs.

Then, to make matters even worse, the dickcheese—who can't be any more than sixteen—who is operating the ride, keeps manually spinning each car, making them turn quicker. It's no wonder there are more screams coming from this ride than any others nearby.

Em looks at me, like she's waiting for something, and that's when my brain catches up and I remember she asked me a question. "Like is a very subjective word. I wouldn't say I like the waltzers, no." I shake my head quickly, as if that helps to add to the statement.

Her face drops a little, and I see her try to hide it with a smile. "Oh, okay. We can try something else," she mumbles, and I can see the disappointment on her face. Even though she's trying to disguise it, I can tell the sparkle in her dazzling bluey-grey eyes has dimmed.

Shaking my head, I pull her towards the queue. "I may not like them, but that doesn't mean I won't go on. They make me dizzy and feel sick afterwards, but I will live."

That bright smile, and the sparkle I've come to enjoy are now very much evident, and as we flash the attendant our wristband, showing we have the right pass to go on the ride, she's practically bouncing. Thankfully the wait isn't too long, as the more I have to stand around and wait, the longer I have to change my damn mind. The attendant lets a couple of people in before us, and then we walk onto the metal structure. Em doesn't hesitate, she heads around the front, past a couple of empty cars, and makes a beeline straight for the bright purple car. I should have known, it's more than obvious it's her favourite colour. Hell, the waltzer colour almost matches her hair.

She climbs in and practically pulls me down beside her, and the energy vibrating through her body has her practically shaking. As soon as we're both seated, she pulls the bar down so it's resting on both our laps, and when I glance over, she's looking down at our hips and the bar, a frown on her face.

"What's up?" I ask her.

She shakes her head, trying to put her mask back into place, but I watch as she shuffles around uncomfortably, and now I'm worried. "It's nothing."

Yeah, I don't believe that for a second, and I make sure my tone reflects that. "Tell me what's wrong. Now!" I don't raise my voice, I just let her know this isn't open for discussion. There's something wrong with her, and I need to fix it.

Her gaze flicks from where the bar rests above my legs, over to hers, and at first I think she's checking out my cock, but as her brows furrow deeper, her frown growing, I realise it's definitely not that. At first she looks like she might disobey me, but with a huff she lets it go, and her voice comes out as barely a whisper. "I'm just worried because I can't pull the bar down any further because of my fucking chunky thighs, and that means the bars not as tight on you. I understand if you want me to get off."

I can see her eyes are filling with unshed tears and it's obvious this is really affecting her. She really means what she's saying, and it's so heartbreaking. To hear the way she talks about her body, you would think she's super obese, which is most definitely not the case. She's a bit curvier in places than what society tells us is normal, but honestly, I think it just makes her look more real. And, she's so amazing to hug. But this is clearly something Em worries about, and she doesn't quite see herself the way she really is.

I don't even really see what she's worried about. Yes, there's a gap of about three inches between my thigh and the bar, as her thighs are stopping it from pulling down any further. But this is the fucking waltzers, it's not like my life is at risk because of this. In the car next to us is a big, beefy guy who must be well over six foot five, with arm muscles bigger than my thighs, and he's just got on with a little girl who can't be any older than six. The difference in the bar for them must be so much worse than ours, yet he doesn't seem concerned, and neither am I. If this made the ride unsafe, they wouldn't allow it to happen, we would all have individual safety harnesses. I need to make Emmaleigh see all this.

"Em, I need you to listen to this very carefully. You are not as big as you think you are. Yes, there's a gap between my thigh and the bar because your thighs limit how far it can come down, but that's not a fucking big deal. If it was, they wouldn't allow the ride to go ahead. Besides, it's barely noticeable. I know you hate your body, but you really don't have to. You are beautiful, and your curves make you even more attractive. So please, don't ruin this amazing day by worrying about things that don't need to be worried about. Okay?"

She takes a big deep breath, and tries to discreetly sweep away the tear that's falling from her right eye. She somehow manages to blink away the remaining, and she gives me a small smile, but this time it does light up her face, and I know I've got through to her—even if it is just for today. If she's had her lack of body confidence for a long time, and has had exes who have added to these feelings, it will take me longer than a day to undo decades worth of pain and trauma. But that doesn't mean I'm not going to try.

As the sun finally sets on our amazing day, I look over at Em, who is watching the enchanting colours of the sunset, like she's never quite seen anything like it before. Obviously there's nothing overly special about the purples, blues, reds, orange, and yellow swirls that cover the sky, but you wouldn't know that looking at Em's expression of awe. Even I have to admit, it looks beautiful.

I let go of Emmaleigh's hand so I can carry on eating my chips, but she doesn't touch hers. She's nibbled on a couple, but mostly she's just been watching the sunset.

We've had the best day. We went on all the rides, from the biggest rollercoaster, to the tiniest tea-cup ride intended for children—we went on them all. We ran from one ride to the next, chuckling like teenagers. Em's laugh really is infectious, and as she dragged me from ride to ride, I couldn't help thinking this is without a doubt the best day I've had in a long time.

I told Em pretty early on, when we started queuing for our first roller coaster, that I don't like heights or big rides like the one pulling the screams from the people riding before us. She asked me if I wanted to skip the bigger rides, and I explained that I like to push myself—I decided to leave out the fact I'm worried I won't look manly in front of her—and she supported me, like I knew she would. She said if I didn't want to ride, that was okay, but if I did, then she would be by my side, holding my hand, every step of the way. So that's what we did. Every ride, no matter how fucking terrified I was, she grabbed hold of my hand and squeezed, reminding me she was there with me. I have no idea what it meant, but I took strength from her grip, and it made me enjoy the day even more.

As the day progressed, holding Em's hand just became easy. We'd done it so much, it almost seemed like second nature, something that came naturally. I know there's a million reasons why that should scare me, and why I should have dropped her hand quicker than I would a red hot poker, but I didn't—I couldn't. I don't even want to know what that means. So, I distract myself by starting up a new conversation, in between the salty bites of chips that are making my mouth water.

"So, what are your plans for this week?" I ask, turning to look at Em as I take another chip that's covered in tomato ketchup and shove it into my mouth.

Em gives me a cheeky smile, waving the chip she's about to eat in my face as she replies, her voice holding a hint of the sarcasm I've come to expect from her. I'm not normally a fan of people who are sarcastic, but Em does it in such a way, you can't help but still like her.

"Oh, Lee, you wouldn't happen to be asking that so you can segway into asking me out again, would you?"

Thankfully I've just finished eating the chip, as her comment causes me to laugh aloud, and I feel sure it would have been difficult to contain the pieces of potato, had I been laughing with a mouthful. "Well, I wasn't, but now you mention it, do you wanna hang out again?"

I watch as Em's bright bluey-grey eyes light up, but she quickly tries to hide her smile by pulling her lower lip between her teeth, biting down. I hate how fucking sexy that simple gesture is. She quickly schools her features and her brow furrows. I'm starting to recognise some of her facial features, but some—like this—are a complete mystery to me. I wish I knew what she was thinking in that pretty purple head of hers.

"I start a stretch of three night shifts tomorrow, finishing on Thursday morning. I may pick up an extra shift and finish on Friday morning instead. It just depends how busy they are. So, during the week probably won't be a good time. I will be asleep all day and working all night, which sadly doesn't do much for a social life. I do have Saturday, Sunday, and Monday off, before I start a few day shifts. But I'm usually pretty tired after nights. What are you thinking?" she explains, as her body droops a little, looking very tired all of a sudden.

I put my arm around Em's shoulders and pull her in until her side is plastered against mine, and she's able to tilt her head to rest it into the crook of my shoulder. She doesn't yawn, or even say that she's tired, but all of a sudden it was like it just hit her and her body started to sag. "Are you okay?" I ask.

She gives me a small smile, looking up at me with her head still resting against my arm. "Yeah, I've just come over very tired, that's all. My body feels a little heavy, with some pins and needles, like I've been sitting on this cold pier for too long. When we start walking again I will be fine. Anyway, I told you what I'm doing this week, and you were going to tell me why you asked," she reminds me, and I can't help but chuckle. Although I'm worried by the way her exhaustion just came along and hit her unexpectedly, I did bring up this topic, so now I need to finish it. The big question remains, what do I want?

I need to keep reminding myself that this is a friends-with-benefits situation only. I don't need to take her on dates—in fact, I'm sure that's one of the things I shouldn't do. I can booty call her, or make plans for when we are next going to have sex—that is perfectly allowed. Hell, under the friendship bit of the term, I can even arrange to hang out with her sometimes.

I just need to remember where to draw the line. But, the more time I spend with Em, the more fuzzy that line becomes. Only, I can't break it. There's a reason I don't want to be in a relationship, and I need to remember that, hold onto it whenever I think of asking her on a date.

"Maybe we can do something when I finish work Friday night? Pizza and a film at yours, sound okay?" I ask, trying to hide how fucking hopeful I sound.

I mean, I could have said I just want to Netflix and Chill, but that just doesn't feel right. Hell, I could have just said I want to come over to fuck, and my good girl would have said come over whenever. But, those aren't what I mean. I really do just want to chill out, curl up on the sofa together, as we watch a movie together. Friday is always an awful day for me, after working hard the whole week.

I mean, I know everyone working Monday to Friday feels tired by Friday, and that my job working as a support analyst in IT isn't the most stressful job, but it is for me. And normally I would come home and sleep as much as possible over the weekend, but now I get to spend it with Em. Yes, fucking her would really help blow off some steam after a shitty week, but so would just being near her.

No! Stop thinking like that. She's a fuck buddy, and that's all. I need to remember that.

"That sounds perfect. Shall we head back?" she asks, lifting her head off my shoulder, only to have it drop back against me. I look at her with concern, but she manages to pull herself up. She stretches her muscles, after being sat on the hard, cold concrete floor, it's not surprising that her body is stiff, and once she's shaken out all her muscles, she doesn't look as tired anymore.

Without thinking about it, I take her hand in mine, interlacing our fingers together with ease. We begin the short journey back to the car, and as we do, I notice Em is shaking her free hand. I look over and she stops doing it, blush spreads across her cheeks as she keeps her eyes down to avoid my gaze.

"Are you okay?" I ask, gesturing to her now still hand with my head when she finally looks up at me.

"Oh yeah, I'm fine. I just have a bit of a numb arm, probably from being sat in the wrong position for too long. It's nothing you have to worry about. Honestly, my body is weird, and it's always doing strange things like that. I have times when I'm so dizzy I faint, but there's no reason for it to happen. My family joke that I'm so clumsy, it's just my body's way of rebelling for all the times I've injured it."

She laughs, but I can't bring myself to. Even just an off-hand comment about being clumsy, it bothers me. I don't know why, but I don't like when she talks negatively about herself. This woman is beyond incredible. She's smart, funny, and incredibly beautiful. In my opinion, she doesn't have anything to be negative about. But, I'm very aware that I haven't known her for long, and we're also not in the type of relationship where I can go against what her family says.

I can feel the lines between us blurring, and it scares the shit out of me. But, even if I somehow miraculously decide I like her, and she's the girl for me, it doesn't matter. I can't be in a relationship. End of discussion.

Fuck, Emmaleigh deserves someone so much better than me. I should let her go, so she can find a guy who actually wants to—and can—give her the world. I'm not, nor will I ever, be that guy. I've also never wanted to before, but as I look at this stunning woman, with the most gorgeous eyes, and silky purple hair, I start to reconsider. Maybe I do want the possibility of forever, but it will never happen. I don't have the capacity to be anyone's boyfriend.

Emmaleigh

The last couple of weeks have passed by in a bit of a blur. Work just seems to be constant at the moment, and I don't think I'm giving my body enough downtime in between my regular shifts and the overtime I'm practically forced to do. I know I'm not eighteen any more, but at twenty-four, my body should still spring back a lot quicker than it is.

In addition to being absolutely exhausted—which can't just be because of the long shifts or not sleeping on nights—my body keeps doing weird things again. When I'm super tired, and I mean to the point where my joints physically ache and it's hard to move, I've been getting blurred vision and an accompanying headache. I've never had migraines before, but that's what the doctor is claiming is the problem now.

Which is fine, but it doesn't explain the times when my right leg feels like a dead weight and I can hardly walk on it. Or when I'm trying to use my hands, but the pins and needle sensation that overcomes them makes them feel as though my skin is burning.

Thankfully, I have Lee to distract me from my failing body. I can't bring myself to do another doctor's trip. I'm sick of them telling me it's nothing, I'm overworked, or my personal favourite... have I considered losing some weight. What a fucking joke. Of course I know I'm overweight, I can see by looking in a fucking mirror, yet they still feel the need to point it out to me. After the last one diagnosed me with migraines, and didn't give a shit about the pins and needle sensations, or the intermittent numbness in my leg, I can't be bothered any more.

Sometimes they look at my job, see I'm a nurse, and assume I either know what the problem is, or I'm overreacting. Of course nurses are more likely to assume the worst, since we spend day after day caring for people who are quite literally living their worst case scenario. But that doesn't mean we know everything. I know what symptoms I have, but I have no idea how they link together or what they could be. Hell, at one point, even I just put it down to the fact I'm clumsy, or I'm overweight. I've always put my faith in medical professionals, so if the doctor doesn't think it's anything, I will have to go with that.

I begin pacing up and down my living room, stopping occasionally to look out of the window to see if Lee's car has arrived yet. Even though he's spent every weekend here since that first night together, he still takes a moment in his car before coming in. I've never asked him why, and honestly, I won't. I pace up and down the living room, mentally preparing myself to act normal and not screw this up. I also have to give my brain the usual reminder pep talk.

This is not a relationship. We are only friends-with-benefits. Don't get any more involved. Don't get your heart broken.

I repeat those things over and over in my head, hoping like hell that at least one of them will stick. This will be Lee's fourth weekend of staying over, and every one is better than the last. It's not even the sex stuff—though that does get more and more mind blowing each time we fool around—it's the other stuff too. Like when we cuddle up together on the sofa to watch a movie. Or how he will text me after a long shift to make sure I'm okay, and that I've eaten.

In my head, those things seem like the actions of a boyfriend, not just a friend. But Lee is very clear in his words—he doesn't want a relationship. So why are his actions a whole lot less clear?

Lee knocks on the door, pulling me out of my own head, and I run to answer it. I stop just before reaching for the handle, shaking myself and giving myself the same pep talk as before. I need to listen to his words, and not get too involved. But, if the way my heart races as I go to the door is any indication, it might be too fucking late. I'm too far gone, which means I'm going to get really hurt.

Opening the door, I allow myself a couple of seconds to run my gaze over Lee, the same way I do every time I see him. Dark jeans hug his thighs, and I know if he turns around the jeans will be pulled across, giving his ass the perfect shape. What can I say... I like a guy with a nice ass!

My gaze travels higher, across his tight black T-shirt that's stretched over his hard abs and is tight around his biceps. He's not wearing a coat, but he never seems to mind. He's always too hot—then again, looking the way he does, I'm not surprised.

Even though his body has me drooling, it's his face that sends my heart fluttering. His plump pink lips are turned up in that mischievous smile, revealing a dimple on one side. He's got stubble stretched across his chin, like he hasn't shaved for a couple of days, but the rugged look really suits him. His bright blue eyes are staring straight at me, glistening as he raises an eyebrow.

Oops, looks like he caught me checking him out.

Blush spreads across my cheeks, causing his smile to widen as he unapologetically rakes his gaze over my body. We've reached the stage now where I don't feel I have to get completely dressed up. I mean, I still make a bit of an effort, and everything is fully waxed, but I opt for some comfier clothes. I'm wearing some black leggings and a baggy T-shirt of Lee's that he left over here last week. It's a Marvel shirt, but the way he's looking at it, you'd think my tits were fully on display.

"Hey." Well, that was the most pathetic welcome I could come up with, but I'm kinda frozen as I think about how good he looks.

His smile widens and his eyes darken, hooded with lust. I open the door wider so he can come through, stepping out of the way. He starts to walk into the flat, and I stand back to give him enough room. The hallway is long but narrow—you can touch both walls with each flattened palm. As he steps through, I try to move away, to give him some space, whilst every nerve cell in my body prickles with anticipation.

It's always like this around him. Whenever he's near, it's like my body connects with his, and for the first time in a long time, I feel alive. I don't give a shit that my thighs look big in the leggings, or that his T-shirt that I'm wearing is a little tight around my hips. I don't even care that I should have washed my hair this morning, but I was so tired I just threw on some dry shampoo instead.

In the past, these are all imperfections that would have given me some pretty severe anxiety, and it would have taken a lot not to make myself perfect for him. But that's the thing about Lee, even looking like shit, as I'm sure I do right now, he doesn't seem to care. He likes me just the way I am, and in turn, that makes me start to like myself just that little bit more.

Lee hears my breath hitch, and that cheeky smile widens as he continues to crowd me. Once he's in, without even looking, he slams the door closed, the latch snapping shut behind him. I reach to put the security chain on, but before I even know what's happening, Lee spins me around and slams my back against the door. He drops the bag he's holding and closes the gap between us, pressing his hard body against mine, caging me in.

I barely have time to register how close he really is before he slams his lips against mine. As soon as his taste hits my tongue, it's like my body just reacts. I throw my arms around his neck, sliding my fingers through the strands of hair at the back of his neck and use that to pull him impossibly closer.

Swiping my tongue across his lower lip, he understands what I want and opens to give me the access I'm craving. As our tongues battle, tasting as much of each other as we can, Lee's fingers skim across my hips, dragging lower until he reaches the hem of the shirt I'm wearing. At first I think he's going to take it off, but instead he scoops his hands underneath the fabric and runs his fingers across my stomach. The feel of his cool fingers on my warm skin causes goosebumps to form, and a moan to escape my lips.

He moves his hands higher, until he reaches the edge of my bra, and my whole body practically vibrates in anticipation over what he will do. His mouth continues to devour mine, as his hand gently swipes across my already hardening nipple, all the while keeping his fingers above the fabric. I want to feel his touch, I need more, which is why I try to arch my back, pressing myself further into him.

Sadly, this doesn't have the effect I'm hoping for, as Lee pulls his lips away from mine, and moves his hands to my hips, pressing me in place against the door. I gasp, trying to catch my breath as he stares at me, that mischievous glint in his eye.

"Tut, tut, Em. I thought you knew the rules by now. I'm in charge, and we go at my speed." He tries his best to sound stern, but I can hear the humour in his voice. He likes the fact he turns me on so much I forget all the rules. Plus, he quite liked to punish me. Over the last two weekends, we started exploring light punishments, as well as other experiments, and I have to say, I love them all. Lee has opened up a whole new world for me, and I'm so fucking here for it.

I drop my gaze as blush spreads across my cheeks. "Sorry," I mumble, though we both know I'm not really sorry. I want him, and I'm not ashamed of that.

Lee leans in until his breath is against my ear, and as soon as his deep, gravelly voice starts, I have to bite my lip to stop myself from sounding even more desperate. "Looks like someone needs to be punished. Do you still want to be my good girl?"

Fuck. Those dirty words cause my stomach muscles to tighten as I try to rub my thighs together to alleviate some of the ache I feel there. I get wetter every time his breath tickles my ear.

"I want to be your good girl," I reply, my voice barely above a whisper.

I brace myself, wondering what he's going to do next, but he just stays frozen, his lips painfully close to my ear. I want to turn my face, to press my lips against his. I want to reach out and touch him, to pull him closer. Hell, I want his hands to move instead of staying frozen against my hips. I want so much more, but I know if I ask for it, he won't give it to me. This is about me learning that to be a good girl, I have to do as I'm told. I have to do things at his pace, not mine.

Catching me completely off guard, Lee spins me around until my face and chest are pressed up against the door instead of my back. It all happens so fast, I can't help the startled yelp that escapes, but Lee doesn't seem to care. Instead, he manipulates my body, moulding me into the position he wants me in. Face and tits pressed against the door, he arches my back as he uses his knee to knock my knees further apart. This angle has my ass sticking out at the perfect angle to show off the curves Lee seems to like so much. And if I weren't wearing leggings, this position would show off my pussy perfectly.

I turn my head slightly so my cheek is pressed against the door, making the position slightly more comfortable for me. Plus, from this position, I'm able to look over my shoulder and see what Lee's doing, and I love what I see. His eyes are dark, hooded with lust, the crystal blue I love is barely visible. Gone is his mischievous smile, now he's completely serious, almost intense, and that sends a shiver of excitement through me.

I watch as he pulls his T-shirt off and throws it onto the floor. I have to bite my lip as I take in the hard ridges of his abs. The bulge in his dark jeans is so obvious it looks almost painful, and I watch as he grips himself over the material, squeezing to help relieve some of the pressure. The delicious hiss that escapes his lips gets me wetter.

I could look at him like this forever—though I wouldn't mind seeing him completely naked, as that's even more of a sight. But clearly he has other things in mind. He reaches over and pulls my leggings and panties down to my ankles, the cool air hitting my bare pussy causes me to groan. I bite my lip in anticipation, and as soon as I catch sight of the glint in his eye, I realise exactly what he's about to do.

SLAP!

The sound of his hand connecting with my right ass cheek echoes all around us, and I bite harder on my lip as the sting spreads. My ass feels as though it's heating up, until Lee rubs his hand over the reddening flesh, soothing the delicious sting.

"What do you say?" he asks, his voice deep and thick, making it obvious just how turned on he is right now.

My brain barely registers what he says, as I'm bracing myself for the next spank. I try to think of a reply, but my brain has lost all rational thought and my lady parts are running the show now.

Clearly unhappy with my silence, Lee slaps his palm onto my left ass cheek just as hard, and this time I cry out louder. As he rubs his hand against my burning flesh, he leans in closer. With his free hand he fists his hand into my long purple hair and pulls my head until his lips are pressed against that sweet spot just below my ear. But instead of kissing it, like he usually does, he holds me in position so he can whisper into my ear.

"You haven't forgotten how you take a punishment already, have you, Beautiful? I can keep spanking this gorgeous ass until it's so red you won't be able to sit down for a week, yet I'd much rather get on with fucking you. But only good girls get fucked. So, are you ready to be my good girl?" he growls, and it's like he's got a direct fucking line to my pussy and I want so desperately for him to touch me.

Clamping my thighs together to try to ease the pressure, I think back to when he first taught me about punishments. I was so fucking nervous the first time he spanked my ass. I didn't think I would like the pain, but I was very fucking wrong. It took my pleasure to a whole other level, one I'd never even thought I could enjoy before. And in between every spank, he made me thank him and count them, building anticipation even further for the next one.

Shit! That's what I forgot to do.

"Sorry, Sir. I'll be a good girl, and thank you every time you spank me. I'll make sure to count them too," I reply, trying to sound as sweet as possible—I know that makes his cock even harder.

"How many spanks do you think you deserve?" he asks.

"However many you think, Sir," I reply. I have no idea when I started calling him Sir during sex. It only happens when we're roleplaying like this. He's in charge, and I will do anything to be his good girl. It just sort of came out naturally, and I saw how excited it made him, and I really do want to please him in any way I can, so I just went with it.

Don't get me wrong, we do still have what some people would refer to as vanilla sex, where we don't role play and it's just Emmaleigh and Lee, kissing, touching, and connecting through sex. But I think we try and avoid that as much as possible—or I know I do—because that's the type of sex you have with a boyfriend. It's the type of sex that leads to feelings becoming involved, and it's the fastest way for me to end up with a broken heart.

The big problem is, I enjoy that sex just as much, if not more, than I do the kinky praise sex that we have. I get more turned on with the kinky stuff, and fuck does Lee know how to drag an orgasm out of me, even when he's causing me pain. But the vanilla sex, that's when we have the most connection, and each time he kisses me, or takes his time devouring my body, I fall for him just that little bit more. So that's what I try to avoid, preferring this rougher side to him.

"I think we will do ten. How does that sound?" he growls into my ear, but before I have a chance to answer, he brings his hand down against my right ass cheek.

This blow is just as hard as before, and the noise that comes out of my mouth is a mixture of a yelp and a groan, but this time I remember to do as I'm told. "One. Thank you, Sir," I cry out, my voice shaky, but I'm not sure if it's from pleasure or pain.

As Lee brings his hand to my sore ass cheek and begins to stroke the reddened area, I can't help but mewl. The way his cool flesh soothes the burning feels fucking amazing. Sadly, I don't even have a minute to enjoy the blissful feeling before he slams his palm down on my left ass cheek this time. Catching me completely off guard, I cry out loudly, but again remember my instructions. "Two. Thank you, Sir."

"Good girl," he mutters beside my ear before kissing my cheek softly. Just those two little words are enough to help me forget all about the pain, and I'm focused solely on making him proud. It's the weirdest feeling, but I feel like I'm soaring.

Lee continues spanking each ass cheek in turn, and as he gently rubs to soothe the sting, I count and thank him for each one. By the end, as each spank gets harder, the pain gets worse and worse. Each blow lands on top of the burn from the one before, until my ass is bright red and I have tears streaming down my face.

Even though the pain starts to feel a little overwhelming towards the final blow, it's still such a fucking turn on. The tears might be flowing, but my pussy is so wet, and it's the most turned on I've been in a while. As Lee is soothing away the final blow, the tip of his finger lightly brushes past my clit, and I whimper. It's the slightest touch, so insignificant that I'm not even sure he did it on purpose—though, knowing Lee, he probably did. Yet, it's enough to cause my back to arch further and whimpers to spill from my lips.

I know he loves hearing my whimpers and cries of pleasure. I can feel his erection straining against his jeans as it presses against my thigh every time he leans over to whisper in my ear. I want more. I want him to free himself. To touch himself. But Lee has the patience of a fucking saint, and if he wants to draw this out, he will.

This time, as his finger slides through my slit, it's clear he's doing it on purpose this time, and fuck does it feel good. It's over before it's even begun, and a frustrated groan rips from my lips, causing him to chuckle. He swiped his finger from my asshole up to my clit, circling around it once before pulling away. It was nowhere near enough, so of course I'm going to tell him that.

"Em... this was supposed to be a punishment. Are you getting turned on?" he chuckles, and I can't help but roll my eyes. Talk about stating the fucking obvious. I mean, I'm surprised I can't feel my juices running down my leg, and we both know the finger that just slid through my slit must be covered, so it's kind of a stupid question.

Before I realise what's happening, Lee grabs hold of my hair in his fist and pulls causing my back to arch further. I yell out at the pain that's currently ricocheting all over my scalp as Lee uses his free hand to grip my chin, forcing me to look at him as he bends me to his will. He seems to know exactly where my line is, and he never goes over it. He never pushes me too far, and even now when he looks like he's pissed, I can see the fire in his eyes that lets me know, this is just the rough side I enjoy coming out to play. He won't ever take it too far, and I know he will stop if I tell him to. But right now, as his fiery eyes bore into mine, stopping is the farthest thing from my mind.

I try to rack my brain, thinking about what I could possibly have done wrong to warrant this. I don't have to wait long before his deep, gravelly voice lets me know.

"Did you just roll your eyes at me?"

Fuck!

I try to move my head to look down, but he has me firmly in his grasp, and I can't move even a little. I could lower my gaze, but that will only get me in even more trouble. So instead, I hold his gaze firmly and reply. "I'm sorry, Sir. I did roll my eyes."

That smile I love starts to get wider, and fuck if that doesn't turn me on even more. He loves it when I'm being good—we both do. No matter how much I like being punished, I prefer it so much more when he looks at me like this, like he's proud of me.

"Why did you roll your eyes at me?" he asks, as he lets go of my chin.

I'm still held firmly where he wants me as his hand is still fisted in my hair, but I could try to move a little, if I wanted. But I don't. I stay exactly where I am, eyes fixed on Lee's, and I love watching his bright blue eyes flash darker every time I do something to turn him on.

"I shouldn't have done it, Sir. I'm sorry. I just thought it was a silly question because my pussy is always wet when I'm around you." My reply slips out, and if I could slap my hand over my mouth right now, I would. I can't believe I just said that. It's like I have no self control, which I obviously do. Just not when Lee's manhandling me like this.

"Is that right?" he asks, the humour evident in his voice.

Before I get the chance to reply, he roughly presses his finger into my wet pussy, catching me completely unaware. It's a good job I am ready, as he doesn't take it slow. He pushes all the way in, quick and rough, and I can't help crying out. Fuck does that feel amazing.

I arch my back further, pressing my hip further into his body, and I can feel how hard he is. When he speaks this time, the humour is long gone from his voice, and now he sounds purely turned on. "Fuck, you really are wet."

I nod my head in confirmation, forgetting he has my hair wrapped around his fist, and the movement causes my scalp to sting. But, I'm too busy concentrating on the feel of his finger moving in and out of my pussy. He's moving so slowly it's almost like torture.

"Does that feel good, Beautiful?" he whispers against my ear, before taking the lobe in between his teeth, nibbling gently.

Arching my back as much as I can, I try tilting my pelvis to meet his finger movements, but it's impossible. He has me fixed in position, and I'm completely at his mercy—just the way I like it. "Yes, it feels amazing. But please, I need more, Sir."

As soon as the words leave my lips, he pulls his finger from my pussy and I can't help but groan. Me and my fucking big mouth. My pussy is pulsating with need, and it feels far too empty. I keep my gaze fixed on his, trying to tell him with my eyes how much I need him.

He lets go of my hair, knowing I won't move from this position, and he adjusts slightly before bringing his finger up until he's holding it in front of my face. I can see my juices glistening over his skin, and fuck is that hot. Knowing he can turn me on that much is intoxicating.

I wait for him to move the finger to his lips, like he's done so many times before. It's one of the hottest things I've seen, so it's not surprising that I stand completely transfixed, just waiting to see the look on his face as he tastes me. But instead of pulling it to his lips, like he always does, he moves it towards mine.

At first I keep my lips together, not quite sure if I want to taste myself. It's not something I've ever done before, or been tempted to do. But the look of pure passion in Lee's eyes makes me want to do anything for him.

Without needing to be asked, I open my mouth for him. As he moves his finger slowly to my lips, the fingers on his other hand cup my pussy, pressing down hard on my sensitive clit. As soon as I cry out, Lee presses his juice covered finger to my lips. I close my mouth around his finger, and whirl my tongue around the tip, just like I would do if it were his cock.

I'm actually pleasantly surprised by how much I like the taste. It's sweeter than men, but it still has that salty kick to it. A little like me, I guess. Lee must see the moment I realise it doesn't taste too bad, and I start sucking on his finger, as his eyes widen, the heat etched across his beautiful face.

Keeping eye contact, I treat his finger just like I would his dick, swirling my tongue around the tip before sucking as far into my mouth as I can. I want to reach down to feel how turned on he is, even though it's plain to see on his face. But I know better than to do something without his permission. This is his game and we follow his rules. I know that, but it doesn't stop me from wanting to feel him. To have him fill me completely.

I'm so lost in his eyes as he watches me clean all my juices off his finger, I almost miss the feel of his fingers sliding through my slit. It's not like he's trying to gather up more of my juices, it's more like he's trying to spread them around. Just as that thought enters my head, and I think about why he's doing that, I feel the head of his cock nudging at my pussy lips.

My eyes widen and a smile spreads across my face—as much as it can with a finger in my mouth—as I feel the tip swipe through my slit. I know he's getting the head wetter, but the feeling is torture. As he presses it against my sensitive clit a cry breaks free and I try to move my pelvis to get his cock where I want it, but he brings his hand to my hip, and holds me tightly in place.

He then moves his cock down towards my asshole, and gently presses against my tight hole. My eyes widen, and I open my mouth to say something, but I'm not sure what. I've never had anyone play with my ass before, and he knows that. We've talked about it, and I did say I wasn't against trying. I'm not sure how I expected it to happen, but I kinda hoped there would be some preparation or warning beforehand. Still... I don't stop him.

Lee pulls his finger from my mouth, and I make sure to suck it clean as he's pulling back. He then takes that hand and places it against my neck, in a similar position to if he were trying to strangle me with one hand. We've played around with breath-play a little over the last couple of weeks, and I discovered how much I like it. I don't like it to go to far, or for him to hurt me doing it, but when he puts enough gentle pressure on that I struggle to breathe for a few seconds—similar to if he shoved his cock deep into my throat—it adds to the feelings of euphoria, and enhances my orgasm.

As his hand lightly presses against my neck—not enough to affect my breathing yet, but enough to cause a bit of discomfort—he leans over and whispers against my ear again. "I do plan on taking this ass, but now is not the time for that. You need to be a lot more prepared, but it makes me very happy to know you would let me have it, right here, right now, if I wanted to. You are a good girl."

Fuck, I can't help the smile that spreads across my face, and he looks at me with a weird mix of pride, and something more. I know I'm not great at reading people, but he was looking at me like he really cares for me. I'm not going to use the L word, as that's dangerous fucking territory, but it looked like something similar.

No, get that out of your head right now!

I try to stop thinking, to focus on the feel of his cock moving away from my asshole, and pressing against my pussy opening. He leaves the tip just resting at the entrance, not quite in yet, but enough that it's stretching me, causing that delicious sting. My eyes flutter closed and I just allow myself to feel, and fuck me does it feel incredible.

I want to move. Hell, I want Lee to move, but I know better than to say anything. Instead, I just wait. That's when I feel him press his lips against mine, his tongue licking along my bottom lip to demand access. Of course I let him, and as he licks across my tongue, I arch my back, a moan slipping from my mouth into his. The movement is enough to press his cock head just that little bit further in, stretching me a little more, until I'm panting with need.

He barely lifts his lips from mine, so when he speaks it's like he's muttering the words straight into my mouth, as he presses a little harder around my neck causing my eyes to fly open. "I can taste your pussy on your tongue, and it's so fucking sexy, Beautiful."

He groans against my tongue as he pushes his cock in a little more, moving painfully slowly. His eyes scrunch together, and he looks like he's in agony, but still he doesn't move. How the fuck does he do that? He must have the patience of a fucking saint because I'm going crazy. It's taking every last drop of willpower I have not to tilt my damn pelvis and press his cock into me fully. But I know if I do, he will just pull out and prolong my agony further.

His eyes open and they're almost completely black, his pupils dilated wide as lust overtakes his body. He captures my lips again, only this time it's not a sweet kiss. This is hard and bruising, and his hand presses harder on my neck, limiting my breathing. All my nerve endings seem to prickle, and I can feel myself getting wetter. I press my tongue against his, tasting him as he devours me.

The lack of oxygen starts to take effect and I can feel my head starting to spin, my lungs begin to burn, and my eyes widen in panic. I'm about to reach down to tap on his side—the sign we agreed on when we first started experimenting—but he's watching me the whole time. He knows my limits, and he sees the moment it becomes too much for me, and pulls his hand away.

I gasp for breath, dragging as much oxygen into my burning lungs as I can, blinking away the spots that had started forming in my vision. Lee kisses along my cheek as I pull in each breath. As soon as my breathing starts to return to normal, Lee catches me off guard by slamming his cock deep into my aching pussy.

Crying out loudly, pleasure evident for all to see, I don't even try to hold it in. If my neighbours hear, so fucking what. I just allow myself to feel the way he pulls his cock all the way out, sitting the tip just at my entrance before slamming all the way back in. The more he does this, the faster he gets, and it feels fucking fantastic.

As he peppers little kisses across my cheek and lips, one hand grips my hip so he can control the pace, while he uses his other to grip my neck again. At first he's just holding his hand there, not even pressing hard, unlike the one on my hip that's digging in so much it will probably leave little crescent moon shaped fingernail marks on my skin. Not that I mind... I quite like having his marks on me.

His thrusts become faster and deeper, and every time he bottoms out, he hits that magic spot that has me crying out. I can feel my body coiling tight, chasing that sweet orgasm I know isn't far away. My whole body feels as though it's on fire, and my pussy gets wetter with every stroke he takes. The sound of our bodies slapping together echoes around the small hallway, and he slams into me so hard, the door begins to shake.

Lee's movements become more uncoordinated and frantic, and that's when he starts pressing down on my throat. I know he's close, and he's making sure to drag the biggest orgasm he can out of me. His thrusts become rougher, just the way I like it, and he keeps hitting that spot over and over.

I force myself to keep my eyes open, despite the overwhelming sensation to close them and just embrace the pleasure, but I know he likes it when I keep eye contact. He looks like he's forcing his eyes open too. The lines around his face look like the kind that appear when you're grimacing in pain, but I know that's not it. He's trying his hardest not to come, until I have. He always makes sure I finish first.

So, I'm not remotely surprised when the hand that was gripping my hip tightly lets go. Slowly, he traces the curve of my hip bone with his fingers, moving down the front of my body, heading towards my pussy. His fingers are moving agonisingly slowly compared to the quick, frantic thrusts of his cock.

As soon as he reaches my bare mound, he slides his fingers in between my wet folds, one sliding either side of his cock. He groans loudly as he can no doubt feel his fingers tightening around his cock as it slides in and out of my pussy. He does that for a few strokes, and his breathing increases. He's panting hard, but because he's so focused on what he's doing, he isn't pressing on my neck all that much. Not that I mind, there's more than enough sensations going on to drive me insane.

My pussy is getting wetter, my juices spreading over his fingers, and I'm not surprised to hear it's driving Lee crazy. His thrusts are frantic, hitting me deep as I beg for more. "Please... fuck... Lee... I-I need...more. Oh fuck, d-don't...stop," I shout in between pants as the sensations begin to overwhelm me. My stomach muscles feel like they're tightening, and my legs are turning to jelly. It's only his body slamming into me that's helping keep me upright.

"You're such a good girl. You feel so fucking tight, squeezing my cock with your wet cunt. Are you ready to come for me, Beautiful?" Lee growls in my ear, before pressing kisses to my cheek.

I don't even get the chance to answer before he moves his fingers from around his cock, and places them on my clit. At the same time he pushes down on my throat, cutting off the oxygen supply instantly. The pain in my neck, combined with the burning in my lungs as I use up the last of my oxygen supply sends my body into overdrive. All my nerve endings crackle, and everything feels so much more sensitive.

I know I'm close, and so I try to focus to get the words out. But it's hard to speak with his hand around my throat. It comes out as a croak, but I focus, determined to be a good girl. "Please, Lee. Can...can I-I come?"

I learnt pretty early on when we started fooling around, Lee gets off on talking dirty, and so do I. I had no idea how to even do it before I met him, having only ever seen the cheesy version that features in porn. But, he made it clear what he expected from me, and to be honest, the rest just came easy. I thought I would find it hard asking him to come, and even fucking harder if he doesn't give me permission. But as soon as I tried it for the first time, it came so naturally. Now I don't even think about it. I know if I want to be his good girl, I can't come without permission, so as soon as I know I'm close, I start begging, and hope like hell I've been good enough for him to say yes.

Rubbing his fingers over my clit, while he continues slamming his cock deep into my pussy, has my body vibrating with pleasure. But he doesn't say a word. I try to cry out, to beg, anything, but he increases the pressure on my throat. His movements are becoming more desperate, and I know he's close too.

"You can come, Beautiful. Come like the good girl you are," he instructs.

It only takes a few more thrusts, and a couple more seconds rubbing my clit before I reach the peak I've been desperately craving. It's like fireworks explode and I see spots in front of my eyes. I'm not sure if it's from the lack of oxygen, pleasure, or both. And right now, I don't fucking care.

My whole body shakes, and my pussy tightens around Lee's cock, clamping so tightly he has to stop his movement. I arch my back, and as he lets go of my throat, I scream out in pleasure before desperately trying to drag air back into my burning lungs. My whole body feels alive, like every nerve cell is tingling, as a pleasure like no other overtakes me.

"I'm coming. Oh my God, I'm coming," I scream, not giving a shit about how loud I'm being. That's how it always is with Lee. I don't think about anything except the here and now. How he makes me feel, and how I affect him.

The feel of my pussy clamping down on his cock is too much, and it's not long before he's grunting and coming right alongside me. He doesn't pull out, instead shooting ropes of cum deep into my pussy. I actually like the feel of him coming inside me. It's like he's claiming me as his, and I don't even want to think about why that makes my heart beat faster.

As soon as I come down from my orgasm, my legs go limp and I struggle to hold myself upright. Thankfully, Lee realises and he grabs hold of me. With one hand around my back, he leans down and tries to scoop me up like I'm a bride he's carrying over the threshold. I bat his hands away with mine.

"No, don't be silly. I can walk. You can't lift me, I'm too heavy," I mutter, hating to admit that as it causes that self doubt and lack of confidence to begin creeping into what was a fucking beautiful moment.

Lee grabs hold of my hand in his, and he fixes me with that hard, stern stare of his. Those bright blue eyes glisten at me, and his brow furrows. He looks almost mad. "Em, listen to me... you don't see yourself clearly. Trust me when I tell you, I can lift you. I wouldn't risk it if I thought I couldn't. If I thought I might drop you and hurt you, I'd never try it. Now, let me take care of you."

He leaves no room for argument, but I can't help but be terrified. I close my eyes and hold my breath as I feel him wrap his arm under my legs. Then, I feel him scoop me up and I can't help but yelp in surprise. Instantly my eyes fly open, and I wrap my arms around his neck in terror.

Fucking hell, he managed to pick me up. But he still has to walk me to wherever he plans to take me. I hold on tight in case I become too heavy the more he moves.

But that doesn't happen. In fact, he moves through to the living room with ease. As soon as he's deposited me on the edge of the sofa he runs into the bathroom, before running back with a washcloth that he proceeds to use to clean us both up. I'm in such a blissed out state, all I can do is stare at the gorgeous naked man as he runs around taking care of me.

He disappears with the dirty washcloth and reappears a few minutes later with the duvet cover to wrap us up in on the sofa, and two cans of Diet Coke from the fridge. He drops down next to me, and without saying anything, he pulls me in so I'm cuddled up against his side as he wraps us up. He opens the can and hands it to me. I take a few drinks, ignoring the burn as I swallow from the pressure Lee used on my throat. He probably pressed a little too hard as he was coming, losing control a bit. Not that I'm complaining in any way. It was hot as fuck.

We sit together for a while, just enjoying being close to each other. I think we both must have nodded off for around half an hour, and we're woken up by the doorbell buzzing. I look over at the clock, and realise it's the pizza I ordered earlier. I go to get up but Lee stops me.

When he returns with the pizza, he's only dressed in his boxers and I lift my eyebrow in surprise. "Did you seriously answer the door like that?"

Lee laughs and nods. "I did try to put your hoodie on, but it was too small, so I thought fuck it. The young guy almost threw the pizza at me, he was in such a rush to get away."

I can't help but laugh, my mouth turning into a bright smile as I picture the scene. "I bet he did. It's just a good thing it wasn't a female delivery driver," I reply, and Lee's eyes widen, that mischievous smile spreading across his face.

"You wouldn't happen to be jealous, would you, Beautiful?" Lee jokes, as he nudges his shoulder against mine, once he's seated beside me again. He hands me a plate as he opens the pizza box, before grabbing his own.

Shit, I probably shouldn't have said that. I don't need him knowing how much I care about him. I like what we have, and I don't want to lose it. But if Lee realises that I really like him, he will run a fucking mile. He's made it very clear he doesn't want more, and I need to stick to that. Or I could lose him for good.

"No. Just don't want the neighbours gossiping." Fuck, that's a piss poor reason, but I couldn't think of a better lie. If the look on Lee's face is anything to go by, he knows I'm lying, but I'm not sure exactly how he feels about it. Normally I can read him like a book, but there have been a couple of times when his face is a mixture of emotions, like he's trying to hide how he feels and I can't even begin to understand him.

We eat our pizza in silence, and I can't help but keep going over and over the stupid fucking comment in my head. Have I blown this? Should I let him walk away? I already know I'm developing feelings, and they're only going to get stronger the more time we spend together, so maybe it's a good idea if I let him leave now. That way I can protect my heart while I still can.

The problem is, I don't want him to leave. The idea of never seeing him again, of him not being in my life any more, that hurts worse than any potential heartbreak. I think this is the moment, the moment I decide that it doesn't matter how much I might get hurt, I have to see this through. I know Lee said there's no potential for a relationship, and if that's true, he will leave me. He may even start dating someone else, and I will have to deal with that when the time comes, but right now, I'm all in. If he's only ever meant to be my friend, then so be it. I don't think I can watch him date someone else, but I will deal with that if and when it happens.

I know all of Lee's words make it very clear how he feels, and what his intentions are, but his actions say something completely different. He holds me like he cares. He kisses me like he's attracted to me. He looks at me like he really does think I'm beautiful. For now, that's what I'm holding onto. I don't know which side of Lee will win out; his words, or his actions. But I'm willing to put my heart on the line to find out. He's worth risking my heart for. I just hope he doesn't destroy it.

Lee

A soft buzzing beside my ear is enough to wake me from one of the best night's sleep I've had in a while. As I look around, I take in the room that is quickly becoming more and more familiar to me. The cream walls are bare, except for the quote that's printed on the one in front of me. *'Happiness can be found, even in the darkest of times, if one only remembers to turn on the light.'*

Em is a massive Harry Potter fan, and the closer you look, the more obvious that becomes. She's got all the books on her bookshelf, as well as the DVDs—despite no longer even owning a DVD player. She has Funko Pop and Lego, all with different designs. And don't even get me started on her wand collection. But, strangely, the more I've got to know Emmaleigh, the more I've realised that's just who she is. When she cares about something, she's all in. I think that's why her jealousy comment bothered me so much last night.

I know she said it was a joke, but I could tell that was her backtracking over what she'd originally said. When she first said it, and it was clear she was jealous, I didn't really know what to feel. My head was telling me I should set her straight, then run a mile. I don't want a relationship, and if Em is starting to feel like she does, then I need to either set her straight or get as far away as possible. I like her, and I definitely don't want to hurt her. I just know I'm not capable of having a real girlfriend. Now I just need to get my body to understand that as well, so we can stop giving her mixed signals.

That being said, even though my head knew those were the emotions I should be feeling, they weren't my first reaction. No... initially, when I realised she was jealous, I felt so fucking good. It was like this caveman style pride washed over me, and I felt on top of the world. I've never had someone claim me in that way, or get jealous over me. It felt kinda nice, but also scary as shit.

My phone buzzes again and I reach over to spot two unread messages. I look at the time and see it's not even nine in the morning on a fucking Sunday. Who the hell is texting me at this time? The only person I text regularly is lying beside me, so I'm fairly confident it's not her.

Opening my phone, I see the first text is from my mum, and I can't help but groan as I read it. Surely she could have waited for me to get home to ruin my day.

MUM

> About your birthday party next week. I've invited your brother. I know we said we weren't going to, given all the trouble he's caused lately, but he's family, and we can't leave him out. Besides, the boys won't come if he doesn't. Are you going to be bringing your new girlfriend? I just need to know for numbers.

Fuck my life. We had a discussion just the other day about who I wanted to invite to the birthday party she is insisting she throws me. If I had my way, there would be no party at all. I don't celebrate my birthday, and if I did, a family party is so fucking far away from what I would chose to do.

Don't get me wrong, I love my family. They're just incapable of all being in one place for too long without wanting to murder each other.

The last gathering, which was Christmas a few months ago, descended into chaos and everyone fell out. My sister brought home her boyfriend, Cain, the father of her baby, Henry. This sounds innocent enough, but while she was pregnant, he cheated on her.

For a while it looked like she was going to be a single parent, but he grovelled and she forgave him. Lena and Henry are still living with us, but Cain is attempting to win his family back, and Christmas was his time to try and make amends to us. Sadly, a lot of my family don't agree with Lena's decision, and that resulted in a massive fucking argument while I was trying to eat my turkey.

My older brother, Leon, seems to think he's entitled to have a say over Lena's relationship, and he does not approve of her forgiving the cheating. This led to everyone arguing and choosing sides. Mum backed my sister and her right to choose, so of course, Dad backed her. Whereas my brother's wife, and my two teenage nephews, they backed my brother—which of course they were always going to. Then I pissed everyone off by saying I wasn't choosing sides. It was a pointless argument. Do I forgive Cain for cheating? No. Do I have a right to say who Lena lets back into her life? No.

This whole argument, which has spiralled beyond belief, is a waste of everyone's time. Cain is still going to be in our lives, as he's Henry's father. My parents recognise that, so Leon needs to fall in line. But since he won't, I've just been advising my family to stay the fuck away from each other. If they can't be in each others company without an argument ensuing, then stay the fuck apart.

I thought Mum was on the same wavelength, and just a couple of days ago, that's what we agreed to. So why does it now sound like we didn't even have that conversation?

I gloss over Mum's thinly veiled comment about Em being my girlfriend. It's another discussion we've had countless times. She obviously knows I spend my weekends here, and have for well over a month now. So in her eyes, that makes Em my girlfriend. I've made it very clear she isn't, and that we're just friends. I don't really want to explain to Mum what friends-with-benefits is, so *just friends* covers it fine. But every time I say that, she rolls her eyes like she doesn't quite believe me, then it's like the conversation never fucking happened all over again.

Groaning, I start replying to her text.

> **LEE**
>
> That's a bloody terrible idea, Mum. I thought we talked about this, but it's done now. Just for the record, when the party descends into chaos and everyone starts yelling at each other, can I just point out I said this is a terrible idea. We should cancel the party entirely. And Em is not my girlfriend, so she won't be coming. And even if she was my girlfriend, there's no way I'd subject her to our family drama.

I've barely pressed send when those three dots appear letting me know she's typing. But I know my mum, she will be ages. So, I click back to see who the other message is from. It's Craig, which is strange because he's never the first to text. It's always me texting him.

> **CRAIG**
>
> Hey, man. How's things going with the new bird? So, I've been thinking. I know it's your birthday next week, we should get the lads together and go out.

What the fuck? I can't even remember the last time we got the lads together for a night out. He's talking about three other guys we grew up with; Jake, Freddie, and Sam. We used to go out a lot, but then they all started dating—girls, not each other—and we got left behind. Not that I really give a shit. The older I got, the more I realised that I was friends with them because of Craig. I don't really have anything in common with them anymore, and so I'm not entirely sure why they all want to celebrate my birthday all of a sudden. Last year, the most I got from them was a 'Happy Birthday, Dude' message on Facebook. So it's no wonder I'm sceptical of their motives.

> **LEE**
>
> Sorry, no can do. I have some family stuff planned. Maybe another time. I'm surprised the guys can even go out.

I know I'm being petty adding that bit at the end, but it's true. Ever since they got into relationships, their lives have changed. They stopped hanging out with us, who are supposed to be their best friends. Jake has started dressing differently. Freddie only ever talks about how hot his girlfriend is—trying to let us know he's punching well above his weight. Whereas Sam, he's obsessed with telling us all about the kinky shit he and his girl like to do.

I mean, I have a kinky side that I'm very much enjoying exploring with Em, but that doesn't mean I'm going to tell my friends about it over a pint. I'm not ashamed of our sex life, but it's ours. Em puts a lot of trust in me, to let me do the things we experiment with, and I can't help but feel that trust would be severely broken if I were to talk about what we do with anyone else.

Two messages quickly appear, and I read them both.

> **MUM**
> We are a family and it's about time we started acting like one. This party will fix everything. Even if she's just your friend, you should bring her. I'd like to meet her.

Shaking my head, I type back my reply, making it very fucking clear there is no room for discussion on this.

> **LEE**
> We can try, but I have a feeling it will end badly. As for Em, she's not my girlfriend. She's just a friend. Introducing her to you guys is the type of thing you do with a girlfriend, and it would give off the wrong impression. So, no, I won't be inviting her.

I quickly check what Craig's reply is, and I'm shocked to see he's even awake at this time on a Sunday.

> **CRAIG**
> Fine. But you have to come over here and play Playstation next week sometime. Okay?

LEE

> Fine. How about Tuesday evening, after work?

There's no point in trying to argue with Craig. When he's got an idea in his head, that's it. I know he's not going to let this night out thing go, but I will fight him on it. It's not just that the idea of spending the evening with the guys makes me want to poke my eyes out, it's also because going out with them would mean giving up my time with Em.

I don't even want to think about what that means. But the truth is, I do enjoy spending time with her, and that's something that scares the shit out of me. Typically I'm a person who prefers my own company, and I hate spending lots of time with people. Yet, with Em, it comes so naturally. As soon as I know she's off at the weekend, I arrange to see her. And it's not just for one night—though that's usually how it starts. I ask if she wants to get some food together on Friday night, and she agrees. That usually evolves, and I don't leave until Monday morning when I head off to work.

I've even come to hate it when she's on shift. When our time together has to be cut short because she has to go into work. And don't even get me started about when she's on nights. I barely get to speak to her, since we're on different times. She's getting ready to go to work when I'm on my way home. Meaning we don't get to talk much for those four days, and they're quickly becoming the longest days.

I know I shouldn't feel this way. That I shouldn't crave meeting her, or miss her when we don't see each other, but I do. There's just something about her, an ease that we have when we're together. Being around her is comfortable and easy, and more than that she makes me laugh. And lets be honest, the fact the sex is fucking phenomenal helps a lot. But there's more to it than just sex.

I try to tell myself it's because we're friends. And as the label suggests, it's okay for us to be friends. It's actually good that we get along so well outside of the sex stuff, as that solidifies that friends-with-benefits is the right option for us. But the more I repeat all this to myself —in an effort to try and make myself believe it—the harder it is to ignore that tiny voice in the back of my mind. The one screaming that this is already something more, we're just using the wrong label.

To anyone looking in from the outside, they might think we are a couple. That we act like a couple. Do activities that couples do. And I'd probably agree with you—a little. But I don't give a shit what other people think. I like things the way they are, and as long as Em knows this is all we can ever be, that's okay. I've never hidden my intentions, or lied about what I want. I've always made it clear I'm not looking for a girlfriend, and that's not going to change any time soon. I'm not capable of having a relationship. Besides, my family is living proof that relationships are more trouble than they're worth.

It always seems like whenever people get into serious relationships, things change between them. They fight more, argue over the stupidest things, and they simply can't deal with the pressure. It's like the love disappears as soon as you add the label, and don't even get me started on marriage. But I've never hidden any of these feelings from Em. So, no matter how we might look to other people, it's only her opinion that matters.

I place my phone back on the side and roll over, hoping I can get a little more sleep before Em wakes up. But as soon as I'm on my side, facing her, I see her eyes are open and she's watching me. Not in a creepy way, but in a cute way. Her purple hair is fanned out over the black and white pillow case beneath her, and her face looks so different without her dark rimmed glasses on.

I've grown so used to her wearing them, it's weird to see her face without them. She only uses them for reading or watching TV, and has contact lenses for during the day, but when she's with me, she's usually more relaxed and just has her glasses on. Without them, her face looks a little pale. But her bluey-grey eyes sparkle all the same. Her eyes look a little droopy, like she's trying really hard not to fall back to sleep, and I don't blame her. We were up into the early hours of the morning, fooling around.

I don't know what it is about this girl, but she's such a fucking turn on. Maybe it's her understated beauty, or the way her body reacts so perfectly to mine. Or it could be that I love watching her shy, lack of body confidence, insecurities melt away as she finds her inner vixen. The way she's so receptive to every little thing I want to try, it's something I couldn't even dream of. And now that she's started voicing her own sexual preferences, things are getting really fucking good.

"Morning," she whispers with a shy little smile creeping up on one side.

Fuck, now my semi limp dick is no longer at half, it's growing harder by the second.

"Morning, Beautiful." I reach out without really thinking about it and pull her over, so her head is in the crook of my shoulder, her cheek on my chest, and I'm able to wrap my arm around her.

I can feel her silky smooth skin plastered against my side, causing my whole body to prickle. She throws her leg over mine, and as she does, she lightly brushes the tip of my cock by accident. The brief sensation of her skin sweeping over the swollen head has my dick twitching in anticipation. I don't think she even realises the effect she has on me.

With my hand wrapped around her, I gently start to stroke her long, silky purple hair, whilst she laces her fingers through the other hand. I like hugging Em, and so this is perfect for me. I also enjoy where I know this will lead.

"Was everything okay? You don't normally get texts this early," she mutters against my chest, the warmth of her breath tickling my hardening nipple. I've never thought my nipples could get sensitive, but apparently having this beautiful woman breathe on them is all they need.

I shake my head at how well she knows me already. She knows I barely get text messages, and never at this time. So to have two is more than a little odd. "Just Mum and Craig. They're both talking about next weekend."

She looks up at me as best she can from that position, and the way her eyes sparkle under her hooded lashes reminds me of when she's on her knees for me. Now my dick's getting even harder. It's a fucking miracle she hasn't realised yet, he's so close to poking her in the fucking leg.

"What's next weekend?" she asks, blush spreading across her cheeks like she's embarrassed about asking me in case it's too much of a personal question. She's trying to seem casual, I think.

"It's actually my birthday. Mum's doing this family party that I am dreading, and Craig wants me to hang out with the guys, which I don't want to do." God, I sound like a fucking grumpy old man who doesn't even know how to be cheery, let alone celebrate his birthday. But I've never liked birthdays. I hate being the centre of attention, and the get-togethers always seem forced. People are only attending because they feel they have to, not because they want to.

"So I can understand you not wanting to spend time with your friends, after the way they've been treating you. Ditching you in favour of their girlfriends is a shitty thing to do. But I don't understand why you don't want to hang out with your family," she says, and before I get a chance to reply, her gaze turns steely. "And don't think I'm just going to ignore the fact it's your birthday and you didn't bother to tell me."

Oops! I actually didn't forget to tell her, I chose not to. I don't want it to be a big thing.

"I know you are working next weekend. Besides, I don't really do birthdays. So it's not a big deal to me," I mumble, averting my eyes from hers, as I'm too afraid to see the hurt I know will be staring back.

"Birthdays are totally a big deal. It's the one day of the year when it's all about you. Where everyone has to celebrate you. And you get to eat cake for breakfast, but that's not really the point," she adds, and I can't help but laugh.

Emmaleigh loves cake, so I'm not surprised to hear she uses her birthday as a good excuse to eat cake for breakfast. My laughter causes both our bodies to rumble, and she smacks my chest, chastising me for laughing at her.

Quickly, I defend myself. "I'm only laughing at you making excuses to eat cake. You're an adult, you can eat cake whenever you like."

Her brow furrows and she glares at me. "I could, but then my thighs would be really fucking massive. Now stop changing the subject. Why don't you celebrate birthdays?"

I release a big sigh, not even realising I'd been holding my breath, as I explain. "I don't like all the attention on me. Plus, if you get your hopes up for things, there's more potential to be let down. And my family have been falling out with each other a lot recently, so this party will be just another excuse for them to drink too much and argue with each other. I don't particularly want to have to sit through the coming shit show in my name."

Although we've been talking for a few months now, and Em does know some things about my family, there's a lot she doesn't know.

There's a lot I've hidden from her. Probably because I don't want her to see my family in a negative way.

Don't get me wrong, I wasn't raised in a bad environment. I have two loving parents that are still together, coming up for fifty years. But, my dad likes to have a drink, and when he does that's when things start to go to shit. He says things he shouldn't. Mum gets pissed off with him, and they argue. I hate it when he drinks, and ever since I got old enough to stay home alone, I've been avoiding any function where they can drink.

When they're sober, my family is amazing. I get on with my mum like she's one of my best friends. She's funny, and we share a sense of humour that very few other people get. She's your typical mum, who loves taking care of people, and as I'm her youngest son—but middle child, since my sister is a year younger—she does mother me a lot. Not that I mind. I even get on okay with my dad, when he's not been drinking.

This is exactly why I don't plan on introducing Em to them at the party. If I were ever to introduce her to them—which I'm not even thinking about—it wouldn't be at an event where they can drink. That's just asking for trouble, and she doesn't need that.

I keep telling myself these are the reasons I'm keeping her away, and that not introducing her to my family is for her own benefit. In reality, I know my family would love her. I think she would love them too. But, then the waters will get really fucking muddy. As I lay here with her in my arms, I already know the lines that define our relationship are a little blurry, I can't make them worse.

"I don't think anyone in your family will ruin your birthday. I know you haven't talked about them all that much, but I can't think any family would do that. Besides, you have to celebrate your birthday. When you know what plans you have this week, let me know if you're free one evening and we can go out, just the two of us to celebrate. We can go to your favourite pizza place, on me?" she asks, and I have to bite my lip to hold back the groan threatening to escape.

Em is working a lot this week, and I know if she's offering to meet me, it will be on one of her few nights off. But, we made a deal early on that this thing between us would be a weekend only thing, so it didn't interrupt my work. If Em was working that weekend, we would do one other evening with no sleep over, or not at all. That's what we agreed. I can't stay up all night fucking her and then go to work the next day, and I know Em can't do that either. And we don't seem capable of spending time together without it escalating to sex. What she's offering breaks all the rules... and I really want to do it, but I can't.

"Sorry, I really can't on a night before work. You know I'm a moody bastard if I don't get enough sleep, and even if we say we're not gonna fuck, we're just going to sleep... we both know that won't happen. But I have a better idea. How about we go away for the weekend in a couple of weeks? We both have a long weekend off in three weeks, so we could do it then."

Where the fuck did that come from?! For someone trying not to blur the lines of our friends-with-benefits arrangement, I'm doing a fucking piss poor job.

Em looks up at me, her bluey-grey eyes narrowed as her brow furrows, confusion clear on her face. "A weekend away together? Where?" Her voice goes really high pitched in the end, like she can't quite believe I would suggest something like that.

It's something I've been thinking about for a while, but I've never been stupid enough to bring it up with her. I have some flexi-time I can take at work, and so I could get a long weekend free that matches the days off she has in a few weeks, giving us more than enough time to have a long weekend away together.

Whenever I think about how I want to spend my birthday, this is what I think of. "I'd like to go to London. Do all the touristy things that we've never done before, and generally have a nice holiday. Three weeks would give us plenty of time to plan something, if you want to?"

A bright smile lights up her face, and my heart starts to race. I like the fact I've made her this happy, and I deliberately choose not to think about what she could be thinking.

Nodding her head, Em looks so excited. "I would love to do that. I don't have any plans that weekend, so it's perfect. There are so many amazing things to do in London. You can pick any activity you want to do, and I will buy it. It can be my birthday treat to you."

Before I have a chance to tell her she doesn't need to do that, she leans up and captures her lips with mine. She pulls away quickly, just a short, sweet kiss, but it's enough to set my body on fire.

I try to lean back in, to capture her lips again, but she pulls away, that shy expression returning to her face. "I take it you aren't going to invite me to the party?" Her voice is barely above a whisper, but she may as well have shouted her question.

Fuck. I thought I had made it very fucking clear where we stand. Meeting families is not something that friends-with-benefits do. Then again, we do seem to be doing a lot of things that are blurring the lines of our relationship, and me asking her on holiday isn't doing us any favours, but it's too late to take it back now.

"You aren't meeting my family," I snap, my voice sounding much harsher than I intended. Em flinches, like my words actually caused her pain, and I wince, hating myself already. "Sorry, that came out harsher than I intended. It's just..."

I don't get the chance to finish my train of thought before Em cuts me off. "It's fine. I knew the answer anyway, so I shouldn't have said anything. Just forget about it."

I can hear in her voice that she's trying to sound fine, but her eyes are a dead giveaway. The fire I usually see there is gone, and they look almost dull—which definitely isn't like her. Seeing this hurts me more than anything, but this is something I can't fix.

"Em..."

She shakes her head before placing her finger against my lips to silence me. I know there's so much more I should say. I not only need to explain myself, but I think I need to reiterate what this is between us. Clearly Em doesn't want to talk any more, as she's quick to press her lips against mine. It's another short but sweet kiss, and it's enough to distract me from the unsaid tension between us. I know what I'm supposed to do, but all of a sudden I'm very aware of how naked we both are, and my skin prickles with excitement.

All thoughts about what the fuck I'm doing fly out of my mind. I stop thinking, and I go with how I'm feeling. And right now, my dick is throbbing, and my lips are tingling begging for another taste of her.

I know I'm wading into dangerous territory, and there's potential for us both to get very fucking hurt, but I can't help myself. Without thinking any more, I pull Em's body until she's straddling me, my cock resting against her slit. All she needs to do is tilt her hips in the right way and my hard length will slip inside. Instead, she grinds herself against my pelvis, moaning every time her sensitive clit rubs against my hard body.

With one hand on her hip, I reach up and circle the other around the back of her neck, clasping her hair into my fist. I use that to control her, manipulating her body into exactly the position I want her in. Her tits brush against my chest, my cock sliding against her wet slit, as I bring her mouth to mine.

Things between us might be very fucking complicated, and I have no idea where the lines even are any more. I'm not going to change my mind. I don't want a girlfriend. And I think if Em's being completely honest, she does want a boyfriend. She wants a guy that's going to introduce her to his parents and be proud he's dating her. This means we're going nowhere good. We will both end up hurt.

Despite knowing this, I'm still willing to jump in head first with what we have now. I don't know what it is, but I crave this. Not just the sex, but the connection we have too. I'm not ready to give her up yet. So, I'm going to hold on for as long as she will have me, savouring every moment because I know we're on borrowed time. I just have no idea how long it will be until we both have to walk away broken.

Emmaleigh

LEE
Show me!

I chuckle as I read Lee's text. In fact, it's the same text he's sent me over the last half an hour. I've become so engrossed texting and flirting with Lee, it's taken me so much longer to get ready than it normally would.

I'm going on my first proper night out in months. The last couple of times the girls from work have invited me over, I've not been able to go. I've either been on shift, my body has let me down in some way, or I had a broken foot. A couple of times they've invited me, and I just haven't physically been able to manage it.

It's no secret to anyone who knows me, I'm a homebody. I joke saying my spirit animal is a sloth, but it's true. My ideal evening would be curled up in my PJs, under a comfy blanket, binge watching some murder TV show. If you can throw in Lee and some good food, that's perfect.

It's not that I'm too lazy to go out. When I say it's my body, I really do mean it. The further into the day we get, the more my body starts to sag. I know everyone gets more tired the later in the day it gets, but mine is something so much more than that. Some days it will feel like I've physically ran a marathon, and in addition to being super tired, my limbs will ache and my body feels so heavy. It's like I'm trying to wade through mud, just to do even the slightest of things. And that's before you add in the dizziness, blurred vision, and tingling sensation I get in my limbs.

I know in my heart that there's something not right, but it's not like that all the time. In fact, some days—like today—I'm barely having any problems. I've been able to get ready for my night out without feeling any of the symptoms I'm used to.

This, of course, is great for me, as it means I probably stand a chance of having a good night. But, it also makes me question how real the symptoms are in the first place. It's hard to argue with a doctor when the symptoms aren't there all the time, and I can't work out what the hell does bring them on. I guess, for now, I have to trust the doctors when they say it's nothing serious.

I push all thoughts of my failing body to one side, and enjoy the fact I feel okay at the moment. I smooth down the front of my navy lace dress, and admire it in the mirror for a second. It's a short navy dress with a beautiful lace overlay. It stops mid thigh, but there's a couple of layers of tulle under the dress, making it flare out the way a ball gown would, if it were full length.

The dress is sleeveless with two thick straps over either shoulder, and the front dips down into a deep V that stops just below my boobs, giving me a very impressive cleavage—thanks to the black push-up bra I'm wearing underneath. There's a matching V in the back, but it goes a little lower, dropping to just above my lower back.

Despite showing off a little more flesh than I'm used to, the dress is incredibly gorgeous, and is the right combination of sexy and classy. I was worried at first that the navy colour would clash with my purple hair, but it doesn't. I've styled my long hair in curls, pulling the front section back into a clip that looks like my hair is half up and half down.

The silver sparkly clip I've used matches the look perfectly, and glistens in the light.

To complete the look, I add a pair of navy high heels, and the height they give me makes my legs look so long. I'm not usually a fan of dresses, particularly short ones as they show off a bit more leg than I typically feel comfortable showing. But today I just knew this was the dress. I've had it in my wardrobe for over a year, and I've never had the opportunity or the confidence to wear it.

As I apply red lipstick that makes my lips pop, I can't help but think about how much being with Lee has helped me. He makes me feel alive, which I didn't even realise was something I needed until it happened. It's like I've spent my whole life half asleep, just wandering around in a daze, until finally he brought me to life. He makes me love myself, and that's a heady feeling. Sadly it's been far too long since I experienced anything like that.

Grabbing my phone off the side, I mess about with camera angles in front of the long length mirror on my bedroom wall. I have to confess, I've never taken a picture of myself using a mirror, but if I am going to do it, you can be bloody sure I'm getting it right.

I take several photos and choose one that shows off the dress the best—which is code for... the image that makes my boobs look the best and pulls in my waist. Once I've picked the best one, I send it to Lee.

EM
What do you think?

I don't have to wait too long before his reply comes through.

LEE
Holy fucking shitballs. You look so gorgeous, Em. And that dress... it suits you perfectly. Are you sure I can't talk you into staying home, so I can come over and get a closer look at that dress? I can see what it looks like on the floor too, if you'd like?

I can't help the fucking grin that spreads across my face. I catch myself in the mirror, and I hate how fucking happy one text makes me.

That's what it's like with Lee, he doesn't even need to try and I can feel my stomach fluttering and my heart racing. It may have only been around six weeks since we met, but there's no denying how I feel about him. Well... I am fighting hard to deny it, but it won't fucking go away. No matter how hard I try, I can't stop myself from falling for Lee.

After what he said last week, it's something I've been thinking about a lot. I think what's confusing me the most is his actions. I mean, we spend every weekend I'm not at work together. We Facetime each other every night, when I'm not at work, and we text when I am. When he's at my house, it's not like he's there as a friend. We cuddle up together, wrapped in a blanket, and binge watch serial killer shows all weekend. I fall asleep wrapped in his arms with my chin on his chest. We go for days out together, and now he wants to go on holiday.

All my friends say this is essentially dating, but without the label. That we're in a relationship, and he doesn't even realise it. But I think Lee knows exactly what he's doing. He keeps telling me to ignore how he acts and focus on his words. We are not dating, and we never will be. I don't know if that means he wants to date someone else, or he will eventually. But for right now, this is not a relationship, and as much as I may want it to, it's never going to go that way. He made that very fucking clear when he said I would never meet his parents.

It wasn't the words he said, as I already knew he had no intention of letting me meet his family, it was the way he said them. It felt like a stab to my heart, and suddenly, all the confidence he'd given me started to strip away. Even though logically I know why I can never meet them, that doesn't stop the evil part of my brain from starting up. I start to think maybe I'm not good enough to meet his family, like maybe he's ashamed of me. I'm not the best looking girl... Why would he want to show off someone like me?

That's why I decided to go out tonight. Normally, if I have a weekend night off, I spend it with Lee. But a couple of my friends from work were going, and they invited me. Though they never expected me to say yes, and neither did I. Lee was equally as shocked that I was going out instead of seeing him. He's become so used to coming over on weekends when I'm not working, he just assumed this weekend would be the same.

I wanted him to come over. If I had a choice, I would choose a night in with him every time. Which is exactly why I didn't choose it. The thing with his parents just reminded me that this isn't going anywhere, and at some point, Lee will no longer be in my life. That scared the shit out of me, and I honestly have no idea what my life would look like without him in it.

Even though it's not even been two full months yet, that doesn't change anything. I can't even remember what my life was like without him, and that scares me. It means I have a fucking lot to lose. And now that I know I have feelings for him too, my heart is well and truly on the line. So this is my feeble attempt at keeping it safe.

> EM
>
> Thank you. I would love you to come over, but it's been ages since I've had a girls night. We can see each other again soon.

I know that sounds vague as hell, and I'm trying to keep it that way. I'm not trying to play games with Lee... Well, not on purpose. Do I hope he will miss me or wonder if I'm hooking up with someone else? Maybe.

I just want him to think about how he really feels about me. I want him to think about why he acts the way he does with me. More importantly, I want him to think of why he doesn't want a relationship with me. I need to know if it's me, or if it's a relationship in general. I guess I'm hoping a night away will give us both time to think.

> LEE
>
> Aren't I coming over tomorrow? I thought we were delaying fajita Friday to tomorrow?

I can't help but groan as I read his message. Thankfully a notification flags up on my phone letting me know the taxi I've been waiting for is here. I quickly send Lee a reply before putting everything in my bag and heading out.

> EM
>
> Sorry, heading out the door now, will text you later.

Well, don't I feel like shit for not answering him. I'm not the sort of girl to play games, but I think this one might be necessary if I'm ever going to get anywhere. I slide my phone into my bag as I climb into the taxi, just as I feel it vibrate again. I ignore it... though I don't know how long that will last. I need to put all thoughts of Lee to one side, and just enjoy my night.

Emmaleigh

After a few random shots that left an awful taste on my tongue, and the vodka I used to wash away the bad taste, to say I'm tipsy is an extreme undersell. I'm wasted, but thankfully so are my friends.

The night started so well. I arrived at the pub and got my usual double vodka and lemonade, and went to meet my friends who were already seated at a table in the corner. It's a typical bar, full of people on a Friday night, all in various states of undress. There's loud music playing, but it's quiet enough that if people shout they can hear each other. I know as soon as I'm outside my ears will be ringing.

As I walk my feet stick to the floor, and I try my best to ignore how icky that makes me feel. I catch a couple of guys eyeing me up—or more specifically I should say, they're eyeing up my impressive cleavage in this dress.

Normally I wouldn't notice a guy giving me attention, or if I did, I would question his motives. Is he looking at me thinking I look ridiculous in this dress? Is he trying to sleep with a fat girl just to see what it's like? Or maybe he's just going to make fun of me at any moment?

None of these things have ever happened, and I can see now, I'm fuelled by my lack of self-confidence rather than evidence of things that have happened in the past. I'm imagining things will happen, but they've never happened before, so it's got to have come from my mind. The toxic thoughts that consume me and prevent me from living life the way I'd like to.

But since meeting Lee, those thoughts don't come around as often. Don't get me wrong, they're still there, and I still have moments where I feel so overwhelmed with things, but overall, I think it's improved. The big problem is that for the first time, I recognise that guys are checking me out, and I'm confident enough to do something about it... but I can't.

I can't bring myself to even look at another guy, because my heart is somewhere else. My heart is pulling me back to the unread message that feels like it's burning a hole in my bag. I like Lee so much, and even thinking about doing something with another guy is the first step on the cheating ladder. I know it's probably not, and that I can't be cheating on him if I'm not even in a relationship with him, but that doesn't change how I feel.

My friends Gemima and Bessy are already here, and given the way their cheeks are flushed and they're both trying to talk over each other animatedly with their hands, I would guess they've had a few drinks before arriving at the pub.

"Emmie!! You're finally here," shouts Gem. I look down at my watch to see it's a little after nine, which is exactly the time we arranged to meet, so I don't know why she's making out like I'm late.

I sit down on the chair opposite Gem, next to Bessy, and I'm about to reply why Bessy cuts me off. "I love that dress, Emmie. It really suits you. I saw a couple of guys checking out your tits," my blonde friend yells far too loudly given I'm sitting next to her.

Gem leans in closer, her shoulder-length brunette locks falling forward as she looks over the table to get a better look at my dress. Her perfectly made up face curves into a slight smile. "Oh yeah, it's nice."

I pinch myself as I try not to roll my eyes. Gemima is one of those people that has to be the queen bee. She has to be the prettiest, with the best clothes, and the hottest boyfriend. Don't get me wrong, she is beautiful, in a very typical sort of way. She knows how to do her make-up perfectly, to frame her almond face. And her brunette locks are always straightened and hair sprayed to the point they barely move at all.

She's the type of friend you can have an easy, shallow conversation with, but if you're looking for anything deep and meaningful, you need to avoid Gem. She's obsessed with gossip, and she'd much rather be the one spreading all the exciting news, than the person they can trust to keep their secret.

I wonder sometimes why the hell I'm friends with her. But the reason stems back to the whole queen bee thing. If you aren't friends with Gemima, then everyone else isn't friends with you.

Normally I can't be assed dealing with her shitty bitchiness, but I really needed a night out, and sometimes she really can be nice. I mean, not often but sometimes.

Besides, Bessy—despite being your typical blonde bimbo—she's a good friend. Always has something nice to say to me, and even if at times I don't believe her, it's good of her to at least try.

Our other friend Kym is probably the one I'm closest to out of the group. She's a tiny girl at just under five feet tall, and she's a bit on the curvier side too. I think because of how short she is, it makes her look bigger. She's got a blonde bob, and wire-rimmed glasses cover her bright blue eyes. She's got one of those reassuring smiles that makes it seem like she's a second away from pulling you into a hug. That's probably why she's so good at giving bad news to a patient's family on the ward.

She's also the easiest out of the three to get along with. She actually listens to what your answer is, and asks how you are doing. Whereas with Gem and Bessy, it's mostly about them and what's going on in their lives. Though, sometimes I like that. I like not having to talk about what's going on in my life, and letting them see what I want them to.

It's hard because even though I call them friends, I'm not sure they really are. I'm not sure I would ever trust them with a secret. They are my work colleagues, and if they found out anything that could put my job at risk, I don't trust them not to use that. And sadly, they're the closest thing I have to friends, and since I needed a night out, these are all I have.

"Thanks. Where's Kym?" I ask, looking around for my small friend, who I know will make this evening just that little more tolerable.

Gem rolls her eyes in that way that makes her look truly obnoxious, a small sneer gracing her lips. But it's Bessy who replies. "She's running late. Apparently Gerry decided to surprise her with some fun sexy time while she was getting ready."

"Well, their dry spell has been going on for that long, I'm not surprised she ditched us for sex. I suspect she will only be a few minutes late. I doubt Gerry is anything fantastic in bed," Gemima snaps, with a sneer. I don't know if she's jealous that they've been in a relationship for over eight years now since high school, or that they are who we think of when we talk about couple goals.

Gem has been with Henry for about four years, and he's definitely what you would class as a catch. He buys Gem anything she wants, he lets her do whatever she wants, and he's hot on top of that. But—and I would never say this to Gem—whenever you are in their presence, it always feels a little fake, like there's something missing.

With Kym and Gerry, it's clear they're in love, and they have been for a very long time. They've only got eyes for each other, but that doesn't mean their relationship is smooth sailing. Of course they go through rocky patches, and times when they aren't having sex. Hell, they've been known to have some screaming arguments too, but they always communicate and work things out. I've never once seen their relationship as rocky.

It's not the same for Gem and Henry. They just seem far too false, too perfect. Like they're papering over some major structural issues, and if they don't accept reality and fix those, everything will come tumbling down around them. But Gem isn't the type of person who likes to admit something is wrong. She also doesn't like to work hard for anything. So at the moment, Henry is working hard to keep their romance going, but that won't last forever. My prediction is that he will leave Gem soon, and I have no idea how she will take it when he does, because she's so wrapped up in her own little world, she won't see it coming.

I can't be bothered replying to her bitchiness, so I down the rest of my vodka, loving the burn as it slides down. "I'm sure she'll be here soon." I say it aloud, to whoever is listening, and Bessy nods her head.

"Why don't I get us a round of shots while we're waiting?" She's up on her feet before she's even finished the sentence, and it's clear it's not really a question. Bessy wobbles a bit as she tries to find her centre of gravity, and as I look down and see she's wearing a pair of what looks to be around six inch stiletto heels, I'm amazed she can stand at all.

As Bessy straightens out, the black bandage style dress she's wearing almost appears to shrink, leaving very little to the imagination. The hem of the tight black dress stops just below the curve of her ass, and lets hope she doesn't need to bend over for anything because that's her whole dignity gone.

The top of the dress is just as bad, and swoops down to reveal a healthy cleavage—well, I think it's healthy. Bessy clearly doesn't, given she has surgery booked for in around six weeks to get them augmented. I have no idea how big she really wants her tits, but on such a small frame, I'm worried they'll look disproportionate. She's almost five foot eight, so is tall enough to cope with bigger boobs, but she's also very thin. I've tried to talk her out of it, but her mind's made up.

"Yes, shots. Then we need to hear all about the doctor you're fooling around with," Gem says, her eyes wide with glee.

Bessy's face drops, and it's clear Gem just divulged a secret that wasn't meant to be shared. Bessy glares at her before turning and stomping off, less than gracefully, with her ridiculously high heels.

I glare at Gem on Bessy's behalf, but I don't bother saying anything. There really is no point because I've come to realise Gem doesn't care. If she can get in on the gossip, she will, no matter who it hurts.

Kym arrives, her cheeks looking very flushed just as Bessy appears at the table with eight shots, all different colours and flavours. There's at least two on that tray that I would like to stay the hell away from, but I don't say that aloud, as I feel sure Gem will somehow make sure I end up with them.

Kym sits down opposite Bessy who is sitting beside me again, a big smile on her face. "What are you smiling about?" I ask.

"You see the guy over there at the end of the bar?" she asks, using her finger to point us all in the right direction. I can see a man who looks to be late twenties, and to say he's hot is a fucking understatement. He looks like a boy band member that's grown up, and now looks like he's all man—muscles for days, and a cute as hell face.

"He's hot," Kym replies, voicing what we're all thinking.

"Well, he actually bought these shots."

My eyes widen with shock. "Holy shit, Bes. You can't let the guy buy shots for us all. I mean, fair enough if he wants to buy your shots, but it's too much for him to buy ours," I say, astonished that she would let him.

Gem narrows her eyes on me, and does not look pleased. "Don't be stupid. If he wants to buy us all drinks, thinking that's how he gets in Bessy's pants, then we let him. I don't think he realises he only had to ask and she would have dropped her panties for him. Isn't that right, Bes?" Gemima chuckles, like she didn't just insult her best friend.

Bessy doesn't even bother acknowledging what she said, and instead lets it fly over her. "Actually, this is the funny part. He didn't buy them for me."

Gem smiles, as she flicks her brunette hair over her shoulder. "I hope you told him I have a boyfriend. I'm okay accepting his drinks, but that's all," she says, looking rather pleased with herself, and if it wasn't for the moral war going on in my head, I would have downed two of these shots by now. I need a lot more alcohol to get me through this evening.

Bessy's face lights up with amusement, as she starts to giggle, and we all look confused. "Actually, he's not interested in you, Gem. He wants to talk to you, Em."

All eyes turn to me, shock clear on all of their faces, myself included. Holy shit. I mean, I've been hit on before in clubs, but never like this, in front of all my friends. And never with a guy that hot.

"Erm…" I don't even know what to say. All I can think about is Lee. Even just accepting the shots feels wrong. I think I need to go to the guy and explain, and offer to pay for the drinks. Bessy should never have let him pay for them.

As I look over at him, he's got the most gorgeous dimpled smile on his face, and he raises his pint in the air, his way of saying cheers to me. I don't think about it, I just stand and head towards him. I can hear my friends muttering in the background. Kym and Bessy are in shock, but are encouraging me to talk to him. I can hear Gem telling me to sit down as I will only embarrass myself. Fuck, she can be mean, but I don't care right now. I know what I need to do.

The closer I get to the guy at the bar, the more muscles he seems to have. I stop just in front of him, and I'm a little nervous to even talk to this guy. He's about a foot taller than me, and he looks out of my league. Like I knew Lee was hot when I met him, but there was something about him that made him real, whereas this guy he's model good looking, and definitely not someone who would be attracted to me.

I realise after a few seconds I've been standing in front of him, not saying anything. I open my mouth but no words come out, and a blush spreads across my cheeks as humiliation overcomes me. He seems to take pity on me. "Hi, I'm Seb. It's nice to meet you."

He holds his hand out, and I stare at it for a few seconds, as my socially awkward ass makes the situation even worse, before my brain finally catches up. "Oh, yeah... I'm Emmaleigh. Erm... so, I-I came over about the drinks. We can't accept them," I say, my voice finding a little more confidence. He looks down and I realise I've been shaking his hand the whole time, and haven't let go.

Okay, I need the ground to open up and swallow me whole now. What the fuck is wrong with me? So what if the guy is hot, that doesn't give me a free pass to act like an idiot!

"I think it's too late for that," he says, gesturing to my friends with his head as I finally let go of his hand. I look over my shoulder to see my friends downing the shots without me. Bitches!

"Fuck. At least let me pay for them then," I mutter.

"No, honestly it's fine. I wanted to get your attention, and it worked. So in my eyes, it was worth every penny." His voice is silky smooth, and I know I should feel something, but I don't.

He's definitely hitting on me, and I expect my heart to race, and my palms to get sweaty as I think about it, but they don't. I mean, I'm more nervous about owing him money since my asshole friends drank the drinks he sent over.

"Yeah, about that. So, I'm kinda, sorta seeing someone," I explain. Well, I think explain is a bit too strong a word, my explanation is about as clear as fucking mud. But then again, the situation isn't exactly clear cut. All I know is that whenever I even think about that unread message I have of Lee's, I get butterflies in my stomach, and my heart races. I look forward to just texting him, let alone how he makes me feel when I see him in person. I don't feel that with Seb, no matter how hot he is.

And I know Lee doesn't want a relationship with me, but I'm not going to settle with someone else.

"What do you mean by kinda?"

"Well, we're not really anything official at the moment, but I want it to be. So, this just doesn't feel right. I'm sorry. I will pay you back, or buy you some more drinks. Whatever you'd like?"

Although his face falls a little at my rejection, he manages a small smile as he maintains eye contact with me. "That's okay. You don't owe me anything. But can I just say one thing?" he asks, and I nod for him to continue. "A beautiful girl like you, who is kind too, deserves a guy who will shout about you from the rooftops. You deserve someone who wants you to be their girlfriend and who will tell everyone he can about it. You're so sexy, and what makes you so gorgeous is the fact you have no idea how appealing you really are."

I have to look away, my cheeks flaring red as I let his words consume me. Before Lee, I wouldn't have believed a word this guy said, but he's looking at me the way Lee does, with hunger in his eyes. The only difference is, this guy wants the whole world to know. He's willing to shout about me from the rooftops, and of course I think I deserve someone who will do this. I deserve to be someone's girlfriend. But the problem is, even with this gorgeous alternative in front of me, it doesn't matter because the heart wants what the heart wants, and my heart wants Lee.

"Thank you for saying that. You deserve someone who doesn't even hesitate to say yes to a drink with you. You seem like a nice guy, and I'm sure there's a girl way nicer than me out there for you. It was lovely to meet you, and thank you for the drinks."

I start to walk away, but he calls my name, getting my attention again. I turn to look over my shoulder as he continues. "He's a lucky guy," he says, a hint of sadness clear in his tone. That's when it hits me; this guy really did want to date me. He didn't just want to have a few drinks and fool around at my place. He really was interested in a relationship with me. I know he was hinting at that, but I didn't think he was serious until I was walking away.

I just turned down a potentially great, serious relationship with a hot guy who thinks I'm beautiful... I must be fucking crazy. Well, not crazy, I'm just falling in love with someone I shouldn't be. Someone who can't offer me the things this guy could have. But, when it comes down to it, none of that matters to me. All I care about is that Lee makes my heart race and Seb doesn't.

I drop down into my seat, and without hesitation, I down the two remaining shots that are on the table. My initial shot is one of the glasses I'd identified early on as one I didn't want to try. So, I drank that first, and followed it up straight away with the second shot. As predicted, the first was disgusting, and a weird milky flavour slid down my throat, making me feel a little ill. Thankfully, the second shot was tequila, and that burnt away all taste buds in my throat, leaving a comfortable burn in my stomach.

"So, it didn't go well?" Gem asks, her voice sounding a little more pleased than it should be.

"Actually, it went well. He said all the right things. He thinks I'm beautiful and said I look gorgeous in this dress. He's happy for us to keep the drinks—which is good, given you'd started drinking them—but I did offer to pay for them. He was super nice, but I made it clear I'm not interested."

Everyone's mouths drop open, and even Gem looks shocked. "What the hell did you do that for?" Bessy snaps, her eyes flitting from me and back over to Seb, who has now gone to sit with a group of male friends in the opposite corner of the bar.

"I'm not interested in him. Besides, I like what I have with Lee," I reply.

"Are you kidding?" Gem snaps. "You know you don't actually have a relationship with this Lee guy, right? He is fucking you, taking what he wants, and has shown no interest in wanting anything more. Why the hell would you turn down a real relationship in favour of the one you're clearly having in your fucking head?"

"Woah, that's a bit harsh, Gem," Kym shouts, but Gemima just throws her hair over her shoulder, that blank mask back on her face, and it's clear she meant every word she just said.

I nip at the skin on my hands, and bite the flesh on the inside of my lip, trying to produce as much pain as possible so my eyes don't fill with the tears that are threatening to make an appearance. Yes, Gem's words were fucking hurtful and harsh, but did she say anything that's untrue? Maybe I really am an idiot, living in my own head. I just turned down a perfectly nice guy, who could have given me everything I've been looking for.

But what if he doesn't make me laugh the way Lee does? What if he doesn't make me kneel before him as he calls me his good girl? What if he doesn't pull me into his arms and stroke my hair until I fall asleep after a long, hard shift? The guy may be able to offer me a relationship, but that doesn't mean we would ever get to that stage.

Being with Lee has taught me that I deserve the best, and even though I could recognise that Seb was hot, and that he seemed nice, I also knew my body didn't react to him in any way at all. I was nervous talking to him, but that's because I've never had to let someone down before. But my heart didn't race, I didn't get sweaty palms, and I didn't get the butterflies in my tummy that I would expect if I'm attracted to someone.

Taking a deep breath, I raise my eyes so I can meet Gem's steely gaze. "I don't know how to explain it to someone who isn't part of it, but I know I have something with Lee... even if he doesn't see it yet. You can call me delusional or crazy. I don't care. Yes, Seb over there is crazy hot, but that doesn't mean I'm attracted to him, or that I should give him what he wants. Even if Lee wasn't in the picture, I would have turned Seb down because I didn't get any kind of feeling towards him." My voice gets louder as I continue to stand up for myself. I can see Kym sitting opposite, the smile on her face growing as she watches me stick up for myself with Gem.

"Well, that settles that. Shall I grab us some more drinks?" Kym asks, clearly trying to move the conversation along, and I nod my head a little as I smile at her, making my gratitude known.

"Yes, more shots," Bessy yells, a lot louder than was necessary, but I think the other shots, combined with whatever she and Gem were drinking before they got here, have started to have an effect on her.

Kym stands to head to the bar. I can already tell by the way my cheeks are flushing, and the way I just stood up for myself, the alcohol is having an effect on me, making me a little looser.

Bessy places her hand on top of mine, grabbing my attention, and as I turn to meet her gaze, she gives me a small smile. "Don't take this the wrong way, because I don't mean it how it's going to sound. But, isn't it a bit of a waste of time holding out for a guy who clearly doesn't care enough about you to want to date you. I mean, I get if he's afraid of relationships, but you deserve better than that, Em. You deserve someone who isn't afraid to call you theirs."

Despite slurring her words a little as she talks, I can hear the sincerity in Bessy's words, and honestly, it makes my heart ache. I think deep down, I've always known what she's saying is the truth, but I don't want to hear them. I came out tonight to get away from all that, not to dive headfirst into it further.

"I know you mean well, but I think we're going to have to agree to disagree on this one. I know the only person who will get hurt is me, but I'm already too far in this now. I have to see how it works out," I reply, and Bessy squeezes the hand that's still resting on top of mine. She nods her head like she agrees, but I can read that smile from a mile away. It's the sympathetic, 'I feel sorry for you, you're making a big mistake' smile. I've used it myself a few times.

I look over at Gem, wondering why she's not having her say on this. Usually she's the first to voice her opinion, but thankfully, she's got her phone out, and that seems to be holding her attention a lot more than any of us.

Kym returns with another two rounds of shots for everyone, and in this line up I see several that I'm sure will result in my stomach contents making an appearance. So I quickly reach out and grab two that look the least likely to make that happen. Everyone looks shocked that I would reach in there and grab first. Usually, my overly polite British ass lets everyone else get what they want first, and I take what's left, but not tonight.

As everyone picks up their drinks, I do the one thing I've been dying to do since I got in the taxi. I grab my phone out of my pocket and see the message from Lee. My heart races, and I can't help but smile. I haven't even read the damn message, and I'm fucking smiling like a Cheshire cat.

> **LEE**
> Have a good night, Beautiful. You really do deserve it. You work too damn hard. Don't worry about me, we can catch up whenever you're free. I will just be sitting here with your picture in one hand while my other is busy.

Fuck. Now my insides feel like they're on fire as I imagine Lee stroking his hard length just for me. Looking at the photo I sent him while he loses control. That makes me feel all kinds of amazing.

I waste no time in texting him back, the plan I had when I came out is now long gone. I'm horny and a little drunk, which means nothing good will come from this, yet I still send the message anyway.

> EM
>
> Ohhh I would love to see you stroking yourself while looking at my picture. And you definitely have to come over tomorrow now. I can take care of myself with BOB tonight, but I'm going to need the real thing tomorrow. I promise I've been a good girl.

Well, I'm actually impressed I managed to spell the whole thing correctly, I think as I put the phone down on my knee. I don't bother putting it away. I'm waiting for his reply now, and there's no way I can put it back in my handbag and pretend like I didn't just start flirting with him.

I look over at my friends, and I try to join in with the conversation. They're discussing our new manager at work, and none of them like her. She's changing things up, and has some new exciting ideas. But the problem is, with our old manager, we were allowed a certain level of freedom in our job to just get on and do our own thing. As long as things got done, she wasn't bothered how we did it.

Whereas our new boss wants things to be fairer and more transparent. So there's spreadsheets and lists. We all have new responsibilities that have been handed out fairly, and we have to make sure our jobs are done by certain times, and we tick it off our list when complete. I notice that nobody is discussing my mini promotion to senior nurse on shift—or at least they're not to my face. It's a bit of a pay increase, and a lot more responsibility. It just means, when I'm on shift, I will be in charge of the other nurses, and will be the one they turn to for support. I will also allocate our workforce and liaise with managers. It's a great step up, and one I've been looking forward to. I've known about it for a couple of weeks, but we've never really discussed it.

Gem's particularly bitter because she went for the job but didn't get it. I'm quite thankful for that, as I can only imagine what life would be like if she were my boss.

I dip in and out of the conversation, and when Kym brings over a round of drinks, I begin sipping on my double vodka and lemonade. But my mind is not really in it, I'm concentrating on my phone, waiting for that telltale buzz to let me know Lee's text me back.

When I feel my leg starting to vibrate, I can't help but smile. I reach down to read his message.

> **LEE**
> Why do I get the feeling you're a little drunk?

> **EM**
> Because I am. But you started it by telling me you're going to wank to my picture.

> **LEE**
> I don't think I quite said it like that. But it's definitely going in my spank bank. You really do look gorgeous.

> **EM**
> I feel it. I think maybe that's why I'm getting a lot of attention. You've helped give me confidence.

> **LEE**
> Are other guys hitting on you?

I ponder that question, wondering what he's thinking. That's what I hate about texts, you can't read between the lines. All you can go on is what the text actually says. I can't tell if he's angry, or if he's jealous. Or if he's just trying to be nice and make damn conversation, and that really drives me fucking crazy.

Before I have a chance to even think about how I want to reply, another message comes through.

> **LEE**
> I like that I've given you confidence, by the way.

Fuck. He's far too nice, and yet he's distant all at the same time.

Why is he asking me about other guys? Does he care? I have no fucking idea. But I think what I really need to ask myself is what do I want him to mean? I think I want him to be jealous, which is probably why I tell him the truth.

> **EM**
> So there was a guy called Seb who hit on me. He bought me and the girls two rounds of shots as a way to get my attention. I'm not kidding you, he was one of the hottest guys I've ever seen.

There's a pause for a while, and Lee doesn't reply back as quickly as he has been doing. Fuck, have I ruined things by being too honest. I mean, I could have told him the rest of the story, about how I turned him down because of how I feel about Lee. But I think part of me wanted to see how Lee would react, if he would get jealous. I know it's a stupid, childish game to play, but it's too fucking late to take it back now.

Thankfully, a few minutes later, his reply comes through.

> **LEE**
> I don't think I like the sound of some hot guy hitting on you. But I also don't think I have any right to say that.

Well... that's not quite the answer I was after. Why is he being so fucking logical? I know I have no right to want it, but I do want him to get angry. I want him to be jealous.

> **EM**
> I think I like that you don't like it.

> **LEE**
> Are you trying to make me jealous?

I pause for a second staring at the screen on my phone, my friends too lost in their own conversation to even realise I'm paying them no attention. At some point another round of drinks makes its way to our table, and as I take a mouthful of my vodka and lemonade, the alcohol burns as it goes down. My vision starts to blur a bit as I blink a few times, trying as hard as I can to focus on the tiny phone screen.

That small bit of alcohol—obviously combined with the huge amounts I downed before—seems to tip me over into the drunk category. It's like my brain is aware of what I'm saying, and it tries to grab a hold every so often to remain rational, but occasionally the drunk side wins out, and I end up replying in a way I wouldn't normally.

> **EM**
> If I am, is it working?

What the fuck am I doing? I'm not the sort of person to mess about like this, but my logical brain has been put to bed for the night, and drunk Emmaleigh is running the show tonight.

> **LEE**
> What happened with you and this hot guy? Are you still with him?

> **EM**
> Why aren't you answering the question?

> **LEE**
> Because I don't want to be jealous. I can't be. I have no right to be. Yet still the idea that you are dressed as fucking gorgeous as you are, sitting with another guy while you text me, it's driving me a little crazy.

> **EM**
> Why do you think that is?

> **LEE**
> I answered your question, now you have to answer mine. Is he still there with you?

> **EM**
> No.

> **LEE**
> Why?

> **EM**
> What do you want me to say? That I turned him down? Because that's exactly what I did, and I don't know why.

I released the breath I didn't know I was holding, and I'm glad I deleted the end of that text—my rational brain grabbing control for a few short seconds. If drunk Emmaleigh had won the text would have looked a little different.

> **EM**
> What do you want me to say? That I turned him down? Because that's exactly what I did, and I don't know why. Well... I think I do, but I'm not supposed to feel this way. I turned down a nice, hot guy who actually wanted to date me, all because I'm falling in love with you. I'm holding out hope that one day you will see sense and realise you love me too. That one day we can have a real relationship together, because it's what we both deserve.

Thank fuck I didn't send that version. This conversation is already going in a dangerous direction, without me deliberately blowing up everything we have right now.

Wait a minute... Did I just say I'm falling in love with him?

I mean, I've been thinking that I might be starting to feel that way, but I thought I was doing a pretty damn good job of telling myself that's not how I feel. I guess my body knows exactly what my heart wants, even if my head tries to pretend differently.

> **LEE**
> I'm glad you turned him down.

> **EM**
> Why?

My heart starts to race, and I sit there waiting on bated breath. Is this the moment he tells me how he really feels? Drunk me definitely feels like this is the way it's going. Sadly, realistic me isn't so sure.

> LEE
> I don't know.

Fuck. Normally I love those *I told you so* moments, but this is not one of those times.

I feel myself deflate, feeling more let down and sad than I ever have before. Maybe my friends are right, and I'm holding out for something that's never going to happen. I'm turning down real life experiences for a fantasy.

I quickly push the phone back into my bag, as I think there's no way to revive that conversation. I hate the way my eyes are glazing over with unshed tears. I can feel my heart starting to ice over and crack just a little.

Luckily my friends don't notice the change in my behaviour, and I don't even think about that. I know it probably means they aren't real friends, but I already knew that. They're work colleagues, and if I'm being honest, I already know I'm using them for this night out. I only have one true best friend, and she's been with me since we met on the first day of school when we were just four years old. But sadly she lives three hours away from me, and that's a bloody long way to go for a night out.

I told her about Lee when we went on our first date, and I told her how well it went. She knows I've continued to see him, but that's as much as I've confessed. She's the sort of person that won't dig for gossip. She knows I'll tell her what's happening in my life when the time comes. I think that's why our relationship has stood the test of time. She doesn't ask questions unless she sees a need to.

I sit quietly, sipping my drink whilst we all listen to Gem talk about the holiday she's trying to talk Henry into. He says he can't get the time off from work, as he's trying to get a promotion, but doing so means working overtime on a big project. Gem hates the fact he's working with a girl called Steph. It doesn't take a genius to work out that Gem is jealous.

"Right, now that I'm sufficiently drunk... I want to go dancing," shouts Kym, and Bessy groans beside me. I can't help but chuckle. This argument happens every time we have a night out. As soon as Kym has drunk enough, all she wants to do is dance, and she's usually drunk enough not to give a shit if she makes a fool of herself or not. Whereas Bessy is a different kind of drunk, and while she will quite happily stick her tongue down the throat of every guy she considers to be above a four, she worries she looks silly dancing.

We always end up going to the same club, Flares, and we get a table right next to the dancefloor. This means I can keep an eye on Gem and Kym as they dance, and I can join them when it's a song I like, but in the meantime, I can make sure Bessy doesn't go off with the wrong guy. Like I said, her standards drop significantly when she drinks, and so I like to make sure she doesn't do anything she regrets.

Though tonight, I'm not sure I can help anyone, maybe not even myself. When we stand up to head out of the pub, I can feel myself swaying. The ground beneath me feels like it's made of the type of padding you find in a kids soft play area, and it's almost impossible to find my footing in these damn heels.

I consider taking them off, but then I remember how much my shoes stuck to the floor when I walked into the pub, and I don't like the idea of my bare feet touching that type of flooring. No amount of showering will ever make me feel clean.

Kym loops arms with mine, and despite her being slightly drunker than me, we both lean on each other for support, and it seems to balance us out enough that we're able to safely walk down the road to Flares.

Gem pulls us along, straight to the same table we always head towards. At first I think we will have to choose somewhere else, as there are two guys already sitting in the booth. But my friends are creatures of habit, and they know no shame—particularly when they've had a few drinks.

"Hey, you don't mind if we sit here, do you?" Gem asks the two startled looking guys. She doesn't even wait for their answer before she's sliding into the booth opposite them, pulling Bessy in beside her.

The two guys, who look like they're barely old enough to be in the club, sit there, just staring between Gem and Bessy. I wouldn't be surprised if they were under eighteen and had used fake IDs to get in here.

They're both thin, and a little geeky looking. The taller of the two has red curly hair, and a narrow face, though his ruby red lips are enviable. His friend is just as small, they barely have a muscle between them, or if they do, they aren't on display. They look like the type of guys who prefer video games to sports.

The smaller of the two actually has a nice face, and when he smiles, a couple of incredibly cute dimples appear. His black hair is spiked up with far too much gel, making it look a little greasy, and I can't help but think if he left off the product and just raked his hands through it, he'd probably look a whole lot better.

Ginger is staring at Bessy—more specifically her cleavage—like he's never seen a girl as hot as her in real life. His friend at least has the nerve to look at Gem's face, although I do catch his gaze raking over all of us.

Kym slides into the remaining seat beside Bessy, and I remain standing. This is probably meant to be a four person booth, but you can squeeze in three each side if you're small enough and not afraid to get a little up close and personal with the person next to you. But the only remaining seat is next to Ginger, and even then I'd need them to shuffle over a little, otherwise just one of my ass cheeks will fit in the booth.

I try not to think about the fact I'm bigger than my friends, but I can't stop the all consuming dark thoughts when they rear their ugly heads. All I can think about is what Ginger must be thinking about now. He's obviously going to be worried about me crushing him, and the fact he's going to have to shuffle so far over to make enough room for my fat ass that he'll practically by sitting on his friend's knee. He's no doubt wishing he had one of my hot friends next to him, so he can admire them while they're next to him.

Just as I feel my thoughts beginning to overwhelm me, Ginger talks to me, pulling me back from the edge of the abyss. "You can sit down here, if you'd like. There's plenty of room. You don't have to stand."

He shuffles over slightly, as does his friend, before he pats the empty seat beside him. I look him over to see any signs he doesn't mean it. Maybe he's doing it to seem like a nice guy in front of my friends? Or maybe he doesn't realise how big my ass really is? Either way, I can't stand here all fucking night, my feet are already killing me, so I lower myself right onto the edge of the seat. I'm shocked to find that even with the entirety of my ass on the seat, and without having to practically sit on Ginger's lap, there's enough room for me.

For the first time in a while, I start to think maybe Lee is right. Maybe I do view myself very differently than how I actually look. He continually says that I think I'm bigger than I really am, and that the person I see when I look in the mirror really doesn't exist. I see myself as this big, plus sized girl, but Lee says, in reality, I'm not as large as I think. Yes, I'm curvy, and I have places with a bit more fat than I should have, but I'm proportionate.

I have to admit, every time he's brought this up in the past, I've ignored him. It's hard to believe that what I see in the mirror isn't reality, but occasionally, I have moments like this, where there's an incident that I just can't explain.

Like right now, my brain told me there was no way in hell my fat ass would fit in the seat next to Ginger, even if he moved right the way over onto his friend's knee. But in reality, he barely shuffled over, and when I sat down, not only did my ass fit comfortably, it wasn't even hanging over the side of the booth like I expected it to be. I think this is something I'm going to have to explore further. There must be a reason why I view my body in a way that's not consistent with reality. Who knows, now I know what's going on, this might be the first step in me finding out how to fix it.

Although Lee has given me a confidence I can't ever thank him for, I know there's a lot more ground to cover. It's more than just feeling confident in how I look, it's about being able to look in the mirror and see myself clearly, and be happy with what I see.

Let's just hope I can still remember this breakthrough in the morning when all the alcohol wears off. As I'm working on my breakthrough, Ginger leans forward, and directs his attention towards Bessy. "Do you come here often?" he asks, his voice coming out far squeakier than I think he intended. I can't help but groan.

"I'm going to go and get a drink, does anyone want anything?" I ask, as I stand up.

Kym shakes her head and mutters something about not being able to take a drink onto the dancefloor. Gem asks for a shot, as does Bessy. The guy sitting next to Ginger turns to me with a big smile on his face.

"Can I get a pint please?" he asks, sounding hopeful and I can't help but chuckle.

"Erm no. I don't buy drinks for people I don't know. Besides with the way you've been staring at our tits, you're lucky we're not making you two buy the round."

They both have the audacity to at least look sheepish, Ginger's face turning an almost tomato shade of red as Bessy laughs at the way they avert their eyes quickly. I turn on my heel, and my head starts to swim, dizziness overcoming me. I grab hold of the edge of the table as I wobble, trying to catch my footing. I knew I'd had a bit to drink, but not enough to be falling down drunk.

I blink a few times, desperately trying to get the spots in my vision to disappear, and Gemima grabs hold of my arm, a rare look of concern etched across her face. Sometimes I forget that she's actually a bloody good nurse, and to be one, you have to care about people. She may come off as heartless, but there must be a kind person deep inside, otherwise you couldn't do the type of job that we do.

"Hey... are you okay?" Gem asks, as my vision starts to improve and the dizziness begins to subside.

I blink a few times to clear my head, taking in a deep breath. "Yeah, I'm fine. I must have stood up a bit too quickly. Combine the postural shift with the alcohol and I'm just feeling a bit faint. It's passing now," I reply, trying to think of myself as a patient. We both know the type of reply I'd give one of my patients would be to stop drinking, drink more water, and go home safely. The problem is, nurses really do make the worst patients, as they think they already know it all.

I get served at the bar, and while the girl behind the counter is getting my drinks ready, I can't resist looking at my phone. I know I put it away in the last pub and didn't reply, but I felt it vibrate. I know he's replied.

> **LEE**
> Sorry. I know that's not the right answer. I do want you to have a nice night. I will talk to you tomorrow. Night, Beautiful xx

Fuck him. Too right it's not the correct fucking answer. He knows how he feels, he's just being a coward. I know alcohol is playing a major part in adding to my anger, but I can't help it. It feels as though my blood is boiling, and I'm so fucking angry at him. Why can't he just admit how he really feels?

The girl hands me my drinks and I take them back to the table. The four of us do our shots before Kym stands up and heads onto the dancefloor. She grabs hold of Gem's arm and drags her along too. She reaches out for mine, but I shake my head. I'm not in the mood to dance at the moment. My skin feels itchy, like I'm only a few seconds away from losing my shit.

Bessy is leaning over and talking to Ginger's friend, who I think she just called Kyle. He's still staring more at her tits than he is her face, but Bessy has drank so much she's now firmly in the making bad decisions phase of the evening. This is normally where I'd step in, but at this moment in time, I can't think about anything but Lee.

Looking at the time on my watch I see it's almost one thirty in the morning. I know he will be in bed already, as he usually gets up early on a Saturday to do the local five kilometre Park Run. I let Bessy know I'll be back in a minute, not that she pays much attention, and I head towards the bathrooms.

To get them you have to walk out of the main room of the club, down a hallway, and then there's a landing with three doors. There's one for men, one for women, and one for disabled. I don't actually need the toilet, I came out here because the music can't be heard. I move over to the corner of the hallway, away from all the drunken people who are trying to get to the bathroom.

As I open my phone, I try to think through what I'm considering. Is this the right thing to be doing? I've got alcohol coursing through my veins, alongside a healthy dose of anger, and all of that is a recipe for disaster. Yet, I can't seem to stop myself. It's like when you drive past a car crash. You know you should look away but you just can't. It's like that. I know I shouldn't make this phone call, but I do it anyway.

Most of the time Lee never gets woken up by his phone going off, he sleeps so deeply, so I'm not even remotely surprised when I get his voicemail. Without thinking it through, I let the alcohol do the talking.

"Lee, sorry to leave this voicemail, and yes, I am a little drunk. But maybe I needed a bit of Dutch courage to actually say this. I like you, and I think you know that. I've liked you since the moment I met you. I agreed to being friends-with-benefits because at that point I genuinely felt like having something with you was better than nothing.

"I love our time together. You make me laugh, and we have so much fun together. I actually look forward to seeing you, which is unusual for me, and I think it is for you too. But as much as I love hanging out with you, I do think the lines have become a little blurred.

"Your words may say we're just friends and will never be more, but your actions say something completely different. You get jealous, and you don't want me hanging out with other men. You spend every free weekend you have at my house, and we hang out like we're a couple. It feels like we're in a relationship, just without the label.

"For a while I told myself it didn't matter. That I'm happy the way things are. That I don't need a label. But I was wrong. It's so fucking confusing, Lee. I think you really like me too, but I need to hear that. I need to know how you feel. It's fucking with my head, and I can't take it anymore. I know I risk losing you with this message, and that's the last thing I want. But I had to tell you how I feel. I guess you could say, the ball is in your court now."

Emmaleigh

That first movement when you first wake up with a hangover has to be one of the hardest. All I need to do is roll over from one side onto the other, so I'm facing my bed side table and I can get the water and headache pills I left there the night before. But the actual movement feels so much harder than it should be. My body feels like it has lead weights attached to it, and just the slightest movement causes the drums in my head to start pounding. Not to mention all the liquid in my stomach that starts swishing around, threatening to make a reappearance.

By some miracle, I managed to roll over and successfully take the pills. I just hope I can keep them down long enough to take effect. Even though the curtains in my bedroom are dark and block out most of the light, the rare strands that are shining through are making my eyes burn. I squeeze them closed, trying to block out the dizzy sensation.

I lay there for a few minutes, my eyes clamped shut as I try to remember as much of the night as possible.

There was dancing, a lot of dancing. I remember Kyle and Ginger, who I think had a night they will never forget as they both went home with Bessy. I remember telling her that she was making more bad decisions, particularly since she's fucking one of the doctors who works on our ward. Apparently he's just a fuck buddy she calls when she wants to try the really kinky shit. My ears are practically bleeding as I think about all the things she told us he's into. I have to see this guy at work again tomorrow. How the hell am I going to be able to look at him again knowing he comes hardest with a finger up his ass?

I don't know how taking home two barely legal teenage boys will help her situation, but apparently she was in a teaching mood last night. I wasn't in the mood to stop her.

I remember Gem bailing early when she called Henry to come pick her up. I remember him being a bit pissed as he'd had to come away from doing his work project with a work colleague. He told her he'd pay for an Uber for her, since she refuses to get in a regular old black cab, but she refused that too, insisting only him picking her up would be acceptable.

Even now, when she's nowhere to be seen or heard, just the mere thought of Gemima was giving me a massive fucking headache. But, after a few drinks, just for a few moments I did get to see the real side of Gem, the insecure side. It was just the two of us, waiting to get in the toilet, but we were queuing in the hallway, making the most out of the peace. The music inside was your typical loud, pounding dance music, and whilst I was in there, the music was intoxicating. I could feel it rippling just beneath the surface, making my heart accelerate as the need to dance along with the beat started to get overwhelming. But I knew I needed the toilet before I started dancing, and as soon as I mentioned it, Gem was the first to jump to tag along. Bessy stayed with the teenagers, and Kym stayed on the dancefloor. We left Ginger with strict instructions to not let Kym out of his sight, or we would cut his bollocks off. If the look of sheer terror on his face was anything to go by, he would definitely do a great job.

Once we were in the hallway and away from the music, it's like she shrunk into this smaller version of herself, all the bravado and bullshit stripped away.

"I think Henry is cheating on me." Her words were barely above a whisper, but the glazing of her eyes spoke volumes. She just voiced the thing we had all been thinking, but none of us ever had any proof. So, why say something if we aren't sure?

"What makes you think that?" I reply, hoping she has more than the hunch we all have. If she's thinking of blowing up her long-term relationship, it needs to be on more than a fucking whim.

"He's been spending a lot of time with this work colleague, Steph. And the other day, I found her earring beside my bed. She obviously left it there for me to find. I mean, she'd spent almost an hour at dinner the week before showing them off to me. There was no doubt they were hers, but why the hell was it in my bedroom? I mean, if she came over to do work, I'd expect to find it in the living room, or bathroom, but she would have no reason to be on my side of the bed, unless she was climbing out of it. And that thought alone makes me want to vomit," she cries, a few stray tears rolling down her perfectly made-up face.

"Shit, Gem. That's tough. I think there's only one thing you really can do and that's to ask him. Have an adult conversation with him about it. I'd like to think after all the years you've been together, Henry won't lie to you if you ask him directly."

She looks up at me with a small smile as she wipes away the rogue tears like they were never there. "You really like this Lee guy don't you?" she asks, and all I can do is nod. "I know there's a risk you might get hurt, but if there's a chance you could find happiness, then I say go for it."

My eyes widen and my brow rises. "That's literally the opposite of what you said earlier. You said he was using me and I needed to face reality and date someone who actually wants to date me."

She lets out a huff and gazes up at me with her big brown eyes. "What the hell do I know? My long-term relationship could be a fucking sham. Lee isn't hurting you. I mean, yes, you do deserve someone who will call you their girlfriend, but you never know, he may get there. I guess you just have to see."

Holy fuck! As I think back over my conversation with Gem, it dawns on me the other stupid shit I did last night. More specifically, the voicemail I left Lee.

Moving far quicker than my sensitive stomach can handle, I roll over and grab hold of my phone, ripping it away from the charger. I scroll straight to Lee's name on Whatsapp, which is where we do most of our talking, and there's nothing since the last messages we exchanged. I look at the top of the screen, and see he was last online around thirty minutes ago. Which means he will have listened to my message, and he's been online long enough ago that he could have done his reply by now, but he hasn't. Well... I've royally fucked this up.

I quickly scroll through my messages app, and the call log on my phone, just to make sure he's not tried to contact me some other way. He hasn't. I wish there were some way for me to take back the damn message, or at least hear it again, so I at least know what I said. I can only remember little bits of it, and the small bits I remember are fucking bad enough.

Okay, so I need to do some damage control. I quickly scroll back through to Whatsapp and type out a message. Naturally, I erase and rewrite it at least twenty times before finally settling on a version I'm semi-happy with. I don't think I will ever be completely happy, but that's the situation—my big fucking mouth ruining everything.

> EM
> Morning. My hangover is on an epic scale, but I'm hoping the pills will kick in soon. Would you still like to come over tonight for Fajita Friday on a Saturday?

I decided to keep it super simple, and make no reference to the message of doom. Which is basically code for the fact I'm holding out hope—and yes, we're talking about one in a trillion odds—that maybe Lee hasn't listened to his voicemail. Some would call me fucking delusional, and they would be right, but it's all I have right now.

> LEE
> Glad you had a nice night. Can't today, sorry.

Oh shit. I've really fucked things up. Just yesterday he was pestering me, telling me he wanted to come over, but now all of a sudden he's busy? Yeah, he definitely heard my message.

> **EM**
> No problem. I'm not back at work until Monday, so if you want to go for Sunday lunch somewhere tomorrow, we can?

> **LEE**
> I don't think that's such a good idea.

Tears begin to pool in my eyes, and my stomach flips as nausea overtakes me. Only this sickness feeling has nothing to do with the hangover, and everything to do with feeling like I've just ruined the best thing I have going on in my life at the moment. I have no idea how to do damage control on this—or if I even should—but I know I need to try.

> **EM**
> If this is about the drunken message I sent last night, please ignore everything I said. I was drunk, and I barely remember ringing you. I do know that by that point in the evening I was being fuelled by vodka, and didn't mean most of what I said. Don't let one drunken message ruin the good thing we've got going on here.

I know it sounds desperate, but honestly, I don't really have a lot of choice. I wish I could stay true to what I said, and be confident in myself, knowing that if he doesn't want me, someone else will. But that's the thing, I don't want anyone else. I know I don't really have Lee, and holding out for something that chances are it won't ever happen is a little crazy. But losing a guy I have here and now, that I really fucking like, or something that might happen feels stupid.

All these different thoughts are flashing through my mind, and my fragile brain can't take it. Even though I'm still lying down, I start to feel dizzy again, those telltale black static spots swimming in front of my vision. I clamp my eyes closed and focus on taking a couple of deep breaths. The more I focus the more the nausea subsides too.

As soon as my phone buzzes, my eyes fly open and I fumble around trying to get the message open. It feels as though someone is stabbing my temple with a red hot poker, and the speed at which my lids flew open has made my eyes burn, but I don't care. I have to read what he says.

I notice Lee's name on the screen, but it's hard to read anything as the message is blurry. I reach over to grab my glasses, though I can usually see my phone just fine, as my issue is with distance. So it's not that much of a surprise that when I do put my glasses on, it doesn't solve my vision issue.

I blink a couple of times, trying to soothe my tired, burning eyes, but nothing seems to be helping. When I hold the phone a little further away, and close my right eye, so I'm just looking out of my left, I can see the phone a little clearer. I swap eyes just to check, and sure enough, it's definitely my right eye that's causing the blurred vision. This isn't usually a symptom I get with a hangover, but that doesn't mean it isn't one. I did drink a fucking lot last night, so it doesn't surprise me. Headaches can manifest in lots of different ways, this one is just a really fucking irritating variation.

Closing my right eyes, and holding the phone a little closer, I quickly fumble to pull up Lee's message, whilst I silently pray to any fucking deity that is listening. *Please give me a little more time with him.*

> **LEE**
>
> I know you were drunk but there's always some truth to a drunken message. I like you too, Em, and that's why I don't want to hurt you. I know you feel my actions can be a little misleading, but my words have always remained the same. I don't want a relationship. Not just with you, but with anyone. I'm not going to change my mind on that. I'm worried that if we keep seeing each other, it will blur the lines for you even more. I don't want that.

I wipe away the stray tear that's managed to break free from the corner of my eye, and try to ignore the sinking feeling in the pit of my stomach. My stomach rolls, and this time I know there's no stopping it. I roll out of the bed, and push through the pain and dizziness as I run to the en-suite.

I make it to the toilet just in time to unload my stomach contents into the toilet. I sink onto the cold bathroom floor, the hardness of the lined floor against my bare legs makes me shiver. As I lean back against the concrete wall, the coolness hits my back sending goosebumps across my body, while I keep my arms firmly locked around the toilet bowl. I'm so sick I don't even have a chance to think of how disgusting it is here on the bathroom floor.

The pain in my head increases, and it feels like that hot poker continues to stab away above the right side of my head, at the back of my eye. With all that pain, it's not surprising that my vision is blurry. I can feel tears trailing down my face, and I try to tell myself it's from vomiting. But we both know it's not. Lee's message hurts worse than any hangover headache ever could.

I know this is the perfect time to walk away. Lee and I are looking for different things, that much is clear. Yes, I hurt now, but he's right, the longer we drag this out for, the higher my hopes will get and the further they will have to fall.

But there's that nagging feeling in the back of my mind that I just can't ignore. The one telling me that I can't let him go. I'm not bothered what might happen, I just can't ignore the part of my brain that's screaming at me not to lose Lee. I don't know how I know this, or why. But Lee is important, and I have to fight for him.

When I finally feel safe that I can stand up without emptying what little is left in my stomach, I move back over to the bed. The room spins, and I curse myself for drinking so much last night. I've never been this hungover where I'm so dizzy I can barely walk, and my vision is so blurry, it's hard to see. I need to sort this thing with Lee and then I need to go straight back to bed.

EM

> I'm a big girl, and I know what I can handle and what I can't. You've made your feelings perfectly clear, and I'm okay with that. If you still want to, I want to keep the whole friends-with-benefits thing going. I know the risks, and I'm willing to take them.

I see those dreaded two ticks light up as he comes online and reads my message. Time seems to tick by at an impossibly slow speed after that as I wait for his response. My stomach starts to do somersaults again, and although it feels like I might be sick again, I don't think I have anything left in my body.

Reaching over I take a sip from the bottle of water on my bedside table, and I'm actually surprised by how nice the cool liquid feels in my mouth. I hadn't realised how icky my mouth had felt until that moment.

> **LEE**
>
> I think maybe we both need to spend some time apart and think about it. I'm not saying no, as I do like spending time with you, and of course the sex is amazing. But I don't want to lead you on.

Too fucking right the sex is amazing, and the mere act he's admitting he likes me is a step in the right direction. I don't know if I'm proving his point by saying this, because of course there will always be a part of me that hopes he changes his mind. I'm still a logical person, and if he's saying that's how it is, then I will believe him. He doesn't have to know I'm holding out for more. Besides, it's my heart that's on the line, so it's my risk to take.

> **EM**
>
> You can't be leading me on if I know where we stand. The sex is amazing, and I can't thank you enough for the confidence you've given me. But I know how to switch off my emotions and just enjoy the sex. We can spend some time apart, but I know I will still want to do the whole friends-with-benefits thing with you. Even if we were to cut out the sex—which I really fucking hope we don't do—you are still probably one of my best friends, and I don't want to lose that.

> **LEE**
>
> You're my best friend too. Let's take some time, but keep texting?

> **EM**
> If that's what you want to do. You know where I stand.

> **LEE**
> Okay, I will think about it.

> **EM**
> Thank you. I'm going to go back to sleep now because I feel like I'm dying.

> **LEE**
> Sleep well, Emmaleigh. Talk soon.

No! My stomach definitely did not do a flip from that. I hate how much I crave hearing from him. I'm falling in love with Lee, and that means I'm really fucked. I can keep telling him my heart isn't on the line, but we both know it is. Now it's just a matter of how much damage it will sustain. I hope I walk away from this with a few little pieces still intact. Either way, I know for sure that a piece of my heart will always belong to Lee, I just hope he looks after it.

Lee

It's been two weeks—two long fucking weeks—since that fucking awful weekend with Emmaleigh. Which means it's been almost three weeks since I last saw her, and fuck me do I miss her. I feel like a junkie going cold turkey, craving that next fix. My skin itches, and it's like I can't settle. I'm constantly looking at my phone wondering if she's texted me or not.

I'm not someone who uses social media, but for the last two weeks I've been stalking Em's accounts so much I'm about a day away from a restraining order.

Since I asked her for some space, she's been great and has done just that. She's never the first to text me, and only responds to what I message her about. But it all just feels wrong. I miss her. I miss the way we used to talk, and the banter we had together. I know I asked for this, but I don't want it to be like this any more. I just don't know what the hell to do. Because as much as I miss her, I can't give Em what she wants.

"Earth to Lee, are you even listening to a word I said?" Craig snaps, as he wafts his hand in front of my face. I have no idea how long he's been doing that, but it's further proof I've been zoning out on him.

I invited Craig over here to distract me, and he's doing a fucking great job. I'm sitting in my gaming chair, while Craig is sprawled out on my bed like it's his own. He's playing on some racing game he brought over, that he knows I have zero interest in. I'm pretending to watch, waiting for it to be my turn next, but in reality I'm staring at the blank screen on my phone. I know she's not going to text me, but I want her to.

I turn my attention to Craig, but he's already back to staring at the screen. "Sorry, mate. Just a bit distracted."

"Is it the naughty nurse?" he chuckles, as he aims a less than discreet wink my way. I fucking hate it when he calls her that.

"Don't call her that, and yes, it is," I growl, my eyes zeroing in on him, but he doesn't seem to care.

"I don't understand you. You say you don't want to date her, and you ask her for space. She tells you she's happy to continue just fucking, but agrees to give you time. And you're sitting here pining for her like a love sick puppy. You clearly miss her, so all you need to do is decide whether you want to go back to just fucking her, or whether you're finally ready to commit. Either way, she's happy to go with the flow. She's the perfect fucking girl for you, but you're ruining it," he snaps, rolling his eyes at me as he throws down the gaming controller, pissed his car just got totalled as he ran it into a wall.

"It's not as fucking simple as you're making it out to be. And I'm not pining like a fucking love sick puppy," I shout, my hands scrunching together into fists as anger begins to pump through my veins.

Craig, the typical asshole that he is, just chuckles. "It really is simple. You miss her, but you don't have to. She's said she's basically willing to do whatever you want, and you still haven't said yes."

"I don't want her to get hurt," I shout, and my best friend throws his legs over the side of the bed, sitting up so he's facing me. Suddenly, he looks serious, which isn't something I'm used to seeing on the face of my easy-going, carefree friend.

"So, date her then." His words sound almost like a dare, and I know he's trying to wind me up. He's been pestering me for a while, trying to get me to tell him why I don't want a relationship, yet I've worked so hard to find a girl. I know it's confusing, but I have my reasons, they're just not ones I plan on sharing any time soon.

"Don't start," I warn, but he just shrugs his shoulders, baiting me further.

"Don't start what? It's clear you like her, so why won't you date her? You are both fucking unhappy right now, and it's all your fault."

His words hit me right in the chest like he's just stabbed me. I know I like Em, of course I do. But I've made it very clear, to everyone that will listen, when I say I don't want a relationship. I know I'm the reason we're both hurting right now, but that's part of the reason I don't want to drag this out further. We will only both get more hurt. I can't ever see my rationale changing.

"Fuck you!" I shout, pushing up from my gaming chair, as I start to pace around my bedroom, suddenly feeling very much like a caged animal. The antsy feeling I already had over missing Emmaleigh, combined with my anger is making me a little volatile right now, and Craig knows exactly what buttons to press to wind me up even further.

"Why don't you just tell me why you won't date anyone? I might be able to help," he says, sounding like the rational one of the two of us, which is not how it usually is between us.

"I have my reasons. I just don't think relationships work. As soon as people get serious, two things happen. They either fall apart, the pressure of being committed becoming too much, or they stay together even when they should be apart. As a couple, they are miserable, yet they think they should stay in the relationship for whatever reason. I don't think I know anyone in a serious relationship that is truly happy. I don't want that in my life. I'd rather just have casual flings that are fun while they last," I explain, as I continue to pace.

The silence in the room is enough to pull my attention back to Craig. It's not normal for him to keep his big mouth closed. When I look over at him, his eyes are wide and he looks almost sad. "Mate, not all relationships are like that. My parents have been together for almost thirty years, and yes they argue sometimes, but if you ask them they'd say they're happy."

"Of course they would. They're not going to tell you they hate being married to each other, and that they resent every fucking minute they have to be in each others company," I snap, my eyes filling with tears as I think back to my childhood, when I first heard those words.

I must have only been around eight years old, and my parents had been in another one of their fights. My dad had been drinking, and Mum was pissed at him about it. They had another of their screaming matches, and me and my sister came downstairs to see what was going on.

We managed to get them to stop shouting, and Lena helped Dad up the stairs, getting him settled in the spare bedroom that used to belong to our eldest brother, Leon, before he moved out. He's fifteen years older than us, so doesn't really feel like a brother. He's married with kids, and we rarely see him. Since he left, his room has pretty much become Dad's. He goes there to sleep off the booze when Mum won't let him in their bed.

Whilst Lena got Dad settled, I helped a very tearful Mum up to her room. I will always remember her reply when I asked if she was alright.

"I will never be alright. I'm in a marriage I can never get out of. We stopped loving each other a long time ago, but it doesn't matter. When we agreed to get married, our own wants and desires stopped mattering. We have to be a couple for our family, and to support each other, even if we can't stand one another. So, always remember this when you're older, Lee. Don't ever get into a serious relationship with anyone, because if you do, even when it all goes pear-shaped—and it will—you're stuck together."

Those words have been in the back of my head my whole life. I'm not even sure Mum remembers saying them, or if she meant them. Although she was mad as hell at Dad for drinking, she'd had a few glasses of wine that night too, and I think she was more than a little drunk. But eight year old me remembered every fucking word, and they've stayed with me as I've got older.

Whenever I've considered looking for a girlfriend, they're the words that always hold me back. Relationships make people unhappy, whereas casual encounters are fun and can never lead to me getting hurt. Or, at least, that was always the case until I met Emmaleigh. No matter what intentions I had with her, the more time I've spent with her, the more I like her.

The more those words get silenced, and all thoughts turn to what it would be like to be in a relationship with her. My brain feels like it's in a tug of war match. One side is the beliefs I've held on to my whole life, and all the evidence I have thanks to Mum and Dad's marriage. But on the other side is Emmaleigh, and the way she makes me feel. The way she doesn't even need to try and my heart races just thinking of her.

It's impossible to fight off years worth of conditioning, but there's one thing I do know for certain, I want her in my life. I know there's a risk of me hurting her further, and I need to do everything in my power to make sure that doesn't happen, but I can't stay away from her.

Craig pulls me out of my own head when he places his hand on my arm, trying to reassure me. "Not everyone's relationships go to shit, mate. You like Em, and I think you owe it to the both of you to at least try. Just don't hurt her any further. She seems nice, and I'd like to meet her someday."

I look up at my friend who has been by my side since we were kids. I suspect he knows a lot of where my opinion has come from, and about the type of relationship my parents have, but he doesn't say anything—which is good because I wouldn't have liked to hear it.

I return his smile, and make my decision. "She is nice. She deserves better than me. But she also has the right to make her own decisions, and if she says she can handle going back to our friends-with-benefits situation, then I have to honour her wishes. We're both adults, who have been open and honest with each other. I can't ever give her what she wants, but if she can handle what we have now, then I'm down for that. I do miss her."

Craig shakes his head, but there's a smile on his face. "I think you're fucking crazy not grabbing a girl like her while you can. You know that she can go off with another guy any time she chooses, and you have to accept that, right?"

I release a big sigh, and I hate the way my heart aches at that thought. "I know. We will just have to deal with that when the time comes."

Before Craig has the chance to reply, my phone pings from the computer table I put it on when I started pacing. I practically run over to it and fumble to get it open as quickly as I can. I have my phone set to alert any time Em does anything online, and for the first time in two weeks, she's posted on Facebook.

I ignore the look on Craig's face, looking at me like I'm an actual fucking stalker, and I open the app as quickly as I can. I get to her post, and I mentally fucking chastise myself for forgetting what day today is. I think I know a way to make things right with Emmaleigh, and hopefully get things back on track between us.

Looking up at Craig with a smile on my face, I fill him in on my plan. "You know you said, you'd like to meet Emmaleigh? What about right now?"

Emmaleigh

"We care, so why don't you! We care, so why don't you," I shout whilst holding on to the wooden banner we spent ages making.

It's the day of the strike. We're only two hours in and it's already going tits up. We have been planning for this day for months, ensuring we find that perfect balance between honouring the nurses' right to strike, and maintaining patient safety.

It's not been easy. We've had to cancel all non-emergency procedures and admissions. We've had to ask family members to come in and help with the basic care of their loved ones, and we have had to strike in stages. I've tried to make sure everyone who wants to strike can, they just have to go and work on the ward for two hours, at some stage during the day, so the ward is staffed at all times. I think it's important we're all allowed to have our voices heard, but we still have a duty of care to our patients, and we would never put their health and safety in jeopardy. As the senior nurse on shift that day, I will also have an emergency pager.

So, if things get too much on the ward, I can step in to help. No matter what, our patients will always be cared for.

It's not ideal to have several different nurses working short two hour shifts, and we have to make sure the handover process is seamless to ensure no jobs get missed, but it's something we as a team have been streamlining anyway. I think our ward runs quite well, and I don't think it will be too much of a problem. Or at least I didn't until one member of staff called in sick, then the whole rota fell out of sequence. But once I got it sorted again, we were able to successfully start to picket.

For the last couple of days, me and a couple of the other girls have spent our free time making lots of placards and signs for people to hold up. We're trying to make it clear that since we give up time looking after our own family so we can care for yours, surely we deserve to be paid fairly for that. I have been doing this job for three years with no formal pay rise—other than the very small one I recently got with my promotion—so with the cost of living increasing, it actually works out that I've had almost a three grand pay cut. Not only that, I probably work more hours now than ever. More unpaid overtime, more shifts with no breaks, more shifts where I never even get to go to the toilet because we're so busy. It's reaching the stage where it's putting our physical health, not to mention our mental health, at risk, and that's not fair on us.

Sadly, that little rant doesn't fit on a placard. So instead I went for catchy slogans like 'We deserve fair pay', 'We care for you, now it's time you care for us'—which is a personal favourite of mine, and is the one I'm currently holding.

As I walk up and down the muddy patch of grass at the entrance to the hospital, I'm glad I had the good sense to wrap up warm. Even though it's June, there's a bitterly cold wind in the air, and if it weren't for the gloves I managed to find in my coat pocket, I think the hand holding my sign would be frozen.

There are almost a hundred nurses who are all standing beside the entrance to the hospital, shouting and chanting about fair pay and equal rights. But what impressed me more than the number of nurses who showed up, is the amount of people who have come just to support us. Patients have stopped by to stand with us for a little while, showing their support. Family members have come and held our hands while they fight for their loved ones. And other clinical members of staff, like ambulance drivers, who have come in their free time to show their support.

We even had a local cafe who came out in their food truck and brought us all free breakfast sandwiches as their way of showing us support.

I'm overwhelmed by the level of love and support we're seeing, and I'm so proud I was part of organising something like this. But I can't help feeling that distant ache in my heart when I look around at the other nurses who have family or friends standing beside them.

Don't get me wrong, most of my family would be here if they could be. My elderly grandparents couldn't get here, and my mum is disabled, so she would have the same issue. My dad is working, and has important meetings he can't miss. They have all texted me, wishing me luck and saying they support me, but it's not the same as having someone here by your side, holding your hand.

After we've been on strike for around four hours, standing in the cold is starting to take its toll. I don't know why my body is feeling so exhausted. I'm used to being on my feet for twelve hour shifts, and so standing on the picket line for the last four hours is nothing. Yet my body feels like I've been running a marathon. My lower back is aching, my legs are starting to feel like jelly, and I'm so dizzy—I guess walking around in circles as I chant is definitely not helping. But it's that fucking awful headache I can't seem to get rid of too.

Ever since that night out a couple of weeks ago, I've had this headache, almost a pressure like sensation, and it causes the eye sight in my right eye to become blurry. Sometimes it goes away fairly quickly, but other times, it worsens to the point I can barely see out of that eye. When the vision is at its worst, that's when all the other symptoms start to kick in. The worst of which is the dizziness and the numbness in my right hip and foot. It makes walking and staying upright incredibly difficult.

Part of me really panics when I feel myself getting like this, wondering what the hell is wrong with me. But the logical side agrees with my doctor. Migraines can cause knock on symptoms, and all my symptoms can be explained by migraines. It just doesn't feel like that's the right answer though. I've been a nurse for nearly six years, and during that time I've learnt to trust my gut instinct, as sometimes that's the best indicator that something is wrong. And my gut is telling me this isn't just a migraine.

Given there's nothing I can do about how I feel now, I try to think of ways I can help myself to remain on the picket line as long as possible. I look down at the cold, muddy grass, and for a fraction of a second, I do consider sitting down. But in addition to getting a cold, muddy ass, I'm also worried I wouldn't be able to get the hell back up, which is why I quickly vetoed that plan.

As I look around, I see there's a lot of people, particularly some of our elderly family members, who are all starting to look a little exhausted, and it's not even lunch time yet. I need a plan, and I need one quickly.

Without thinking about it, I open my Facebook and Instagram accounts. I barely use them, and the feeds are full of random pictures of people I haven't spoken to in ages. I scroll to the top so I can make a post, trying to think back to the last time I did it. Luckily I find a setting that replicates whatever I put on Facebook onto my Instagram, so I don't have to worry about using that system. I can barely remember how to use Facebook.

I find the picture we took just a couple of hours ago. It's the group of nurses from my ward—including Gem, Kym, and Bessy—and we're all standing together holding our signs. I start writing the post.

This is the amazing nursing team from Sunflower Ward. It breaks our heart that we aren't caring for our patients today, but we are doing this to help us give better care to our future patients. All we are asking for is what we're fairly owed... a pay rise.

We miss out on special days with our family to take care of yours. We work long days, with countless hours of unpaid overtime. We work all day without breaks, under very stressful situations. And we do it all with a smile on our face, even if we're crying inside.

Today we are taking a stand. Going on strike wasn't the easy option. And we want you to know that our ward will remain staffed today to ensure the current patients receive the best quality of care—because that's what this is all about. We want to be able to give you the best care. To do that we need help. We need more nurses, and we need fairer pay!

If you want to help, you can come and support us today. We will be outside the entrance to the hospital until nine this evening. If anyone has any chairs laying around that they can spare for a couple of hours, please help us by bringing them over. There are a lot of people here, and we don't want anyone to have to sit on the ground.

Thank you to everyone who has already supported us, and to everyone who will support us throughout the day—we appreciate you all. Stand with nurses!

I send the post, and then honestly, I don't even think much more about it. I can hear my phone sending me notifications that people have either liked or commented on the post, but I will have to check them later. Even though I'm on the picket line, I'm still here to support my staff, and my work phone is constantly ringing as the nurses try to navigate working under such extreme pressures.

Thankfully, everyone is doing a great job, and all the patients that are still on the ward are receiving such good care, I'd be surprised if they even realise we're on strike.

I also meet up with other senior members of staff every hour to discuss how things are operating in the hospital overall. Although we asked patients not to attend the emergency department unless it's an absolute emergency, they still are. So we've had to send a couple of nurses to help for one or two hours, just to try and clear the backlog of patients. There are some agency nurses, who have no loyalty to the hospital or what we get paid—since they get almost double what we get per hour by working for a private company—and they come in to work for a few hours. It may be costing the hospital a fortune, but I think it's a small price to pay for people to realise how much nurses really do, and how integral they are to the running of the hospital.

It's around eleven in the morning when I hear a loud horn blaring as a big van turns the corner into the hospital. I don't know why this captures my attention so much, given people have been honking their horns to show support for us all morning. But this one is louder than all the others, and as the van pulls up beside us, that's when I see the sign on the side of the van. It looks like an old white bed sheet, and painted on it in black are the words, 'We care about nurses, do you?', then below in smaller red paint it reads, 'Honk if you love and support nurses.'

The noise from every passing car is deafening as people show us their support, and I realise there must be an identical sign on the other side that people entering the hospital by car can see. Everyone that passes shows us their support, and it's just what we need to rally the troops who were all starting to deflate a little through cold and exhaustion.

I don't recognise the man who climbs out of the driver's side, but I could hug him for this. I'm about to walk towards him, when I see a man coming around the front of the lorry, wearing a homemade T-shirt. It's white, except for my face that's printed in the middle of the shirt. There's text around it that reads, 'This is Emmaleigh. She's kind, caring, and an amazing nurse. She cares for others without a thought to her own wellbeing. Today I stand for her. I stand for all nurses. Nurses deserve fair pay and we will not back down!'

My eyes begin to mist over as I take in the picture of myself, exhausted after a long day, but still smiling in my nursing uniform. I look tired, but incredibly proud of my job. I look up and see Lee's beautiful, smiling face and I don't even hesitate, I rush towards him and throw my arms around his neck, pulling him into the biggest hug.

To say the last couple of weeks have been awkward as hell is a fucking understatement. I've been trying to give him the space he asked for. I only ever reply to his texts, and never deviate from the conversation he starts. The short version of that is I've hated every second of the last few weeks.

I've missed Lee. I've missed talking to him like we used to. I've missed us having banter together. Of course I've missed the sex. But mostly I've just missed him; the way he hugs me, the security I feel when I'm around him, and the comfort.

He pulls me in for a tight hug, and I can't resist taking in his scent. Lavender, cinnamon, and something that is so completely Lee, I can't even describe it. But as his scent envelops me, it's like I can finally relax. I hadn't realised it, but it's like my body had been on edge this whole time. Like a piece of me was missing, and it's not until I'm in his arms that I feel complete.

I'm so totally fucked. A girl who is just in this for sex doesn't say shit like he makes me feel complete. They're the words of a girl who is falling hard. I just need to hide that from Lee.

If this past two weeks have taught me anything, it's that I fucking miss him like crazy, and if I have to hide how I really feel so I get just a little of him, then that's exactly what I'm going to do. I have no idea if I can protect my heart like this, but I'm going to have to give it a go.

Reluctantly, I pull away from him, and he reaches up to wipe away one of the stray tears that are threatening to escape. I give him the biggest happy smile I can manage, and I try to ignore the way my heart races when he smiles back at me. "What are you doing here?" I ask, though it seems a bit of a stupid question.

We've talked about the strike before, but he never said he wanted to come and support me. But he must have been planning this for a while, as it's not the sort of thing that's put together on a whim.

As he pulls back, my mouth dips into a frown, but he laces his fingers through mine, like it's the most natural thing in the world. I can feel the eyes of my friends boring into my back, but I don't even think about it, I don't think about what this could mean. I just focus on the here and now.

"I've been planning this for a while. There's someone I want you to meet." Lee pulls me towards the back of the large lorry, and that's when I see the doors are open, and a couple of young lads are unloading chairs. Lots of wooden chairs that they are passing around for everyone to sit on.

Lee walks towards one of the guys, who is just a little shorter than Lee, making him probably around five foot six. His longish brown hair has waves that make him look like he's got a messy mop on his head, but at the same time, it really suits him. As soon as we approach, he stops what he's doing and looks down to where our hands are connected, before he turns his gaze onto me. He looks me up and down, assessing me, before giving me a big, cheesy smile that lights up his forest green eyes.

"You must be Emmaleigh?" he asks, holding out his hand for me to shake.

I nod and take hold of his hand, shaking it with a smile. "I am, and you are?"

He turns his steely gaze to Lee, his brow furrowing into a frown.

"I'm offended that she doesn't know who I am. How have you never told her about your life long best friend?" His voice raises in mock disgust, and it's clear he's messing with Lee. As soon as he says that, I know exactly who he is.

"You're Craig," I reply, hoping that will save Lee.

Craig turns his attention back to me, and I go to drop my arm when I realise we're still doing that awkward handshake thing. Lee just chuckles as he watches our uncomfortable interaction.

"I am," Craig confirms, nodding his head.

Thankfully, Lee decides to step in and save our conversation. "Craig's family own an event planning agency. One part of that is that they hire out chairs ready for weddings. Craig's family heard about your strike, and they wanted to do something to support you, and this was the best we could think of."

I shake my head in disbelief at the charity and support of strangers. I'm just about to thank him when Craig speaks. "It's the least we could do. We also got in touch with one of the companies we work with, and a catering company will be arriving in about an hour, and they will be supplying free lunch for anyone on the picket line. We don't want anyone starving while they're fighting for what's right."

My eyes start to well up, and I'm literally overcome with the kindness of others. Reluctantly, I let go of Lee's hand and I pull Craig in for a hug. He lets out a startled yelp that sounds very feminine, and I can't help but chuckle. "Sorry, I'm a hugger," I explain and Craig starts to chuckle.

"It's nice to meet you, Em. You're as awesome as I expected you to be." Even though his words are aimed at me, he's giving Lee a pointed stare, like they're having a silent conversation they don't want me to be part of. And it's actually kind of cute. I quite like having this insight into Lee's life that I've never had before.

I let them have their moment, and Lee seems to end the silent conversation with a shake of his head, to which Craig simply rolls his eyes and turns back towards the van when Lee casts his gaze back over to me. "Better let them get set up. Want to make sure the chairs and tables are all set up for when the food comes."

I shake my head in disbelief once more, before clasping my fingers back through Lee's. We've held hands before, but this is in front of our friends and my work colleagues. He moves his gaze down to where our hands meet, and I expect him to pull away, but he doesn't. Instead he looks up at me with a sad look on his face. "Em, I'm sorry about the way things have been this last couple of weeks."

"Hey, you don't need to apologise. I was the one who ruined things. You asked for a break, and I gave you one. You are entitled to that," I explain, cutting him off before we have to dive further into this. I know we probably have a fucking bucket load of issues we need to address, but all of that can wait. I'm having a cloud nine moment right now, and I don't for even one second want that to be ruined.

"I do, and I know now isn't the time for us to talk. When you are free this week, I'd like to maybe take you out for dinner and have that chat, if you'd like? But for now, I want you to know that I have missed you and I'm sorry I wasn't here for this sooner. I had it all planned, but I just assumed you would have told me when it was happening, not on the day. But I know that's my fault because I asked for space."

My cheeks scrunch as I try not to grimace. He's right, I have been deliberately not telling him about my shit, but mostly because I want him to have his space. I want him to have me in his life but not really. I wanted to make him miss what we had before. To make him realise he misses me.

Before I get the chance to say any more, my work phone starts to ring, and one of my colleagues, Kayla, announces she thinks one of the patients on the ward is about to code. I spring into action. I know most people wouldn't act until it's actually happening, but I trust the instincts of the nurses I work with. We have watched patients deteriorate rapidly, and we know exactly when a patient is going to code—have their heart stop beating.

I call for Kym to come with me, as she's the nurse next due to do a shift on the ward, and we both set off running as fast as we can. My legs ache and my lungs burn, and I'm reminded very quickly that I'm not fit. In fact, I'm in fucking agony, and we aren't even close to the ward yet. I could have sworn I wasn't this unfit usually. But the more I push myself, the more the pressure in my head seems to intensify. I try my best to ignore the headache and just concentrate.

I realise after a few minutes, Kym was speaking to me, but I couldn't hear any actual words over the ringing in my ears. But as we get into the lift, and I can stand still for a second to catch my breath, I apologise and ask her to repeat herself. She's basically asking for a plan, which I can answer easily. I need her to keep the ward running, whilst I help Kayla, the nurse currently working on the ward, and if the patient does code, I will run the resuscitation until the team gets here. Kym agrees with my plan, and I'm grateful I don't have someone with me that bitches and moans when they get given a task.

With Kym, she follows instructions really well. But more than that, if she ever were to voice a different opinion, I would listen to her. She qualified a couple of years after me, but she's worked on Sunflower ward since she graduated, so she knows the place just as well as I do.

As soon as we get onto the ward, Kayla shouts out for our help, and the patient begins to deteriorate rapidly. I ask for a quick handover, which Kayla gives, as the Health Care Assistant on shift, Lesley, begins chest compressions. I shout for Kym to call the resuscitation team, and when she lets me know she already has, relief washes over me.

As I listen to the handover, trying to formulate a plan of action in my mind, I think about how I'm going to keep this patient alive until the senior team gets here and takes over. I have to push aside the way my body is hurting right now. I mean, I know I have a bit of fat on my bones, but I've never seen myself as super unfit. Yet, that short run has knackered my body completely.

My legs ache, there's pins and needles in my feet, as well as in my left hand. I keep having to blink repeatedly to chase off the deteriorating vision, thanks to the spots that keep appearing. Obviously the pressure at the back of my eye is making my vision blur, and as soon as I rest and get rid of the migraine, it will all right itself. But this doesn't feel like a normal response to running just that short way. I've had to run the full length of the hospital before, when I've been in a meeting at one side, and then I'm needed back on the ward. I don't remember ever having these types of symptoms when I ran back then.

I have to force myself not to focus on the way I feel, and instead just concentrate on keeping the patient alive. Once Kayla has finished her handover, I start firing out instructions to the team. Another nurse who was working the other side of the ward has come to help along with her assistant, giving us just enough people to get all the jobs done. I'm very aware that it leaves only Kym out there on her own, with no proper handover of tasks that need doing, but I know she will be able to handle it. The resus team will be here any minute, so we just need to hold on.

Around an hour later I manage to get back to the picket line, breathing a sigh of relief that we managed to get the patient back, and they've been moved to the intensive care unit, where they will get one-to-one, higher level care. Just as I arrive back, I see the catering van has pulled up, and people are queuing to get their food. The tables and chairs are all set up, banners hanging from all the tables, and everyone who enters the hospital sees the sign on Craig's van, they all beep their horn in support.

We've been blown away by the amount of people who have come to sit with us. Patients who have been discharged, some that are just visiting, and others that have come just to support us after seeing about the strike on social media. We've even had a few patients who we discharged a while ago come back to show us their support.

One lady I looked after for almost four weeks after she had surgery, and we only discharged her home last week. When I first saw her I was worried she was ill again. Her prognosis isn't good—grade four bowel cancer that has already spread to her brain, liver, and lungs. She doesn't have long left at all, but since she's not even fifty yet, and has three children, she's been fighting.

I grew close with her, visiting her every day I was at work, even if I wasn't the nurse caring for her. I could see what cancer was doing to her body, and I knew that no matter how hard she fights, she can't beat this. All she's doing is giving herself more pain and suffering, but I know she's not ready to give up yet. She just wants a little more time. So while she's fighting, we will too. I knew she'd be back on the ward, needing more care, I just hoped it wouldn't be this soon.

Though as I make my way over to her, she's quick to tell me she's not here for medical reasons. She dragged herself out, even on a day when her pain levels are through the roof, and she came to support the nurses who have been fighting for her.

My heart swells as I look around at all the people who have come to support us. Not just family members, friends, or other work colleagues. There are patients and members of the general public who all support us.

When we first decided to strike, there was a lot of bad press, and even today, I feel sure some news outlets will be reporting the negative side of this story. The one where patients have suffered, had operations and appointments cancelled, all so we can strike. But they never show the other side, looking at why we are striking, and what we are doing to make up for today. Most of us are putting on extra clinics this weekend, so we can catch up on the patients who missed out today, making sure they don't have another long wait to be seen.

What the news always fails to mention is that we are doing this for our patients. Patient care is our number one priority, and the emergency services and maternity have full staffing levels to cope with emergency situations. Other services have been rearranged for the weekend, when most nurses are working overtime. But we are doing it because we want to be able to give patients better care. As I look around, I'm just glad that the people who really matter—our patients—know the truth and are behind us.

I find Lee and flop down into the chair beside him, resting my head on his shoulder without thinking about it. I'm exhausted, and we still have all afternoon to go. Lee wraps his arm around me, and I allow myself to sink into him. I can feel some of my friends and work colleagues looking, no doubt wondering what the hell is going on between us, but I don't care. I'm just glad he's here.

"I know you're busy, Em, and we do need to talk properly about this, but I need to get this out now. I like you, but I'm never going to change my mind about being in a relationship. I know you say that doesn't bother you, but we both know you want a boyfriend and I can't give you that," he explains, and I go to reply, but he cuts me off before I even have a chance to start. "I trust you when you say you know what you can handle and what's best for you. So, if you really think you can be friends-with-benefits, and not want more, then I'm happy with that. But I don't want you to get hurt."

I give him a small smile and squeeze his hand, pulling strength from his warmth. "That's the thing. I might get hurt, and yes, that will suck. But right now, without you, I am hurting. I miss you and that hurts. So for me, I can either be friends with you and risk getting hurt in the future. Or I can leave right now, and I know I will be in pain. And as much as I like a bit of pain when we have sex, I'm not generally a masochist, so I choose possible future pain over the guaranteed pain I have now."

As soon as I mention sex, Lee starts to chuckle, and I watch as he tries to make his face turn serious. "I get the feeling this is going to end really badly for us both, but I'm the same as you, I can't seem to walk away."

He reaches over with his free hand and cups the side of my face, rubbing his thumb across my cheek. I can't help but lean in to his touch, the coolness of his palm causes my skin to prickle as a shiver ripples down my back. I lean closer to him, hoping he's going to close the gap between us and press his lips to mine. I know I can't make the first move here, it has to all be on Lee.

Leaning forward, he places his lips right beside my ear, and the feel of his warm breath against the sensitive spot on my neck causes me to shudder. "I want nothing more than to press my lips against yours. You have no idea how much I've fucking missed your taste these last two weeks. But, I can feel our friends staring at us, trying to read into our behaviour in a way I didn't want. I need to have you again soon though," he growls, and it's like he's got a one-way ticket straight to my core, which begins heating up with his words. I can feel myself getting wetter as I think about it.

"Well... I'm not working tomorrow, but I know you are. I think the first day we both have off together will be Saturday," I reply, and Lee very deliberately begins to shake his head. A mischievous smile slides across his face.

"I think I feel a bit of a cold coming on. I better take tomorrow off, just to be on the safe side," he states, adding a fake as fuck little cough on the end just to really sell the story, and now it's my turn to chuckle.

"Back to mine after this?" I ask, and Lee nods his head so much I worry he might actually hurt his neck.

"Absolutely. I can't wait to get you on your knees. You've been a very good girl these last couple of weeks, and now it's my turn to show you how grateful I am for that."

His words are dark and dirty, and they call to me. Hearing him say I'm his good girl, it pushes away all the other thoughts I have going through my brain. I push aside the pain, the weird feelings in my body, even the fact I'm at work and should be thinking about all the ways today could go wrong, so I know how to fight against it. Instead I focus on Lee, and what we have to look forward to.

I lean in, my lips against his ear this time, and I place a slow but chaste—almost innocent looking—kiss on his cheek, right next to his ear. I feel him shiver beneath my touch and I can't help but smile as I think about the effect I have on him. "I wish I could kiss you right now. Instead, I will make a list in my head of everything I've wanted you to do to me over the last couple of weeks, so I know what we should try together."

His head tilts rapidly and his gaze fixes with mine. His normally bright blue eyes are swimming with lust, and I have to shuffle discreetly in my chair to relieve the ache I feel between my legs. "And what things have you been wanting to try?"

I give him a shy smile, but it's impossible to keep the mischievous glint from my eyes. "Well we were talking about exploring anal and I think I may be ready for that now. Plus, I really want to try outdoor sex sometime," I whisper, making sure nobody around us can hear a word I'm whispering in Lee's ear. This is my work, after all. Can't have them learning all about my kinky side.

The anal thing isn't too much of a big deal. I mean, I've never tried anything like it before, but I know a lot of women get lots of pleasure from it, and it's just something I have to try. I trust Lee to do it properly, slowly, and not hurt me.

The outdoor sex, on the other hand, is not something I ever considered. I guess my lack of self-confidence played a part in that, and my fear of being caught. But I know it's something Lee thinks he'd enjoy, and it's something he's never really explored with other partners, so it's a first that we'd both be able to explore together. And if the look of pure sex on Lee's face by now is anything to go by, I'd say he's interested.

I notice him trying to discreetly shuffle his trousers, no doubt to try and get his erection to sit a bit more comfortable, and I can't help but smile. Obviously the fact he's getting hard in the middle of a nursing strike—and my workplace—isn't ideal, but I do love that I have this effect on him.

"Oh, Emmaleigh. You have got yourself a deal, and I can't fucking wait. But you should know, getting me hard right now, when you can't do anything to help me is called being a tease. Only bad girls are teases, and so I think I'm going to have to punish you for this. You are going to spend all night making sure my cock gets taken care of every time it gets hard. Do you understand?" His voice has taken on that authoritative tone, deep and gravelly, and fuck me does it make me melt.

I struggle to find the right words, and try to just nod my head in confirmation, but as he holds me frozen to the spot with his glare, I know he wants my words. I lean forward and whisper the words just beside his lips. A few millimetres to the right and our lips would be touching. "I promise to be a good girl just for you. If I have to be punished, I understand and I will take it like the good girl I am."

A groan escapes from Lee's lips and he pulls away from me, shaking his head like he's trying to knock some sense into himself. I know why he's doing it. When we're together like this, and we're so caught up in our own lust, it's like everything around us just disappears. We get into our own bubble, and we never want to leave. But here and now is not the right time to be getting each other turned on, so I'm not surprised when he pulls away, but his whole body, his eyes, and his words make it very fucking clear I'm in for one hell of a night tonight.

Emmaleigh

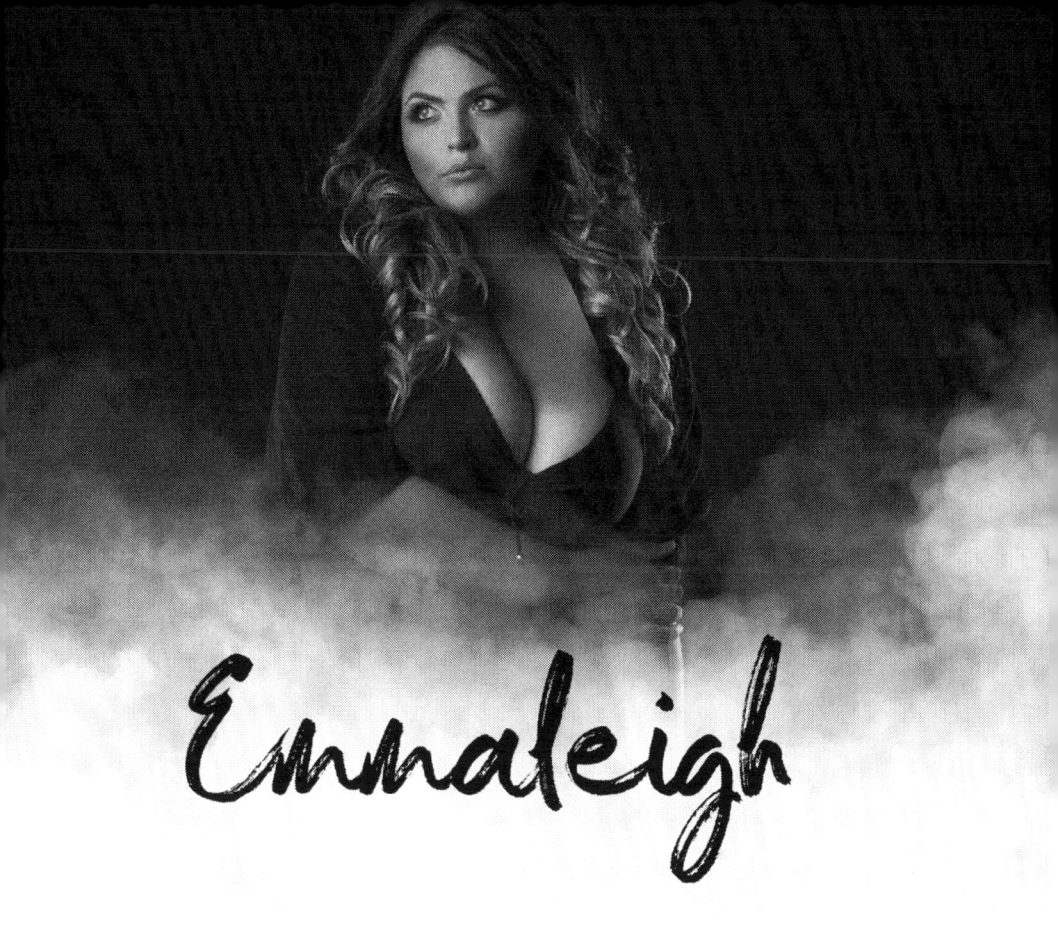

We barely make it through the door before Lee's lips collide with mine. We have two weeks worth of sexual chemistry that has built up, and fuck did I miss him. If the way his hands are wandering over my body are any indication, he missed me too.

We're almost frantic, kissing and devouring each other as we move through the flat, discarding items of clothing straight onto the floor as we make our way to the bedroom.

When we make it into the bedroom, I'm standing in just my black lace boy-shorts style panties and matching bra, while Lee is in his tight black boxers, his cock bursting to break free. Thankfully, the black colour of my panties means the wet patch that I know is there, won't be visible. Not that I care, he must be able to tell how turned on I am—or he will when he removes my panties.

Reluctantly, Lee drags his lips away from mine, and takes a step back from me. I try to follow but he shakes his head, making it very clear I have to stay here. He doesn't move too far away, just enough for him to rake his gaze across my body. It's almost like I can feel his touch as my skin burns in every place his eyes cover.

He starts at my toes, and by the time his eyes meet mine, his pupils are so blown they look almost black. Holding my gaze, the corner of his mouth lifts up into that devilishly sexy smile of his—the one that tells me I'm going to enjoy what comes next.

He rakes his hand down his stomach, tracing his fingers over his hard abs, and I have to bite my lip to hold back the groan. You have no idea how much I want that hand to be mine. I want to touch him, to kiss him, to feel him all over me. But I know by now I have to do as I'm told, and right now he wants me to hold still, so I do... reluctantly.

As his hand reaches the waistband of his boxers, and slowly slips inside, I feel myself starting to squirm. As his fist circles his hard cock, he lets out a deep moan that sets my pussy on fire. I watch transfixed trying to work out what he's doing, and it looks like he's squeezing his hard length, no doubt trying to stop himself from losing control too quickly.

Just then, a thought occurs to me, and even though I try to push it out of my mind, Lee must see the moment on my face. "What just happened? You thought about something and it changed your entire demeanour," Lee asks, pulling his hand free of his cock as he steps towards me. He's so in tune with me and my body, he can read even the slightest of mood changes.

I'm almost too ashamed to voice this thought aloud, but if I want to be able to touch Lee's cock tonight, I'm going to have to talk about it. He won't rest until I do. My voice is barely above a whisper, but I know he can hear.

"I don't know where the thought came from. I was thinking about you squeezing your dick, and that you were probably doing it so you didn't come too soon, as two weeks is a long time to go without sex. Then, of course, my fucked up brain couldn't help wonder if you did go without sex the last two weeks. I don't know if you saying you needed a break meant you needed to fuck other women."

As soon as the words leave my lips, I regret them and I know how wrong they really are. Lee's face falls, like I've just stabbed him, and he looks genuinely hurt. I know Lee would have told me if he were with anyone else—at least, I hope he would, but in that moment, my insecurities got the better of me. I try to apologise, but Lee cuts me off.

"Don't apologise. I didn't really use my words well enough to describe why I needed space the last couple of weeks, and honestly, if I had used my words, it wouldn't have stretched on for this long. There's a lot we need to discuss, but just know, when I say I don't want a girlfriend, it's not just with you. It's with anyone. Hell, if I were ever to try getting into a relationship, it would be with you, I think. But it's not what I want, and one day I will explain it all to you, but for now, please trust that I only ever see one girl at a time. For me, getting space didn't mean fucking someone else. I already know the answer, but did anything happen with you and another guy?"

I shake my head profusely, making it very clear I don't want anyone else. "I told you what happened with the guy on the night out. He asked for my number when I saw him later on that same evening. I said no, and that was it."

The bright smile that spreads across Lee's face is more than enough to get me hot again, but then his words hit me harder. "So, you've been my good girl this whole time?"

Nodding, I confirm. "Yes, I have. Other than what you have said I need to be punished for, obviously."

"Well, the punishment will have to wait. It's been two weeks since I felt your tight, wet pussy. Do you mind if we do this hard and fast, and I will make it up to you the rest of the night?" he growls, as he begins moving the hand circling his cock again.

I try my best to look at his face, but with each stroke, his cock captures my attention even further. I can't even form words, I just nod, and Lee takes a purposeful step towards me. He tries to keep the stern look on his face, but I see how the corners of his lips turn up at the side in that mischievous grin I love.

He stops so close I can feel his breath on my cheek and the warmth from his body. I want to minimise the already small gap between us, but I know better than to do anything without his permission. He leans in until his breath is tickling my ear. "That's another punishment for not answering me. You know you're supposed to use your words. Now, do as you are told and remove your bra."

The deep, gravelly tone to his voice calls to me, and I can feel my core heating, my pussy getting wetter. Not wanting to have any more punishments adding on, I reply to his earlier question, as I slowly and purposefully remove my bra. "I like the idea of fast and rough, Sir. And I apologise, I will take any punishment you need to give me like a good girl."

I smile at him sweetly, as I drop my black bra to the floor, gently tugging on my nipples in a way we both love, making sure to get them hard and erect. He can tell by the way my mouth falls open in a silent O, I love the way it feels when my nipples are played with. I love a bit of pain with my pleasure, and having someone tug or nip at my sensitive nipples, is exactly the right way to go about it.

He doesn't bother to give me any further instructions, instead he closes the gap between us and places his hand over my pantie-covered pussy. I bite my lip to hold back the groan. Even though he's not doing anything other than holding his hand over my mound, it's the fucking anticipation that has me on edge.

"If I put my finger in here, am I going to find you wet, Beautiful?" he asks, before pressing little kisses along my jaw, his hand rubbing just enough to cause some friction, but not enough for it to give me the pleasure I crave.

"Yes, Sir. I'm wet… just for you," I reply, my voice deep and thick with lust. I want to tell him my pussy is craving him, that it's been lost the last couple of weeks without him. But that sounds crazy, so I keep that to myself.

Keeping his hand outside my panties, he presses his finger into my slit, forcing the fabric inside my lips, and it's not long before the lace is soaking wet.

"Fuck, you're so wet," he growls, and before he's even had chance to finish his sentence, he roughly pulls the sides of my panties until the fabric rips in half, and he throws the ruined garment onto the floor.

"What the—" I start to ask him what the fuck he's doing, but before I get the chance he cuts me off by roughly grabbing my hips and turning me so that I'm facing the bed. He then pushes the top of my back down and kicks my legs wider apart at the same time.

I'm leaning over the bed, my tits crushed against the duvet, my face turned to the side so my cheek is pushed into the fabric. I have no choice but to arch my back, which sticks my newly exposed ass out even further. I can feel the air against my exposed core and a shiver ripples through my body as anticipation builds. I need him to touch me.

Both his legs are pressing against mine, keeping them spread wide, and I feel as he lightly trails his fingers up my spine, creating tingles wherever he touches, until finally he grabs my hair into a fist.

With one hand on my hip, and the other controlling my upper body using my hair, Lee has me exactly where he wants me—and I love it. I love feeling completely under his control, and I can feel myself getting more turned on the longer he draws this out.

Slap!

Catching me completely off-guard, I'm shocked when I feel his hand make contact with my ass cheek. He spanked me enough that I know a red mark will be left over, and it takes a while for the delicious stinging to go down. Normally, he soothes my skin by rubbing his hand over it, but not this time. Instead, he spanks the opposite cheek with the same force, catching me unaware again, causing a startled yelp to escape.

Even though my ass is stinging like crazy, and my heart is racing as he builds anticipation over what's going to happen next, I do my best not to forget my training. "Thank you for spanking me, Sir," I say, making sure to keep my ass up high, presented for him in case he wants to spank me more. I am due a punishment, but he said that would come later. Maybe he's changed his mind?

"You are my good girl," he purrs, as he lightly drags his fingernails down my spine, ripples of pleasure spreading along behind his digits.

My face lights up with his praise, and I give him the best smile I can manage from this position, but I know he's seen it. And he keeps those piercing blue eyes locked on mine, as his fingers begin to explore my slit.

His fingers slide through my folds, getting wetter, before reaching my engorged clit. Slowly he circles around it, driving me crazy, before they travel back up. When he reaches my hole, he slowly presses his fingers inside. Not too far, but it's enough for me to feel the beautiful stretching. It's over far too quickly as he pulls them away, and they're no doubt now dripping with my desire.

I expect him to travel back down to my clit, to drive me even more crazy, but he doesn't. His fingers keep travelling upwards until he reaches my puckered asshole. My cheeks are wide open in this position, and so it's easy for him to swirl his finger around my rim.

Initially, I'm a bit embarrassed, as I've never been touched there before. He knows I want to try it, though. So, when I feel him spreading my juices all around my ass, I should be excited for what's to come... but I'm terrified. What if his cock's too big for me? What if it hurts?

My heart races and my breathing starts to come out in pants as I begin to hyperventilate. Those damn spots appear in front of my vision again, and I try to blink them away, but they just cause the blurred vision to worsen. If I keep going at this pace, it's a certainty that I will pass out.

That's when I hear Lee's voice. I know he's right beside my ear, but he feels so far away, like he's a distant whisper. "Hey... Em. Listen to my voice. Come on, Beautiful. You can do this. That's it, deep breaths," he instructs as I do my best to listen to him and do as I'm told. "Good girl."

His praise is exactly what I need to hear, and I start to breathe normally, which helps calm me down. I'm still bent over the bed, but Lee is kneeling down beside my head, stroking my cheek as he makes sure I'm okay.

He asks me how I'm doing, and so of course I lie and tell him I'm fine. I can't tell him that the pounding in my head is worse than anything I've ever had before. That I have pins and needles in my limbs that have nothing at all to do with sex or this position. Or even worse, how do I tell him about those damn spots and the way my vision blurs sometimes.

My doctor has said I'm fine... that it's just anxiety, and it might be. Hell, after what just happened, I'm probably leaning more toward agreeing with the doctor. I was getting nervous and anxious about doing anal when my body kicked off.

Instead of unburdening all my problems on him, I choose a lie. "I'm fine. I'm sorry, I don't know what came over me."

Lee nods. "Look, Em. We don't have to do anything tonight. We can get into bed and just cuddle, if you'd like?" He's looking at me full of concern and a little sadness, which I hate. I want to go back to a few moments before when he was gazing at me like I'm sexy, full of lust and desire.

"I want you to fuck me, like you said you would," I snap, making sure all he see's when he looks in my bluey-grey eyes is determination.

At first he doesn't say anything, he just looks at me like he's trying to read what I'm not saying. But, despite me not being completely honest with him about what caused the anxiety, his question was whether I wanted to have sex or just cuddle. My answer to that is one hundred percent genuine, and there's no denying that. I know he can see it clearly on my face.

"So why did me playing with your cute little ass make you anxious?" he asks, as he stands back up and moves behind me again. I feel his thighs hit the back of my legs, and my breath hitches in anticipation. I love when his body is this close to mine.

As he's waiting for me to answer, he rubs the head of his hard length through my slit, spreading my juices as it goes. As soon as the head presses against my sensitive clit, my back arches and a loud moan rips free.

"Answer me, Emmaleigh. Or I will take it away!" he snaps, as he continues to drag the head of his cock through my folds.

"I was just a little anxious because we've never done anal before. I've never had anyone play with my asshole. It started off as just the normal embarrassment of having a guy—you—looking and touching such an intimate part of my body. But then my brain just went into overdrive. All I could think about is how big your cock is. I was worried it wouldn't fit, or that it would hurt me. You don't get wet in your ass to produce the natural lube like you get in your pussy, and I know we can use lube, but I don't have any. I know I probably should have bought some because we did talk about doing anal. And I do really want to try, it's just—"

It's like I have verbal diarrhoea and I just can't stop fucking talking. Luckily, Lee interrupts me by spanking my ass. I yelp as he startles me. It's not a hard spank like it normally is, this is just enough to get me to shut the fuck up, and I'm grateful for it. Who knows how much more crap I would have talked about if he hadn't stopped me. It's an awful trait I have, I talk when I'm nervous.

"So, you do still want to do anal, but you have reservations?" he asks, summarising my long speech into just a couple of words, and I can't help but chuckle.

"Yes, that's the short version."

I don't need to look back to see him smiling, I can feel his body move as he tries to hide his little chuckle. "Okay, so how about we discuss anal later. Right now, I want to sink my big, hard cock into your tight, wet pussy. Can we do that?"

"Yes, please," I whimper.

He barely lets me finish my plea before he presses the head of his cock against my hole. I cry out with pleasure as the engorged tip spreads open my entrance. Pausing for a second, I can feel Lee's breathing increase as he rakes his fingers down my spine before travelling back up again to fist my hair into his hand once more.

As he tugs on my hair, a harsh sting spreading across my scalp, he pushes his hard length further and further in. At first he moves painfully slowly, but as he pulls harder on my scalp, it forces me to lift my head up off the bed and arches my back more. My tits are just scraping across the fabric of the duvet, the friction creating a heady sensation.

It doesn't take him long to bottom out, and as soon as he does, Lee freezes for a few seconds, no doubt giving me the time I need to adjust. It doesn't take me anywhere near as long as it used to, my pussy more used to him now. I can hear Lee trying to slow down his breathing, and I try to do the same. It's been two weeks since we were together, and I have a feeling this is going to be a quick one for us both. Not that I'm bothered. I just want to feel him.

"Please, Lee. Move. Now," I beg, not giving a shit about the rules. I need to feel more of him, as this is like fucking torture.

Lee's grip on my hip tightens to the point it's almost bruising, and he pulls back on my hair just that little bit more, the stinging on my scalp paling into insignificance when he starts moving his hips. At first he pulls back so fucking slowly I want to scream at him, and when he stops, just the tip still inside me, I almost do. But before I get a chance, he slams back inside me, his cock hitting so deep I can't help but yelp as his balls smash against my clit when he bottoms out.

He feels so fucking deep I can barely catch my breath before he really starts moving. Long slow strokes as he pulls back before slamming inside me, hard and fast.

Both our breathing increases as he hits that sweet spot deep inside again and again, and each time I squeeze the walls of my pussy around his cock, he loses control just that little more. His movements become more uncoordinated and frantic, in between his thrusts loud grunts fill the air.

As we both chase our release he starts to move faster, thrusting into me harder each time. He pulls back on my hair even more, and the pain shooting through my scalp only adds to the overwhelming sensations. He pulls until I'm standing upright, my back still arched, and this new position changes the angle his cock hits, causing a loud, guttural moan to rip from my throat.

Once he has me upright, he lets go of my hair and moves that hand around to wrap around the front of my throat. His other hand continues its bruising grip on my hip as he uses that to control me, pulling my body back hard so that I slam harder on his cock—which I fucking love.

He continues his frantic pace, and I can feel my pussy getting wetter, so close to my impending release. Given the desperate thrusts, I think Lee is close too. As I feel the sensation deep within my lower stomach start to grow, the tightening of my muscles I feel whenever I'm getting ready to come, Lee begins to squeeze my throat with his hand.

At first the sensation feels amazing, having him dominate and control me, taking his pleasure whilst giving it to me at the same time, it feels incredible. I can just about drag in a little oxygen with each breath, but it's not quite enough and I start panting. That's when Lee presses down hard, cutting off my air supply completely.

As soon as I try to take a breath and realise I can't, I start to panic. I can feel my lungs starting to burn, as I try and fail to drag in some air. That's when I feel Lee's breath against my ear. "Trust me, Beautiful. Don't panic, just let yourself feel." His voice is deep and throaty, like it's full of sex. I don't even hesitate, I do as I'm told. If he tells me to trust him, then that's absolutely what I will do. We've experimented so much over the last couple of months, I know he won't hurt me. He knows what I enjoy, and so I'm willing to put a little faith in him knowing I will like this.

I stop trying to breathe and just let my body relax, allowing myself to simply feel everything like Lee told me to do. He must be able to feel me submit, as he whispers in my ear, "Good girl."

The magic words help me even more, and I just let myself enjoy the sensations. The feel of his cock hitting deep inside, the burn in my lungs, and the feel of his body enveloping mine. Each thrust is more intense, and I feel it so much more. As I start climbing closer to my release, the burn in my lungs worsens, and spots begin to appear in the corners of my vision—those damn fucking spots. Only this time I know it's because my body is desperate for oxygen.

I bring my arm up and grab hold of Lee's wrist, but I don't pull it away. I want to let him know I'm reaching my limit, but I'm not quite there yet. I trust him to know when I've had enough. Still, it can't hurt to give him a little hint.

I feel him start to move the hand that was on my hip down to the front, across my lower abdomen, before he gently slides his fingers in between my soaking wet folds. It doesn't take long for him to reach my swollen clit, and even just the slightest touch from him is too much.

I try to scream and moan, but thanks to Lee's grip on my throat, I can't. All it does is waste precious resources and the burning worsens, which in turn creates more spots. That's when Lee doubles his efforts, thrusting harder and deeper, while his fingers rub over my clit.

It's not long before I'm losing control, my pussy walls beginning to tighten as I near that cliff. I'm so close to the edge... I just need more. "Come for me, Beautiful," Lee growls as he bites down on my neck just as he releases my throat.

A rush of air fills my lungs at just the right time and fuck me does it feel incredible. My whole body feels on fire, but so much more alert. It's like I can feel everything, every nerve ending is prickling with excitement as I lose myself. The orgasm rips through me, and I scream loudly, my body vibrating with need. "Fuck!"

My body trembles as my pussy walls clamp down on Lee's cock, preventing him from moving, but he continues to rub my clit through my orgasm. This causes more waves of pleasure to ripple through my soaking pussy. All those sensations are too much for Lee, who holds onto me tight as he falls apart. With a loud roar against my ear, his cock explodes deep inside me.

As soon as it becomes too much, and my body sags into a heap that's only being held up by his arm around my waist, Lee takes his fingers from my pussy and helps me lay on the bed. As his cock slips out, I feel so wet and empty. I always hate this feeling. It's like I'm missing a part of me.

I watch as he licks his fingers clean of my juices before walking into the bathroom, collecting a washcloth that he brings through to help clean us both up. I can't believe it wasn't too long ago I found this whole process embarrassing. Now, I'm just laying here with my legs open, my cum-filled pussy on display while I let him take care of me.

Once we're both sorted, he runs through into the kitchen and brings us both some water, which I gladly accept. It's been a long fucking day, and everywhere hurts. I reach into the bedside cabinet and grab some pain killers. Lee looks at me concerned. "Don't worry, it's not from the sex," I tell him. "Today was just a really long day and I ache. Who knew going on strike and helping the entire NHS healthcare system collapse for the day would be such a headache."

Lee chuckles as he climbs into the bed beside me. We both sit with our backs against the headboard, and he pulls the duvet up over us both before holding his arms out wide. "Come here. We can rest for a while. I've already told work I'm not coming in tomorrow, so I'm all yours for a bit. We can get to the sexy time again soon, but for now we rest."

Mmm, that's like music to my ears. I curl up into his arms, my head resting against his warm, hard chest. I don't know what it is about Lee, but he always runs hot. Seriously, the guy never gets cold. There will be evenings where I'm sitting there in jumpers and blankets, and he's shirtless. On the plus side, I always have something nice to look at, and when I cuddle up to him, he's always warming. He's like my own personal radiator.

I try not to think about how much my body is hurting right now. I mean, the pins and needles in my right leg are getting so bad, a couple of my toes keep going numb. I know I've been on my feet a lot today, but it's no worse than normal. And don't even get me started on the headache behind my right eye, and those fucking spots on my vision.

Even now when all I'm doing is lying quietly with my head on Lee's chest, it's like I can feel my heart pulsating in my head. The pressure behind my eye makes even just moving it sore. Closing it and getting some sleep sounds like the best idea all around. I just hope this has all gone away by the time I wake up because Lee has been tempting me with some very kinky sex acts, and I think I might be ready to try some of them now. But first I need a little sleep, and I need my body to start behaving a bit better.

Emmaleigh

They say nobody knows your body better than you. I know some medical professionals—and yes, I'm thinking about doctors—will argue otherwise. But I've been a nurse for several years, and the one thing I've always learnt is to trust the patient's instinct. Obviously that's not going to apply to everyone, as I've met more than my fair share of hypochondriacs. But those that are really ill, usually they know.

As healthcare professionals, we get taught the average. So we know what the average range for a good blood pressure is. We know that the optimal resting pulse should be on an average person. We know roughly what weight people should be, based on their height. But these are all completely generic, made up of statistics and maths, rather than taking real people into consideration.

According to the BMI scale, I'm obese, and I can either lose a couple of stones to reach a healthy weight—which is a number I don't think I've ever seen on the scales since I became an adult—or I can grow an extra foot taller. Take the ideal heart rate for example, I've looked after ninety year old men with perfect pulses of fifty beats per minute, which is on average the same as someone who runs a couple of times a week. Obviously, the old man isn't running marathons, but he did have a quadruple bypass a couple of years ago, so it's like he has a brand new heart.

We learn the average, but the patient knows what *their* average is. People who have epilepsy often know when they're about to have a seizure because they see auras, or they feel a certain way, and I genuinely believe this is something we, as healthcare professionals, should listen to more.

So, when I woke up this morning, I just knew there was something really wrong, and it terrifies me. I've known for a while that my body hasn't felt right, and was behaving oddly. I have been trusting of the doctors when they've said it's migraines, or anxiety, but I know that's not what this is.

Lee is softly snoring beside me in bed, and I roll over to take a look at him. I love watching him sleep—not in a creepy way—but he has this peaceful serenity that crosses his face, and it's actually kinda beautiful. In fact, rolling over and looking at him before he wakes up has become one of my favourite things to do.

I think it's because, for that moment, anything could be real. I can convince myself that this is ten years in the future and we're still sleeping beside each other. Only now, I'm wearing a ring on my finger, and he tells me he loves me as soon as he wakes up.

I know dreaming like that is dangerous territory, but it's one of those moments, those little glimpses into what I really crave in life, and that's not something I can control.

But this morning, as soon as I rolled over, I knew something was different. My vision was wrong. Blinking open a couple of times, I reach over to the bedside table to grab my glasses, wondering if that will make a difference. It doesn't. In fact, as I try to concentrate, I realise I can't see anything out of my right eye. Gone are those fucking annoying spots, which I should be pleased about, but instead there's just nothing.

I try to get my remaining eye to focus, and thankfully, I can still see a little out of that eye, but it's not right either. I have to blink a few times to get it to focus, to stop things from blurring or appearing in double vision. My heart starts to race, and I can feel myself starting to panic. I try to tell myself it's nothing serious, that it's just because I've been overdoing it a lot lately, but I know I'm just lying to myself.

The pressure behind my right eye is immense, and whenever I move my eye, it feels like it's grating against glass. It's painful just to move it, and that's not normal. I know I could take a handful of pills and none of them would take away the pain I'm feeling in my head at the moment. But it's not like a normal headache. It's unlike anything I've ever experienced before, and that's why I just know something is wrong.

Even though I've only been up less than half an hour, and I haven't even got out of bed yet, I can feel my body trying to draw me back into sleep. My whole being just feels exhausted. I don't run marathons—or run at all—but I imagine this is what people feel like when they've run too far too quickly. It's an exhaustion you can feel deep in your bones, and I can feel my eyes starting to droop. It's like I don't have any choice, I have to go back to sleep.

As I let sleep pull me under, I pray to whoever is listening that when I wake up, this will all be a distant memory. Something caused by not enough sleep, and that the pills I've just taken will help take away the pain. Mostly, I just want to wake up and have my vision back.

"Morning... or should I say, afternoon, sleepyhead," Lee says, as he gently strokes the hair out of my eyes, sweeping it off my face to tuck it behind my ear.

The feel of his warm fingers as they sweep across my skin feels delicious, and I try to smile at him, but once again I'm hit by that impending feeling of doom. I try to push it away, and blink a couple of times to try and get my eyes to focus, but the more I blink, the more my eye starts to hurt.

That's when I'm flooded with the memory of how I felt when I woke up earlier, and I realise, not only is my eyesight still missing in my right eye, but other parts of my body feel weird too. Specifically, my right leg. I can feel it, but it feels so unusual, like it's not really my leg. Like it's an alien leg that doesn't actually belong to me. I know that sounds crazy, but there's no other way to describe it.

I think if I tried, I'd be able to move my leg, but it wouldn't be the same. It feels heavy in places, but also numb in others. I can feel a numbness around my hip area, and that gets me thinking whether I've ever been able to feel my hip area before or not? It's one of those things that have always just been there. I get pain in my hips when I've over extended my legs, or pushed myself too far, but that's pain. This isn't pain, it's numbness.

As a result of the numb joint, and heavy feeling in my leg, my foot has this weird pins and needles sensation going on. How the hell can one leg have all three separate situations going on at the same time?

I say good morning to Lee, giving him a small smile, and I try to pretend that everything is normal. I don't want to freak him out by telling him how I feel. Besides, he's made it really clear that we're just friends-with-benefits. If I tell him about this, he'll feel like he has to look after me, and I don't want that. I don't want him to feel pressured into anything.

As I talk to Lee about yesterday, my brain is on autopilot as he tells me about how things have been at his work, my brain is somewhere else entirely. I'm running through every abnormal feeling I have in my body, and I'm trying to switch on as much of my medical brain as I can in an attempt to work out what the hell is wrong with me.

I'm not stupid. I know my ass should already be in the hospital where a real doctor can examine me and tell me exactly what the hell is going on. But, when they say nurses make the worst patients, that's not an understatement.

I know how busy hospitals are, and there's no way I'm wasting valuable time and resources if this is just a really severe headache. Personally, I feel as soon as the staff in the emergency room learn I'm a nurse they expect me to already know what's wrong. Maybe that's all in my head, but it's one of the reasons I haven't already dragged myself to the hospital, despite being sure something is really wrong.

I've ruled out major things like heart problems or a stroke. I have to admit, at the moment, I'm stuck on a brain tumour. But I know that's fear talking. The problem is, without more tests, it's impossible to tell what this is. The symptoms are wide and varied, meaning only more tests will give us more information to add to help make the diagnosis.

Lee touches my arm, pulling me back into the moment, as I notice his brows furrowed and he's looking at me with concern. "Are you okay?"

"Yeah, of course. Why do you ask?" I try to sound as casual as possible, but I can hear a quiver in my voice that I hope he can't pick up on. Though, given the way his beautiful blue eyes are assessing me, I can tell he is trying to work out what I'm hiding.

"I've been talking to you for the last ten minutes, and it's like you're zoning in and out. Normally when you wake up, you are up and talking. It's me who usually takes ages to wake up. I've never known you to sleep in this late. Are you sure you're okay?" I can hear the concern in his voice, as his finger lazily strokes my forehead, in the most soothing of ways.

Fuck, for just a few second, I really wanted to tell him everything. I don't want to lie to him, or keep things from him. But that's just what I'm like with these sorts of things. I'm the same with my family. There's no fucking point worrying everyone if it turns out to be nothing, and that I just need some more sleep and pain killers. Deep down, I know it's more than that, but I guess, ignorance really is bliss. When nobody else knows I can pretend it's not real.

"I'm so sorry, Lee. I guess it's just been too much for me lately, with all the stress and lack of sleep these last couple of weeks, as I prepared for the strike, and all the other things I had going on. I think maybe I just need a day to catch up on my sleep. I know you took the day off work to spend it with me, and I really do want to, it's just—"

Before I can finish my sentence, Lee interrupts me by pressing his lips to mine. It's only a short, sweet, chaste kiss, but it's perfect. I've noticed this is something he's started doing whenever he thinks I'm talking too much. He silences me with a kiss—and I'm okay with that. I hate when I get verbal diarrhoea like that, so kissing me to shut me up is the perfect way to get it under control.

"Hey, don't you worry about me. You look really exhausted. How about I get us both some breakfast, then I will head home and you can get a bit more sleep. I know you have work tomorrow, and so do I, but how about I come over Friday after work and we can spend the weekend together. We still have to plan our London trip. I know we were supposed to be going next weekend, and I know it's my fault we haven't planned it. But, how about we get together this weekend, look at our days off, and get something booked?" The bright smile on his face, like he really is looking forward to going on holiday with me is infectious. I can't help but smile back at him.

"I would love to. And don't blame yourself about next weekend. You had your reasons for needing space, and I will always honour that. So, if you want to wait a while until you're sure you want to go away with me, then we can do that." I don't know why I'm encouraging him to back away, but I want him to know that the ball is in his court. He's the one with the decisions to make. I've made mine. I'm all in. I know my heart is on the line, and I will most likely get really hurt, but I can't walk away. I know the way I feel about him is dangerous, and that waiting for Lee to realise he likes me and wants a relationship with me could be the wrong move, but it's far too late now. My heart is already all in.

Maybe I need him to walk away because I'm not brave enough to? Maybe that's why I'm encouraging him to walk away because I can't? Either way, it's all on Lee.

"As long as you know we're just friends, and you're okay with that, then I'm happy to just keep going as we are." I don't know what it is, but he has this almost hopeful look in his eyes, like he's really hoping I don't say no. And it's the cutest fucking vulnerable look I've ever seen on his face, and so of course I say yes.

Lee gets up and heads into the kitchen to make breakfast, and while he's not in the room, I know I have to try moving to see what the hell is going on with my leg. I'm really hoping it's just dead from the position I've been sleeping in, but as I try to stand at the side of the bed, it quickly becomes apparent, this really is serious.

It's so fucking alien, it's like I know my leg is there, but I can't get it to work the way I want it to. The movements I make seem almost exaggerated, and even then it's like my leg doesn't quite lift up fully and I feel like I'm dragging it along behind me. I can move, with a bit of a limp, but it's hard— like really hard—and I feel really unsteady on my feet, like at any moment, I'm going to topple over.

I manage to drag myself into the bathroom to get cleaned up, and then into the living room so I can have breakfast with Lee. Luckily, he's got his back to me buttering the toast as I enter the large open plan kitchen, living room, dining room, and so he doesn't see my limp. I would never hear the end of it if he does.

I manage to have breakfast without him knowing anything is wrong, and I force myself to keep up with the conversation. No point dwelling on how I feel, it's not going to get better on its own, and I'm not suddenly going to work out what the hell it is without getting more tests done at the hospital. I've already decided that's my next stop, I just have to wait for Lee to leave first.

How I manage to behave as normal for the next hour while we have breakfast and Lee gets ready to leave is a fucking miracle. I try to move whenever he's not looking, hoping if he does see me, I can pass off the very obvious limp I have as a dead leg from all the protesting yesterday. But, I see him watching me with those piercing blue eyes of his, and I think he can tell there's something wrong, but thankfully, he doesn't say anything.

He leans against the side of the front door, getting ready to leave, and he takes my hand in his, clasping our fingers together. My heart races and my stomach does a little flip that even a school girl with a cheesy crush would be impressed by. Even just the slightest of touches from him has me behaving like a lovesick teen.

With his other hand, he reaches forward and sweeps my hair out of my eyes, pushing it behind my ear. I try not to panic as his hand disappears from view completely when he gets closer to my right eye. It's the scariest fucking feeling in the world to have a whole portion of sight just gone, yet it was there just a few hours ago.

"You look tired, Beautiful. Are you sure you're okay?" he asks, leaning closer as he continues to stroke the side of my face. What's really fucking worrying is that on top of not being able to see what he's doing out of my right eye, I also can't feel his touch properly either. It's like I know he's doing it, and I can feel the ghost of his touch but not the usual warmth that I get from his skin against mine.

With a sigh, I give him a small smile. "Yeah, I promise, I will be fine."

Giving his hand a reassuring squeeze, he leans further, closing the gap between us. The feel of his lips against mine is a much needed and welcome distraction. It starts off just a simple kiss—a sweet goodbye—but as soon as we taste each other, he begins to grab at me pulling me closer, and I barely manage to grab hold of him before my leg becomes wobbly.

I try to hide it by kissing him, and it works for a few seconds before he pulls back, and that knowing smile is there all over again. His voice is deep and full of concern as he talks. "Are you sure you're okay? I'm worried about you. I can stay, or I can take you to your mum's if that will help. Hell... I'll even take you to the emergency room, if you think it's that bad. Just, please, let me help."

Don't get me wrong, I've always known that Lee cares about me in his own way. But as he stands in front of me right now, that serious look in his dazzling blue eyes, I can tell he really does care for me, and that warms my heart so much more than it should.

"Honestly, I just need some sleep. I will be fine. Go home and enjoy the rest of the day. I will see you in a couple of days and we can spend the weekend together. We can do whatever you want," I reply, and Lee's smile turns higher in one corner, that sexy smirk I love spreading across his face.

"Well... if we can do *anything* I want, I'm sure I will be able to think of something good." The way he says anything, it makes such an ordinary word seem so completely sexual, and I can't help but smile.

Lee leans over and seals his lips against mine once more. This time it's me who deepens the kiss, slipping my tongue in to taste him. I have to pull away far too quickly, because I know I can't stand at the door for much longer. My numb leg already feels like it's starting to quiver, like it might give way at any moment, causing me to collapse to the floor, and I really don't need that happening.

We kiss goodbye, and as is the same every time he leaves, my heart feels empty. In fact, it's not just my heart, it's everywhere. I've lived by myself for the last couple of years, and I never wanted a roommate.

But, as I watch Lee walk away, I feel like he's taking a piece of me with him. It's like he was always meant to move in here and be with me, and when he's not here, the place just feels empty. I feel empty without him. Yet, this time as I watch him leave, I know it's for the best.

He's made his feelings perfectly clear—he doesn't want any kind of serious relationship. And if this medical issue is as bad as I suspect it is, my life is about to get a whole lot more complicated, and I don't want to have to deal with him as well as everything else.

As much as it breaks my heart, I know I can't have him in my life if this is something serious. I need people who want to be here, who want to care for me, to love me. Not people who feel like they're doing it out of a dumb sense of loyalty.

So, as I get myself dressed and call for a taxi, I repeat over and over in my pain filled brain, telling myself I have to let him go. I need to be strong enough to fight whatever this is, and I can't do that if I'm worried about my fucked up love life. I think maybe I knew it would end this way. Maybe that's why I stole one final kiss from him, because I knew this would have to be our goodbyes. Maybe if I'm wrong and this isn't anything major I can forget these thoughts ever occurred and I can move on with Lee. But if I'm right and this is something serious, he can't be a part of my life, and this was our goodbye.

Lee

I knew as soon as I walked out of Emmaleigh's flat that something was wrong. I can't even explain it, but she just wasn't herself at all. When she thought I wasn't watching, I'd catch the look on her face, once the mask she was wearing for me dropped, and it became blatantly obvious, something was going on with her and she didn't want me to know what it was.

I tried on numerous occasions to get her to talk to me, but when she didn't, I tried to leave her alone, and I just watched. I noticed how there were times when she was walking with a limp, almost like her right leg was dragging behind her slightly. Then I'd catch her putting her hand to her head, like she had a real bad migraine, and was just too polite to tell me to shut the fuck up.

Honestly, I hated leaving her, but I trust in the fact she's a nurse and can look after herself. She knows where I am if she needs me, but that doesn't stop me from worrying about her. In fact, that gnawing feeling in the pit of my stomach, telling me that something isn't right, it's consuming me.

I try to pass the time when I'm home by hanging out with my mum. I don't see her much as we both work different hours, so to get home early on her day off, it's nice to be able to just sit with her and see how she is.

Even though we live in the same house, it is possible to go a long time without properly seeing each other. I get up for breakfast in the morning just as she's going to work. Despite me being twenty-three years old, she still makes me porridge for breakfast and packs me some lunch to take to work. I've repeatedly told her I'm old enough to sort myself out, but she's one of those mum's who will always find something to mother over, and for my mum, this is it—well, and she does my washing, ironing, and cleaning. So, I guess you could say I have a very easy life.

When I come home from work, Mum and Dad have usually already eaten, and have left mine to be reheated. They settle to watch something on the TV, while I go on my computer. I'm not much of a gamer, but I like some. My real passion is making useful YouTube videos that can help people. The fact I work in IT probably gives it away how much of a tech geek I am, and the YouTube channel I have is designed to help people with all their tech needs.

Although I see both Mum and Dad for a short period of time on an evening, with me spending more time at Emmaleigh's whenever I can, particularly at weekends, my time with them has dwindled a lot. So, I'm not even remotely surprised that Mum is shocked I'm there early enough to spend time with her. I didn't tell her I called in sick to stay home with a girl. I might be an adult, but Mum will still get mad at me for that. Can you imagine if I told her I did it because I wanted to spend all day having make-up sex with Em, only for her to have to cancel due to being unwell? My mum would be so pissed, and I would get a massive lecture on how no girl is worth my job.

As I sit here thinking about yesterday, I remember the conversations we had about the sex we were going to try. Em genuinely seemed interested in experimenting, even going as far as to promise trying anal. My dick gets hard at just the thought of that.

I've known Em for a while, and even though I haven't seen her in the last couple of weeks, I still think I can read her. I don't think this is her way of getting back to me because of the last two weeks. She's not the type of girl to get me all hot and bothered and then walk away because she wants me to suffer. That's not Em at all. She only ever says and does what she means. So when she promised me a day of kinky sex, that's exactly what she intended to do. The fact she wasn't able to fulfil that promise has me even more nervous.

My mum places her hand over mine, where it's resting on the table in front of us, bringing my attention back to the here and now. "So, are you going to tell me anything about this girl?"

My eyes flick to Mum's, and the piercing blue eyes I see staring back at me are exact replicas of my own. "What girl?" I ask, trying to play things as casually as I can.

Mum rolls her eyes and I bite my lip to hold back a chuckle. "I wasn't born yesterday, Lee. I'm the one who cooks, cleans, and tidies up after you, which means I notice when your bed hasn't been slept in. I know you've been spending weekends away from here," she explains, her voice sounding firm, like she will be pissed that I'm trying not to answer her.

"It's not serious, Mum. That's why I've not mentioned it to you," I mumble, looking down at the table, suddenly feeling like a teenager who has been caught doing something he shouldn't.

Mum's short, sharp, sarcastic laugh jolts me back into the moment, and I raise my gaze to hers. "Lee, we both know that's rubbish. For the last couple of months, it's the happiest you've ever been. I never said anything because I didn't want to jinx it. I know how much you have problems trusting people, but somehow this girl was able to crawl under your skin, and I was pleased because she brought you to life." She squeezes my hand, giving me a sad smile.

"I saw how lost and upset you've been over the last couple of weeks. Combine that with the amount of time you've been home, and it wasn't hard to guess you had a falling out. I wanted to say something, to support you. But you've always been independent, wanting to make up your own mind. So when I saw you this morning, that bright, happy smile on your face, I knew you'd sorted things out. I know I probably shouldn't say all this, and I don't want to interfere in your relationship, but I would like to meet her. I'd like to thank her for making my son so happy."

Fuck! Mum has got the complete wrong end of the stick, and now I need to break the news to her about what Em and I really are. I never wanted to have this conversation with Mum—or anyone—which is why I haven't told people about Em.

"Mum, I'm not going to be introducing her to any of the family. She's just a friend, but if she starts meeting you lot, she might think this is more than it is," I explain, but I can see that stern look on her face growing in only the way a mother's can. She looks like she's a second away from grounding me, and despite being old enough to ignore her, I still shrink down a little under her piercing gaze.

"Lee, that's a load of rubbish and you know it is. With the exception of the last couple of weeks, you've practically been living with that young lady. You say she will get the wrong idea about things, but to me, it sounds like you're the one with the wrong idea. Call it whatever you want, but you are in a relationship with this girl," Mum snaps, and my breathing starts to accelerate.

Is Mum right? Have I been giving off the impression we're in a relationship this whole time, and that's why Em thinks the way she does? I mean, my words have always been crystal fucking clear, but I guess my actions have muddied things a little.

"Look, Mum. I appreciate what you're saying, but Em knows what this is. She knows I never want a relationship."

Mum squeezes my hand, her way of demanding I stop looking down at the table and meet her gaze again. It's not easy discussing this with her. I worry she will see the real reason behind my belief. Nonetheless, she is my mum, so of course I do as I'm told and meet her gaze. There's a sad look on her face, and I hate knowing I put that frown there.

"Why don't you want a relationship?" she asks. Her brow furrows, and her eyes are laser focused on mine as she waits for my answer.

"I just don't," I mumble in reply.

Mum tuts. "Lee, don't lie to me."

I can't hold back the huff that leaves me, and I know I sound like a stubborn teenager having a strop. "I'm not lying to you," I snap. "I just don't see the point in relationships. They always turn to shit, or people stay in them when they shouldn't."

Mum's eyes widen and as she realises I'm talking about her and Dad. Her blue eyes that match mine perfectly start to glisten with unshed tears as she slowly releases her hold on my hand. She doesn't look like she's going to get up and leave—like she should after what I just said—but she doesn't look like she wants to stay either.

"Is that what you think? That your dad and I stayed together when we should have split up?" she asks, her voice barely above a whisper.

Dad is in the living room. I can tell that by how loud the TV is blaring out. He's in his late sixties now, and his age is beginning to really affect him. His hearing is by far the worst, but the idea of wearing a hearing aid does not appeal to him. I'm not worried about him listening in on this conversation, yet as soon as Mum sees me looking in his direction, she gets up and closes the door, sealing us away in our own bubble. Maybe she thinks this is all I need to start confessing a lifetime of issues.

"Well... you do argue a lot. Less now than you did when I was younger, but still..." My thoughts trail off as Mum's face droops, the mood in the room turning sombre. I love my mum to pieces, and I really wish she'd never asked me this question because I can't lie to her, but at the same time, I hate seeing that look of pain on her face. Knowing that my words put that there.

She takes hold of my hand again, only this time she tries to pull me a little bit more toward her, so I have to shuffle forward in my seat to get closer. "Listen to me, Lee. Me and your dad have had our issues, and I'm so very sorry that you, and your brother and sister ever had to witness them. We would argue whenever your dad drank, but it was never because we didn't love each other, or that we didn't want to be with each other. I was frustrated because the man I love was harming himself by drinking. Every time I yelled, it was because I wanted to make him see the pain he was causing with his drinking. As much as it hurts me—even now—that he still drinks, I would never leave him. We've been together for over forty years, and not because I'm too afraid to leave him, or that I stayed for my kids. It was never about that. I stayed because your dad is the love of my life. Yes, at times, our relationship is chaotic, and I'd love him to make changes—I'm sure he'd change some things about me too—but that's what love is. We work at it, even when it's hard. I don't know what you have with Em, but if she's worth it, you will fight for her. And if she thinks you're worth it, she will fight for you."

"I still remember what you told me one night, when I was just eight-years-old, Mum. In the middle of one of your arguments, you told me to never get into a relationship, as they will always turn to shit, I will get hurt, and I will be stuck with the girl for life. They're not the sort of words a kid forgets, Mum," I snap, and as her eyes widen in shock, I regret the words as soon as they're out.

"Oh, Lee. I should never have said that. In fact, you and your sister should never have seen half as much as you did. I can only apologise, and say that those words were fuelled by anger and alcohol. I would never have said them and meant them. You're one of the kindest, sweetest people, Lee. You deserve to be happy, and I think Em makes you happy. Please, don't let some stupid drunken ramble ruin your future, I won't ever forgive myself," she pleads, her breath catching as she tries to hold back her sobs. I hate that I've made Mum so upset, but I think this conversation has been a long time coming.

It's like Mum's words strike an arrow to my cold, black heart, and it's trying to break down all the walls I've spent the last few years erecting. All of a sudden, everything I've ever thought about relationships has all been smashed to shit, but in a good way.

As Mum's words fully register, I realise she's right. Emmaleigh has been fighting for us all along, and now I just have to decide if I want to fight alongside her. But, the more I think about Em, the more worried I become that I haven't heard from her. I know the most likely option is that she's gone to bed, and she's sleeping off whatever illness is creeping up on her, but that impending feeling of doom I have whenever I think of her, it's starting to feel overwhelming.

Mum pulls me out of my own head by pulling me into her arms for a hug. It's then, when I feel her tears on my cheek, that I realise I've managed this whole situation with Mum very badly. I've been so caught up worrying about Em, I didn't see the full extent of the pain I caused Mum.

"Oh, Mum. I'm so sorry. I never meant to upset you. You know I love you and Dad, and I've always said I had an amazing childhood.

Ignore what I said," I apologise, as I pull her closer. My mum's only around five foot, if that, and so she always feels tiny in my arms.

She gently pushes me out of the hug, keeping her arms on my shoulders, so she can make sure I'm looking at her. A few stray tears fall down her cheeks, but otherwise she looks to have gained some control over them. I can see she keeps taking big, deep breaths, which I'm sure is what's helping her.

"Lee, honey, you don't have anything to be sorry for. I can't change what happened between us growing up, but you can't let that warp your view of relationships. We have had way more happy momemts, times when we're so in love and are making memories together than we have ever had sad memories. And even if we were arguing all the time and we hated each other, that's our relationship, not yours. You and this girl are the only ones involved in your relationship. If it goes wrong, it's because of you two, and nobody else. I'm not saying you have to date this girl. What I am saying is that your reasoning for not ever wanting to date anyone is massively flawed, and I would appreciate it very much if you would think it through. Again, you don't even have to date this girl, but I need to know that when the time comes, you will be ready to date."

Nodding my head, I make Mum a promise, and I know I can stick to it because I'm already thinking about it as we speak. "I promise, I will think about what I really want from her. I will think about whether I'm saying I don't want to date her because I really don't or because of my warped view. If it is because of how I thought, then I can work on fixing things with her. But if it's because I don't see myself ever dating her, I need to end things with her. I know she wants to date me, and I don't want to lead her on if I know we will never end up together."

Mum reaches over and cups my cheek with her hand, stroking under my eye with her thumb. "You're a good boy, Lee. This girl, or the next one, will be lucky to have you," Mum says, before leaning forward and placing a light kiss on my cheek. Without any more discussion, she gets up and begins making a hot drink for herself and Dad. I decline and head back upstairs to my room. I have a lot to think about. I've been thinking about things all wrong for all these years.

As soon as I'm in my room, I distract myself from my thoughts by playing one of my video games. I don't play often, but when I do, I become fully immersed in the experience, which is exactly what I need to stop myself from thinking about Em. Why isn't she texting me? Is she alright? Do I want a relationship with her? Should I walk away and never see her again?

Too many big questions to deal with, and so I allow myself to fall into the video game. I know I will have to deal with the questions eventually, but not today.

> **LEE**
> Hey, Em. How are you feeling this morning?

As soon as I wake up the next morning, when I realise I've not heard from Em, I send her that message. I've been staring at it for the last eight hours while I've been trying to work. Those fucking annoying two ticks are blue, which means she's read my message, she just hasn't replied.

All manner of thoughts are flying around my head. I'm thinking she's collapsed alone in her house, unable to ask for help. Or she is just being too fucking stubborn and doesn't want to ask for help. I'm also thinking this is her way of finally getting rid of me. My punishment for those fucking awful two weeks we spent apart. There's only so many times you can tell a girl that you don't want to date her before she listens, leaves you, and finds someone else. Maybe that's what this is? Either way, it's driving me fucking crazy.

I try to tell myself not to text again, that it's pushy and it will make Emmaleigh run a mile if there's actually nothing wrong. But that impending feeling of doom I feel in my stomach is worsening, like deep in the pit of my gut it's telling me to keep checking on her.

I pull out my phone once more and type another message.

> **LEE**
> Hey, Beautiful. Just checking that you're okay. I was worried about you yesterday, and now I'm even more worried today. Just let me know that you're okay, so I don't come all the way to your flat just to check on you.

I wait, and the longer I wait, the more concerned I become. I was only partially joking when I said I would drive to her flat to check on her. It's not like I have contact details for any of her family so I can check on her. I'm stuck, so I just have to keep focusing on my breathing to hold back the panic I can feel drawing closer.

When my phone eventually does buzz, I almost jump out of my own skin.

> **EM**
>
> Sorry for making you worry. After you left I realised I wasn't feeling well. Bad headache that was making my vision poor, and one of my legs was numb. I thought it would go away, but it didn't. So I went to the hospital. They've admitted me to run some more tests to try and find out what's going on. I didn't want to worry you.

> **LEE**
>
> Holy shit, Em. Are you okay? You should have told me, I would have taken you to the hospital yesterday. What ward are you on, I will come visit you? Are they any closer to knowing what's wrong?

Fear really is taking over my body right now as I spring to my feet, trying to find some more comfortable clothes to change into, since I'm still in my work suit. Before I have a chance to take my trousers off, Em replies.

> **EM**
>
> Honestly, it's fine. I didn't drive, I got a taxi. Don't worry about visiting. My family is here, and meeting family is against your rules. I'm having a scan this afternoon, so hopefully I'll get some results tonight, but tomorrow morning is more likely. I can keep you updated, if you'd like?

LEE

> Of course I want to be kept up-to-date. I've been so fucking worried about you, Em. It doesn't matter to me that your family is there, I just want to come and see you.

EM

> I'm sorry I worried you, but honestly, I didn't know what I was supposed to do in this kind of situation. We're not together in that way, so you don't have to worry about me when I'm sick. You might be okay with my family being here, but I'm not. I can't handle all their questions and opinions about our lack of relationship right now. I'm sorry, we can Facetime though, if you'd like? I'm in my own room, so that would be easy enough.

Fuck! I've read that text over and over, God knows how many times, and my heart breaks each time. All this bullshit over defining our relationship, placing a label on it, that's what has caused all this. Surely she knows I care about her, even if it is only as a friend.

I don't have the mental capacity to worry about Em, and think about what this means for the two of us. I know we're going to have to make some big decisions soon because we can't go on like this. But while Em is ill, and emotions are running high, is not the time.

LEE

> Of course I want to Facetime. If you change your mind about me coming to visit, I can be there in half an hour. I care about you, Em, and I want to make sure you're alright. You don't have to be alone.

EM

> Thank you. That means a lot. I'm not alone, my mum's here, and the rest of my big, crazy family keep rotating in and out. I will Facetime you later this evening when they've all gone, if that's okay?

I wait around for a couple of hours, just staring at my phone, waiting for her to call. I try to distract myself with other things, but it's never enough. All I can think about is Em. Wondering when she's going to Facetime, and if she's okay.

My heart breaks knowing she's in that hospital bed, and I can't be there to check up on her. But I guess that's all my fault. I told her I didn't want to blur the lines, to make her think we were more than we are. Turns out, I was wrong all along. I'm the one blurring the lines.

As I stand here, all I can think about is hearing from Em, caring for her, making sure she's okay. I want to be with her at the hospital, I want to hug her until she's feeling better, and I want her to know she's not alone. I'm very aware those are the actions of someone who is way more than a friend, but I'm just following how I feel.

When Em does finally call we talk for almost an hour, but I can tell she's not really herself. I also know she's hiding things from me, not telling me the full extent of what's going on with her. She looks so tired, and drained, and I just wanted to be there to support her. But since I couldn't do that, I did the next best thing. I tried to distract her.

I spent most of the time we were on the phone together making jokes, forcing Em to laugh. I figured if she didn't want to talk about the serious stuff—and she made it clear very early on that she didn't—then the least I could do was distract her by making her laugh. By the time she is ready to hang up, I'm pleased to see a smile on her face, even if it is just a temporary one.

We say goodnight to each other, and I make her promise to text me all day tomorrow, even though I'm at work, keeping me updated with what's going on. She didn't have the results of her MRI scan, so we think the doctor will come tomorrow. I promise that if she keeps me updated, I will keep her laughing and distracted. I may not be happy with the deal, but she is, and to me, that's all that matters.

The next couple of days pass by in a very similar pattern. She texts me throughout the day, while her family are visiting her, and then we Facetime at night before the nurses tell her off and make her go to bed. Every day I ask if I can come and visit, and every day she makes an excuse as to why I can't.

She doesn't even really talk to me about what's going on with her. I ask if she's got any test results back, and all she says is they're doing further tests. They are still unsure what's going on. I know she's got some sort of medicine being administered into her arm via a drip, and with each passing day, I can see it's wiping her out. She's getting more tired quicker, and generally she's looking more unwell. I've never seen her this pale, and given she's always had a beautiful, creamy alabaster skin tone, that's saying something.

Every day it physically hurts me that she won't let me see her, and that she won't open up to me. I keep telling myself that the role I play is far more important, that she needs someone to make her laugh, as that will help her get through it. But it still doesn't make me feel any better.

After five days, she's finally allowed home. Her dad drops her off at her flat around four in the afternoon. I know she's had an argument with her family, as they think she needs to move into her grandparents' spare room, so they can look after her while she's not well. But Emmaleigh is a stubborn woman, who of course wants her own independence, and so she demanded to be allowed home.

I didn't bother asking her if I can come over, as I have a sneaky suspicion I know what she would say. So instead, as soon as work is over, I drive straight to her flat. Once I'm upstairs and outside her door, I knock and wait for her to answer. I can hear movement inside, but it seems to take forever for her to get to the door. That's when the sinking feeling overwhelms me and I worry I've just woken her up.

Over the last five days, one of the things we've talked about repeatedly is the lack of sleep she got in the hospital. The nurses were waking her every hour at night to check on her, and then during the day there was so much going on, she didn't have any chance to nap. So, of course she would have wanted to go to bed as soon as she got home.

As Emmaleigh finally opens the door, I realise she's been holding back a lot more than I thought. She's using two crutches to hold herself up, and even then she looks like she's seconds from collapsing. The bags under her eyes attest to how fucking exhausted she really is. Her normally fair skin has a grey tinge to it, and her cheeks begin to flush as she sees me standing there. Her eyes drop to the floor, like she's embarrassed.

"What are you doing here?" she snaps, before turning around and beginning to hobble slowly towards the living room. She doesn't even bother to hold the door open for me, making it very clear I can come in, but I'm not invited. I don't care. I close and lock the door behind me before following her. My instinct is to pick her up and carry her, but I know that would only piss her off more, and believe it or not, the purpose of this visit was not to offend her.

"I've been worried about you, Em. I wanted to come and see you," I explain, as she sits down on the sofa.

I'm so used to this place now, I feel completely at home, which is why I don't even hesitate walking over to the fridge. I look over at the table beside Em and see it's empty, so as I grab a can of Coke for myself, I offer her one. She nods her head, which is very much unlike her. Normally, she'd make a sarcastic comment about me offering her one of her own drinks. I actually find myself missing the old Emmaleigh. But she clearly has a lot going on, so I can understand why she's not in the mood to mess with me.

"You should have asked before you just showed up. What if I had people here?" she snaps, as I hand her the can of Coke.

I sit down beside her and take hold of her hand. She tries to shuffle and pull away, but I don't let her. "I don't care. I've been so worried about you. I just needed to make sure you're okay. I don't give a shit who knows that."

Her breath hitches, and I can tell she's seconds away from breaking down. Her exhaustion combined with this whole scenario are getting the better of her. "I'm not okay, Lee. I don't know if I ever will be," she cries, and that's all it takes for the floodgates to open. She begins to sob hysterically, and even though I want her to explain what she means, I know I won't get anything out of her while she's like this. So, I do the only thing I can do, I pull her onto my lap, rest her head on my chest, wrap my arms around her, and I hold her while she cries.

I don't know how long we sit like that for, but I definitely can't feel my legs. This position became uncomfortable at least half an hour ago, but Em is still sobbing, so I keep soothing her. When she eventually calms down and stops crying, all she can do is yawn. Her exhaustion overtaking her. So, I shuffle around with great difficulty until I'm in a position where I can pick her up safely. She tries to protest at first, but even that's weak, and she gives up almost immediately.

I carry her into her room and tuck her up into bed, pulling the leggings she is wearing off, leaving her in just my baggy T-shirt that she's been wearing since I got here. I hadn't noticed she was wearing one of my old T-shirts when I got here. It must have been one of the few I leave here for when I stay over. I love seeing her in my clothes, it does something almost primal to my body, but I push that to one side. Right now is definitely not the time for my cock to be hardening.

Once she's tucked in, I turn to leave. I know I'm not going to leave the flat, but I can sleep in the spare bedroom. That way I can be here for her if she needs me, but I can still give her space. I don't even manage to take a step before she grabs hold of my arm, pulling me towards her. I don't move because there's no strength at all behind her pull, but I do look at her.

"Please, Lee. Stay with me, just for tonight. I just want one more night with you." Her words are almost incoherent, the tears have only made her exhaustion worse. I don't know whether she's talking about me going home tomorrow and tonight being our last night. Or whether she doesn't want to see me again. I would take either of those two over the worst case scenario that's invading my brain as we speak. What if she's dying?

Surely her family wouldn't be stupid enough to leave her on her own if she is dying? Then again, Emmaleigh is so fucking stubborn, she might not have told anyone what's going on with her. Like me, she might have told her family that she's fine. She's been trying to tell me it's all because of these bad migraines she's been getting, but we both know that's not true. I don't doubt she hasn't been having migraines, but I've never known a migraine to leave someone needing crutches to be able to walk around. I have an awful feeling that whatever is going on with Em, it's something very serious, and she has no intention of telling anyone what's wrong with her.

Emmaleigh

Waking up the next morning, in Lee's arms, caused the gnawing ache in my chest to worsen. I'd come up with a plan when I was in the hospital. I need to push him away. Lee only wants to be friends, but that was before. He wanted to be friends with the normal version of me that he met a couple of months ago. The one who can go on fun days out together, and who isn't bothered that he doesn't want more.

I'm in a position now where I don't want anything serious, and the more time I spend with Lee, that's exactly what I want. I know he said he won't ever change his mind, but I can't risk it. I'm not strong enough to close off my feelings and still have him in my life, so he has to go. That thought alone cuts me deeper than every fucking nightmare I've encountered over the last week—and believe me, I've been living some of my worst nightmares. But with Lee, I can't risk it.

I know I should have told him that I don't ever want to see him again before I left the hospital, but I never expected him to turn up at my fucking doorstep. I shouldn't have let him in. I shouldn't have cried on his shoulder. And I definitely shouldn't have fallen asleep in his fucking arms. I remember he was going to leave, and my weak little heart begged him to stay. I've never felt so completely vulnerable, yet I trusted him not to hurt me.

For just a fraction of a second, I wanted to tell him everything. Not the piss poor version of events I've been practising for the last couple of days, that I've used on my friends and family. I'm not in the mood to tell everyone the ins and outs of my business, so I have told them what they need to know, which is not a lot. But as Lee held me in his arms and just let me cry, I really wanted to open up to him.

I wanted at least one person to know the whole truth, so I can have someone to speak to about everything, but he's not the right person. He only wants to be friends. I have to keep reminding myself he's not my boyfriend. If he was, I would tell him everything, but he's not. I don't want him to feel sorry for me when he finds out. I can't take having him look at me with pity, like he finally sees just how broken I really am.

He makes me breakfast that morning, and he does an incredible job of skating around the important subjects. There's been a couple of times, I've caught him looking at me, concern etched in those crystal blue eyes of his, and I've thought he would ask me what's on his mind. It's clear he has a lot on his mind, yet he doesn't even try to ask them, which is good because I don't want to lie to him.

"How are you feeling today?" he asks, in between spoonfuls of Coco Pops.

"Fine," I mutter, as I too take some small spoonfuls from my bowl. I can't bring myself to say anything more, I'm too busy rehearsing my speech in my head.

I hate the painful look on his face at my reply, but he skirts past it like a pro, and just starts telling me some stories about his work. I'm actually kinda pleased with the distraction. I know I need to do this, and soon, but I keep telling myself that a few more minutes won't be a problem.

After we've had breakfast, and Lee has put all the dishes in the dishwasher, without asking me, he takes hold of my hand and helps me to the sofa. I must have left my crutches over there, because they were definitely not within reach, and so I did appreciate his help, and I told him as much.

"You don't need to thank me, Beautiful. I want to help you, to make sure you're okay. You tell me what you want, and I will do it," he says, his face completely serious as he sits down beside me, taking my hand in his like it's second nature. Neither of us really thinks about what we're doing, we just clasp our hands together like that's exactly what our bodies were made to do.

This is it, this is the in I've been waiting for. But the more I tell myself I have to do it, the harder it is. Lee must see the war happening on my face, and he reaches out, taking my cheeks into his hands, and the feel of his warm palm against my skin sends shivers down my spine. As much as I hate it, I have to ignore how he makes me feel.

All I can do is stare at his alluring pink lips. I will always remember the last time we had sex, and I promised him anal. I will always remember the last night he held me in his arms as we slept. But I can't remember our last kiss. Or, at least, that's what I tell myself as I lean forward and capture his lips with mine.

At first Lee seems a bit unsure whether he should kiss me or not, but as soon as I swipe my tongue across his lower lip, all thought of him turning me down must have gone away. He allows me access and I deepen the kiss. He pulls me closer until our bodies are flush against each other, and I get lost in his taste.

I know I shouldn't have kissed him, especially knowing what I was about to do, but I couldn't help myself. I needed to feel him one more time. The only problem with getting one last taste of him is that he's my drug. Even just the slightest taste of him has me craving more. At this moment, I feel like I need his kiss just as much as I need air to breathe.

I'd like to say I'm the one who pulls away first, that I suddenly developed a backbone and the willpower to do the things I know will hurt me, but I haven't. I keep telling myself I just want one more minute. So when Lee pulls away, and we're both desperately trying to drag in more air, I allow myself one final moment with him.

"Did you mean what you said just now, that you'd do anything for me?" I ask, my voice barely above a whisper.

Lee glances at me, his big blue eyes looking hopeful. "Of course. Anything."

"I need some space. I'm so grateful you came over last night, but you can't do that again. I need some time to just deal with everything that's going on. When I'm with you, I can pretend it's not happening, that my body isn't failing me in the worst possible way. But, living in that dream state, it's not real. I have to deal with everything that's happened," I explain.

Lee shakes his head. "But I want to be here. I want to help you."

"No!" I snap, my voice is much harsher than I intended, but he's not listening to me, and I have to get this done, no matter how much I might hate it. "You didn't sign up for this, Lee. I'm not your girlfriend, remember. You didn't want a serious relationship. If you were my boyfriend, I wouldn't hesitate to let you in and have you help me, but you are not. You made that perfectly clear. I can't risk opening up to you, only for you to fuck off and start dating someone else. Believe me, if you aren't all in on this, you should walk away. I don't think my life is going to get any easier from here on out, so please, just let me go and forget all about me. It was fun while it lasted."

Lee's beautiful blue eyes widen with each word that falls off my tongue, and as soon as I finish talking, his face falls, leaving devastation in its wake. He looks like I just stuck my hand in his chest and pulled out his heart. I know because that's exactly how I feel right now.

It doesn't matter that I'm falling for him, or that he makes me feel more like myself than I ever have done. Even if he were to feel the same way about me, I'd still be pushing him away. He doesn't need to tie himself to someone who has no future.

"Em—" Lee tries to speak, but I cut him off.

"Please, don't argue with me on this. Keep looking, I know you will find a girl who means the world to you, and who makes you want to settle down. That's not me, and I can't keep pretending that it will be. It hurts too much, and I can't take that on top of everything else I'm dealing with," I explain, and as soon as I mention how much it's hurting me, I see Lee physically sag. The hurt is spread across his face for all to see, and my heart is breaking. I didn't know what pain really was before my heart snapped in two.

"We can't even talk about this, can we?" he pleads, his head shaking like he can't quite believe this is happening.

"We have talked, Lee. You know how you feel, and I know how I feel. I thought I could carry on pretending, hoping for the day you'd change your mind. But my life is different now. What I'm looking for is different. Besides, trust me when I tell you, getting as far away from me will be the best thing you ever do."

His head drops and he breaks eye contact with me, but just for a fraction of a second before he did, I thought I saw the ghost of a tear forming in his crystal blue eyes. We both sit there in silence for a few minutes, the awkwardness between us growing in a way it never has before. We've always been comfortable together in each other's silence, but this is different.

After a short while, Lee takes a big deep breath and shuffles away slightly before standing. "I better go." He doesn't move, so I reach over and grab one of the crutches to help me get up off the sofa. I watch as Lee starts to move forward, as though he's going to help me, but then he thinks better of it and stays where he is.

Once I'm upright, I try to give him a small smile, but even that's too painful. I feel like I'm ripping out a piece of my heart, and he's going to take it with him when he leaves. I will never be whole again, and my heart will never beat properly. I didn't realise it was incomplete until I met Lee, and suddenly this hole I've had my entire life was filled. My heart started beating properly for the first time, just for him. But now, he's going to take that piece of me with him, and I will never be whole again. I just wish he could leave a piece of himself with me, so I will have a part of him with me always. But it doesn't work like that. He doesn't care for me the way I do him, and so him leaving is the best thing for everyone.

Lee starts moving towards the front door, and I notice he goes slow as he walks, giving me time to follow along behind him. As soon as we're at the door, instead of opening it, he turns to face me. "Can I ask, do you know what's wrong with you?"

I take a big deep breath before I reply. "No, though they have their suspicions. I'm going for another test on Tuesday that will tell us for sure. I'm not going to say what it is until we know for sure. I don't think my brain can take any more maybes. That's all I heard in the hospital; it might be this or it might be that. I don't want any more maybes, only definitives."

I'm not just saying that because I don't want him to know. The honest answer is that I haven't been able to say it out loud yet, and I won't, until we know for sure what the diagnosis is.

"Okay, that's fair enough. I accept you will find it too hard for me to be in your life, when it's not the way you want, but for me, I'm going to find it so hard losing you. Over the past few months, you've become my best friend, and I will be lost without you. I'd like to text you from time to time, if you'd be okay with that? Maybe one day we can be friends?" he asks, that hopeful tone back to his voice, his eyes wide, almost pleading with me.

It's the look on his face that almost has me falling to a puddle on the ground. I want to let those big puppy dog eyes have whatever they want, but it doesn't work like that. I need to move on.

My face crinkles into a grimace and Lee sees it—he always notices even my slightest change. "I don't know, is my honest answer. Give me a little space, and if I can, I will text you and we can go from there. How does that sound?" I ask, hoping that will be good enough for him because it's all I have.

"Yeah, I can wait. But I really will miss you, Beautiful. Please know I'm here if ever you need me, just send me a message. You don't have to be alone." There's no judgement in his tone, but I can hear the inflection. He knows I plan on dealing with whatever the hell this turns out to be by myself.

I have always been someone who takes care of other people, and if I let people into my world right now, I will spend more time helping them to deal with my illness than I do actually looking after myself. That's exactly what happened at the hospital. I love my family to pieces, and I was grateful they took time out of their day to come and see me, but I ended up spending more time comforting them than they did me. It's how it's always been, and usually I can cope with it just fine, but with all this going on, I need to concentrate on myself. No distractions.

"Thank you," I say with a smile, but it doesn't quite reach my eyes.

Out of habit, Lee leans forward as though he's going to kiss me goodbye, and my breath hitches. My heart starts to race as my brain whirls, and for just a fraction of a second it's like everything freezes and I wait for him to kiss me.

It's like this every time, like my world pauses while he kisses me, but today is different. He seems to catch himself when he's almost in touching distance and at the last moment he turns his head to press a kiss against my cheek. It's so close to my lips, I can almost feel him right on the edge, but it's not enough. He lingers for just a moment before pulling back, leaving a burning spot on my cheek where his lips just were.

Tears begin to well up in my eyes, and I need him to leave so they can fall freely without him knowing. As he turns, I hear his breath hitch and I wonder if he's feeling the pain as much as I am.

"Goodbye, Em."

"Goodbye, Lee."

The door closes and I just about make it so I can collapse on my bed before the tears start to fall. Sobs wrack my body, and I don't ever think they will stop.

Emmaleigh

"Em, I swear to God, if you don't get your ass out of that bed right this damn second, I will come and drag you out myself," my best friend, Lucy, shouts loudly from the kitchen.

It's been almost two weeks since Lee left, and for the first few days, I actually had to take the SIM card out of my phone to stop me from texting him. I genuinely felt like an addict struggling to go cold turkey, thinking of all the different ways I could survive without my fix. I didn't just miss him, I craved him. And being without him, not having him in my life, even just a text, it hurt worse than any physical wound. Take it from the clumsy accident prone girl who has broken more limbs than the average person, pain in the heart hurts worse than anything else.

Naturally, when people couldn't get in touch with me, they started to panic. This led to a very long lecture from my mother, who threatened to move in with me if I ever worried her like that again. So, I got my phone up and running again, but my desire to hear from him was still there. Well... until a couple of days after the appointment I told Lee about. I hate when my mind drifts back there.

The doctors, after a lot of backwards and forwards whilst I was in hospital, they thought they knew what I had, but they needed me to have a lumbar puncture, which isn't a procedure they do at my hospital. So the following Tuesday, my dad drove me an hour down the road to our nearest specialist facility.

To say I was terrified is an understatement. As a nurse, I know what a lumbar puncture is, and I know how to perform one—not that I do, that's a job for specialist doctors—but I know nothing at all about what it feels like to have one.

As I laid there in a ball, with a nurse trying to keep me calm, while another nurse stuck a large needle into my spine, I tried to think of better things. They told me to find my happy place, as that helps. But in all honesty, I pushed my happy place away, and thinking about it—about him—does nothing but hurt.

After sticking the needle in my back repeatedly over around an hour, the nurse finally admitted she was unable to complete the procedure, and that I would need to come back in an hour and have it done under guided X-ray. Neither myself or my dad, who had been waiting for me, were very happy. My back was so bruised already, and I didn't like the idea of them trying again.

Thankfully, under guided X-ray they were able to do it within minutes, and I couldn't help but wonder why they didn't do it this way to start with. But if I thought the pain of the procedure was bad, it was nothing compared to the appointment to discuss the results.

My dad took me, and I was actually glad it was him. My dad hates hospitals, and so to make up for being uncomfortable, he always tried to make me laugh. I've been in and out of hospital since I was a kid, and we've developed a little routine now. He never talks about anything heavy, and instead spends his time trying to distract me.

This includes playing the hardest game of Eye Spy that anyone has ever played. You would think playing with a sick child means you dumb it down a little so they can win, but no. My dad is insanely competitive, and it actually became funnier trying to guess his really obscure answers. One of his more difficult, and therefore funniest, was in the very hospital waiting room we were in, and he said the letters 'EWS'.

I don't know how long I spent guessing before I finally conceded, and he told me the answer was 'Emergency Warning Sign'. How the hell a ten year old was supposed to get that, I will never know. But it made me laugh, which I think was the point.

Though, at this appointment, now that I'm older and a lot more knowledgeable, it's harder for Dad to distract me. Still, he tried, and he did manage to make me laugh a few times, which made the waiting time a little less anxious.

We were in with the doctors for almost fifteen minutes, but it may as well have been just a few seconds. As soon as he confirmed their suspected diagnosis, my world fell apart. A ringing sound blurred my hearing, and those fucking spots in my eyes started up again. My stomach rolled, and I didn't know if I was going to be sick or if it was just anxiety.

I have a condition now. A label. Something that will follow me around wherever I go. My life will change forever after this very moment, even if I don't want it to.

"The tests confirm you have Relapse Remitting Multiple Sclerosis. It's a neurological condition where your immune system attacks the healthy cells in your brain when they shouldn't. Depending on which area of the brain is affected, will determine what symptoms that relapse produces. I know this is a lot to deal with all at once, so we will refer you to our MS specialist nurse. Once you have come to terms with your diagnosis, we can get you started on treatment," the doctor explains, his voice displaying no emotion at all.

It's almost like he's reading from a script, and I'm the tenth person he's read it to just today. he sounds almost bored, but this is my fucking life. I don't want some cookie cutter explanation, I want something real.

I can feel the anger building the whole time he's talking, and I only pick up on bits as the rage is making me lose focus. When he finally stops his speech, I snap. "Why the hell do I have to come to terms with my diagnosis before I start treatment? You've just diagnosed me with a condition that will one day kill me, but in the meantime, my life will just deteriorate to the point it's unrecognisable. That's not something you come to terms with overnight, so why the hell do I have to wait for treatment?"

My dad places his hand on top of mine, but I shrug it off. I don't need *comfort, and I don't need him trying to calm me down. I'm anything but calm, and I want some fucking answers.*

"Treatment is long term and can be very strenuous on the body depending on which you choose, and most are still experimental with very little research. We need to know you're in the right place to make those kinds of decisions. And MS is not necessarily a disease that will kill you. Research is advancing—" he explains, but I cut him off before he can give me any more bullshit.

"Research may be expanding, but MS is still an incurable condition. It's still a degenerative condition. And most people with MS die on average ten years before people who don't have it—or sooner if they kill themselves, which is a high probability given the awful nature of the disease. Don't forget, doctor, I'm a nurse. I've cared for people with MS, in all stages. I know what it does to your body."

"Enough, Em. Please, just let the doctor speak," Dad snaps at me before turning back to the doctor. "Sorry about that, it's a lot to take in."

Fucking understatement of the century. Even though they told me this is what they suspected I had when I was in the hospital, I never let myself believe it. Hell, I would have taken a brain tumour because at least they can cut that shit out. This was probably the worst case scenario, and so of course it came true.

"I don't hear your ass getting out of bed," Lucy shouts again, pulling my brain out of the darkness that seems to be consuming me. No matter how hard I try, I can't stop reliving that moment. The moment my life changed, and since then, darkness has overwhelmed me.

I've spent most of my time wallowing in my room, refusing to answer the phone, simply sending texts every so often to let people know I'm okay. They sent me an appointment with the MS nurse, but I cancelled it. I told them I would rebook when I'm ready, but I'm nowhere near there yet. I know she's going to want to talk about me accepting where I'm at, but I don't accept it. All I can think is why the hell did this have to happen to me?

After over a week of radio silence, my best friend turned up on my doorstep and refused to leave until I let her in. She's been here for two days now, and I can tell she has a plan. We've been best friends since the first day of school at five-years-old. I know her, and I can read her every move. When she first arrived, it was all about showing me sympathy. Holding me while I cried, eating ice cream with me while we watched movies that made us cry even more.

Lucy hoped that having me cry it out would work, but when it didn't she's now moved on to tough love. Sadly for her, she's rubbish at being tough. I'm the tough, bitchy one. She's the nice one out of our little duo. So when she tries her best stern voice, I almost want to laugh. She comes stomping through, her long ginger hair flowing behind her and she cocks her hip when she reaches my bedroom.

"I'm serious, Em. You need to get your ass out of bed and have a shower. You stink," she snaps, before the guilt creeps in as it's not in her nature to be nasty. "Sorry, I just mean it would do you some good to shower and go outside."

I narrow my gaze at her and try my best not to be an asshole, but it feels like it's the only mode I have at the moment. "I will shower because even I feel icky, but I'm not going outside. If you're not happy with that you can fuck off."

My best friend flinches at the harshness of my words, but she holds her ground. "I will take the shower as a win, and we can work on the rest. I know you're struggling, Em. You need to talk to me, or if not me then someone."

"Talk about what?" I snap. "About how my life is over. About how I have to shower with a fucking old people's chair because I can't even stand up in my own fucking shower. Talk about how I'm too fucking scared to go to sleep because I don't know what state I will be in when I wake up. Talk about how I know I'm going to have to give up my dream job because people who are disabled can't work as nurses. Or talk about the fact I miss the one person in the world that I can't ever have."

She walks over slowly until she reaches the bed, where she perches on the edge. She moves slowly, so I can see what she's doing, and she reaches out with her arm to wipe away the stray tears I didn't even notice were falling. I've cried so much the past few days, they're almost like a permanent feature.

"Oh, Em. Most of those things are way out of my ability, and I think a specialist would really help you. But there is one of those I can help with. Why don't you just send him a text. He asked you to message him when you felt ready, so why don't you do it?" she asks, her face suddenly looking very naive.

"We both know that's a stupid fucking idea," I shout, the anger rippling just under the surface where it always is at the moment, forces me to lash out. "He didn't want a relationship with me before, so he really isn't going to want one now. I'm far too fucking broken to ever be in a relationship."

I didn't mean to say that aloud, but it's the truth. I genuinely believe nobody will ever want me knowing the condition I have. I don't know when, it could be soon, or it could be years in the future, but one day I will become a liability. I might lose the ability to care for myself, or even lose control of my bladder and bowel. I don't want a partner who has to be my carer too.

Even just thinking about all the ways my life will change, causes the darkness to descend. Going to the shop will no longer be a fun outing, it will result in unimaginable pain. Getting out of bed every fucking day will feel like a chore, one I'm not sure I want to complete. Even going on a night out won't be the same. I will need to prepare for it days in advance, and accept it will knock me out for a few days afterwards. Little things people take for granted are now big tasks for me. I don't want to become stuck in the shell of a body that continues to fail me.

No matter how many medications I take, no matter how much I try to fight it, this is my future. Well… it should be my future, but there's no way in hell I will ever allow myself to get that bad. I will not become a burden on anyone. I will end things long before they ever get that bad.

The more I think about ending things before they get worse, the more that idea becomes appealing to me. I'm at the start line now, and I have no idea how long it will take to get to the end, but I know it's not going to be a pleasant journey. I just don't know if I can keep going knowing that things are going to get a lot worse.

The more these thoughts circle through my mind the more the darkness begins to descend. I get up, and with the help of Lucy, I shower and get myself freshened up, but it's like I'm just on auto-pilot. I don't even remember doing half the things I did that day. It's like I'm just going through the motions, just existing.

When I get into bed that night, and I hear Lucy's light snores from the room next door, I pick up my Kindle and start reading the book I put down earlier. I lose myself in a world of shifter wolves, vampires, and a whole lot of sex. A world where there's no disease or depression, and where the main character isn't rejected by the man she loves.

I keep reading long into the night, not only desperate to escape the world I'm living in right now, but also because of the fierce need I have to stay awake.

The way multiple sclerosis happens, most of the relapses will occur while you're asleep. When your immune system should be protecting you, instead it's working overtime and has got confused, resulting in it taking out healthy parts of the brain that you need. This causes the white matter of the brain to become scarred, and the nerve pathways stop working.

Meaning, whatever bodily function that part of the brain controls, it won't be working anymore. No clue as to whether that will be permanent or temporary. I will just wake up that morning and MS will have taken something else from me. This relapse was the vision in my right eye, and the strength in my right leg. But who knows what will be next.

Although most of my sight has come back, my eye is definitely weaker. Same goes for my leg. I also have damage in my hip caused by walking funny for a couple of weeks. You see, when you do something your body doesn't like, you feel pain telling you to stop doing that, but when my leg was numb, I didn't have the pain receptors telling me what to do, and so it caused damage.

If I thought this relapse was bad, I can only imagine what the next one will bring. I know it's not sound logic, but it's all I have at the moment. My brain is a mess, clouded by darkness, and so even though I know I'm not thinking straight, it's all I have.

All I keep thinking is that if I don't sleep, I can't wake up with another relapse. You know you've hit rock fucking bottom when you're too afraid to even sleep.

When my fiction books don't keep me awake any more, I pick up my phone, and scroll all the way back to that first ever message with Carlos, AKA Lee. I read every message we ever sent each other, and I laugh at all the jokes and fun times we shared. My heart breaks a little more with each message I read, but I can't stop. Maybe I'm a glutton for punishment, or maybe I want to embrace the pain.

Or maybe it's just that I miss him so much I will take him any way I can get him. Either way I keep reading until my body gives out. As I feel sleep start to grab hold of me, I shed a tear. This time not for the life I've been dealt or my diagnosis. No, this one is for Lee. Because I think I've just realised that I'm in love with him, and we can't ever be together.

Lee

"For fuck's sake, Lee. I'm sick to death of you moping around. I'm bored," Craig moans as he picks up a random sock sitting on the side of my bed, rolls it into a ball and throws it at my head.

I'm sitting on my computer chair, just looking at my phone. I created a folder with all the pictures I ever took with Emmaleigh, and over the last few weeks, I've just been looking at them on repeat. I can't even begin to describe how much I miss her. If I thought the two weeks we had apart when we didn't see each other was bad, it's nothing compared to this.

At least during that time I was able to speak to her, text her, and I still felt connected to her in some way. This is torture. I think the worst thing is that I don't know if she's okay. My mind keeps replaying all her symptoms, and I kept looking for signs of ones she might not have told me about. Then I did the only thing a sleep deprived man could do, I Googled her symptoms. Let me tell you now, no good can come from trying to diagnose on Google. Now I'm not sure if she has a fucking brain tumour or a migraine.

I feel like the past couple of weeks I've just been existing, going to work, coming home, and just waiting. Waiting to hear from her. But I never do, and that fucking kills me.

"Fuck off, asshole. You sound like a petulant child, and I didn't even invite you here," I snap back at Craig, who has that annoying fucking grin on his face, like he knows exactly what he's doing by winding me up.

I put my phone away, because as much as it calms me to see her picture, it also drives me a little crazy just waiting for a text to come that I now realise isn't going to. I know I need to move on. Hell, Craig tells me I have to every fucking day, but I'm not ready to yet.

"I came to make sure you are alright. I may be an asshole, but you're still my best friend and I'm worried about you," he says, and it's the first time in a long time that I can hear he genuinely means it.

"I'm fine," I grumble, though I know he deserves a lot more than me being a dick to him when he's actually making an effort to be a nice person, which isn't something he does very often. It's just this is a really hard subject matter for me.

Craig chuckles, and I'm back to wanting to punch him. He must be able to see the scowl on my face as he holds his hands up, palms facing me in an effort to calm me down. "Relax, I was just going to say that you are definitely not fine, and I don't blame you. But, I do have some news for you."

"What news?" I ask.

"Emmaleigh has had a diagnosis, although it's not something she's divulged to people yet. She's on long-term sick leave from work, but they believe she will be starting treatment soon. I got the impression that this isn't something she will be cured of, but she can manage it. That's all I could find out for you," Craig explains, and I sit there with my mouth open wide, a mixture of shock and concern plastered across my face.

"How?" I mumble, unable to even get a full sentence out. Has he been talking to Em, but she won't talk to me? If so, I don't think I will be able to hold myself back from killing him.

"Remember when we went to the strike?" he asks, and I nod. Of course I can't forget that day. It was our last proper day together. "Well, she introduced me to a few of her friends that day. One of them, Bessy, well... I took her out last night to get the information you needed."

I shake my head, wondering why the hell, even just for a minute, I thought he'd changed. "Please tell me you didn't fuck one of Emmaleigh's friends just to get answers."

A sheepish look spreads across his face and I can't hold back my groan. "I didn't sleep with her, but only because she didn't want to. Apparently she's doing this new thing where she doesn't sleep with people on the first date," he grumbles, and now it's my turn to laugh.

"Ooh, she turned you down!"

Craig shakes his head. "No. No she did not. We're going to see each other again."

"When?" I ask, my brows raised in question.

Craig's brow furrows like he's doing a complex maths puzzle. "Erm...we didn't agree on a date yet."

I bite my lip to help back the chuckle that's fighting to break free. My friend is so used to being the one who lets people down, and who uses women, he doesn't even realise it's happening to him. Emmaleigh told me all about Bessy, and even before this I couldn't help but think she's the type of girl who would give Craig a run for his money. She likes to play around, and clearly Craig didn't measure up.

I see the moment Craig realises he's been played, and his face drops, only to be replaced quickly by his usual mask of indifference. "Enough about me, what about the information about Em? Was that not useful to you?" he asks, and my heart aches every time her name is mentioned. I appreciate he was just trying to do something nice for me, but it's hardly going to help me to move on from her.

"I'm grateful, honestly. It's just I still don't have any answers, only more questions, and it's the lack of answers that's killing me," I admit.

Craig shakes his head. "That's not it, man. I'm sorry to be the one to tell you this, but I had hoped you'd have worked this out by now. Of course you want to know what's going on with Em, and to know that she's okay. But the main reason you are pining after her like a love sick teenager is because you have feelings for her. You can say all you want that you didn't or that you didn't want a relationship with her but that's all bullshit. You were in a relationship, and the only person who didn't realise that was you. You care about her—maybe even love her—and that's why you miss her so much. You just have to be honest with yourself."

With each word Craig says my heart starts to race. He's saying things I've only thought about in the dead of night, when I'm alone in my room and all I have to keep me company are her memories. I've been bullshitting myself for a while, telling myself I didn't like her in that way. Even after the talk with Mum, and she had me reconsidering what it actually means to be in a relationship, I still wasn't sure. It's hard to undo years of negative thinking.

But the more I think about it—her—the more I think it is possible I had real feelings for her. Because the truth is, I do miss her. I miss her to the point it physically hurts me, and I don't have a fucking clue what to do about it.

Thankfully, Craig doesn't press the issue any further. That's not who he is. He's the sort of person who will say just enough to get you thinking about it, but not enough to actually have an adult conversation. Don't get me wrong, I think if I wanted to have a proper talk with him about my feelings—which I absolutely fucking don't—he'd do it, because he can be a good friend when he wants to be. I just can't think of anything worse than opening up about my feelings while he sits there trying not to laugh.

He does manage to distract me with a new Playstation game he brought over though, and we lose ourselves in the game for a couple of hours. The great thing about gaming is you really do have to immerse yourself in the game, which doesn't leave time for thinking about anything else. I can lose myself for a while, and all thoughts of real life fall away. I don't have to talk to Craig about anything other than the game, which is perfect.

Just as the current battle we're in ends, my phone buzzes from in my pocket. I don't even hesitate, I drop the controller and pull my phone out. The only people who ever text me are my parents, who are downstairs, Craig, who is sitting next to me, and Em.

My heart skips a beat as I quickly type in my passcode to open the phone, but then I see the text is from a number I don't recognise and I can feel my body sag. It's not her.

I open the text anyway, getting ready to delete it straight away, as I'm convinced it's just spam. But as soon as I read the first line, I'm hooked.

> **UNKNOWN**
>
> Hi Lee, I'm Lucy. You don't know me but I'm Emmaleigh's best friend. She would kill me if she knew I was doing this, but I took your number from her phone. She's in a really bad place right now, and her stubbornness means she's refusing to ask anyone for help. I'm really starting to worry about her. I can't tell you what's going on, as that's not my story to tell, but I can tell you that her refusal to deal with her situation is leading to depression. We have all tried to help her, but we can't. I know she misses you a lot, and I also know she thinks she has a good reason for pushing you away. I've never met you so I could be wrong about this, and I'm sorry if I am, but I think Emmaleigh means more to you than you maybe let on. If that's true, please don't let her push you away. More than anything right now, she needs people who will fight for her. But, I only want you to do this if you truly care about her, in the way she deserves. If you can't go all in, then don't bother. But if you can, she will be at home all day tomorrow. I know you don't normally work Saturdays. If you want her, please come and fight for her.

I don't know how many times I read the message, I just sit there frozen staring at the screen. I must have sat there for a bit too long, clearly ignoring whatever Craig was saying to me, as he snatches the phone out of my hand to read the message himself. His face lights up and he starts to cheer.

"What the fuck are you cheering about?" I ask, my brow furrowed in confusion.

Craig laughs that cocky laugh, and I have to clench my hand into a fist once again. The urge to punch my best friend is growing stronger every time he opens his mouth. "I'm cheering because now you can stop fucking moping. You can finally go and get your girl."

I shake my head. "It's not that fucking simple."

Craig dramatically throws himself onto my bed with a groan, his hands flying to grip his head, like he's trying to tear his own hair out. Talk about being dramatic. "Are you fucking kidding me? This is exactly what you've been waiting for. You know Emmaleigh is missing you the way you're missing her. You know she needs your help. So you have to go to her." He says it like it's so obvious and simple, but it's really not.

"It's not like that, Craig. First of all, this is Lucy telling me this, not Em. Em hasn't texted me like she said she would, which means she still wants space from me. Even if I believe what Lucy is saying about Em pushing me away, there's still the big fucking obstacle in the way. Lucy said it herself, I can only go to Em if I'm certain I want to be with her. I don't want to hurt her more."

My head sinks into my hands, and I feel like it might explode. Craig shuffles over to the edge of the bed and places his hand over mine, directing me to look at him. I know he can see the pain in my eyes, because he gives me a small smile.

"Look, I know absolutely nothing about relationships, but one thing I consider myself a bit of an expert in is you. You've been my best friend for almost fifteen years, and I know you. I saw you with Emmaleigh at the strike, and even if you aren't sure how you feel, take it from me when I tell you that you are perfect for each other. Both of you lit up whenever the other one was near. I know the idea of a relationship terrifies you, but I truly believe you will regret it if you don't give this a try."

I mull his words over and over in my mind, wondering if he's right. After Craig leaves for the evening, all I'm left with are my thoughts. Pretty soon tomorrow will be here, and I will have to make a decision on what to do. The truth is, it physically hurts not having her in my life. I miss her with every fibre of my being, and the more I think about it, the more I realise what that probably means. I think I was falling for Em all along, I just didn't realise it.

Lee

I woke up early the next morning. After my revelation the previous night, it became obvious what I needed to do. Emmaleigh has spent the last few months fighting for us, and now it's my turn. How the hell did I not notice I was falling for her all along?

I realised, much to my annoyance, that Craig was right in what he said yesterday. We were in a relationship, and I was the only one who didn't know. Em knew, and she was fighting for us, even when she knew she could get hurt. I could—and probably will—berate myself over how I treated her, but that's not going to fix anything. Instead I need to get my ass over to her flat and show her that we still have something, and now I'm fighting for us. I will not let her push me away this time.

I'm ashamed to admit I sat in the car outside of her apartment for far longer than I should. Nerves are getting the better of me, and my heart is racing so much I can hear it beating in my ears. I do the usual breathing techniques that help, but it's barely making a dent this time. My hands are clutching the steering wheel so tightly my knuckles are white, and I'm pretty sure they're going to slide off any minute if they get any sweatier.

After giving myself yet another mental pep talk, I finally open the door and walk up to Em's flat. I straighten down the band T-shirt I'm wearing, and make sure I look decent. I haven't dressed smart because Emmaleigh would think that was weird, but I've obviously tried to look nice. I'm wearing the dark jeans that are tight around my ass and thighs, because I know Em loves these. The band T-shirt I'm wearing sits snugly over my abs, and the dark colours suit my skin tone—or at least that's what Em has always said. I've spiked my black hair a little, too, so it's the perfect messy style she likes.

As I knock on the door, I'm not only filled with the sense of dread and anxiety, as I wonder if she's going to reject me, I'm also filled with excitement that I get to see her again. It's been just over three long fucking weeks, and I have missed her every single day. Even if she weren't sick, she would still have been on my mind and I would have been thinking about her, wondering how she is and what she's doing. But add her sickness into the mix, and it's a wonder I have any fingernails left at all. My nerves are frazzled as all I've done for the last three weeks is worry about her, wondering if she's okay.

Even if she doesn't take me back, and this Hail Mary attempt fails, I would just like to know if she's okay. Maybe then I can get some sleep at night.

It takes a while for her to get to answer the door, but when she does, a look of pure shock spreads across her face. For a second, I'm sure she almost looks pleased to see me, but that's quickly replaced by a scowl I'm not used to seeing on her pretty face.

"What are you doing here?" she snaps, her tone sounding much nastier than I ever would have thought she was capable of.

I take in the prickly girl in front of me, and I'm shocked by what I see. Her long purple hair now looks dull and lifeless, and it's pulled up into a messy bun on the top of her head. Her normally bright bluey-grey eyes look dark and sunken in, with big black circles surrounding them. Her face looks pale and almost ashen. I can still see her natural beauty, but it's hiding behind the girl standing in front of me.

It's obvious she's lost a little weight, and she doesn't have as many curves as she usually does. She's wearing a baggy T-shirt, and my heart stutters a little when I realise it's one of mine. I must have left it here some time. She's wearing a big black cardigan over the top, and as soon as she sees me looking at the shirt, she pulls the cardigan closed so I can't see it anymore. She's paired those with her usual black leggings and bare feet.

I'm pleased to see she's not using crutches anymore, but it's clear just from the way she's standing, her posture isn't quite back to normal. Not only does she look unwell, she looks to be in pain. Not just physically, although that is plain to see, it's also obvious she's struggling mentally too. Her eyes that are normally so vibrant, showing off her amazing personality, now look dead and almost lifeless. What the hell happened to my beautiful, vibrant girl?

"I came to see you. Are you going to let me in or are we just going to stand here?" I ask, trying to hold firm. If she's going to try and push me away, I need to make sure she can't.

She doesn't say a word, just leaves the door wide open, turns her back on me and begins to walk into the living room. I don't miss the slight limp and hobble she has going on when she moves, or the fact she has her hand out on the wall, guiding her. Clearly walking isn't easy, but she's given up on using the crutches. So fucking stubborn.

I follow behind, closing and locking the door once I'm inside. As I walk into the living room, I look around, and it's obvious Lucy has been here cleaning up. The place looks far too clean for Em. I always used to joke with her that although her house was never dirty, given she always dusts and hoovers, neither of our parents would class it as tidy.

Emmaleigh has a habit of just leaving stuff lying around. Normally you can't even see the dining table, as when she's finished with stuff, that's her dumping ground. Hair curlers, hair brushes and products, even a discarded bra, are all usually left on the table. But not today. Today it looks immaculate, and that's not at all like Emmaleigh.

She throws herself onto the sofa, trying her hardest not to look at me. I take off my jacket and shoes, leaving them where I always do and walk into the kitchen the same way I always did. I turn to face Em, and I notice the way her brow is furrowed, like she can't quite work out what I'm doing.

"Do you want a drink?" I ask, holding up the can of Coke I've just taken out of the fridge.

Her eyes bore into mine, and she looks pissed. "Are you really offering me one of my own drinks while you help yourself?"

"Well, you weren't exactly playing the dutiful host by offering me a drink, so I thought I'd get my own. Offering you one was just my way of being polite. So do you want one or not?" I reply calmly, trying not to let her snarkiness get to me.

"Fine," she snaps, and I just roll my eyes at her. I take a second can and place that one beside her on the coffee table, before sitting next to her on the sofa. I crack my can open, take a drink and wait for her to do the same.

She picks up the can and tries to lift the ring pull with her thumb. After a couple of failed attempts she tries with her other fingers but is unsuccessful. She doesn't even look at me, she just slams the can back down on the table in a huff.

"What the fuck are you doing here? I told you I didn't want to see you again!" she shouts, clearly taking her anger out on me instead of the Coke can.

"Would you like me to open it for you?" I offer, completely ignoring her childish tantrum. It's so unlike Emmaleigh, and I can see the hurt in her eyes. Whatever is going on with her, it's really getting to her.

Wordlessly, she passes the can over to me, and I open it before passing it back. She takes a drink, places it on the side and mumbles a quick thank you, which makes me smile. "I'm serious, why are you here?" This time, instead of sounding snarky or angry, she sounds almost despondent, like she's a second away from crying, and it takes every ounce of strength I have to just sit here, to not pull her into my arms. But I know she's not ready for that yet. She needs to know I'm here for good, no matter what is wrong with her. And I really mean that.

"I gave you some time to call me, but you didn't, so I decided to come to you. Not because I want to know what's wrong. You can talk to me about that if you decide you want to. But the reason I came here is because I miss you so fucking much. Every single day since I last saw you has been consumed by thoughts of you. Every time my phone has beeped, I've hoped it was you. Every night I fall asleep wishing you were by my side, and every morning that I wake up without you feels wrong."

I've practised what I wanted to say to Emmaleigh a million times over the last twelve hours, but no amount of preparation could have made the words sound that powerful. Looking into her beautiful bluey-grey eyes, no matter how dull they look, I'm reminded of the girl I care so deeply about, and I couldn't help but put all those emotions into my words. I'm clearly not great at telling people how I feel, and the idea of doing this scares the shit out of me, but I want her to feel how much she means to me just by my words.

Tears start to form in her eyes, and I hope like hell they're happy tears. She blinks them away before they have a chance to fall, but even just for a moment, I saw how much she appreciated what I had to say. I saw the happiness shining in her eyes, but that was quickly replaced by the dark cloud that seems to be hovering over Em.

"It doesn't matter if you miss me. It doesn't change anything. We can't be together, and all you're doing is making things worse by dragging everything up again," she snaps.

I shake my head, ignoring what she's saying, even if her words are like knives to my heart. "It's not too late. I know I should have realised how I felt before, but maybe it took losing you for me to finally be sure how much I really do like you. We can talk about all the reasons I had for not wanting to be in a relationship another time, but the thing you need to know is that it was because of my issues. Some life long prejudices that I've had, that I'm working on. But never, not once, were they about you. In fact, I always used to say that if ever I were to get a girlfriend, it would be you. What I never realised is that I was already in a relationship, I just couldn't see it, but you could," I explain, as I slowly reach over and take her hand in mine.

At first I expect her to pull away, and I think for just a moment, she considers it, before eventually she relaxes and allows me to lace our fingers together. Where our palms meet, I can feel electricity humming through my nerves, and it feels like my body is alive for the first time in weeks.

I look up to see Emmaleigh staring down at where our hands are connected, and now she's not holding back the emotions. Tears are rolling down her cheeks, and I want to reach over to wipe them away, but she beats me to it with her free hand. When she looks up at me, I've never seen her look so lost and in pain. My heart aches for her, and I want to hold her in my arms until the pain goes away.

"I wish you'd have had this epiphone sooner, Lee. Before, I wanted nothing more than for you to realise we were in a relationship, and for you to commit to us fully. It's all I wanted, but now it's not an option. I'm not looking for a commitment, Lee. I'm sorry," she explains, as she lowers her gaze back down to staring at our hands. She can't make eye contact with me because she knows I will see that she's lying. She thinks she doesn't want a relationship, but that's not true. It's just another way for her to push me away.

"That's bullshit and we both know it," I snap, and her eyes fly up to meet mine, startled by my tone. "You can bullshit yourself as much as you like, but we both know the only reason you're saying this is because you want to push me away. I have no idea why you think you need to, but you don't. I've made my mind up. You fought for us at the start, now it's my turn. I'm fighting for you, Emmaleigh, and I'm not going to stop."

She snatches her arm back, pulling her hand away from mine, before pushing me hard against the shoulder. "Fuck off, Lee. If I tell you to walk away, you have to trust I'm doing what's best for us both."

"Why? Because of your illness? Is that what this is about?" I ask, but she stays silent, so I continue. "I have no idea what illness you have, but no matter how bad it is, I will stand by you through it all. If you will have me."

Her eyes fly back up to meet mine, and now she looks so vulnerable it breaks my heart. I can see the hope reflecting back at me, the emotion she's so afraid to feel. "You say that because you don't know."

"Well... tell me then. What do you have to lose? I will either run away like you think, I will let you push me away because I'm too scared to stay, or I'll be true to my word and stand by your side. Either way, you have nothing to lose, right?" I ask.

This time it's Em who reaches over and grabs my hand, her eyes wide and pleading. "I will tell you, but you have to promise me something. Please don't stay with me out of pity. If you find out what it is, and genuinely still believe it doesn't matter, then that's okay. But don't stay because you feel you have to."

I nod my head and give her a small smile. "Em, over the last couple of weeks I've been going crazy wondering what you might have wrong with you. In the notes app on my phone, you can see the illnesses I've narrowed it down to. I've also made a list, under each illness, of ways I can help you to deal with it, if I got the diagnosis right. But even if I didn't and the diagnosis isn't in my phone, the point I'm trying to make is that I've thought through a million different scenarios, and no matter how bad it is, none of them ever resulted in me leaving you. I want to be with you, and I'm not letting anything get in the way," I explain, handing my phone over to her so she can take a look. She takes it from me with her free hand, but she doesn't open it. Instead, she puts it on her knee and takes a big deep breath. I can see the fear and anxiety in the way she shuffles around in her seat.

"I have a neurological condition called Multiple Sclerosis, but people call it MS for short. Without going into too much detail, my immune system doesn't work correctly and it attacks healthy parts of my brain. It's a degenerative condition, meaning each time I have a relapse, I have no idea what part of my body will be affected. I could end up in a wheelchair, unable to move, unable to eat, unable to talk or control my own bodily functions. I will be trapped in my own failing body," she explains, trying to keep her voice as controlled as possible, but I can hear the shaking as tears flow freely down her cheeks.

As soon as she's finished, her tears turn into sobs, and I can't hold back anymore. I reach over and pull her over into my arms. At first she resists, but I stand firm, and it doesn't take long until she's curled up in a ball on my lap, her cheek against my chest as I stroke the silky purple hair out of her eyes, before wiping away her tears. I hold her while she cries and cries, and my heart breaks for her.

As she's crying it gives me a moment to think about what she just told me. That she has MS. It was one of the conditions I had on my phone, and I have to admit, it's one of the ones I was praying she didn't have. The idea of her having something incurable is like a stab to the heart because I know, no matter what I do, I can't make her better. Still, it doesn't change what I said. I still want to be with her.

I think about everything Emmaleigh said about MS, all the ways it can affect her body. I knew a little of that from my research, but I didn't know all that. The idea that her body could fail her in such a way is heartbreaking, but it doesn't change my mind. If her legs fail her, I'll carry her. If she can't eat, I'll feed her. If she can't speak, we will learn sign language together. If I want to be with her, which I very much do, then I will just have to learn to deal with this part of her.

I don't know how long she cries for, but when she's finally finished, she looks up at me, a shy almost sheepish expression on her face. Her cheeks are bright red from all the crying, her eyes puffy, but she's still the most gorgeous girl I've ever seen. "Sorry about that," she mumbles.

Em tries to crawl off my lap, but I hold her firm, and as she looks up at me through hooded eyes, I can see she's confused. "You aren't going anywhere, Beautiful. I meant what I said, I know MS is a serious condition that will affect you for the rest of your life, but you don't have to battle it alone. I will be with you every step of the way. I'm here now, and I promise you this with all my fucking heart. I'm going nowhere, Beautiful. I was always yours."

As soon as the words are out of my mouth, I lean down and seal my lips over hers. It starts as a sweet kiss, but as soon as we both get a taste for each other it deepens quickly. Her tongue sweeps across my lower lip and I grant her access. The kiss is deep and bruising, like we both can't get enough of each other.

Em shuffles in my lap until she's straddling me, her knees either side of my hips, her core sitting right over my hardening dick. I can't help myself, I grab hold of her hips, pulling her down onto my shaft, hating the fact we're separated by our clothes. Her moan rings loudly, but is swallowed by my mouth as I kiss her more feverishly.

Her hands rake down my front, right the way down until she reaches the hem of my T-shirt, and she pulls it up, exposing my abs. She lightly trails her fingers over every hard ridge, and I can't hold back the shudder of pleasure that rips through me. That's when she reaches down and begins to pull my shirt up.

I pull away slightly, both of us panting as we try to catch our breaths, and I take her cheeks in between my hands, forcing her to look at me. "Em, we don't have to do this. We don't need to rush. I meant what I said. I'm not going anywhere."

"Lee, if you really mean that, you will give me this. I promise to try and make this work with you—even though I'm convinced you're going to leave if it gets too hard—but right now, I need you to make me feel like the girl I was before. I don't want to think about my MS. Please, can you do that for me?" she pleads.

"I hate that you don't trust I'm going to stay. But I know I brought that on myself. Only time will show you I'm serious. If you're sure this is what you want, then I'm all in. So... do you want to be my good girl?" I ask as I pull her down against my hard length once more, rubbing against her covered clit.

She moans loudly as her eyes flare for the first time since I got here. "Yes, please. I want to be your good girl. Please can you fuck me hard and fast. I need you to make me feel like I did before."

I pull her lips to mine, just a short but passionate kiss that tells her everything she needs to know. "You are still the same girl, Em. I will fuck you hard and fast now, because I've missed you so fucking much over the last few weeks, I don't think I will last. But after that, I'm going to spend all day and all night loving you the way you should be loved, and you're going to do exactly as I tell you. Understand?"

She nods her head, but then remembers she's supposed to use her words. "Yes, Sir. I will be your good girl."

As soon as she says those words, it's like we both spring into action. I move her so she's kneeling above me, and it's just enough for me to pull all the clothes from her body, and throw them on the floor in the middle of the living room. As she leans over to her right side, putting all her weight on her right hip, she winces, and I grab hold of her.

"Are you okay?" I ask, as she continues taking off my shirt, and unbuttons my jeans. She's clearly not bothered by the pain, but I am. Any pain she has should only be there to heighten the pleasure, nothing else. I hold her body firm, one hand on each hip, making sure not to press too tightly on the right side.

"My right hip just twinges sometimes. It's okay now," she says, as she leans in and presses a kiss to my neck. I know she's trying to distract me by going for that sweet spot, but it's not going to work.

"If it hurts—"

She cuts me off before I can finish my sentence. "I will tell you. Now, please will you fuck me."

I reach down and pull my cock out, shuffling my jeans and boxers down enough that I can flick them off with my legs. My cock's rock hard, the purple head appears engorged with pre-cum leaking for the tip. I wrap my hand around the base, and slowly move my hand up and down a couple of times, causing more pre-cum to pool on the tip.

Em, who is still straddling my lap, looks down at my cock as it stands tall between us. I reach over with my free hand and run my finger between her pussy lips. As I drag my finger through her slit, as soon as I feel how wet she is, I can't help but groan. "So wet, Beautiful. Is this all for me?"

She nods her head. "Yes, Sir. It's always for you. Please can I ride your cock?" She bites her lip, her eyes dark with desire. Fuck, she's the most gorgeous girl I've ever seen.

"You can, but only if you tell me that you're mine," I say, as I continue to rub my finger lightly over her sensitive nub.

"What?" she asks, clearly confused with all the sensations going on in her body.

"You heard me, Beautiful. We can talk about it properly later, but I want to know that you are mine. That you are my girlfriend."

Her breath hitches, and this time I don't think it's caused by my finger on her clit, though I think that may be helping a little. I have to stop fisting my cock, as it won't be long before I blow my load right here, if she keeps looking at me like that.

"You really mean that, don't you? Even after everything I just told you?" she mutters, in between whimpers as I continue sliding my finger through her wet folds.

"I really mean it. I'm not going to say those three special words until I know I mean them for sure, but I don't think I'm far off. You are mine, Emmaleigh, and I am yours," I tell her, as I place a kiss on the side of her lip.

"You are?" She sounds almost shocked.

"Beautiful, like I said before, I was always yours, I just didn't know it."

As soon as I finish my sentence, her mouth is on mine, and I let her take every bit of pleasure she wants as she devours me with her tongue. "I was always yours, too," she says, as she uses her knees to raise herself off my lap, just enough, whilst still straddling me.

Making her intentions clear, I help her line up my cock with her hole, making sure to spread some of her juices around the tip so it will go in easier. Em slowly lowers herself down, and as soon as her hot, wet entrance touches my tip, I throw my head back in a groan. I have to force myself to pay attention, as I want to watch her tight pussy swallow all of my cock.

Em lowers herself slowly, but it doesn't take her long to envelop all of my cock until it's seated deep in her pussy. Once I've bottomed out, she sits there for a moment, just getting used to my size. This position allows me to go deeper, and her hot cunt clamps around my shaft like a vice. It feels fucking amazing.

As Em adjusts to the sensation, I lean over and take one of her nipples into my mouth, while I tweak the other with my free hand. I suck and nibble on her engorged nub until Emmaleigh is panting and moaning. It doesn't take her long to start moving.

Slowly she pulls herself up off my cock, leaving just the tip inside, before she plunges all the way back down. Each time I hit deep inside her, she cries out loudly, and my groans mingle with hers. She does this a few times, and I let her take what she needs, but as I feel the tell-tale tingle in my balls, I decide to take over.

Taking hold of her hips, I use them to help lift her on and off my cock, whilst also tilting my pelvis to thrust even further. I control the pace, giving her all the help I can as she rides my cock, her tits bouncing away in front of my face, and she's never looked more beautiful or confident.

I still remember the girl a few months ago who was afraid to show me her body, but not this girl. This Emmaleigh is using her body to take what she wants, and fuck does she look amazing doing it. Her cries of pleasure, as she begs me for more, and to let her come are loud and proud. She knows what she wants and has no reservations about telling me.

"Are you going to come, Beautiful? Do you want to be a good girl and come all over my cock?" I ask, as I reach down and press my finger over her sensitive clit. That's all it takes to get her to the edge. I bite my lip, determined to hold off until she's come first.

"Fuck... yes. Please, Sir. Please... can I-I... come on your cock?" she begs, her voice breathy as she moans loudly each time I brush my finger over her clit.

I can feel her pussy walls starting to clamp around my cock, as she gets impossibly wetter. I know she's close. She's just waiting for me. "Yes, Em. Be a good girl and come now," I demand.

That's all it takes to throw her over the edge, a loud cry filling the room as her body trembles beneath my touch. Her pussy clamps around me so tightly, and the feel of her walls pulsating around me is all I need to come alongside her.

My cock explodes, shooting my load deep within her pussy as my cries of pleasure mix with hers, creating the most beautiful symphony as we fall apart in each other's arms.

We both gather our breaths, but we stay like this, clinging to each other like we're afraid this might be over the minute I pull out. I guess, maybe there's a part of me that is worried about that. We didn't exactly talk things through before we threw ourselves into the sex.

Our sex life has never been a problem. In fact, it's fucking amazing, but we do still need to communicate with each other. Clearly Em is on the same wavelength as me because just as I open my mouth to say something, she beats me to it.

"Did you really mean what you said before? That my MS doesn't bother you? Because I would totally understand if you want to walk away. We weren't really together when I got diagnosed, so you're off the hook. You can leave and never look back, and that would be okay." She tries her best not to make eye contact with me, but I'm not going to let her get away with that. I place one hand on her chin and tilt her head until she's looking at me. Her beautiful bluey-grey eyes have some sparkle back in them, and I can see how hopeful she looks.

"I know all of that, but I stand by what I said. I don't care that you have MS. I'm not going anywhere," I state firmly and a smile spreads across her face. It's so gorgeous, I can feel my exhausted dick beginning to spring back to life, still warm in her wet pussy.

"Things might get worse before they get better. But, whatever happens, please don't leave me. I think I really need you, Lee," she says, her voice full of a million promises, each one I vow to keep.

"I promise, no matter what. I'm here for you."

Emmaleigh

The next few days with Lee pass by in a blur. It's like we're both just existing in our own little bubble, the outside world going by around us while we ignore it all. And as much as I've enjoyed the last couple of days, in so many ways, that's exactly what we've been doing. We've been ignoring everyone, but we both know the time is ticking closer and very soon we're going to have to see if this relationship we've created for ourselves can survive under the pressures of the real world.

I would love nothing more than to stay in our own little bubble. I mean, the sex alone is enough to keep me hooked. I eventually talked him into trying anal with me, and despite it stinging a lot to start with, I actually really like it. It made me want to try so much more with Lee. I think I would trust him with any sexy, adventurous thing he wants to try.

But the longer it goes on, the more I can tell Lee knows this little bubble we've created isn't real. I really do love the sex, but if I'm being honest, I'm using it to avoid dealing with my issues. What better way to keep me up all night, than sex?

But as each day passes, I can tell Lee notices more and more of the health-related things I try to hide. He's giving us this time together because not only do we need it, we deserve it. But pretty soon, we have to get back to reality, and that scares me. All that means for me is that the darkness will return and it will cast its ugly shadow over the happiness I've found with Lee.

On Sunday night I expect Lee to go home, but he doesn't. He tells me he has some time off work, and he stays with me. When it gets around to Wednesday, and we're sitting across from each other having breakfast, Lee bursts our bubble.

"Don't you have an appointment with your MS nurse today?" Lee asks, and my mouth drops open.

"How did you know about that?" I ask. I do have an appointment, but I have absolutely no intention of attending. I wanted to cancel last week, but Lucy wouldn't let me. Then, if I'm being completely honest, I allowed Lee to distract me and I forgot all about it.

"I saw it on your calendar," he says, pointing to the calendar I have up on the wall in the kitchen. It's the one I make for myself every year, full of family photos. I turn to look at it, and see Lucy has written the appointment on it, along with big red words that say, 'DO NOT CANCEL!' and 'YOU HAVE TO ATTEND!'. I'm not surprised Lee saw the bloody thing.

"I'm not going," I mumble, deliberately not meeting his judgemental eyes.

"Em, nobody can force you to do anything you don't want to do, but from all the reading I've been doing, people with MS say that the support they receive from their MS team is invaluable. Surely their aim is to help you?" he asks, and my eyes snap up to meet his. His stunning blues are looking back at me, and I'm surprised that they're not filled with judgement like I thought they'd be. Instead, he just looks concerned.

I take in his words for a moment, and I know he's right. Whenever anyone from the MS team has come on to the ward to help a patient, they've always been one of the more helpful, more knowledgeable teams that we deal with. But in all honesty, I've only maybe looked after two patients with MS, in my whole career, probably because they would usually end up on a specialist neurological ward, as opposed to my emergency treatment ward.

I think that's part of what scares me. People in the hospital are going to read that I'm a nurse and at first they're going to feel sorry for me because I'll end up losing my job over this, but then they'll look at me like I should know the answers. I should know what the best treatment option is, or even how MS works. I was taught the basics in medical school over eight years ago, but as it's not something I've worked with or specialised in, it's not something I know a lot about.

Lee clears his throat, trying to get my attention, since I must have drifted off into my own little black hole—something I've been doing regularly. Lee helps keep the darkness at bay, for now, but it's like the dark cloud is just waiting around the edges, getting ready to descend.

"They told me when I was diagnosed that I couldn't start treatment until I've come to terms with my MS. I think it's fair to say, I couldn't be further away from dealing with my diagnosis, so I just didn't want to waste their time," I admit, being honest about my reasons for the first time. I didn't even tell Lucy this is why I cancelled last time. If this thing between myself and Lee is ever going to work, I have to be honest with him about everything.

He reaches over the table and takes my hand in his, slowly brushing his thumb across the back of my palm. It's such a soothing gesture, but I can feel my body starting to heat at the same time.

"I don't think you're wasting their time, Beautiful. I think that's exactly what their job is, to help you deal with it all. And I know you probably think they will be judging you because you're a nurse, but they really won't. If that is something that's worrying you, why don't I come along. Then they will have to dumb it down to my level," he asks with a smile on his face.

"You'd really go with me?" My voice becomes much higher in pitch than I intended.

"Yeah, of course. I'm off anyway, so why not. Honestly, I'd like to hear if there are any ways I can be helping to support you. You don't have to do this alone," he states firmly and I scrunch my eyes closed.

Whenever he says things like this, it creates a range of feelings; I'm overwhelmed and so fucking happy he wants to take an interest in my life, but I'm also so terrified, it's scary. I know he keeps saying he's in this for the long-haul, no matter what life throws my way, but it's easy to say that, it's harder to actually live it.

"Fine, we can go," I mutter, while trying my hardest not to think of all the ways this can go wrong.

Once we get to the hospital, I'm already exhausted from the effort of showering—my new nemesis—getting dressed, and making it down the stairs to my apartment and into Lee's car. Honestly, I probably should still be using crutches, or at the very least, a walking stick. But I'm far too fucking stubborn to use those, much preferring to force myself to manage, even if it causes me physical pain.

As soon as we make it inside the hospital, and I realise how far away my appointment is from the front door, I realise I'm fucked. Lee must have seen the expression on my face too, and for just a fraction of a second, he looks over at the wheelchairs lining the wall next to us, but thankfully he thinks better of that.

Instead, he grabs hold of my arm, his elbow crooked through mine, and he forces me to put all my weight onto his side. This new position takes away a lot of the pain in my hip, and although I look like a drunk person being supported out of a nightclub, at least it's not the wheelchair.

Sitting in the waiting room, I can't help but jig my knee up and down, anxiety of the situation getting the better of me. I can't believe I actually miss my dad's fucked up games of Eye Spy.

So, instead, I tell Lee all about it, and he laughs at my dads antics. "I would love to meet them someday. It doesn't have to be soon, but eventually," he exclaims, and I know this is what people in relationships do, but it's the first time I've ever heard him say he wants to meet them. It catches me off-guard a little.

"My family are a little crazy, you know." I don't really know what else to say, but it's true. From what Lee's told me about his family—which admittedly isn't a lot—they seem normal. Mine really isn't.

"It's a good thing I like my girls a little crazy then," he jokes before pressing his lips to mine. Thankfully, he pulls away fairly quickly because I was about to deepen the kiss the way I always do when I taste him, completely forgetting that we're in the middle of a busy hospital waiting room.

When I hear my name being called, I take several deep breaths, trying to gather the courage to even stand up. "Here," Lee calls for me, so the nurse doesn't think I'm ignoring her.

Lee takes hold of my hand, laces our fingers together and squeezes tight as he holds his other hand out to help pull me up. "You are stronger than you know," he tells me, as he helps me to my feet. I can't help but smile. I love the fact he believes in me so much, even when I'm not quite sure I believe him.

The nurse is waiting for us in her room, and as soon as we enter, she stands to greet us. She's a small lady, wearing a specialist nurse's uniform. She has a short brown pixie cut, and it frames her face perfectly. She looks to be in her fifties, the lines around her eyes and mouth showing her age a little more than I think she'd like. Her mouth is turned up into a kind smile, not the fake kind I was expecting.

Holding her small hand out towards me, she introduces herself. "Hi, Emmaleigh, my name is Kate and I'm one of the specialist MS nurses that works here in the hospital. I work with another nurse called Lesley, but I'm what we call your 'appointed named nurse'. Please, have a seat," she says as she points to two chairs beside her desk. "What would you like me to call you?"

"Emmaleigh or Em is fine. I answer to either," my words are barely above a whisper, but I do reach out to shake her hand, hoping like hell she can't see the way my hand is trembling.

She takes her hand back and reaches towards Lee. "And may I ask who you are?"

Lee reaches over and shakes her hand, that sexy as hell bright smile on his face, and I can tell, just for a fraction of a second, that she noticed it too. When he turns on the charm like that, his face looks so beautiful, and it's hard to miss. "I'm Lee, Emmaleigh's..."

He trails off, gazing over at me. It's like he's looking at me for answers, and that's when it occurs to me, this will be the first time out of the apartment that we've admitted we're together. And I'm guessing if I use the term boyfriend, it will make it into my hospital records. But if I say friend, it feels like we're taking a step back. Even though I hate having to make this decision, I'm grateful Lee cares and respects me enough to see this should be my choice. It's my hospital care, after all.

"He's my boyfriend," I say proudly. I've fought for a month to get to this stage in our relationship, and now that I can finally call him mine, you can sure as shit bet I'm screaming that from the rooftops. I can't keep the smile off my face as the word comes out.

Kate obviously sees my smile too, as I see her lip turn upright, almost into a smirk. "Thank you for coming. I always think it's important that family members come and are part of this journey too. I know this is your first appointment with us, Emmaleigh. I can also see you've cancelled it twice since your diagnosis. Do you want to talk to me about why?"

Taking a deep breath, I explain about what the consultant said, and how I don't feel like I've come to terms with things, and I didn't want to waste anyone's time. And since I was on a roll confessing things, I told her about being a nurse, and worrying people would judge my knowledge based on that, and I don't know shit about caring for someone with MS. She listens intently the whole way through, never once looking over at the clock.

I have no idea how long our appointment was scheduled for, but that never seemed to matter to her. She wasn't distracted looking at my notes, or making her own. She gave me her full attention the whole time, and I couldn't be happier about that.

"Em, I'm sorry you had that experience. The doctor who gave you your diagnosis is a locum, meaning they're just covering that clinic for us because our regular doctor was on sick leave. You should never have been told in that way. I mean, the information you were given is accurate, but there was a better way to give that to you. I don't expect you to come to terms with the condition overnight, but my job is to help you understand it. Today, all I'm going to do is give you a lot—and I mean a lot—of leaflets for you to take home and read at your own leisure. Call it homework, if you will. But next time we meet, we will go over the information, and at that point we will look at how we can help you next. My goals for you right now are: give you a basic understanding of MS and how the symptoms might affect you, dispel any horror stories you may have in your head as they're most likely untrue, get you stable enough that we can judge which is the best medication for you, and ultimately my goal is to get you back at work. Do you have anything you'd like to add? Any goal you feel I've missed?" she asks, and my head feels like it's swimming.

"You really think I can go back to work?"

Kate nods her head so much it's almost funny. She looks like one of those solar powered bobble heads, but her smile is genuine. "Emmaleigh, as I said, one of my biggest tasks will be dispelling preconceived thoughts on what MS is. Just because you've been diagnosed doesn't mean your life is over. You don't have to quit your job, or stop doing things you love. You are not all of a sudden going to end up in a wheelchair, unable to care for yourself. Yes, MS is a horrible condition, but there are lots of versions, and you are at the good end right now. My job is to keep your relapses few and far between, and making sure when they do come—because of course they will—we can keep it as minor as possible, with no lasting effects.

"This isn't a pipe dream. The medication that you will start soon has good research behind it, and it is working for people. I have a patient who was diagnosed ten years ago now, and she is living the best life. She is travelling all over the world, climbing mountains, and jumping out of planes. She doesn't let having MS hold her back, and that's my aim for all my patients. Of course, when the relapses come, it's a hard time, but I will be here when that happens to help you through. For now, I just want you to read as much as you can and come next time with a bunch of questions. I also have some leaflets for you, Lee, and you have the same homework. I'm here to support the family just as much as my patients."

She hands over the biggest stack of leaflets I've ever seen and I wonder how the hell I'm going to get through all this. My brain is still stuck on everything she just said. The idea that my life doesn't have to change, and that it might not worsen the way I think it will is a light I really need about now.

"Can I just ask something?" Lee asks, as he takes his pile of leaflets out of Kate's hand. She nods for him to continue. "Is it safe for Em to delay treatment? Isn't it better to start as soon as we can?"

"That's a good question, Lee. We actually don't like to start medication while the patient is still recovering from a relapse. We need them to be completely stable otherwise it's hard to measure baseline stats that we then compare against. Emmaleigh looks like she's on the mend, but some of the symptoms she's still experiencing leads me to think the inflammation hasn't quite gone down yet. It will probably be another month before we consider treatment," Kate replies.

"What happens if I have another relapse in that time?" I ask, crossing my fingers underneath the pile of papers in my hand, hoping like hell she can give me a good answer to that.

"The high dose steroids they gave you in the hospital, they've reset your immune system, and it takes a while for that to become fully functional again. It's highly unlikely to have a relapse while recovering. But there is such a thing as a pseudo relapse, that's where your body forces all your old symptoms back on you, usually during a period of extreme stress or exhaustion. So, if your vision suddenly goes in your right eye, or your right leg becomes weak again, it doesn't necessarily mean you're having another relapse, it is more likely you're tired or stressed. All of the leaflets in your hands will tell you how important it is to get lots of sleep, and take care of yourself mentally."

"But... erm, aren't I-I more likely... to have another relapse... when I wake up?" I ask, exhaustion obvious as I stumble over my words. I think I need her to tell me the answer to this, to give me permission to sleep properly because all this lack of sleep is making me feel worse.

"It's true, you are more likely to wake up and find that you've had a relapse, but it's not the actual process of sleeping that causes it. People can wake up from a fifteen minute nap and find they're having a relapse. But, not sleeping won't prevent it from happening. If anything, the lack of sleep will only make a relapse more likely," Kate explains, and I can feel her eyes assessing the black circles under my eyes.

I had hoped my thick-rimmed glasses would hide them, but apparently not. She answered the question like she knew what I was implying. All the unsaid things, she addressed. She knew I'd been avoiding sleep, and now I need to try and get it in my head that, what I see as my coping mechanism, my way of controlling an uncontrollable situation, might actually be the thing that's making me worse.

Kate talks a little more about the condition, and both Lee and I sit there, listening to every word she says. But it's not at all like she's lecturing us, it's like she really wants to help us to understand. She isn't just reproducing an answer we could have read on Google either, she makes reference to real people and real situations, giving me hope that if others can beat this, then so can I.

We arrange to meet again in two weeks, giving us more than enough time to read all the leaflets and come up with some questions. As we were leaving, with Lee's hand firmly clasped in mine, I'm overwhelmed by a feeling I didn't think I'd feel for a while—hope.

I'm hopeful that I can learn about my MS and how it affects me, and in doing that, I can learn to get it under control. I can learn what things trigger my symptoms. Like when I go in the shower, I'm so exhausted afterwards because my body doesn't handle extreme changes in temperature too well. I also know, no matter how scared I am, I need to get some more sleep. All these things will hopefully get me back at work and living a normal life again.

Before meeting with Kate, I had lost all hope. Even with Lee, I was still convinced he will leave as soon as things get rough, but after today, I'm not so sure he will. I have hope he really means what he says, and plans to stay with me, no matter what.

Emmaleigh

It's been over a month since I first met Kate, my MS nurse, and we've met a few times now. Every time she gives us homework, both Lee and I work hard at reading and learning the leaflets she gave us. And I have tried so hard to come to terms with my diagnosis, but it's not going how I would like.

We've reached the stage where medically I can start treatment, but Kate wants me to be assessed by a counsellor first. No matter how good an act I put on for her when we meet, she can see through it. I want to be okay with everything, but it's harder than I thought it would be.

The lack of sleep is still a massive problem. No matter how much I tell myself it's safe to fall asleep, even when I'm in Lee's arms, I still can't get more than half an hour before my body wakes me up, terrified of what could be heading my way.

Obviously the lack of sleep is taking its toll on me, and it's making me a little irrational. Lee spent all week with me when we first got together, but after that, he had to go back to work, which meant going back home. I wanted to tell him not to leave, to ask him to move in with me, but I didn't want to sound like a crazy person. I mean, we've only been dating properly a week at that point—it's far too soon.

Lee promised he would do the same as before; sleep at home Monday through Thursday, and come to mine over the weekend. It's only four days, but it felt like an eternity. Whenever Lee was here, it's like I could easily keep the darkness at bay, or should I say, it was easy to distract myself and get lost in Lee. Whether it was chatting to him, watching TV with him, or all the sex we had. Being around him gave me the spark I needed to survive. But, sadly, every time he left, so did my spark.

I know it sounds very anti-feminist to rely so much on a man, but I don't think that's completely what it is. It doesn't necessarily have to be Lee here. I think the problem is that when I'm alone, all I'm left with is my intrusive thoughts. My sleep deprived brain gets the better of me and the darkness descends.

Over the past week or so, that darkness has become so bad, it's hard to push it aside when Lee does come over. I can see he's worried about me. I'm not showering, I'm barely sleeping or eating. I'm so consumed by depression, it's hard to function normally.

The whole thing came to a head two days ago, when Lee came home from work to find me, quite literally, hitting rock bottom. As painful as it is to remember, the memories flash in my head so vividly.

"*Hey, Beautiful. I'm home,*" *Lee shouts as he walks through the front door, but I can barely hear him, or make out what he's saying.*

I'm in my own little bubble, and I don't even know how long I've been here. It's like I have spaced out, and I can't remember much of what happened to get me here.

I try to look around a little, but the more I move, the worse the buzzing in my ears becomes. It's so loud it's almost deafening, and I want to move my hands to place them over my ears, but I can't. Why can't I move my arms?

My head feels so spaced out, and it genuinely feels like a black cloud has descended over me, making me forget about where I am, or what the hell I'm doing.

As I look around a little, I realise I'm sitting on the kitchen floor, my back against the cupboard door. The lino feels cool under my ass, which now that I think about it has gone a little numb. How long have I been sitting here?

I try to think back to what I was doing before this dark cloud claimed me. I remember it was lunch time, and I came into the kitchen to make myself a sandwich. I had a real craving for a tuna mayo, so I gathered all the ingredients. I placed the tin opener on the tin of tuna, and tried to clamp it down with my hand. But every time I tried, it wouldn't clamp onto the tin. Or when it did finally clamp on, I couldn't press down hard enough to have the opener cut through the metal.

The more I tried to open the tin of tuna, the more my hand started to tremble. For the last few days I've had intermittent pins and needles and weakness in my hands. Kate assures me it's caused by my lack of sleep and stress. But that doesn't help me right now. I've never had my MS affect me in such a simple way. All I kept thinking is that if I can't even open a fucking tin of tuna what's the point in living.

As soon as thoughts of ending my life began taking shape, the darkness latched onto that feeling, making it ten times worse. I'm so lost, not even thinking about anything except how much better everyone's lives would be without me. That's when Lee comes into the kitchen.

I'm barely even aware of him kneeling down in front of me. It's not until I feel his cold hand pressing against my arm, does he pull me back from the abyss. I look down at where his hand is, and I'm shocked by what I see.

In my left hand, the one Lee is now holding, I have a large kitchen knife that I'm pressing against my right wrist. I don't know how long I've been sitting here, pressing the blade down into my flesh, but there's blood dripping from the wound, pooling on my leggings beneath my arm.

Lee moves his hand slowly, so as to not startle me, and he places it over the knife handle. For the first time since he knelt down with me, I look Lee in the eyes. His bright blue eyes are filled with tears, and a few have escaped and are streaming down his cheeks. He looks so scared as he glances between my face, the knife, and my bloody wrist. When he finally talks, his voice is so low it's barely audible, and it's not hard to hear the way he *quivers as he speaks. He's scared.* "Em, Beautiful. Please will you give me the knife?"

His eyes bore into mine, and as my brain catches up, I can't even understand why I still have the knife. I look down again, taking in the cut across my forearm, and my heart races as I realise what I've done. It's like the mist that was clouding my judgement finally dissipates and I'm left with the aftermath. Blood drips from my wound, my hand shakes with fear as I realise how close I just came to ending my own life. Worst of all is seeing the tears my boyfriend has allowed to fall. How the hell could I have been so selfish to even think of leaving him?

But the point is, I never thought about it. It's not like I sat down on the kitchen floor, with the knife in my hand, and purposefully attempted to kill myself. I'm a nurse for fucks sake. If I were going to end my own life, I'd know how to do it. But there's no other way to explain it. I genuinely didn't know what I was doing. It's like the darkness, and those fucking scary feelings, just took over me, and I let them.

I hand Lee the knife and he throws it to the other side of the kitchen before grabbing a clean tea towel out of the drawer. As he's about to place it over my wound, I quickly look down and try to assess how bad it is. "I don't think it's deep enough to need stitches," I mumble, as he places the towel over the wound. I can't help but wince as the fabric hits my open cut.

"Em..." I look up into Lee's eyes, and there's so much pain there. His emotions are so strong, I feel like I'm suffocating. But he has every right to feel them after what I put him through. He doesn't say any more, and I know it's because he can't find the right words. Lee's the sort of person that if he can't find the right words, he won't say anything at all.

I owe him to be the one to speak, to try and make this right. "I'm sorry, Lee. I know this isn't much of an excuse, but I really didn't intend on harming myself. It's just that the darkness took hold, and I didn't even realise it."

I tell him everything, how it started with the tuna, right up to how I'm feeling in this moment, and we both cry with each other, overcome by so much emotion it almost feels too much for me.

"Em, you have to promise me you won't ever do that again. If you feel the darkness coming, you have to ring me, or anyone. Is it okay if I ring Kate to get some advice? I think this is bigger than we can deal with, just the two of us. I know you hate asking for help, but this is you hitting rock *bottom, Em, and if you don't get help, there's only one step further down, and that's death. I feel like I've only just found you, and I sure as fuck am not ready to lose you yet,"* Lee cries, opening up to me about his feelings.

I agree to him calling Kate, and she tells us we need to get an appointment with my GP to start medication for my depression, and she will make a referral to counselling.

I absolutely don't want to do any of those things. I'm still the same old stubborn me, hoping I can fix myself. But, I don't want to see that pain in Lee's eyes ever again, and so I agree to do whatever it takes, for him. He keeps telling me not to do it for him, to do it for me, but I can't. I hope soon to get my self-confidence back, but for now, I'm happy living for him.

I've been working through that particular memory, as well as so many other issues in my counselling sessions. I went to the counselling appointment by myself, though I would have preferred Lee to be there. He wanted to come, but Kate told him it would be better for me if I did this alone, so I don't have him as a crutch to lean on. She was right.

The more I talked to the counsellor, the more I realised I'm the person holding me back. I'm scared to accept that I have MS, because then I'd have to let go of that 'why me?' feeling. I would no longer have that as an excuse, something to blame. I also would have to admit that the fear I have over Lee leaving has very little to do with my MS.

Don't get me wrong, MS will always play a part in most of my decisions and will affect how I feel, but it's not the only factor. When the counsellor dived into it, I realised I was scared about Lee leaving me long before he even committed to me, and before I was ever diagnosed.

The self-confidence—or lack of it—has been there for a long time. I know Lee has been working on building it up, and I couldn't be more fucking grateful for that, but in a way, it's just been papering over the cracks. I needed to look seriously at why I don't feel I'm worthy of being loved.

Laying in bed that night, Lee is here again, as he has been the last couple of nights since he found me with the knife. I love falling asleep enveloped by his warmth and his scent, and well, everything that makes him Lee. I'm still terrified to fall asleep, but having him here helps a little. The problem is, now I've been faced with addressing every thing in my life, and I realise I'm using Lee as a crutch. I need to be able to get to sleep and to generally survive without him holding me up—no matter how fucking terrifying that is.

"Lee?" I ask, turning my head just enough that I can look up at him while still keeping my cheek on his chest. "I love you being here, but I think it's time you went home. Just for a night or two. I need to know if I can survive on my own."

Lee reaches over and turns the bedside light on a little. It's one of those touch lamps where the more you touch, the brighter the light gets. He turns it on to the lowest level, but it's enough to see the cautious look on his face. "Is that why you think I'm here? To make sure you don't hurt yourself again?"

I close my eyes, not having the courage to look at him as he talks about that night. Even when I was talking to the counsellor, I can't call it a suicide attempt, because I wasn't actively trying to kill myself. Or at least I don't think I was. That's the problem, I don't remember what the hell I was thinking. But I did self harm myself, and it could have been so much worse. That I can't deny, but I also can't say that weird black out moment where I'm overcome with the sensations of the moment won't happen again. I hope I'm learning the tools to deal with it, but I can't make any promises.

"Yes," I admit.

Placing a hand over my cheek, he swipes his thumb under my eye, stroking at the skin until I look at him. His touch is so tender and soft, it causes tingles to spread across my face. "Em, I'm not still here because of that. Obviously I want to make sure you're okay, but that's not the reason. I'm here because I want to be. Because the idea of going home fills me with dread. I don't sleep properly in my own house any more. It doesn't feel like home. You feel like home," he explains, as he presses his lips to my forehead and my heart starts to race.

"You feel like home too," I admit, giving him the most genuine smile I have. "But, after talking with the counsellor, I realise I'm using you as a crutch. So I don't have to stand on my own, and I need to know if I'm strong enough to do this by myself."

Lee tilts my face to make sure I'm looking at him, and the fire in his crystal blue eyes has my heart skipping a beat. "Em, I will do whatever you need, but I already know the answer to that question. You are so fucking strong, even when you don't know you're being strong. We can have some space, but not too much. I've been apart from you, and I never want that to happen again."

Using my hand on his chest to lift myself up slightly, so I can look at him fully, I give him my sternest glare. "This is not us breaking up, Lee. No fucking way. This is just me saying we need to go back to how it was before where you would only sleep over on weekends. We can talk on the phone, or meet for dates, if you'd like. But for me, night time is the hardest. I need to learn to sleep again, and I need to do that without you here to hold me. I want you here, but I have to be sure that I don't need you. That I could survive on my own, if I really had to. Does that make sense?" I ask, hoping he understands where I'm coming from and doesn't see it as any kind of insult because it's not.

He strokes his thumb over my cheek, giving me that gorgeous smile of his. "We can do that. We can do whatever you need, but I want to make something very clear. I already know that you don't need me. You are so fucking strong, Emmaleigh, and you will beat this. You will realise how strong you are, and when you do, you will be a force to be reckoned with. So you can bet your ass I'm never letting you go."

Lee

> **EM**
> Are you sure you want to do this?

I read the text on my phone and chuckle to myself. I don't know which of us is more nervous. This is about the fifth text I've received from Emmaleigh in the last few hours. I thought I was nervous, but it's nothing on her.

> **LEE**
> Of course I do. What time will you be getting here?

I look down at my watch, and see there's only about half an hour before the party starts. It's my parents fiftieth wedding anniversary, and to celebrate we're hosting a family gathering in the garden at my parents house. The sun is shining, and I can't keep the ridiculous grin off my face.

It's been well over two months, almost three, since that awful day when I found Em with the knife. We agreed just a couple of days later that we had to go back to our original arrangement of me only staying with her on the weekends.

Her counsellor felt we rushed into our relationship, since we weren't properly dating before Emmaleigh's diagnosis. Then when she pushed me away, it made me realise how I really felt. I didn't ask her to be my girlfriend because she was diagnosed with MS. I did it because I realised during our time apart that I really did like her, and that I wanted us to be together.

After that our relationship progressed very quickly, her situation throwing us together faster than if we did just meet and start dating. So when her counsellor suggested we take a step back, and learn to just be a couple without all the extra drama, of course we agreed. But, in addition to that, Emmaleigh needed some time to work on herself.

When Em found her will to fight, it was a magnificent thing to witness. It was like the dark cloud that had descended over my beautiful girl finally lifted. Obviously she has a way to go, and each time her MS symptoms flare up, she's faced with new challenges. But overall, she's fighting them head on.

She made such great progress in her counselling, it only took around a month before her MS team felt she was well enough to begin treatment. She takes a pill called Tecfidera twice a day. In all honesty, even after reading every leaflet I could find, I have no idea how it works. And after listening to her neurologist, I don't think they really understand how it works either, all they know is it does.

Em has had to get used to taking it, and learning how to deal with the side effects that come along with it. If she eats or drinks too soon after taking it, her stomach cramps so badly she has to take deep breaths to try and control the pain. She also suffers really badly from flushing when that happens. Whenever she describes it, she says it feels like fire is ripping through her body and setting fire to her from the inside out. Thankfully, the side effects pass quickly, and the longer she's been on the medication, the more she's getting used to it, which is helping a lot.

Just under a month ago, she made the biggest step, which was going back to work. Emmaleigh was absolutely terrified to return. She'd been off on sick leave for a couple of months, and was worried too much would have changed. Her boss has been really kind, and agreed for her to go back on a phased return, to build up her strength and get her ready to be back there properly.

I think the other thing that really upset her, and that she was worried about, was going back to her so-called friends. None of the people who claimed to be her friends stood by her. They came to visit her once in the hospital, and once at home when she was diagnosed, but after that, she rarely heard from them.

Gemima actually said to her that having MS means she won't be able to go out and have fun like they used to, and that's boring. My beautiful girl was struggling to come to terms with a life changing condition, and her so-called friends—who are all nurses, may I point out—actually called her fucking boring. I wanted to skin them alive. I've never felt such rage until I had to hold Emmaleigh in my arms while she cried over that. Thank fuck it didn't take her too long to realise they weren't her real friends to start with.

So, when she finally went back to work, she made it clear they were nothing more than her work colleagues. In fact, given her seniority status, she was their boss, and they may not have respected that before, but they sure as shit did after Em stood up for herself. Before, they used their friendship with Emmaleigh to get out of doing jobs they didn't want to do, and because Em saw them as her friends, and she didn't have the confidence she does now, she let them manipulate her. But not any more. If anything, they got even more of the shitty shifts to make up for what they missed out on before.

My phone pings again, pulling me out of my reminiscing.

EM

> I will be there in about five minutes. I'm stuck at the lights around the corner from your house.

Emmaleigh has been to my house many times, but we've always been sneaky about it. She either comes when my parents are out or away, or she sneaks out while they're sleeping. Generally we prefer to hang out at her house. We can be as loud as we want when nobody else is there, and the walls at my house are far too thin for any sexy time.

Mum has been pestering me about meeting Emmaleigh since we

made it official. She stopped talking to me for two days when she found out I met her parents last week. It wasn't even planned. We were supposed to go by her parents house and pick up their little Daschund, Milo, and Shih-tzu, Hector, to take them for a walk while they were out at the football match they were going to. But when we got to the house, they hadn't left yet. Her dad was running around trying to get ready, which I quickly came to realise meant he had to find as many items of clothing as he could that featured his football team's logo.

The meeting was quick, and her mum made me promise I would come over and meet them again properly when they weren't in such a rush to leave, given they were already late. Since I fell in love with Hector and Milo from the moment I met them, I knew I'd be back. Those little dogs may be crazy, and Milo literally eats everything, but from the first moment they met me, and started licking my ear, I knew I had friends for life.

No matter how much I told Mum the meeting with Em's parents wasn't supposed to happen, she was still pissed. That's when Emmaleigh accepted the invite to come to their party. She was invited weeks before, but had been on the fence about coming. She's nervous about meeting all my family in one hit, and I have to admit, it's not something I'm thrilled about either. Family parties—specifically my family—are always a bad idea, in my opinion.

They always drink too much, then a petty squabble from years ago will turn into a big drunken argument that I have to spend months trying to fix. So of course I don't want Em exposed to that. But I want her to meet my family. I think it's the next logical step in me showing her how fucking serious I am about our relationship.

EM

I'm outside your house. Fuck! Lee, there's an older lady with white hair, holding up a camera heading straight for me. You better get out here quick!

Shit! I need to go and rescue Em from what I'm sure is one of my crazy aunties. I quickly look at myself once more in the mirror, smoothing down my tight black jeans, and the plain black T-shirt I've paired them with. I twist a few rogue strands of hair until they're standing up perfectly, and dab on a little of my Calvin Klein Defy because I know Em loves it.

She often comments that the woodsy scent topped with hints of lemon and lavender always reminds her of me. As soon as I'm ready, I run as quickly as I can down the stairs and out the front door to intercept my auntie.

Sure enough Em is sitting in her car, while my Auntie Connie knocks on the window. Em's eyes are wide, like she doesn't quite know what to do, and my aunt is holding her ancient camera up as though she's going to take Em's picture.

"Aunt Connie, what are you doing? Back up so she can at least get out of the bloody car?" I shout, as I run across the driveway.

My aunt, who is in her early nineties, though you wouldn't know that, turns to face me, pointing her finger at me as she does. "Don't use that language with me, young man. You are not too old for me to give you a clip around the ear," she threatens and I can't help but chuckle. My aunt's had the same threat since I was a rowdy kid, but never once has she followed through with her threat.

"Auntie Con, please go into the garden. We will be along shortly," I say, as I gently guide my auntie back across the road, down the path at the side of the house, and into the garden. Instead of following behind, I take Em in through the front door. I know Mum will want to meet her first, and I will never hear the end of it if she doesn't.

Before we go into the house, I turn to Em and pull her in for a kiss. As soon as I taste her, I want more, but as I try to wrap my arms around her to bring her closer to me, Em pulls away, a blush spreading across her beautiful cheeks. As she moves back, it gives me a moment to properly take her in. She's wearing a black dress that falls to just above her knees.

It's a scoop neck with no sleeves, but it's modest enough not to show off too much cleavage—not that I'd mind, but she thinks my family might. The dress is tight on top, and flares out from the waist down, showing off her amazing figure. She knows I love her curves, and now that she's confident in her own body and can show them off, I love them even more. She's paired the dress with some lace ballet flats, and I tell her I'm shocked to see she's not wearing her Converse.

Chuckling, Em reaches up and pushes a stray strand of hair out of my eyes. "I've just changed out of my Converse in the car. I wore them to drive in, but didn't think they were appropriate for meeting your family. I want to look nice."

Now it's my turn to laugh. "Beautiful, you could wear a black bin bag and would still be the most gorgeous person in the room. My family will love you, I have no doubts about that."

Taking hold of her hand, I feel as she takes a deep breath, no doubt to help settle her nerves, and I pull her inside behind me. I lead her through into the kitchen where my mum is running around like a headless chicken. Every damn time she throws a party, we offer to help, but she doesn't let anyone. She insists on doing it all herself, and then moans that the party was stressful. Every time she tells us she's never doing another, and she always does.

"Mum," I shout, trying to catch her attention. She puts down the bowl she's holding, her face twisted in anger. No doubt she was about to chew me up for disturbing her, until she saw Emmaleigh standing beside me. Her face lights up and she rushes towards us. "Mum, this is my girlfriend, Emmaleigh."

I hear Em's breath hitch as I say the word 'girlfriend'. I guess this is one of the first places we've had to use that phrase, outside of Em's hospital appointments. I need to make a point of calling her it more often, since she seems to like it. Using my free arm, I needlessly point to Mum as I introduce her. "Em, this is my Mum, Sharon."

Em holds her hand out for Mum to shake, but she completely ignores it, and instead pulls her in for a big hug. I can't help but chuckle at Em's startled yelp, but she hugs Mum back nevertheless.

"It's nice to meet you, Mrs—"

Before Em has the chance to call her by our surname, Mum cuts her off. "None of that. We're family now, so you can call me Sharon. It's so lovely to meet you, and you really are just as beautiful as Lee said."

The blush on Em's cheeks spreads as she looks from Mum to me, lost for words. I decide I better save her now while I can. "I'm going to go get us a drink, Mum, and introduce her to everyone. I know you were busy when we interrupted you, so we will let you get back to it. I just wanted to make sure you were the first to meet her."

Mum smiles, her whole face lighting up like this is the happiest she's been in a while, and she reaches up to pinch both my cheeks. "You're a good boy," she says, before releasing my now stinging cheeks and turning towards Em. "I will come and find you later when I'm not so crazy busy. I want to find out all about you. Lee has told us a little, but you know what men are like. They don't know how to tell a good story, missing out on all the juicy details."

Em chuckles nervously and tries to hide the apprehensive look on her face. "I look forward to speaking to you later."

We say our goodbyes, and just as we're about to head out, Mum calls me. Turning my head over my shoulder, she says, "Don't forget you're doing the speech later, Lee. Please tell me that you have something ready to go?"

She looks worried, and it has been for the last two weeks since she asked me to do it. Mum is a massive control freak, and she's organised every single piece of this party, to make sure it goes off without a hitch. My sister wanted to bring the cake, but Mum would only let her if she got to pick the design. My sister wanted it to be a surprise for Mum and Dad, but she wasn't having any of it, and in the end, Lena actually took Mum to meet the baker, so Mum could make sure she got the design she wanted. I, on the other hand, refused to be a pushover. No matter how many times she's demanded to see my speech over the last two weeks, I've held firm.

At one point she told me I couldn't do it unless she approved it, and so I told her she could find someone else. She backed down in the end, but it's still been a sore subject between us ever since.

"I have my speech ready, Mum. Don't you worry, just enjoy the party," I say, as I lead Em out of the kitchen and into the fire—I mean garden.

I don't even know how long we spend going around to all the guests. It feels like fucking forever, but everyone wants to meet Emmaleigh. She's like the star attraction of the party, and I can tell being in the spotlight is hard for her. But she does so well, talking to everyone, answering all their questions. Honestly, I think I'm losing my patience a lot quicker than she is.

Once we're sure she's met everyone, we take our seats beside my sister. She's a little like me, and she doesn't make meaningless conversations. So I know she'll only talk to Em if she has something important to be said. It gives me and Em some time alone to chat and catch up.

After an hour or so, Em starts to settle in, and everyone stops looking at her like she's the main event. It also helps when Mum says the buffet is open, as food is always a good distraction. As we walk to the back of the buffet line, I notice Em's limping a little more than she was before. I pull her closer to me and whisper in her ear, trying to ignore the way she shudders when my breath touches her neck. "Are you okay? I saw the limp just now."

She turns to face me, the corners of her lips turned up, but I can see the pain she's trying to hide. "I'm fi—"

"Don't you dare say you're fine," I say, cutting her off before she can finish her sentence. My eyes widen, giving her the look I usually reserve for the bedroom. The one that tells her I'm not taking any shit from her. She rolls her eyes, and I make a mental note to punish her for that later.

"Fine. We were standing a lot while you introduced me to everyone, and it hurt my hip a bit. I just need to get my food and sit down for a little while," she explains as she picks up two paper plates. I grab the cutlery and serviettes for us both and we swap.

"Okay, but in the future, just tell me. I'm sure everyone here would have come over to us, they're all that damn nosey," I grumble as Em laughs, nodding her head.

Leaning over, she places a quick kiss on my lips. It's not nearly enough for me, but given we're surrounded by my family, more eyes on us than I would like, I understand why she pulls away.

The rest of the party passes by in a blur. Emmaleigh fits in with my family like she was meant to be there. The only thing they couldn't get onboard with is the fact Em wouldn't have an alcoholic drink. She had to tell my mum at least three times that she can't drink because of her medication, but she finally stopped pestering her in the end.

As the sun started to set, and the music got louder, my family party got a lot rowdier. The women of my family had moved all the chairs to the side and they created a make-shift dance floor in the middle of the garden. Thankfully, half the neighbours were at the party, otherwise it wouldn't take long for the noise complaints to start.

My sister walks over to where I'm sitting, my arm thrown over Em's shoulder while she snuggles into my side. I love that she feels comfortable being like this with me in front of my family. I'm not the sort of guy who is bothered by public displays of affection. If I want to hug my girl in the middle of a supermarket, I will.

"Hey Lee, Hayden is getting a little ratty—which is code for he's being a little shit because he's tired—so we're gonna head off soon. Shall we get the cake and speech done now? If we wait much longer, everyone is going to be too pissed to even remember," she points out, and as I look around the garden at the people in attendance, I can't help but agree with her. Some of my family—mostly the ones on the dancefloor—are already too far gone. One of my uncles is asleep in the corner, and I see at least two more who are close to nodding off too. She's right, it's now or never.

Suddenly, the nerve I wasn't worried about earlier comes flooding to the surface. My heart's racing so fast I can hear it beating in my ears. I try to slow my breathing down, taking some deep breaths, but it's not until Em lays her hand on my arm that I start to calm down. She always finds a way to ground me.

"Don't be nervous, Lee. You've got this," Em whispers into my ear as my sister and Cain head into the kitchen to grab the cake.

Once I see them standing at the door, ready to bring it out, I stand up, and with a few big deep breaths, I shout loud enough to get everyone's attention. To help, Em hits her knife on the side of her glass, and everyone turns to face us. "Sorry to interrupt your evening, but it's that time of the night. Will you all take your seats, please."

Everyone waddles back to their chairs, and I guide Mum and Dad over to the front of the garden, beside the table which has room to hold the cake. Once everyone is seated, I begin. "Firstly, I want to thank you all for coming. I'm sure you will all agree this has been an amazing party, and Mum has done such a great job organising it."

Applause and cheering interrupts me, while Mum waves her hand away, like she's trying to act modest. She loves it really. As much as she moans, she lives for her family, and having everyone together like this, it's what she loves. Even me, who fucking hates any kind of family gathering, has to admit this one hasn't been too bad. Probably because Em's here.

"As you all know, we're here to celebrate Mum and Dad's fiftieth wedding anniversary. Which is a bloody long—"

My dad interrupts me by shouting loudly. "I would have got less time for murder!"

Laughter fills the garden and Mum playfully hits Dad around the shoulder, telling him he's an asshole.

"Mum asked me to say a few words, but before I do, I think I should hand it over to my sister. There's no song to sing for a wedding anniversary, but we are going to celebrate like there is," I say, pointing over to my sister, Lena.

Everyone either shuffles around or turns their head until they can see my sister. Her boyfriend is holding the cake, which looks beautiful, and she's got Hayden in her arms. "The only song I could think of is 'Congratulations' by everyone's favourite, Cliff Richards. So, we're going to go with that," she shouts as she lights the candles on the cake. I can't help but laugh when she mentions Cliff. The majority of the people in the garden are the right age range to know this song, so it's not a bad pick. In fact, I notice out of the corner of my eye that Aunt Connie, one of the eldest in attendance has actually stood up so she can sing.

"Congratulations and celebrations. When I tell everyone that you're in love with me. Congratulations and jubilations. I want the world to know I'm happy as can be."

As everyone sings, Lena lights the candles on cake and they walk over towards where Mum and Dad are standing. Cain places the cake on the table and Lena comes to stand next to me, Hayden looks like he's going to fall asleep in her arms at any minute. For just a moment, I feel sad Leon, his wife and their two boys decided not to come. I fear the rift within my family may never be fixed, and even though we never really discuss it, I can tell it hurts my parents, but they don't know how to fix it.

Mum and Dad blow out the candles and everyone cheers. Mum asked the baker to make a white square cake, like the one she had when she got married, and it's decorated in pretty pink flowers. I heard Mum say they're the same she had in her bouquet. They both look at the cake and say how amazing it is, before hugging my sister.

Once they've said thank you, and a few people, including Aunt Connie and her fifty year old camera, have taken pics of the cake, I start my speech. "As you all know, I'm not much of a talker, and honestly, giving a speech, even in front of family is terrifying. But, if ever there's a time to do it, it's now. I can't believe mum and dad have been together for fifty years. Some of you had the pleasure of going to their wedding, and I bet a lot of you thought it wouldn't last. Two teenagers getting married. Everyone thought they were too young, some even thought Mum must be pregnant for them to get married so young. She wasn't, they just knew they were in love.

"Up until recently, although I've always loved the story, I've never really understood it. I always thought that falling in love would take time. That you have to date for a long time, get to know them at their worst, and only when you're sure can you then fall in love with them. So to hear Mum and Dad married without even living together, that blew my mind.

Growing up I had to listen to Mum lecture dad about putting the toilet seat down, or about picking up his socks. He moaned about how she continually nagged him to do things like take out the trash, which he wanted to do in his own time. I couldn't help but think, if they lived together for a bit first, they would have known all these annoying features. But now I know it wouldn't have made a difference, they would still have got married.

"Most of you have had the pleasure of meeting my girlfriend, Emmaleigh today. She's the reason I now understand everything Mum and Dad went through. Don't get me wrong, we certainly aren't rushing into marrying each other, but being with Em has opened my eyes to what they experienced.

"Love is something that can sneak up on you and bite you in the ass. It can happen at any time, but when it does, there's no denying it. Sometimes it's obvious, but other times it takes a while for you to see it. With Mum and Dad it was instant. They knew in a heartbeat that they didn't want to spend another moment apart, and so they married. For me, my story is different."

All eyes are on me, but I turn towards Em, as she's the only person I'm interested in right now. I am very aware I'm hijacking my parents speech, but I know my mum will approve. I take Em's hand in mine, and she looks at me, confusion marring her beautiful face.

"When Em and I first met, we were just friends. This went on for longer than it should have, until Em told me she wanted more. She felt we already were in a relationship, and she needed it to be official, but because I was terrified of commitment, I turned her down. That's when life pulled us apart, and every minute of every day that we were apart, she was all I thought about. I missed her like I needed her to breathe. I genuinely felt like a part of me was missing, so I fought to get her back. After a lot of grovelling, she agreed," I say, and cheers ring out around the garden.

"Em, I have never told you this because nothing ever felt like the right time, but I realised while we were apart that I love you. I think I probably have since that first night in the pub when I hit you with my pool cue, and you still kissed me goodnight. Every weird joke that we share together, every time you ask me how my day's been, I fall in love with you a little more.

"Now that I know how I feel, I don't want to spend another moment apart from you. I'm not going to propose yet, because even though it worked for my parents, I still think it's too soon. But, I will someday. Until then, I would like to ask if you want to move in with me?"

Her eyes widen and tears make her bluey-grey eyes glisten. She nods her head as the biggest smile lights up her face. "I love you too. I'd love to live together. And, just so you know, whenever you do decide to propose, the answer will be yes," she says with a wink.

My family erupts into loud cheers, but I drown them all out as I pull my girl into my arms before I press my lips against hers. I've captured her and I don't ever plan on letting her go.

She pulls away before I deepen the kiss, and I reach up to wipe away the tears that are threatening to fall. She leans in to whisper in my ear. "You better finish your speech and then I'm taking you home." There's so much that goes unsaid in the sexy way she bites her lip at the end, and suggestively shrugs her eyebrow.

I lean in, pulling her ear lobe into my mouth, I give it a little nibble, and I love the quiet moan she tries to stop from breaking free. "I can't wait until we get home. I'm going to worship every part of you. I'm going to turn you into a hot, needy mess, who can think of nothing more than me and my cock. You're going to be screaming my name like I'm your God. I'm going to devour your pussy, mouth, and ass in every room of our home, until you beg me to let you come. How does that sound, Beautiful?"

Her eyes flick around to make sure nobody heard me, but I can hear how loudly they're still cheering. I whispered for only her to hear, and nobody else is near enough. She bites her lower lip even more, and I don't miss the way she squirms a little, rubbing her thighs together like she's looking for some release.

"That sounds perfect," she mutters, and I waste no time in finishing my parents speech. I hope like hell people are too distracted celebrating to notice the growing bulge I have trying to break free from my jeans. It was not a good idea to get us both so worked up in the middle of a fucking family party, where there's literally no way we can do anything about it. In my defence, she started it, and I intend to fucking finish it.

As soon as the speech is over, and my parents have thanked us, we spend a few moments saying our goodbyes, much to Mum's annoyance. She made me promise she would come over next time she has a weekend off for Sunday lunch, and so of course Emmaleigh agreed. I think she'd like the opportunity to get to know Mum in a much smaller, more quiet situation.

As we head towards the front of the house, it suddenly occurs to me that we will have to drive back in separate cars as I will need my car. "I'm gonna go and pack some of my stuff, so I can officially move in with you, if that's okay?" I ask. For a moment, as nerves get the better of me, I really hope she didn't say yes to us moving in together because I put her under the spot.

"You can bring everything, and then I know you will never have to leave again. But, make sure you don't wait too long. I have some really sexy underwear on under this dress, and I don't want to have to take it off all by myself," she taunts as she turns and walks towards the door.

I grab hold of her hand, twirling her as I pull her back around to face me, her back to the door. With my free hand, I trail my fingers up her thigh, under the hem of her dress, right the way up to her lace panties. Gently I slide my finger over the fabric, pushing it in between her puffy lips. I can feel she's already wet, and we both groan quietly at the same time. I twirl my finger around her pussy entrance, before doing the same with her ass. Even though the fabric separates me from her silky skin, her juices have made her panties so wet, it's like they're not really there.

"If you even think about starting without me, I will have to punish you badly. Are you going to be my good girl and do as I say?" I ask, trying not to think about how much my dick is throbbing right now.

"I will be your good girl," she whispers, and as I reluctantly pull my hand away from her wet pussy, I can't help but smile because life really doesn't get any better than this.

If you've enjoyed reading about Emmaleigh and Lee's love story, and you want to see what their HEA looks like, keep reading for a bonus epilogue, exclusive to people who sign up to my newsletter. Get it here: https://dl.bookfunnel.com/lyefsyr392

Acknowledgements

I hope you enjoyed reading I Was Always Yours, and loved Emmaleigh and Lee as much as I did. These characters have been living rent free in my head for quite a while now, just demanding to have their voice heard. So, when the time came that I wanted to step back and write something a little less dark than I usually do, I knew this was the story.

In actual fact, I found this book so much harder to write than my darker stuff. This is about people and their feelings, and how they can be influenced by the slightest of things in their past. I wanted to create two characters that were broken in their own little way, and watch them start to heal with each other. I'm hoping that's exactly what I did.

There are so many people I need to thank for helping me with I Was Always Yours, and if I miss your name from the list, please don't think that means I don't value you. I just have a terrible memory!!

AMBER NICOLE - my editor - you helped me make my words shine, and I thank you for that. Getting rid of all the repetition definitely made this book so much better. I'm so grateful for you, and I can't thank you enough.

ABRIANNA DENAE - my proofreader and friend - I'm so lucky to have you in my life. You get my characters, and have helped to make their journeys even better. I can't thank you enough for your love and support!

MY BETAS - Kerrie, Zoe-Amelia, Amanda, and Daniela - thank you so much for taking the time to read my work, even when I don't give you much notice. Kerrie, Zoe, and Amanda, have been with me from the beginning, and are amazing. Daniela is the newest member of my team, and despite never having done a BETA read before, she let me push her into it, and now she's stuck with me. Thank you to all my team for all your support. I love and value each and every one of you.

SARAH AT THE BOOK COVER BOUTIQUE - thank you so much for creating such a beautiful cover. As soon as I saw it, I knew it was perfect for this story. You are a great talent, and a pleasure to work with, so thank you very much.

DANI RENÉ AT RAVEN DESIGNS - Thank you for creating all the beautiful teasers, banners, and countdown graphics for this book. Your gorgeous designs have helped me promote the book so much. Thank you for working with me, even on such a tight deadline. It's always appreciated. You're a very talented woman!

LOU J STOCK - Thank you so much for working with me to design the interior graphics used to create the gorgeous paperback. You took the time to listen to how I see my characters, and were more than happy to make any changes I had. Even when I was being picky, you were still amazing, and I'm so delighted with the final product. The paperback is going to be gorgeous.

TALK SPICY 2 ME - Thank you for agreeing to work with me on my very first TikTok Tour. I can't wait to see how far we're able to spread the word about my book and I'm excited to be part of this new venture of yours.

ENA AND AMANDA AT ENTICING JOURNEY - as always, thanks for helping me get my hands into all the amazing bloggers and bookstagrammers. Your help and support with each release is invaluable.

NIKKI WESLEY - my PA - thank you for all you do in keeping me organised and on track with things. I wouldn't be able to do this without you, so thank you!

MR LUNA - thank you so much for your support. You are the reason I'm able to keep living this crazy dream. You push me on days I don't think I can write anymore, and you have faith in me, even when I'm not so sure I do. I'm very lucky to have you by my side on this crazy life journey.

MY LUNATICS - thank you for taking a chance on this book. I know it's not your typical Emma Luna book, but I love it, and I'm so proud I pushed myself to write outside my comfort zone. I hope you enjoyed it too. I can't thank you enough each time you pick up one of my books, it means the world to me, and I'm so humbled whenever I hear you liked it. Please, keep reading, and I will keep writing. I love you all, and I'm forever grateful for you.

About Emma Luna

Emma Luna is a USA Today Bestselling dark romance author from the UK. In a previous life she was a Midwife and a Lecturer, but now she listens to the voices in her head and puts pen to paper to bring their stories to life. In her spare time, when she should be sleeping, she also loves to edit, proofread, and format books for other amazing authors.

Emma's books are dark, dangerous, and devilishly sexy. She loves writing about strong, feisty, but underestimated women, and the cocky, dirty-mouthed men they bring to their knees.

When Emma isn't writing, promoting, or editing books she can be found napping, colouring in adult colouring books, and collecting novelty notebooks. She also enjoys coffee and gossiping with her mum, playing or having hugs with her gorgeous nephew, who is the light of her life, and curling up on the sofa to watch a film with Mr Luna. Oh and for those of you that don't know, Emma is a hardcore Harry Potter fan—Team Ravenclaw!!

Thank you for taking a chance on a crazy Brit and the voices inside her head. That makes you a true LUNAtic now too!

Follow Emma Luna

I absolutely love chatting and catching up with readers. I love letting you know what books I'm working on, what I have coming up next, and my new releases. So, don't be afraid to come and say hi, or drop me an email. If you love my characters, tell me!!

If you want to find out all things Emma Luna before anyone else, you can join my newsletter here:

https://www.emmalunaauthor.com

If you have facebook, you can join my reader group for exclusive news and giveaways:

https://www.facebook.com/groups/emmaslunatics

If you would like to check out any of Emma's other books or stalk her in more places, you can find everything you need here:

https://www.linktr.ee/emmaluna

facebook.com/EmmaLunaAuthor
instagram.com/emmalunaauthor
amazon.com/Emma--Luna/e/B082GNYLM4
bookbub.com/profile/emma-luna
goodreads.com/emmaluna
tiktok.com/@emmalunaauthor

More Books By Emma Luna

SINS OF OUR FATHERS SERIES

Broken
https://geni.us/SouF-Broken

MANAGING MISCHIEF

Piper
https://geni.us/MM-Piper

BEAUTIFULLY BRUTAL SERIES

Black Wedding - Bree and Liam's Story
https://geni.us/BW-BB

Dangerously Deceptive - Kellan's Prequel
https://geni.us/DD-BB

Trust In Me - Kellan and Mia's Story
https://geni.us/TiM-BB

The Ties We Break - Declan and Belle's Prequel
http://Geni.us/TTWB-BB

Fighting To Be Free - Kian and Freya's Story
http://Geni.us/FTBF-BB

The Time Is Now - Ryleigh and Shane's Story
https://geni.us/TTIN-BB

The Lies That Shatter - Finn and McKenna's Story
https://geni.us/TLTS-BB

Together We Reign - Evan and Teigan's Story
https://geni.us/TWR-BB

WILLOWMEAD ACADEMY - CO-WRITE WITH MADDISON COLE

Life Lessons
https://geni.us/WA-LifeLessons

STANDALONES

Under the Cover of Darkness
https://geni.us/TL8-UtCoD

I Was Always Yours
http://Geni.us/IWasAlwaysYours

ANTHOLOGIES

Ours To Keep: A Why Choose (RH) Anthology
https://geni.us/OursToKeep